Loverl

MW00896650

Loverboy

Loverboy

Dartmoor Series Book V

by

Lauren Gilley

LOVERBOY

ISBN -13: 978-1537317564

HP Press®
Atlanta, GA

The Dartmoor Series

Fearless

Price of Angels

Half My Blood

The Skeleton King

Secondhand Smoke

Loverboy

Loverboy

Trigger Warning

Dear readers, welcome, at last, to Tango's book. His is a story that has been simmering slowly in the background as the series progresses. It's the book I'm most often asked about, and has without a doubt been the most emotionally straining to write. If you're coming into *Loverboy* as a fan of the series, then you will know that this story will be difficult to read. PLEASE read the list of (potential) triggers below and consider them seriously.

This book contains mentions, suggestions, and a few scenes of: kidnapping, imprisonment, child abuse: emotional and physical, underage sex, non-consensual sex, sex slavery, rape, self-harm, drug use, addiction, and suicide. This book is intended for MATURE audiences, and contains scenes that are disturbing.

Throughout the novel, Tango struggles with feelings of self-loathing, worthlessness, and depression. Please note that all the characters' viewpoints are clouded with strong emotion, and their thoughts and actions are not *condoned*, merely presented in a way that is true to life.

Please note, however, this isn't a book *about* abuse and horrors. Rather, about surviving them, and emerging stronger on the other side. And I strongly suggest that anyone who has experienced trauma of any sort seek out appropriate clinical help. Thus forewarned, please enjoy Tango's long-awaited time in the spotlight. He and I thank you for your readership.

~LG

Loverboy

LOVERBOY

Loverboy

One

The craving. It had transcended that small voice in the back of his head, grown beyond the itch, the pull. Now it was a full-fledged, snarling, beastly thing, gnawing at his bones, snapping up every other sensation until there was room only for the fix.

The blue door of the house at the end of the driveway beckoned him, tempting as neon. A long walk, a slow one, the way the ground seemed to shift beneath his feet. He shut his eyes and forced himself on. Finally his boots struck the porch steps, and he scrambled up them. He knocked three times, then waited, then knocked a final time.

Peter answered the door with what was becoming a usual frown. He sighed. "Again? Does your boss know you're doing this shit?"

"You gonna tell him?"

"How do you even stay on your bike these days?"

"Are you gonna sell it to me, or do I need to go somewhere else?"

Peter made a face. No, he wouldn't want that. As one of Ghost's newly-inducted dealers, he couldn't afford to lose business – even this kind of business, from one of his overseers.

"Whatever." He went to the hutch that served as his oversized medicine cabinet.

It was a tiny house, but up to Ghost's cleanliness standards. The tradition of letting dealers live how they wanted to had died with Fisher. Every ounce of product had to be hidden at all times. Regular inspections were held to ensure that the houses and apartments looked normal and well-kept. The goal was to keep suspicion to a minimum, and barring that, keep the police from turning the place upside down.

Peter's cottage had warped, but well-scrubbed pine floors, rag rugs, secondhand furniture that had been trendy in the eighties, and a comfortable assortment of lamps and knick-knacks. Peter himself was on the thin side, and sometimes a little glazed like he smoked his own weed, but overall professional and clean-cut.

The hutch held several sets of dishes, a collection of cookbooks, usual kitchen things. But behind this were removable panels in the back of each cabinet, and that was where the weed, coke, and ecstasy was kept, all of it bagged and catalogued. There was also a small stash of heroin, and that was what Tango had come for.

Peter tossed a reluctant glance over his shoulder. "He's gonna catch on, you know. Ghost. And when he comes and wants to put my head through the wall for selling it to you, what am I supposed to say?"

"Say it wasn't your fault." Tango's palms itched and he curled his fingers up tight. "That's the truth."

Peter snorted. "In my experience, the truth don't mean shit."

~*~

The nightmares had started a few weeks after he was rescued from Don Ellison's basement. He'd known they would, and stupidly, he'd thought he was equipped by now to handle them. What was a dream sequence compared to what he'd been through physically? Not just at the hands of Ellison's men, but at the hands of *all the* men. The ones who'd shamed and ruined him since childhood. He hadn't stood a chance, had he?

And so as the bruises faded from his skin, the nightmares had crept in, soft-footed and insidious. First the vague sense of panic, a weight across him in his sleep. He'd awakened tangled in the sheets, his t-shirt soaked through, clawing to regain his equilibrium. These had lasted for several months, and then the real night terrors had begun.

Particular memories, in vivid color and crystalline detail. The low bass thump of the music. Diego's muffled voice over the speakers as he announced each feature and invited gentlemen to get out their wallets for special time in the back. The soft brush of the velvet upholstery on the couches in the private rooms.

Stink of male arousal and sweat. Crackle of money against his skin. Clammy grip of a hand…

He woke screaming, almost always. The first time it happened at the clubhouse, Carter and Jasmine had come stumbling in from the dorm next door, half-dressed, eyes wild with fright.

"What is it?" Carter had asked.

Jasmine had made a move toward the bed, face concerned, holding Carter's shirt closed against her breasts.

"Go away," he'd told them, and hadn't been polite about it. He couldn't handle them, individually, or as a couple. He just couldn't. If anything that even smelled like sex came toward him, he'd go into a full-on panic attack.

He couldn't live in the clubhouse after that. He managed to scrape together enough to put a deposit on an apartment.

Maggie brought him a casserole the night after he moved in, took one look around the place, and her eyes had filled with tears. "No, baby," she'd whispered. "Oh no, you can't live here." And she'd cried quietly while the massive water stain on the ceiling above her threatened to give way and dump the upstairs waste water line on their heads.

By some miracle, Mercy's old apartment above the bakery downtown was available, and Aidan and Mercy had strong-armed him into moving into it one Saturday afternoon.

He owned a double bed, two sets of sheets, and a sad excuse for a sofa. But somehow a table, chairs, towels, dishes, and lamps appeared, like exotic plants sprouting in his landscape of blacks and grays. Maggie scrubbed the bathroom until it sparkled. Ava baked a chicken and they had a big family dinner at his tiny new table. Before they all left for the night, Aidan squeezed his shoulder and gave him an unsubtle look of assessment.

"You want me to stay over? We can get drunk and watch bad movies."

Tango shook his head. "No. Go home to Sam and Lainie."

The club was paying his rent, he had no doubt. The girls kept forcing food on him. His brothers made too-cheerful overtures of friendship at every turn.

But he stood on the other side of a fine steel mesh. He could see them, hear them, smell their skin and shampoo. But none of them could touch him. And wasn't that what he'd always craved? Touch?

Still nothing but a sex toy.

He was suffocating.

It had been inevitable, really, reaching for the needle again.

He sat down now at his table and opened up the shaving kit that held everything he needed to send himself to oblivion. The lights were off. A glimmer of neon from Bell Bar filtered through the window, sparkled against the kit's zipper. He pushed his hands through his hair – it was long all over now, down to his shoulders, a tangled mess – and clasped his hands against the back of his neck. His pulse throbbed just beneath the skin, a tattoo against his fingertips.

He was going to die.

The knowledge came to him suddenly, heavy and certain. Maybe not tonight, maybe not the next time, or the time after that – but at some point soon, he was going to put the needle in his arm, and it was going to kill him. Because he knew himself inside and out, with an intimacy most men never dreamed of. He knew a little bit was never enough. He always had to have more. Always, always.

What was he doing here? Besides delaying the inevitable.

Time unspooled; glimmered faintly in the dim kitchen, a long rope of habit and repetition laid out before him. Heroin. Crippling, toxic sex. And wanting. Craving.

Craving, craving, craving.

His phone was in his hand before he made the decision to reach for it. Whitney picked up on the second ring.

"Kev."

Oh, God…her *voice*. He hadn't remembered the beautiful soft tone of it. Hadn't thought it would hit him hard as a punch.

His eyes filled with tears and he shut them.

"Kev?" she repeated, worried now. "Are you there?"

He took a deep breath. "Yeah. I'm here."

A pause, but a warm one. He swore he felt her sweetness through the cell connection.

It was two in the morning and he hadn't talked to her since the last time he'd made one of these sad, desperate calls a month ago. She would have been within her rights to hang up on him. But instead she said, "How've you been?"

"Fine."

"Well that's good. But you don't sound very fine."

"What are you doing? Did I wake you up?"

"No. I'm painting."

He went back to the basement in his mind, the cold concrete and the comforting press of her hand against his. She'd told him about her painting then, when he'd been foggy with pain and would have listened to her give the traffic report for eight hours straight.

"Oils," he said. "Right?"

"Uh-huh." She sounded pleased he remembered.

"What are you working on?"

"A landscape." She went on without prompting, like she knew he wanted to hear. "It's a photo I took last winter, when we had snow on the ground. There's a farm about a mile from my brother's house and" – her voice caught at mention of her brother, killed by Ellison's men a year ago – "they have this old fashioned big red barn." Deep breath, and she pressed on. "I've always wanted to paint it, and I couldn't sleep tonight, so…"

"Why can't you sleep?"

He heard a sad smile in her voice. "You're not the only one who has nightmares, Kev."

"Right." He'd tried to spare her that. He'd taken the physical punishment, and she hadn't been touched. He'd kept her safe, yes…but he'd hoped he'd kept her mind easy, too.

"I go back there sometimes, when I'm dreaming," she said, quietly. "And I remember–"

15

"Don't remember," Tango said. "Just don't. Wipe it out of your head. Stop thinking about it."

"Like you did, you mean?"

Had she been anyone else, he would have hung up on her. Instead he gripped the phone tighter and took a deep breath, tried to calm his racing heart. "That's different."

"How? Kev, you're torturing yourself. I know you are. It isn't healthy."

"You're twenty-one. What do you know about healthy?"

"I know it doesn't look like you," she shot back, firm, but caring. Like Maggie. Or Ava. Like one of the tough girls in his life.

Desire spiked in his belly. A hard kick of longing and sexual frustration. With his eyes closed, he could envision what she must look like now, up late painting in her pajamas. He wanted to peel them off of her, feel her skin against his hands, find out how warm and wet it was between her legs. Wanted her to hurt him, dig her nails into his shoulders and bite the jagged scars down his ear.

No! He couldn't want any of that. Wouldn't allow himself to direct his insatiable urges toward Whitney, who was sweet and wholesome and had never been with a sexually deviant junkie like him.

"No what?" she asked, and he realized he'd said it aloud. "Kev?"

"I can't," he said, and disconnected the call.

"Wait—" she was saying before she was cut off.

Tango cupped a hand to his mouth and breathed through it, air whistling between his tattooed fingers.

No, no, no, no, no. He couldn't think that way about Whitney. It made him feel vile. She was just a kid, and a good, decent, sweet one at that. Who'd comforted him, and held his hand.

Just like Ian had, all those years ago at The Cuckoo's Nest.

For him, the sexiest thing in the world had always been shared trauma, and the comfort traded back and forth in the aftermath.

Because he was fucked up. Wired incorrectly.

And now he was going to fuck Whitney up. He could see it unfold before him, her future, if he stayed a part of her life. She would have a weakness for him; she would let him in, stroke his hair and tell him she cared. And he would poison her, and take away every shot she had at a substantial life.

His many ghosts crowded around him in the dark kitchen where Mercy and Ava had cooked for each other right after they were married. His father. His clients. Miss Carla. Ian. The other boys. His brothers. Whitney. A cacophony of voices, competing and shouting to be heard above one another.

It was Carla's voice that finally broke through: *"He's damn pretty."*

Oh, if only he'd been born an ugly child. If only...

In the bathroom, he flipped on the lights and caught a glimpse of his achingly feminine face in the medicine cabinet. His big, dark-lashed blue eyes; slender jaw; narrow, sharp nose, the curve of his mouth.

He opened the cabinet, pushed aside the shaving cream, and found the razors.

~*~

Whitney didn't stop to consider the wisdom of her reaction until it was too late and she was knocking on Aidan and Samantha Teague's door. She'd stared at her half-finished landscape for five full seconds after Kev hung up on her, and then she'd made a decision. She knew the note in his voice; the same note she'd heard in her brother's voice before he'd plunged headlong into total addiction and eventually gotten himself killed because of it.

She'd dunked her paintbrushes in the water cup, tugged on clothes, and dialed Kev five times on the harried drive through the deserted streets of Knoxville to get to Aidan's.

"Please be home," she murmured, and knocked again.

17

The apartment was a walk-up in a semi-sketchy part of town, and wind funneled up the concrete stairwell, plastering her jacket to her back. She shivered and raised her hand to knock again.

But the door swung open on Aidan in his boxers, scrubbing his hair, still half-asleep. She got an eyeful of ornate tattoos across the entirety of his torso, and then heard the high thin cry of a baby from behind him.

She winced and wanted to kick herself. But there was no help for it. Kev trumped babies and sleep right now. "Hi, I'm sorry it's so late, but—"

He'd been staring at her blearily, but now his eyes flipped wide. "Shit. Whitney? What are you…?"

"It's Kev," she said, and his mouth snapped shut. "He called me just a little while ago, and he sounded wrong."

"Wrong?"

"Upset. He cut me off and he…" She had to swallow a rising panic; it got caught in her throat and she blinked furiously. "I think he's going to *do something*, Aidan, and I'm so sorry I showed up like this, and I know you don't owe me anything, and I'm sorry I woke your baby, but he—"

"No, you should have come." He came fully awake then, shivering.

"I don't know where he is, but I figure you do."

"Yeah."

Aidan's wife, Sam, appeared behind him, glasses perched haphazardly on her nose, long dirty blonde hair cascading down her back; fresh from bed and worried. She had the baby in her arms, patting her back and shushing her quietly.

"What's going on?"

"Tango," Aidan said, and Sam's face echoed his panic.

"Oh."

He turned from the door. "I'll go get him."

"I'll come with you," Whitney said.

"No." Aidan paused and sent her a hard look over his shoulder. "You'll wait here with Sam."

"He was talking to me. I want to go."

18

"You want to see the mess?"

Her stomach quivered and her panic ratcheted another notch. "I want to see *him*. Make sure he's okay."

His eyes flashed – admiration? – but he shook his head, and she knew he wouldn't budge. A firm man, Aidan, like his father, who scared the hell out of her. "No, kid. Stay here with Sam, and I'll let you know when I've got him safe."

"Come on in." Sam pushed the door wide and waved her in, holding the baby in one arm. "I'll make us some tea."

~*~

Three weeks from her due date, Ava couldn't sleep for shit. The baby, so sedate and calm thus far, had decided that she was ready to come into the world, and seemed to be doing somersaults in the womb, kicking at her kidneys and making her belly heave in the dead of night. She lay on her side, facing her sleeping husband, hands pressed to her belly, willing the little bean to quiet down. She was exhausted and restless and more or less miserable. *I want to meet you, too*, she thought. *But let's get some sleep, okay?*

Mercy turned onto his side to face her. His eyes glimmered in the dark. Okay, so he wasn't sleeping.

His voice was clear, free of sleep. "What's wrong, Mama?"

She smiled, though she didn't know if he could see it. "She's spinning around in there."

His massive hand cupped the swell of her belly. "Yeah? She getting ready?"

"Slowly. Not yet. Not tonight."

He curved his big body around hers, spoke in French to the baby.

Ava's smile widened, and she felt herself relaxing, safe inside his physical protection. Their little girl seemed to sense it too, settling. "What did you say to her?"

His breath stirred her hair, warm and smelling faintly of his last cigarette. "That she's gonna be as beautiful and tough as her mama."

"You and your sweetness."

"You don't like it?"

"Oh, I love it."

A cellphone went off. They both froze, fear streaking through her and radiating into him; she *felt* his fear, the fast grab of worry in his palm against her stomach.

"It's mine," he said, and rolled away from her to answer it.

~*~

For possibly the first time in his life, Aidan felt obscene driving down the streets of his own city. It was after three in the morning and his headlamp cut a bold swath through the dark; the growl of his bike engine echoed off the building facades as he turned down Main and then Market.

No lights on in the apartment above the bakery.

Mercy pulled in behind him in Ava's truck as he hit the alley. He tore impatiently at his helmet and gloves, meeting his brother-in-law at the base of the iron stairs.

"You talked to him yet?" Mercy asked.

"I tried before I left home, but he didn't pick up."

Aidan went up first, heart in his throat, pulse throbbing in his hands. *Please*, he prayed. *Please, please, please.*

He'd known this night was coming. For months he'd watched his best friend withdraw deeper and deeper into himself. He'd tried again and again to drag him out to Bell Bar, to get him to play pool at the clubhouse, had tried to force him to come have dinner with him and Sam. When that hadn't worked, he'd recruited Mags and Ava. Had gotten Ghost on his side. He'd done everything short of commit Tango to some sort of rehab program.

Or had he? he wondered as he reached the door. Had he done everything? Had he truly tried to save his friend and brother? Or had he been consumed with his wife and child?

"Jesus," he whispered, one last prayer, and fitted his key into the lock.

Empty living room, cold kitchen, no lights. But Tango's bike was in the alley below.

"Kev?" he called.

No answer.

"Look," Mercy said, and the lights flipped on above the kitchen table.

Aidan squinted down at what lay before him. A leather shaving kit, unzipped, full of needle, syringe, and rubber tourniquet.

"No," he whispered. "Oh, shit."

Mercy's hand landed heavy as lead on his shoulder, and squeezed in a comforting way. "The bathroom."

"Yeah."

The lights were on there. The bathtub was full. Tango's rail-thin body seemed to float in the crimson water. One arm lay white as death outside the tub, dripping blood – *drip, drip, drip* – down onto the hexagonal tile. His eyes were shut, face white as porcelain, long hair plastered to his forehead.

"*Kevin!*"

Two

"I'm a bit of an Earl Grey addict," Samantha said as she started a tea kettle one-handed. She looked like she did this a lot, moving around the kitchen with the baby in the crook of her arm.

Lainie, Whitney reminded herself. The little girl was Lainie.

Not that she gave a crap about that right now.

"Do you take milk?" Sam asked.

Did she? "I…uh, I don't normally drink tea, so I don't know. I…"

Sam glanced over at her, and then her eyes widened behind her glasses. "Whoa. Okay. You look about ready to faint."

"Do I?"

Sam abandoned the tea and came to take her arm. "Let's go sit down."

"Okay…" Her head *did* seem a little light, suddenly.

Sam steered her to the couch and sat down in the chair across from her, juggling a now-quiet Lainie up higher against her shoulder. "You can lie down if you need to."

Whitney shook her head, which was a mistake. But said, "No, I'm okay." She knotted her hands together in her lap and tried to tell herself that Kev was okay, that she was just overreacting, that Aidan was going to find him and tell him that she had been stupid to worry so much.

But dread lay like a coiled snake in her belly, and she couldn't shake the sense that something was irretrievably wrong with her…

Her…

Well, what was he to her?

She could find no label in her mind, only knew that she cared for him deeply.

"Whitney," Sam said in a careful voice. "How have you been doing since…everything happened?"

It seemed an odd question, given what was happening with Kev.

"I've been fine."

But Sam didn't look convinced.

"Do you think Aidan should be there by now?"

"Maybe. I'm sure he'll call soon."

As if on cue, her cellphone rang, and she fumbled it off the arm of the chair to answer it. "Hey, what's up?"

Whitney watched her face, saw the bright spark of emotion in her blue-green eyes, and she knew what had happened.

All the air left her lungs. *No*, she prayed. *Oh no, please no.*

~*~

She refused to believe it until she saw the blood on Aidan's clothes. Then her steps faltered in the hospital corridor and she braced a hand against the cool block wall to steady herself.

No.

Aidan's white t-shirt and hoodie sported bold patches of blood, the stains dark as they dried. Blood smears down his jeans. Blood coloring the black and white inked side of his neck. Blood all over his hand as he pushed it through his hair and turned a haunted look toward his wife.

Mercy was crimson-streaked too, face grave.

So much blood. It didn't seem possible that there could be enough left to keep his heart pumping.

But they were at the hospital, and not the morgue. Which meant he wasn't dead yet. Which meant she wasn't going to give up on him.

With a deep breath, Whitney pushed off from the wall and walked up to meet the men alongside Sam. "How is he?"

Aidan's eyes broke her heart. He shook his head and glanced away from her, down to the floor.

"We found him in the tub," Mercy said, voice heavy. He drew a long finger across his own wrist, as if she'd needed the explanation.

"What have the doctor's said?"

23

Mercy didn't flinch away from her, gaze sympathetic and devastated. "That he's lost a lot of blood."

"You shouldn't be here," Aidan said, suddenly, head lifting.

"Aidan," Sam said quietly.

His dark eyes shone beneath the tube lights, and Whitney could detect no malice in them. He thought he was being kind, turning her away. He expected Kevin to die, and he wanted to spare her the gut-punch of hearing it straight from the doctor.

Well, that was sweet of him, but she wasn't having any of it.

"No, I should be right here," she said.

His head kicked back a fraction, nostrils flaring. He couldn't believe her, she guessed.

"Maybe…" Sam started, laying a hand on Whitney's shoulder.

"Fine," Aidan said. He turned and slumped back against the wall, head hanging. "Whatever."

So she settled in to wait.

~*~

Sam set Lainie's carrier down at his feet, and then laid a comforting hand against Aidan's chest, like she was touching his throbbing heart. "I'm going to go and get everyone coffee," she said, and then slipped away down the hall.

Aidan nodded too late, after she was already gone. It had just seemed like so much effort to make his head move up and down.

Someone – a nurse, maybe – had steered them into a small family waiting room. Possibly because Mercy's pacing was making patients and staff nervous. It was like watching a large, restless panther; one of those big paws could come darting out at any moment. Aidan knew better, after all these years, but he guessed other people didn't. Other people, after all, were stupid.

Almost as stupid as his best friend.

Aidan pitched forward in his chair and stared down at his daughter. She was awake, but barely, perfect smooth eyelids flagging. She was an unnerving child, the way she always stared at him. The first months had been fraught with crying, colic, and a haphazard routine of three Teagues trying to learn one another and fit together like mismatched puzzle pieces. He'd had his secret fears that this disjointed family of his was an experiment in disaster; that Sam might come to her senses one morning, hand his squalling baby back to him, and get on with the life she was supposed to have led all along. He'd held his breath against the inevitable; he'd become a praying man, asking God nightly to allow him to keep this new terrifying world he'd snagged for himself.

And the newness had worn off, the storm had passed, and now they were as solidly fused as a husband, wife, and baby could be. Lainie was turning into a serious, contemplative baby. She was smarter than her father, he had no doubts. Perhaps, by some miracle, she'd inherited all the best parts of him.

Though what those were, he had no idea. He was many things. A good friend obviously wasn't one of them.

The chair across from him groaned as Mercy settled into it.

"Try not to break the furniture, Hercules," Aidan said out of habit, voice flat.

"Try not to be a crybaby douchebag," Mercy shot back.

They shared worried, exhausted half-smiles.

Mercy's gaze dropped to Lainie. His face brightened, and Aidan was suddenly glad she was there. Something innocent and sweet in the midst of a black moment. "She's being quiet."

"Yeah, that's her new thing. She just stares at us. It's kinda creepy."

"Cal's like that too. When he's not screaming." He shook his head. "That one…"

"Yeah."

They had nothing to talk about. Nothing was as important and urgent as whatever was happening with Tango, and discussing baby stares, or the weather, or work seemed irrelevant.

Where the hell was Sam with the coffee? This was where she excelled: distracting from disasters and keeping everyone warm and hopeful.

Aidan glanced down the line of chairs to Whitney. She sat three seats away from him, an oversized wool jacket wrapped tight across her front, purse held on her lap. Everything about her struck him as unlikely. Her slender ankles slopping around in a pair of scuffed suede booties. The small hands and chipped nail polish. Her heartbreakingly sweet face with its guileless blue eyes. And her age, above all. Only just able to drink in public and looked like she'd gag on her first sip of beer. She looked exactly the sort to fall to pieces at any provocation. And she looked nothing like the worldly, hypersexualized women Tango had always gravitated toward within the club.

And yet, here she sat, steely-eyed, and straight-backed.

Mercy snapped his fingers to get Aidan's attention. When he had it, he tipped his head toward the girl. *What's going on there?*

Aidan shrugged. He hadn't known Tango was still in contact with her.

Or that Tango was shooting up again.

There were a lot of things he hadn't known.

"Whitney," he called, and her head turned toward him slowly; she was stuck in her head, just like they were. "You don't have to sit all the way down there."

She studied him, assessing his sincerity. "I didn't want to bother you."

He felt a small kindling of warmth for her, then. She was just a baby, and she had no business aligning herself with an ex-stripper, ex-prostitute, mentally-fucked junkie who'd slit his wrists tonight.

But she was brave. He'd give her that. And he'd learned, in the last few years, that the world was short on brave girls. It was always best to have them on your side.

"Nah, it's alright." He patted the chair beside him. "I want to ask you some things."

26

Guarded, she moved down next to him, careful to keep her arms around her purse so she wasn't touching him. "What things?"

Keeping his voice gentle, he said, "For starters, how long have you been talking to Kev?"

"Since it happened." And she didn't have to remind them what "it" was.

"You thought he might do something like this."

She nodded, and her eyes brightened with a sudden rush of tears. "What happened to him?" she asked. "I don't mean in that basement. I mean before then. What happened that made him want to…to…sacrifice himself, like that?"

He sighed. "That is a very long story. And I only know part of it." And he'd always had a feeling that the part he knew was the very least of it.

~*~

Ian dreamed of home. Not his modern high-rise, nor his offices above the funeral home, nor even the place someone had designated his home when he'd first come to America. But his family's house in London. The four-story, whitewashed brick façade with its iron railings and window baskets of flowers. He recalled with perfect detail the blue door with its brass knocker, the permanent scuff marks on the steel threshold left by the piano when it had proved too big to come in the service entrance in back and was forced, between three men, into the front door, much to his mother's social horror.

He stepped into the black-and-white tiled entryway, with its hall tree and the antique mirror passed down from Auntie Emerson. He looked at his reflection: twelve, thin enough to slide through the bars of the garden gate, knees like building blocks and a face too narrow for his nose. A strong nose, regal, like his father's. But his mother's eyes, large and blue, "pretty as a girl's," his father had said. Altogether too pretty, that was him, with his auburn hair and his long eyelashes, skinny as a ballet dancer.

27

That was why he had chosen dance over fencing, he supposed. One of two boys in Madame Clarice's studio, a prized possession of the company. He was to dance in Madame's production of *Swan Lake* at the end of the month, and his stomach fizzed with excitement when he thought of it.

Deeper into the house. Past Father's study, and the good parlor where his mother entertained her book club. He heard Dottie laying the silver and china out for supper in the dining room; heard her drop something with a clatter and curse her own clumsiness.

Upstairs he went, past the closed door of Mother's bedroom – she would be taking her evening nap at this time – and past his sister's, and then his brother's room. Down to his own. The high street-facing windows welcomed him, poured late afternoon sunlight across his crisp blue counterpane, his desk and the open notebook of sketches on top of it.

He dropped his rucksack and went to the desk immediately, drawn by the open cover of the sketchbook. He could swear he'd closed it that morning, before he left. He had. He was sure. Someone had leafed through it, probably Mother, and had stopped on the piece he'd done in ballet class: his classmate, Ren, stretching at the barre. It was a hurried, many-stroked sketch, a sort of impression, a suggestion of her features. The real focus was the movement. A lively piece, if melancholy in its penciled darkness.

Ian touched it with a fingertip, and a perfect crimson drop of blood landed on the paper. *Plop.* From out of nowhere. Then another. Another. It became a stream, thick tendrils that ruined his sketch.

He turned his hand over, and along the inside of his wrist saw the deep slice where the razor had opened his vein.

But that wasn't right. He hadn't tried to kill himself until he was fourteen. And that was after...

He woke with a start, jackknifing upright in bed. The breath sawed in and out of his lungs, burning his throat, and sweat poured down his naked skin; he felt a drop quivering at the end of his nose and he dashed it away, reeling. His hair lay plastered against the back of his neck. The sheets were glued to his thighs.

Shaking, he flung out a hand, searching for a warm body beside him. But there was only cool, vacant linen. Kev was going to be celibate now, after all.

"Damn," he said to the empty room.

He hadn't dreamed of Mayfair in years. The boy he'd been then was long since dead; it was no longer painful to venture back through the halls, only impossible, because that had been another life, another person, derailed.

So why now? Why could he still smell his mother's cigarette smoke creeping from beneath her door? Why could he hear Dottie's tuneless humming as she set the table?

Why was he awake, heart galloping?

Something was wrong. Badly so. But damned if he knew what it was.

Aside from…well, from everything. Nothing had ever been right, had it?

~*~

Was this the other side? This sense of cold and light and exhaustion? Somehow he hadn't expected it to be so bright. He'd thought, in those last minutes as he sank down to his chin in the warm water, that he'd be headed somewhere dark, and hot, and unfriendly. But he came to with the sense of cool, sterile surroundings, and a heaviness in his limbs that defied comprehension.

"Hey," Aidan's voice said, and he knew then. This wasn't the other side at all, but the hospital.

"Kev." Whitney. That was her pretty voice.

"Brother." Mercy. Of course, Mercy; someone had dragged him out of the bathtub, after all.

He'd failed, then.

Three

It was morning. The light at the window hinted at rain later, watery and weak as it fell across the floor. An arrangement of white lilies with a cheerful Mylar balloon attached had arrived in the arms of an orderly moments before, the note from Ava. No one else knew about what Kev had done, Aidan had explained to her out in the hall. None of the club could know. This was a family-only situation. Aidan, Sam, Ava, Mercy, perhaps Aidan and Ava's parents – they were the only ones who'd been told. She must keep it completely to herself, Whitney had been made to understand, with lots of direct eye contact.

Bless his heart, Aidan hadn't been intimidating…but he'd been earnest, and she understood, now that he'd enlightened her. Suicide wasn't allowed in an outlaw biker club. There would be no choice but to excommunicate Kev if all his brothers found out what he'd done.

What he'd done. That made it sound like some sort of crime.

Well, it was a crime against himself, she figured.

The bed was propped up and he was awake. His eyes had fluttered open about fifteen minutes ago, and so far, he'd said nothing, just stared at the ceiling, swallowing in a way that looked painful, Adam's apple jumping in his skinny throat.

Whitney couldn't believe how thin he was. Nothing but bones and a shocking headful of greasy long hair. His tattoos stood out stark and black against skin gone white and papery with malnutrition.

She'd thought she could be patient, and wait quietly until he was able to make eye contact. But she wasn't.

"Kevin," she said, and her voice cracked.

His gaze came to her then, distant and haunted, his eyes a shocking pale blue in the morning sunlight.

There were dozens of things she wanted to ask, but all she could say was, "Why?"

He stared at her, unblinking, until she thought he didn't mean to answer. Then he said, "Because I can't do this anymore."

The lump in her throat thickened. She fought back the hot press of tears. "Do what?"

"Live with it."

Live with what? she wanted to know. But fear strobed through her, bright and blinding. Maybe she didn't want to know. But she suspected she already did, a little.

"This is about what happened to you in that basement," she guessed. "What those monsters did to you."

"They weren't the first monsters. It goes way back before that basement."

"Tell me," she urged.

He didn't answer.

"Then you can tell the psychiatrist when she comes." He looked startled. "They aren't going to turn you loose until you've been evaluated."

She saw emotion in him for the first time, faint stirrings of unease. "No. I won't do that."

"You have to, or they'll commit you to the psych ward."

"No."

"You tried to kill yourself, Kev." Her voice shook. She had to stop and swallow back the tears. "That isn't okay."

Silence, again.

"Do you care that your friends are upset? That they would have grieved for you?"

"Are you upset?"

"I'm *furious*."

"Then why are you here?"

"You didn't just ask me that, did you?"

He stared at her.

She *was* furious with him. Intensely so, suddenly. She stood. "I'm going to go tell your doctor that you're ready for your psych eval."

She was at the door when he said, "Whitney."

She glanced back over her shoulder, and felt so sorry for him, so afraid that he was beyond salvage, that she almost rushed back to his bedside.

But she refrained.

"You don't need to stay," he told her.

She took a deep breath. "No offense, but shut the hell up with that 'don't stay' business. Talk to the psychiatrist, and I'll see you after lunch." She shut the door soundly on her way out.

~*~

"Your messages, sir."

"Thank you, Alec."

Alec, a sharp and sensitive employee, picked up Ian's empty teacup and bowed his way out of the office with a professional quickness. Ian knew that fresh tea would be brought within a reasonable period, after he'd been allowed to sort through the messages in private for a few minutes. A good one, Alec; he deserved a Christmas bonus this year.

He didn't have a direct phone line in his office. He could dial out if he wanted to, but all the answering was done by his staff out at the reception area. Messages were taken down on notecards and brought to him on a tray, once in the morning and once in the afternoon. He craved the orderliness of it; the old fashioned tradition of it.

He was glancing over the first in the stack, anticipating his next cup of tea, when the door to the outer sitting room opened, earlier than expected, and he heard raised voices.

"Mr. Shaman will not—Sir! *Excuse* you!" Alec exclaimed, and then came the heavy tread of biker boots across the rug.

"Mr. Shaman!" Alec called, scurrying after. "I tried to—"

"It's fine, Alec," Ian called back. He laid aside the messages and was ready when Aidan Teague burst into the office.

"That little bastard," Aidan said, jabbing a finger toward poor ruffled Alec.

"Don't insult my staff," Ian said, calmly. Then, to Alec: "It's alright. You've done a fine job. Go back outside, and I'll handle Mr. Teague."

Aidan made a growling sound at mention of his name.

"Come off it, everyone knows who you are," Ian said. "Alec, please."

Flustered, red-faced, Alec straightened his glasses, said, "Yes, sir," and bowed out of the room.

Aidan tugged his cut straight and gave him a sharp look. "Just announcing my name, huh? These people around here know who you really are?"

Ian smirked. "To what do I owe the pleasure today, Aidan?"

The man's face – it was such a nice face, very masculine, dark slanted eyebrows, stubble – blanked over. He took a deep breath. "Kev tried to kill himself last night."

The words hit him as a physical blow, right up beneath his ribs; punched the air from his lungs and threatened to take his vision. "No." He tried to swallow and couldn't. "No, I don't believe that."

Aidan sighed and dropped down into the chair across from him. "Yeah, well…he did."

He couldn't breathe. Couldn't think. Couldn't…

"He's okay," Aidan said, gaze becoming worried. "Don't pass out or anything. I ain't giving you CPR."

"I…" Ian gripped the edge of the desk, hard, until it hurt. Concentrated on his thin white knuckles. He could see the blood pulse through them, beneath his pale English skin, with each beat of his heart.

Blood. It always ended in blood, didn't it?

"How?" he asked, and didn't recognize his own rough voice.

"In the bathtub," Aidan said, quietly.

The dream. The dream of home, of his Mayfair house, of his own scrawny reflection, of his sketches, and then of the blood. His wrist throbbed now, the old scar gone livid and insistent beneath the skin. The blood wanting out.

"Jesus."

"The doctors say he'll be fine. Physically. We found him in time. But–"

"Where is he now?"

"At the hospital. Waiting on his psych evaluation."

"He'll lie to them. Tell them it was all a mistake and that he doesn't want to hurt himself anymore. He'll say whatever it takes to be let out."

"You think?"

"I know so."

Aidan frowned. "I don't believe that."

"You should. It's exactly what I would do. He wants to get out…so he can try again." And next time, he added silently, Kevin would succeed. You didn't botch suicide more than once.

Aidan studied him, eyes looking raw, jaw clenched. "You did it too, didn't you?"

"A long time ago," he said, softly. "When you're fourteen, and a fat, smelly American day-trader pins your face to the floor and takes your virginity, you lose all love for living."

Aidan said nothing.

"I want to see him."

"I figured you would. That's why I came."

~*~

The psychiatrist was straight from Central Casting. Pear-shaped, buttoned up in a dark green wool winter suit, gold loops in her ears and a multicolored scarf draped around her shoulders. Her makeup was tasteful, hair conservative. Her sensible flats made low clipping sounds across the tile as she came to take the chair beside his bed. Everything about her was by-design; she was meant to make you feel safe and sheltered. Styled to be someone you'd spill secrets to.

"Hello, Kevin." Soothing voice. Kind expression. "I'm Dr. Beverly. But I'd like you to call me Dana."

He didn't respond.

"I'd like to talk about what happened last night."

"I wouldn't."

She cocked her head. "I think it would be helpful. I'd like to help you, Kevin, that's why I'm here."

"You're here because the hospital won't release me until I talk to you." At another time, he would have been appalled by the cold, blunt force of his voice. But that time had slipped down the bathtub drain with all the bloody water.

She took a breath and her shoulders settled. "Well, that's true. You can't leave the hospital until I think you're ready for release."

He glanced down at his lap, plucking at the covers around his waist, pleating the stiff sheet into little folds. He didn't want to look at her. He felt almost guilty that he was unreceptive to her efforts, and he didn't want to be so openly defiant. None of this was supposed to be happening. He wasn't supposed to be alive at this point.

"Was this your first attempt?" she asked.

"No." He turned his arm toward her, so she could see the silvery razor scars up the insides of his arms.

"You're a cutter."

"I was."

"Did it help?"

"Some."

"When did you try to kill yourself for the first time?"

"When I was sixteen."

"Why?"

"I was afraid my best friend would hate me because I was a stripper and a prostitute."

Professional though she was, Dr. Beverly hadn't been expecting that kind of admission. She blinked, then covered her surprise. "That must have been traumatic for you."

Tango folded the sheet again, and again, smile tidy folds. He hadn't meant to handle it this way. He'd meant to be sorrowful, full of remorse, a changed man who no longer wished to take his life. He'd known this meeting would come. But in the moment, he was too consumed by the need for the razor to play the game. The irony wasn't lost on him: he was too desperate to say what he needed to say in order to do what he needed to do.

"Kevin."

He hated the way she said his name. That practiced note of concern.

"Why don't you tell me about the first time? When you were sixteen. Maybe then we can understand what happened last night."

A hard, hot kernel of anger formed in his chest, gaining layers and momentum as he met her gaze once more. "We can understand?"

"Yes."

"Do you think" – his hands started shaking and he clenched the sheet – "that I don't understand *what happened?* Do you think it's some sort of mystery to me? Huh?" His voice rose, shrill and furious, shaking with fright. "Do you think I want to kill myself because I *don't understand* something? You stupid bitch!"

He didn't know when he reached for it, but suddenly the pitcher of water on the nightstand was in his hand and he was throwing it at Dr. Beverly. It hit her in the shoulder, and the top popped off; water plumed upward into the air. Dr. Beverly shouted in alarm and shoved her chair back, leaping out of it.

He was still screaming, his voice seeming to come from a great distance. Was this an out-of-body experience? "You're the one who doesn't get it! Don't you dare fucking talk to me, you've never had shit happen to you! What the fuck could you ever tell me?!"

This was it. He'd finally snapped.

The door swung open and in came the people of his life: Mercy, Aidan, Whitney. He didn't want to see them; couldn't bear the thought of making eye contact.

But then...

There was Ian, dressed for the December cold in his long black coat and cream cashmere scarf, long hair windblown. He pushed past the others, face grave and ashen.

"Kev. Darling."

He buried his face in his hands, felt the erratic pulse in his fingers, fought the heaving tide of grief inside him, the way it wanted out, a howling beast of an emotion that wouldn't quiet.

Ian's arms went around his shoulders. His coat brushed Tango's face, fine and masculine-smelling.

"Stop," Ian said in a quiet, firm voice. "Stop, this isn't the way. You know it isn't."

But that was just it: he didn't know anything.

~*~

As Aidan shooed her back out into the hall, Whitney's mind went blank save for one image: the tall, narrow man with the long auburn hair cuddling Kev against his chest like a child, whispering against his matted hair. She recognized the man – he'd been there the night she and Kev were rescued. And even if she was only twenty-one and innocent, she recognized the energy between the two of them: that was no brotherly, friendly embrace. It was like a parent with a child. It was like lovers.

"You brought him into it?" Mercy asked when the room door was shut.

"I had to," Aidan said, throwing up his arms, expression defeated. "I'm so out of my depth with this. I've got no idea how to get through to him. If nothing else, Ian's been there too. Maybe he can..." He trailed off, shaking his head, scrubbing the back of his neck.

Dr. Beverly brushed water droplets from her jacket, flustered and unsure. "I'm recommending he be committed," she told them, tidying her hair. "He's in no shape to be released."

"Yeah, recommend," Mercy said, rounding on her with a black look. "See how that turns out for you."

Her eyes flew wide.

"Merc, don't threaten the shrink."

"The shrink needs to mind her own damn business."

Dr. Beverly drew herself upright.

"Bye," Mercy told her, and what could she do in the face of such a terrifying specimen? She walked away.

Mercy turned back to face them. "Have you ever seen him get physically violent with someone like that?"

"No." Aidan sighed. "Shit. No, never."

"He doesn't need to be more upset," Mercy reasoned. "If he doesn't want to talk to her, then he doesn't have to."

Whitney wanted to feel sorry for the doctor, but she couldn't, too preoccupied with what she'd seen. "Who is that in there with him?" Both men glanced toward her. "He was there when you broke us out of that house. Who is he?"

Aidan's lips compressed. "He's an old friend of Kev's."

"Is…is Kev gay?"

"He goes both ways." Defensive edge in Aidan's voice, daring her to say something against it. "Is that a problem?"

"No." And it wasn't. It wasn't something she'd ever considered, but she felt no revulsion.

But she did feel…something. A tug of emotion in her belly. Loss? Perhaps loss. Because she hadn't spent the night in this hospital just because it was the right thing to do.

"Damn. Baby," Mercy said on a sudden breath, voice changing. He was staring down the hall, and coming toward them were Ava and her mother, Maggie.

Maggie pushed a double stroller with Mercy and Ava's two boys loaded into it. Ava was wearing a dress and leggings, tall boots, a long black wool coat, the dark ensemble ruined by her very pregnant belly.

"You didn't have to come," Mercy said, moving toward her.

Her expression pained, she laid a hand on the side of her stomach. "Oh, but I did. It's time. She's coming."

Four

"I've got the boys," Maggie told him, patting his shoulder. "Go with your girls."

And Mercy went, because there was no separating him from his old lady in this kind of situation, and because he trusted no one more than Maggie when it came to his children.

It was a familiar scene at this point: a pink-toned labor and delivery room, the bed with the surgical lamps glaring overhead, a brisk staff of nurses, led by Ava's obstetrician, Dr. Leeds. Mercy was bundled into the drape and cap, wanting the nurse who helped him to hurry, damn it.

This was the third time for Ava, and everything was progressing quickly. Too quickly – his common sense couldn't catch up to his panic.

Ava's hand fluttered up into the air and he captured it in his own, fingers closing carefully around hers.

"Alright, Dad," Dr. Leeds said, smile kind. "Do you want to help her push?"

"Yeah."

As he had twice before, he hooked her behind the knee with one arm; a nurse stepped up on the other side to do the same.

He met Ava's glazed eyes once, before it started. Her grin was more of a grimace.

"Love you, *fillette*," he said, and ducked to kiss her forehead.

"Ready?" Dr. Leeds asked.

Ava pushed.

~*~

Ghost found his son in a small family waiting area down the hall from Tango's room. Sam sat beside him, fatigue and worry marring her pretty features. Lainie was in her carrier at their feet.

Sam spotted him first. "Mr. Teague." She smoothed her hair, hitched her glasses up her nose. She looked exactly like someone who'd spent most of the night in the hospital.

"What did I tell you about that 'Mr. Teague' business?" He motioned for her to stay seated and patted the top of her blonde head in greeting.

Aidan stood, face haggard, eyelids drooping.

Ghost pulled him into a fast, masculine embrace on impulse. "How is he?"

Aidan pulled back and shook his head. "Physically, he's gonna be fine. But he was throwing shit at the therapist a few minutes ago."

Alarming to consider. Of all his men, Tango was the most placid, the most troubled by violence, the absolute least likely to be picked up for a bar fight.

"Shit."

"I've explained it to him," Aidan went on. "But he's snapped, Dad. He doesn't give a shit about anything anymore."

As evidenced by the suicide attempt.

"Let me talk to him."

Aidan's brows lifted, and an unfamiliar hardness moved through his dark eyes. After Sam, after Lainie, after Tango's rescue, Aidan had lost the shine of youth and impetuosity. Gone was the trod-upon young man who'd stood up to his father in half-measures.

Thank God.

"Hey," Ghost said, careful to soften his tone. "I know what's at stake here. I'm not his president right now." He plucked at his black and white Lean Dogs sweatshirt as proof: no cut, only soft colors.

Aidan gave him a long, hard stare.

"Take your girls home," Ghost urged. "Grab a shower." He was crusty with dried blood. "Get something to eat. I'll stay with Kev 'til you get back."

Aidan sucked at his lip, torn between brotherly and husbandly duty.

Sam stood and laid a hand on his shoulder. "I can take Lainie home, and you can stay."

He turned his head toward her, expression softening. "I don't want you driving if you're tired." He exhaled; sounded completely done in. "Come on, baby." Sharp look at Ghost. "You'll stay?"

"Cross my heart. Mags and I are gonna be here a while anyway, with Ava having the baby."

"Shit. Right. Kiss her for us."

"I will."

Sam stepped forward and kissed Ghost's cheek in parting. "Love you."

"You too, sweetheart."

He watched them go, Aidan carrying the baby seat, free arm around Sam's waist. Two people very much in love. A biker and the support he needed from his old lady.

Not for the first time, Ghost sent up a silent thanks to the powers above for bringing Sam into Aidan's life. He knew exactly how lost he'd be without Maggie.

Then he took a deep, bracing breath and headed down the hall.

He knocked once on the door, then let himself in.

Tango, propped up with pillows, swallowed by a pale blue hospital gown, looked nothing less than skeletal. His hair hung in tattered streamers down his neck. His eyes stared into the middle distance, glassy, lifeless.

The change hadn't occurred overnight, but it had been so easy to dismiss the slow decline: the weight loss, the hair growing out, the deepening detachment from everyone and everything. A slow transformation, yes, but one that had been unfolding beneath all their noses. Half-denial that they were losing him, half-unwillingness to strap the boy down and force their love down his throat. They'd been trying, all of them, but they hadn't taken the necessary drastic measures.

Tango had been drastic instead.

The sense of failure was crushing.

Ghost's chipper greeting died on his tongue. "Ah, Christ, Kevin." He walked to the bed, sank down into the chair that waited.

Tango didn't acknowledge him, but his throat worked as he swallowed.

Ghost reached to cover one bony, tattooed hand with his own where it rested on the sheets. "Kev. No." His throat felt tight. "Son, no, this isn't the way. This won't help you."

Tango closed his eyes. His narrow jaw trembled.

Ghost tightened his hand. "Aidan says you won't talk to the shrink. He says you blew up at her."

He took a shivery breath, eyes still closed. "What am I supposed to do? Tell her – tell her how I used to suck cocks for a living?"

Ghost knew he didn't have the tools to handle the snakes in the boy's head. There was a possibility he would do more harm than good. But someone had to break through these self-destructive walls. "I want you to talk to her about whatever you feel like talking to her about, so you can come home with us."

Tango's eyes popped open, tear-bright and wild when they slid to Ghost. "But don't tell her too much, right? 'Cause I can't say anything about the club. Or about Don Ellison's basement."

Shit. "I'm not worried about any of that right now."

"Do the others know?" Faint note of defiance. "Do they know what I did? You'll have to strip my patches now. They'll never let me stay."

Ghost sighed. A large part of him wanted to take Tango by the shoulders and shake him until his teeth snapped together. But that would solve nothing. Swallowing the impulse, hoping for patience, he said, "No one knows but the family."

Tango stared at him with his eerie, fevered gaze.

"Mercy, and Aidan," Ghost explained, "and Mags, and Ava, and Sam. And me. Aidan and Merc brought you in the truck so there wouldn't be a call on the scanners. None of our brothers know where you are or what you did."

"Why wouldn't you tell them?"

Snapped was right. Snapped was a damn understatement.

Ghost said, "Because if I have to rewrite the entire goddamn MC rule book, I will to keep you from getting excommunicated, but for starters, I want to try keeping it secret."

"You should tell them."

"No."

~*~

"Mind if I join you?"

Whitney jerked, startled from her deep contemplation of her coffee cup. She sat at a small table tucked up against the wall of the ground floor hospital café. A warm, cheerful place, with honey walls and potted ferns, strategic lighting. The bakery cases and buffet line were full of unexpected treats: huge sticky cinnamon rolls, gourmet cookies, grilled chicken and asparagus, some sort of Asian dish in dark sauce that looked like it would be heaven spooned over rice. She hadn't been able to stomach the idea of the cafeteria, but this little place was charming, full of human chatter, and smelled of rich cooking things. Wall-to-wall tinted plate windows looked out onto the hospital drive, cars crawling past, ribbons of gray exhaust snaking from cold tailpipes. People bustled up and down the sidewalk, wrapped in jackets and scarves. She could almost pretend she was at Stella's, and that she wasn't in a hospital, worrying about her suicidal, bisexual...whatever he was.

Maggie Teague stood beside her table with the double stroller that held Mercy and Ava's two wriggling boys. She was, as always, pretty, unselfconscious, and smiling, and for those reasons a little intimidating.

"Sure," Whitney said, surprised to see her. "How's Ava?"

Maggie took the chair across from her and put a hand on the stroller, pushed it idly back and forth, which made Cal giggle. "She's great. The baby was born about twenty minutes ago. Ten fingers and toes, screaming like a banshee." She beamed with maternal pride. "Ava's a trooper. I said I'd give Mama and Daddy some alone time to catch their breath."

"That's wonderful. I'm so happy for them."

Maggie nodded, then grew serious. "But you're not happy in general, are you?"

Whitney blinked, surprised again. Maggie gave the impression that she'd eat you alive if the occasion called for it, and there would be no warning. By the time you noticed her fangs, they'd already be sunk in your throat. "I'm sorry?"

"What's happening with Tango has you all upset," she observed. "You looked ready to cry when I walked up."

Whitney tried and failed to smile. "I was."

Maggie leaned her elbow on the table, cupped her chin in her hand, expression thoughtful, and penetrating. "He's special to you."

"Very."

"Can I ask why?" Her eyes said she knew exactly why, but there was the question, thrown down like a gauntlet between them. Tell her why…and risk revealing herself as young, and shallow, or worse, the kind of girl who romanticized fixing broken boys.

Whitney took a deep breath and stared down into her untouched coffee. She'd poured too much creamer, and it trailed in lazy swirls across the surface. "When we were…when we were in that basement." It was physically painful to go back there in her mind. "He kept me safe. He sacrificed himself for me. And I was just a stranger, and he didn't have to do it, but that's just who he is, isn't it?"

Maggie nodded.

"But that's not why he's special to me." The tears threatened, and she swallowed them down, chased it with a fast sip of coffee. "My brother's heroin addiction killed him."

"I know that."

"I couldn't save him. I didn't do enough, or say enough, or try everything that I could. I lost him. Because I let him push me away." She shook her head. "But maybe I can save Kev. Maybe, if I don't quit, and I won't leave him alone, and I won't be pushed away, I can keep him here on earth with us."

Maggie sat back, hazel gaze hard to read. "You know, most doctors would say that you can't save a person. That he has to make the decision to save himself."

"What do you think?" Whitney asked.

"I think when you hate yourself badly enough to slit your wrists, you can't haul yourself out of the hole. You have to be pulled out." She offered a bare smile. "Keep pulling, sweetheart. We can always use an extra set of hands."

~*~

The next afternoon, the most unusual of lunches took place at a few pushed-together tables in a back corner of the hospital café. Untouched mugs and plates cluttered their haphazard table, and a strange sense of togetherness had them all leaning toward one another, as if drawn by magnets.

Mercy, a just-released Ava, in sweats and cradling the new baby. Maggie, Ghost, Aidan, Sam, Whitney, and Ian. Bruce the bodyguard sat alone at the next table, enjoying coffee and an oatmeal cookie the size of his considerable head.

Ian had the floor, his crisp British accent heavy with sadness. "I was much like this when I did it. I didn't want to be alive anymore." His composure almost slipped, lean jaw clenching. "But finally the breakthrough came, and the ice melted, and I wanted to live again."

"What was the breakthrough?" Ghost asked.

The Englishman met the president's stare boldly, big blue-green eyes full of grief. "He was."

"Hmph."

"But...." A tremble in his breathing, a fast glancing away. "I don't think it will be me for him this time. I don't...I don't..."

"We've got to get him out of this damn hospital," Aidan said. "And Jesus Christ, he needs therapy, but he won't agree to that."

"Discharge first," Maggie said, "therapy second."

Ava said, "I have an idea."

~*~

His memory had gone fuzzy around the edges. That was the morphine they'd dosed him with. The past and the present flickered together and then apart, like dancers, legs flashing, feet catching behind knees. Together, the embrace, and then the spin, fingertips clinging. Everything was now: the razor, the hot enclosing water of the tub, the therapist with her professional sympathy. And there was Miss Carla, too, with her cigarette breath and her stained teeth grinning at him. And Ian, not of the expensive suits and cashmere scarves, but the Ian of old, with eyeliner and bronzer, and the delicate kiss he pressed to the hollow of Tango's throat.

Now was the cell, and the broom handle, and the stink of sweating men. Now was the thick red dirt of Mama's front yard, and the gleaming white steel of the fancy car pulling up at the mailbox. Now was yesterday, and tomorrow, and twenty years ago. The future took on the shapes and colors and sounds of the past, and he would never escape, he realized. The nightmare would never be over; a pretty boy...he was just a pretty boy...someone's little loverboy.

It became a song in his head. First Whitney's clear sweet voice. And then Miss Carla's. He thought he would scream.

But instead, the door opened, and Ava poked her shining dark head into the room. "Kev?" And he remembered where he was, and all the dancing images snapped back into place. This was now, and they wouldn't let go of him, his people.

He blinked against the grit in his eyes, and struggled to sit up higher against the pillows. "Yeah?" His voice was an awful croak.

"Can I come in?"

"Sure." What the hell did it matter at this point? Aidan, Mercy, Whitney, Ian, Ghost...what was one more person telling him how important it was that he get out of this bed?

She eased the door wide with her shoulder and came into the room, and that was when he realized something was off. The last time he'd seen Ava, she'd been very pregnant. Now, the bulging belly was gone. She was dressed in yoga pants and a sweatshirt, and carried a white-wrapped bundle in her arms. She walked slowly, gingerly, wincing he saw, as she drew close. Still sore.

"You had the baby."

"Yesterday." She beamed, proving that even exhausted and haggard, new mothers were the most beautiful of women. "Can we sit?"

He shifted over on the bed. "Yeah." And she took a careful perch on the edge, hissing a little through her teeth.

"The third time, and it doesn't get any less painful, only quicker," she said with a wry grin. She twisted so the baby was right in front of him, almost in his lap. "Here, hold her."

"Oh, no, I shouldn't…"

But Ava was putting the bundle in his arms, and he had no choice but to cradle the small body, and cup the back of her little beanie-covered head. A pink beanie because, as Ava said, she was a girl.

When his hands were safely full of baby, Ava curled a hand around his forearm. "Uncle Tango," she said, voice bright and official, "meet Camille Nanette Lécuyer. Nanette for Mercy's Gram," she explained. "Three weeks early. She just couldn't wait to come out and meet everybody."

Camille. Pink, and new, and perfect. She yawned, tiny mouth opening wide, eyelids fluttering.

"She's beautiful, Ava."

"I think so, too, but I'm her mama, so I'm a little biased." Then her voice changed, and her hand tightened on his arm. "Kev."

He tore his eyes from the baby to meet her mother's serious, dark gaze.

"When my boys are your age, they're going to be Dogs too. And sometimes it scares the hell out of me, but I won't deny them their legacy. And when they're grown, and patched, and the clubhouse is theirs, they'll walk through the rooms and find all the old framed photos on the walls, the ones of members past. And their father and uncles will be in those pictures. They'll find

47

one of you and Aidan standing together, and they'll say, "That's Aidan, and that's Tango."

She smiled sadly. "And I want both of you to be gray, and wrinkled, and too arthritic to get on your bikes in that photo. I want you to be an old man in that picture, Kev. We all want that. I want to sidle up next to you at Camille's wedding, and make some stupid remark about the good old days being long gone."

He had to look away from her then, back to the baby, Camille's pink new face blurring as tears filled his eyes.

Her voice changed again, tear-choked now. "The world is full of terrible things. But there are beautiful things, too, and you're one of them."

She stood and put her arms around his neck, held his head against her breasts. "Come home. Just please come home."

Camille squirmed in his arms, and now was just two pretty girls who loved him like family. That was the beginning of the next, the longest, the last chapter of his life.

Five

The apartment welcomed him back in pristine condition, warm, the central heat chugging and the windows fogged with steam. Maggie had baked white chocolate chunk blondies, his favorite, and left them cooling on the counter; the whole apartment smelled like vanilla and sugar. Night was falling, and the Christmas lights strung up in the businesses across the street were coming on with multicolored twinkles.

"Home sweet home," Aidan said behind him, and dropped his keys on the counter.

Tango did a slow revolution, taking it all in, as though seeing it for the first time. There were changes since he'd gone to the hospital: the old bookshelves under the window were now full of books, tattered second- and thirdhand paperbacks. A new curtain in the window. Several warm throws were draped over the back of the sofa. Magazines – car, bike, and gun – were spread artfully across the coffee table.

He looked down at himself: skinny pale arms full of track marks, bandages on his wrists, still. They'd kept him in the hospital until he was done detoxing. For the first time, food sounded good, and he was thirsty for a drink, and the feel of air moving across his skin didn't make him want to scream. But…look at him. He was a bundle of scarred sticks, haphazardly held together with tape and well-wishes.

"Alright." Aidan slapped his palms together and chafed them back and forth, all excitement and anticipation. "First, beer. Then this awesome shit Mags baked. Then not one, but all three *Expendables* movies. Make popcorn," he directed. "And I'll set up the DVD player."

"I don't have one."

"You do now. Present from *moi*."

"Mercy teaching you French?" he asked with a snort.

"Ha ha, asshole. I'm married to a professor. I'm cultured and shit now."

Tango smiled. It was exhausting to do so, taxing to the muscles in his skinny face, but he couldn't fight the urge. "You didn't have to do that."

"Call you an asshole? No, that was kinda bad."

"The DVD player, I mean."

Aidan shrugged and wouldn't meet his eyes as he slit the tape on the box with his boot knife. "I did if I wanted to watch movies."

Deciding his best friend was never going to be comfortable with gratitude, he went to make the popcorn.

~*~

Miss Carla's bony fingers running down his cheek. Her fetid breath against his face. *"What a pretty little loverboy you are."*

Tango woke with a shout, jackknifing upright. It was dark, and the TV was still going, and as the nightmare faded, the reality of the night returned. He'd nibbled on popcorn and Maggie's blondies in front of a movie marathon with Aidan. They'd dragged the sofa cushions and bedroom pillows and blankets and the sleeping bags Aidan had brought to the center of the living room floor and made a pallet in front of the TV like little boys. He hadn't thought he could fall asleep, but he had, and then, of course, the nightmare.

He sat with his head between his knees, trying to catch his breath, trying not to throw up. Carla couldn't pass through his mind without making him want to gag.

Beside him, the blankets and pillows rustled, and for a second, he thought it was Ian. But then Aidan's work-rough hand touched his arm, and somehow, that was more comforting: the presence of his best friend rather than his lover. It was more real. More pure.

"Nightmare?" Aidan asked.

The air felt still, without temperature, a vacuum around him. Nothing stirred. There were no sounds save those out on the street. And the thumping of blood in his ears.

"Yeah."

More stillness. And then…

Aidan shifted closer, and put an arm across his shoulders. A firm, reassuring hold. Brotherly, platonic, sweet. Tango felt his friend's chin against the top of his head.

"What do you usually do when you have a nightmare?" Aidan asked.

Shaken, enjoying the physical comfort – the first he'd had in the dark of night for a long time – he couldn't guard against an honest answer. "Usually, I call Whitney."

"Do you want to call her now?"

Again, the honesty. "Yeah."

"Hold on." Aidan withdrew, stood, and fumbled around a bit. "Do you want the lights?"

"Not really."

Aidan returned, as did his arm, and he put Tango's cellphone in his hand. "Here. Is she always awake this late?"

"Yeah. It's when she paints."

~*~

The house was blessedly quiet in the wee hours. During the week, Whitney arrived home at her dead brother's house after six every evening, and it was early December, which meant it was full dark by then, the lawn and driveway shifting with dubious shadows. She hustled through the chill night, purse clutched to her chest like a weapon, boot heels rapping the concrete. She had unlocking the door, whirling inside, shutting and relocking it down to a science. Only once the lock was engaged could she breathe properly. Safe. Guarded. It wasn't a bad neighborhood, but she didn't much trust crime statistics or orderly landscaping anymore. The world was brimming with danger.

Just like this house – full of landmines and booby traps.

Most evenings, she could hear the kids arguing, crying, or fighting over the TV remote. Their mother, Madelyn, sat off to the side, ignoring the drama, nursing the first of several drinks of the night.

51

Whitney settled the squabble, greeted her sister-in-law as cheerfully as possible, and set about starting dinner. She was no chef, but was improving. Madelyn would shuffle in, tumbler of vodka in-hand, to tell Whitney that the potatoes were overdone, or that the chicken wasn't seasoned properly, and then she would take over.

Dinner was always a sullen affair. And then the chaos of bathing and putting the girls to bed. After, Madelyn bearing a fresh drink and swaying side-to-side, they tackled laundry-folding, or furniture-dusting, or mail-sorting, bill-paying. The house, always so spotless and cheerful before, was rapidly becoming a dungeon. And only when she was finally alone, locked away in her bedroom, could Whitney allow herself to feel the weight of depression.

Then she turned to her paints.

Jason had sought relief in heroin.

Madelyn in booze.

But for Whitney it was the glide of rich oil paint across canvas.

She was a perfectionist, and she leaned close to her easel, squinting, face screwed up in concentration. She chose narrow, delicate brushes, feathering in precisely-blended colors. Minutes slipped into hours, the night melting beyond the window. She would be exhausted, face shadowed the next morning, but the peace was worth it.

Tonight she had a photo of a yellow iris clipped to her easel. She had sketched the flower with graphite first, and now filled the petals with a rich canary-colored base coat, broad strokes of the brush. So quiet, the window rimmed with frost, she heard the brush against the paper, the liquid movement of the paint.

Her phone rang.

She almost dropped her brush. She didn't have to check the caller ID, just fumbled the phone up to her ear. "Kev."

A ragged breath. A pause. "Hi."

A dozen questions crowded her mind, so many things she wanted to ask him. More than that, she wanted to be beside him, put her insubstantial arms around his skinny shoulders. But she knew she couldn't let her worry and stress bleed onto him. He couldn't be ready for that yet. So she kept her voice calm. "Are you back home?"

"Yeah."

"That's good. Are you alone?" she asked, fearing he was.

"No, Aidan's sleeping over."

Thank God. "Tell him I said hello."

"I will."

"Are you guys having a good night?"

"We watched movies. Mags left us stuff to eat."

"That sounds nice." Infinitely nicer than her own night, eating half-burned spaghetti while her nieces looked sadly upon their drunk mother. When he didn't respond right away, she said, "You had another nightmare."

"Yeah."

"Are you going to tell me what it's about this time?"

He hesitated. He'd never offered up an explanation, and so she had no idea what plagued him. Not exactly, anyway. She had a feeling broom handles and the mysterious Cuckoo's Nest played a part.

"Is it that you don't want me to know?" she pressed, gently. "Or that you don't like to talk about it?"

"Both."

She held the phone in one hand, and resumed painting with the other. Even, careful strokes, as soothing to her as being petted. "I think you probably need to talk to someone, though."

No response.

"If you don't like Dr. Beverly we could find someone else."

He hesitated, and then: "We...?"

She thought about the tall, elegant, long-haired man who'd come to Kev's bedside, his gentle lover's touch. And then she thought about meeting him formally at breakfast: Ian. Insanely gorgeous, like Kev, but healthy and clean and taking care of himself.

What was she doing? There was no place for her in Kev's life.

But then she thought about Maggie Teague in the café, just the two of them, Maggie asking her not to give up.

"Yes, 'we,'" she said, firmly. "All of us who love you. We're going to help you through this, whatever that means."

When he spoke, it almost sounded like he was smiling. Or at least trying to. "You're bossy."

She smiled back, wishing she could see him, that he could see the encouragement shining in her eyes. "Not usually. My coworkers would never believe you. You must just bring out the boss in me."

His chuckle was pitiful, but it was there, and that was a start. The tension she'd felt at first – the vise-like grip of the nightmare – eased, melted slowly away, as she kept smoothing paint across the paper.

"What are you doing tomorrow?" she asked, and felt like it was safe to do so.

"Oh, uh…."

She heard Aidan's voice, distant, but shouting toward the phone. He must have been listening. "He's doing whatever he wants to," he said, voice almost excited, egging her on. Oh, thank you, Aidan. "You wanna come over?"

"Why don't I come make lunch?"

"Perfect," Aidan said. "All I can make is Eggo's."

"Twelve-thirty?" Her heart was pumping with anticipation, smile splitting her tired face.

"Awesome."

"Kev?" she asked, to make sure.

He said, "Yeah, that sounds good."

~*~

Silence. Among so many other things, money could also buy silence. A wall clock that never ticked. A Rolex that never made a sound. Top of the line refrigerator that kept quietly to itself. No sounds intruded upon his conscience save that of the scratch of the pencil against the paper.

A thick, dark graphite, fresh white paper, and the marks he made that were like wounds inflicted upon the sketchpad. It had been so long, Ian wondered if he could pick it up again, resume with the same old flair.

He could.

A face stared up at him, rendered from memory. A female face, wide blue eyes, a small mouth, the portrait of innocence. Not club-related, not part of Kev's adopted family. But someone important. The girl from the basement.

He hated her.

Six

"Hey, you wanna grab gyros?"

Whitney pressed the power button on her computer and stood, stretching the kinks from her lower back.

Her coworker, Mark, stood with his arms folded over the top of her cubicle, shirt rumpled, tie askew as usual, bright orange-red hair standing up like he'd raked his fingers through it. His expression belied the casual tone of his question: he really wanted gyros.

"I can't today," she said, reaching for her jacket and purse. "I promised a friend I'd make him lunch."

His brows quirked above the rims of his glasses. "A friend, huh?"

"Yes, just a friend." But her stomach fluttered.

"Uh-huh."

"How's April?" she asked, and he flushed with adorable happiness, cheeks going redder than his hair.

"She's good. I'm introducing her to my parents this weekend."

"That's awesome, Mark." She smiled and he blushed some more. "They'll love her, I'm sure."

"I hope so," he said as she joined him and they started toward the elevator. "She's really nervous."

"I guess I would be too. But your parents are really sweet." Both of them had come to the company picnic back in the summer, both of them doughy, kind, and redheaded, like their son. They'd looked like a family of sunburned leprechauns, standing off to the side of the impromptu softball game.

"I told her she could borrow a Xanax from me," Mark said.

Anti-anxiety meds: good idea for Kev? Probably not, given his drug history. She swept it from her mind.

"Hopefully she won't need it," she said, and hoped she didn't sound too distracted.

Mark, always good company, rode down with her in the elevator, and walked her across the parking lot. They wished each other happy lunches, parted ways, and went to their respectfully crappy cars.

She would have to hurry, she saw, as she checked the dash clock. Her manager wouldn't mind if she was a few minutes late getting back, but she didn't want to waste any time.

Southern Decembers were fickle. They could be mild, sunny, and reminiscent of spring. Or they could be wicked, overcast, and biting. This was shaping up to be a wicked month, and she drove in cotton gloves, shivering as she waited for the car's heater to take the chill from the air. Early Christmas garlands flapped like flags along eaves. Tattered leaves cartwheeled across the street.

She stopped in briefly at Leroy's to grab supplies, reveling a little in her new ability to buy alcohol, then made the short trip to the address Kev had given her.

The apartment was above the bakery, and she parked in the alley as instructed. She braced herself, climbed from the car, pushed the errant windblown hair from her eyes...

And there was Kev. Right in front of her. Come all the way down the iron staircase to meet her.

Her heart actually skipped a beat. Before she could greet him, analyze her appearance, or guard her chemical reaction, her pulse leapt. That was probably all she really needed to know about her relationship with him.

"Hi," she said, too bright, too hopeful.

It looked like it took effort, but he smiled. "Hi."

He was still painfully thin, and his hair needed cutting. But it was clean, and slicked back from his narrow, finely-carved face, his eyes standing out like bright clear jewels. He was in jeans and a baggy sweatshirt. He smelled – as the wind shifted and brought his scent to her – faintly of soap.

"I brought some groceries," she said, lamely.

He reached for the back door of the car. "I'll get 'em."

"Oh, you don't have to." She leaned toward him, half-afraid his matchstick arms might collapse under the weight of their lunch.

But he managed, hefting both brown paper bags. "I got it."

"You sure?"

He sent her a fleeting smile. "I might be all fucked up, but I can manage carrying things." He obviously meant it as a joke, so she didn't counter him, only followed. Up the tall narrow iron steps, through the door, into his apartment. He circled behind her to hip-check the door shut, and the raucous breeze was mercifully cut off.

She loved the place immediately.

From the door, she could see the living room, kitchen, and two doors – presumably a bedroom and bathroom. The appliances were dated, the furniture bachelor pad-standard. But she saw the cleanliness, the shining white baseboards and crown molding, the natural light, the scraped pine floors, the bookshelves under the window.

She also saw Aidan, getting up from a leather recliner. "Hey." His expression said a wealth of thanks. A silent acknowledgement of their shared goal: saving Kev.

"Hey," she greeted. "Are you hungry? I thought I'd make burgers. And I brought wine."

His eyes flicked over her shoulder – to Kev – and back. "Actually, I was thinking I'd clock a few hours at the shop." He gave her a look: he wanted her alone with Kev, for some reason. "If that's okay."

"Sure." She glanced behind her at Kev.

He shrugged, awkward beneath the weight of the bags. "He's got mouths to feed besides his own."

Her heart lurched. Going by Aidan's expression, so did his. *We love him*, she knew. *And we just want him to live.*

"That's fine," she said. "You go ahead and we'll be fine."

She watched, feeling like an interloper, as Aidan took the bags from Kev, set them on the counter, and then smothered his best friend in a hug.

"I can't breathe," Kev protested.

"Shut up," Aidan said. He smacked him on the shoulder and drew away. "I'll be back."

"You don't have to be," Kev said.

"But I will be."

And then he was gone.

Whitney knew a moment's fear, wondering if she could possibly be vibrant and lively enough to keep Kev in a good headspace. But she knew she couldn't afford to worry about that; she could only try her best.

So she said, "Hungry?" and gave him an encouraging smile.

"A little bit." His smile was thin and apologetic. "I haven't had much appetite lately."

"It'll come back," she assured. "Come here and you can help me figure out how to work this stove top. How old is it?"

"From the fifties, I think."

"Wow."

"It works, though. Mercy always liked to cook."

"He did?" It was hard to imagine that giant monster of a man stirring up brownie batter.

"Yeah, and then I guess he and Ava cooked together..." His brows crimped as he stared down at the stove. In the wash of incoming sunlight, she could see the faint blue tracks of veins in his temples, down the pale column of his throat. His skin was almost translucent, white and smooth as a pearl, seemingly fragile as tissue paper. She thought if she touched him, her finger might push right through, straight into meat and blood.

A disturbing image, one she chased away. She turned to the grocery bags, and began laying things out on the counter: the hamburger patties, a block of sharp cheddar cheese, red onions, lettuce, buns.

"You weren't kidding about burgers."

"All the fixings," she promised, setting down the jar of pickles. "I would have made fries, but that takes some time, so I brought the frozen kind instead."

"Frozen's good." He surveyed her purchases with some distress. "But I don't want you to go out of your way. I really won't be able to eat much."

"Eat what you can, and we can put the leftovers in the fridge for later."

He took a deep breath and met her gaze. "Thank you."

"You don't have to say that."

"And you don't have to be here."

She felt the sting of sudden tears, and turned away, blinking. "Okay. So. The stove?"

"Right."

~*~

Years ago, in the cramped apartment where Miss Carla's boys slept three and four to a mattress, there had been a blue Lava Lamp in the windowsill. He would stare at it, as he waited for the day's exhaustion to overwhelm the lingering taint of depravity and carry him off to sleep. He'd found great comfort in the slow, liquid movements of the lamp's contents: never once the same, but predictable none the less. Mindless, soothing.

That was Whitney. Always saying something new and sweet, surprising him, but more or less predictable in her goodness. She reminded him, in her own small way, of Maggie, or Ava, or even Holly. The women in his life who were brave enough to be kind, and tough enough not to quit. But the difference was, Whitney wouldn't leave here and head to one of his brothers' homes. He wasn't borrowing someone's woman; she was all his.

Huh. He'd never had a woman who was his.

Probably still didn't. There was a wealth of difference between sympathy and love.

He sat on a stool drawn up to the counter, smoking, tapping ash in a teacup saucer she'd found in the cabinets. He hadn't even known he had dishes; someone, probably Mags, had provided him with an entire set, even dainty little teacups to go with the saucers.

"You really look like you know what you're doing," he teased, exhaling a long, settling drag.

She tossed him a quick, light grin, and went back to turning the burgers in the cast iron skillet – another cabinet find. Go Mags. "My mom taught me how."

"Do y'all cook a lot?"

"We did. Before she passed away."

"Oh shit. I'm sorry. I didn't–"

"It's fine," she said. "You didn't know."

He felt like a heel. He'd never asked about her family, knew nothing outside the drama of her junkie brother. "I'm sorry," he repeated.

She sliced open the cheese package with a knife and tugged it off with a loud crackle. "My parents were older," she explained, tone conversational. She didn't seem traumatized by it. "I mean, much older than most people's parents. They thought Mom was infertile, so they finally gave up trying. My brother was conceived when they were forty. The doctor was completely surprised; Mom said it was a miracle. And then eight years later, she wound up pregnant with me."

"Man."

"I know, right?" She sent him a wry smile. "They were very kind, and very sweet together – high school sweethearts. But their friends' children were all off to college when Jason and I were still on the playground, and I don't think Mom and Dad knew quite what to do with us."

Tango ran the numbers in his head. If they'd been alive, her parents would have been seventy by now, but seventy wasn't that old in the grand scheme of medicine these days.

"What happened to them?" he asked, quietly.

"Mom had cancer," she said, tone becoming distant, matter-of-fact. "And when she died, Dad spent the next two years drinking himself to death."

"Shit."

She sliced the cheese in thick, perfect squares, knife clacking when it hit the wooden cutting board. "Dad was selfish. He didn't want to live without Mom, even though he had Jason and me. And turns out, Jason was that selfish too. The pain was more important than his family."

She paused, knife hovering in the air, the sunlight glinting down the edge of the blade, now gummy with cheese in places. "You know," she mused, "I've never thought of it like that. That they were selfish. I don't even really think that." She shook her head, and went back to slicing. "It's just that sometimes I'm so angry they did that. Mom couldn't help dying, but they could, and I just…" She paused again, and sent him a helpless look. "I'm sorry. I didn't mean to talk about this sort of stuff. And I don't mean that you—"

"No, I get it." Strangely, he wasn't having a reaction to her words. He'd thought this topic might tie a knot in his gut, leave him sweating and nervous. But two people in Whitney's life had killed themselves. He found himself not wanting to be the third, suddenly.

She stared at him, with her huge pale eyes full of sweetness. "I didn't do enough for them. I couldn't save them, and I hate myself every day for that. So I'm sorry, but I'm not going to give up on you, and you're just going to have to deal with it."

He felt a stir of warmth in his chest, felt the sharp tug of a smile. "I can deal."

~*~

"Kev still with his aunt?" Carter asked, and Aidan nearly jumped out of his skin.

He had a bike up on the rack, and turned away from it, toward Carter who stood eating a PowerBar with dirt-smeared hands. Was that suspicion in the guy's eyes?

"Yeah," Aidan said, careful to keep his voice flat, disinterested. Nothing going on; nothing to get excited about. "He is. Said he might be a little longer than he thought."

"Hmm." Carter shoved the rest of the bar in his mouth until his cheek bulged. "That sucks."

"Yeah." Aidan watched him retreat, feeling the faint vise of panic close around his throat.

He and Ghost and Mercy had concocted a story to tell their brothers. Tango's aunt was ailing, and Tango had gone to Spring City to be with her, since she had no other relatives. The call had come in the middle of the night, and he'd had to leave in a hurry, with only time for a quick call to Aidan for explanation.

Everyone had shrugged and taken it in stride, but the lie made Aidan itchy. It was a lie he'd tell to the bitter end, but he wondered if some of the others suspected anything.

There was one bright spot, though, and that was Ghost's stance in all of this. Sometimes Aidan didn't give his old man credit for slowly pushing the clock ahead, and letting some of the more preposterous and prejudiced MC practices die quiet deaths. Their womenfolk, for instance, exercised more autonomy and influence than the women of Duane's time. With Maggie, Ghost had set a precedent: he wanted a strong woman, and he worshipped her for that strength. Gone were the days of property patches and naked groupie Bitches on the backs of bikes. Gone too were the days of abject club poverty. Ghost had steadily built an empire, and sought to create a public image that was poised, dangerous, and powerful.

But some old traditions and superstitions persisted. Suicide was a sign of weakness in their brutal world. Brothers laid down their lives for fellow brothers, but they didn't take their own lives. The punishment for such a sin was excommunication.

Aidan didn't doubt that his fellow Dogs loved Tango. But they didn't love him unconditionally, the way their own small family did. So it must be kept secret, what Tango had tried to do. And when he came back to work and to church, no one would ever know, save the three of them who'd long kept Tango's other secrets.

Ghost protecting Kev? That earned big points in Aidan's mind. It almost made him love the man.

His phone rang, startling him, and he went outside to answer it, thinking it might be Tango.

It was Ian instead.

63

"How is he?"

Aidan sighed and leaned back against the side of the shop. He was getting tired of this British asshole's dictatorial phone calls. "He's alright. Why don't you call him yourself and ask?"

Ian made a delicate noise. "I'm not sure that's wise. Not now, anyway. Soon."

Another sigh. This time because he couldn't really argue with that, and he couldn't really fault the man for being concerned. "He's not back to his old self," he consented. "But he's better."

"Are you there with him now?"

"I'm at work."

"And Kev is alone?" Ian demanded. "You know that he–"

"He's not alone, okay? Do you think I'm that stupid?"

Deep sigh of relief. Then: "Would you like me to answer that question?"

"Look, I need to get back so I can clock out soon."

"Yes, of course. But tell me, who's with him?"

"A friend," Aidan said, firmly. "He's having lunch. It's fine."

Ian's voice hardened. "It's that girl, isn't it?"

A warning signal pinged in the back of Aidan's mind. He himself had no opinion of Whitney outside her ability to make Tango happy. But Ian was coming from a very different place on the friendship spectrum.

"She's in the same boat as us," Aidan said, firmly. "She wants Kev to get better."

"What does some starry-eyed child know about 'better'?" Bitterness now. Anger. Jealousy.

"Hey, listen to me. Leave her alone. Understand? Don't bother that kid."

"What would I possibly want with her?" Ian asked, and the call disconnected.

~*~

It was just a cheeseburger, but it was the best thing he'd ever tasted. He hadn't been hungry before, but the first bite changed his mind. The meat was juicy and well-seasoned, the cheese sharp, the bread soft. Like an animal, he choked down bite after bite, putting away two thirds of it before his shriveled stomach grew full and protested.

He laid the burger down and wiped his mouth, took a deep breath. "God. That's fantastic." His stomach cramped, and he willed it to still, to hold onto the food Whitney had prepared for him.

"Good." Her cheeks pinked with pleasure.

They sat at the scrubbed plank table that had been here back when Mercy rented the place. The sunlight did radiant things to Whitney's eyes, her delicate complexion; it chased rivers of auburn and gold through her dark hair.

She was only an arm's length away, but seemed a whole different species. Something vibrant, young, clean...alive. He was breathing, yes, and eating, sipping on a Coke, reaching for his cigarette in its saucer ashtray. But he wasn't alive. Not like Whitney.

"How have things been with you?" he asked, soothing his belly with a long drag.

She nibbled a French fry. "I'm still living with my sister-in-law. Helping her out with the girls." A shadow crossed her face. "She's...she's having trouble adjusting."

"Drinking?" he asked. Maybe it was too blunt, but he didn't have much grace left to offer, not even to someone as special as Whitney.

But if he was too blunt, she didn't seem to mind. She nodded. "A lot, actually. I know I need to confront her about it, but she hates me so bad I don't think she'll listen."

"If she hates you, she's stupid. And a bitch."

Her brows lifted. "She lost her husband."

"And you lost your brother. But you aren't lying in the gutter."

"Not yet."

"You would never. That's not you."

65

She set the fry down, spread her hands on the tabletop and studied them. It sounded like she chose her words carefully. "Some might say you're being hypocritical."

"And what do you say?"

Her head lifted, eyes shiny. "I say I don't know why the people I care about keep giving up on themselves."

"It's not the same," he said, tapping ash, frowning. "I don't have kids."

"You have people who love you. There's no qualifying *that.*"

His chest tightened. He felt her sadness, a physical presence, and wanted to do something about it. "You have to confront her," he said. "Get her in AA if you have to."

Whitney nodded. Picked up her burger, took a small bite. "I know," she said once she'd swallowed. "She couldn't hate me any more than she does. And I can't let her do this to Ashley and Charlotte."

"How old are they?"

"Seven and five." Her expression softened. "They're actually pretty fun kids…"

She told him about Ashley's wish to be a ballerina, and her little sister's contrasting obsession with horses. She talked about taking them to the fair a couple of months back, about the way they'd wanted to ride the Ferris wheel eight times, and the way they'd begged for candy apples, then been unable to bite through the hardened sugar.

Tango smiled because she smiled, because seeing her happy warmed his insides. "You like kids, don't you?"

"A little bit." But her bright blush and modest smile said more than a little bit: she wanted kids of her own.

Why are you here with me? he wanted to ask her. *You deserve the world, kiddo.*

"I thought I wanted to be a teacher for a little while," she said. "But I don't think I want to be in charge of *that* many kids at a time."

"Just a few."

"Yes."

"You'll be a wonderful mom," he said, and her blush deepened.

"Why would you say that?" she asked, looking self-conscious.

"Because you remind me of all the wonderful moms I know."

Her eyes widened, pleasure radiating from her in a visible aura. "Thank you."

He took another drag off his cigarette.

"You've never talked about your family," she said in a quiet voice.

"The club is my family."

Her expression became sympathetic.

The sight of it put a lump in his throat, for some reason. "Don't feel bad for me, Whit." He had to clear his throat.

"Never," she said. "It's just that sometimes, I want to hug you."

He allowed himself to fantasize about it: her small shape bundled against his chest, her sleek hair under his chin. The softness of her breasts. Beat of her heart, sound of her breathing.

"That's probably not a good idea," he said, and sucked down the last of the cig.

~*~

"Oh no," she said when she checked the time and realized she had to leave.

"You have to get back?" Kev guessed, and his cautious smile dimmed down to nothing.

"I wish I didn't have to." And she meant it. Because though she'd come today with the intent to cheer Kev, she felt sure the opposite had happened. Coaxing smiles, even a chuckle or two, from him had warmed her in a way nothing had been able to lately. And now she felt sadness return, as well as the persistent worry that he shouldn't be left on his own.

She stood and collected their plates.

"I can do that," he said, pushing his chair back.

"I don't mind."

But he followed her to the counter, took the plates from her one at a time, and dumped the scraps into the garbage, stacked them in the sink.

Whitney found tin foil in a drawer – Maggie really had thought of everything – and wrapped up the leftovers, put them in the fridge while Kev washed the dishes and skillet.

"I forgot the wine," she said, spying the bottle on the counter.

"I can open it now," he offered.

She shook her head. "I better not, since I'm driving."

They were done, suddenly, and all that was left to do was leave.

The prospect made her chest ache.

Kev came to stand in front of her, hands in his pockets, face a little bashful, blonde hair swinging forward to brush against his chin.

How beautiful he was. Pretty and perfect as a marble bust.

"Thanks for lunch," he said. "And for the company."

"Thanks for listening about Madelyn," she returned. "It felt so good to talk about it, and get if off my chest."

His brows lifted. "Is that a hint?"

"Not a very subtle one, huh?" She wanted to touch him. Instead, she hitched her purse strap up her shoulder. "I wish you would get some help. Then I wouldn't worry myself sick."

"Sick?"

"Just please say you'll think about it."

He glanced toward the door. "I'll walk you out."

Outside, the afternoon had become grayer, colder, the wind snatching at their hair as they descended the iron stairs. Whitney shivered as she fished out her keys, pulled her jacket together. It felt ominous, this change in the weather, portentous somehow.

She hit the remote and Kev opened her door. "Drive safe." And then, more personal, making eye contact again, "Text me when you get back to work and let me know you're there."

The wind caught his long hair and he smoothed it back, the domino tattoos standing out in dark relief against the white of his fingers.

How thin he was, how underfed and defeated.

How sweet he was, how gentlemanly and thoughtful.

Her throat tightened.

"Whitney?"

She flung her arms around his neck, a sudden, impulsive hug. He smelled of smoke, and clean laundry, and feminine shampoo. He felt frail in her arms, muscles like water, bones hard knobs and cylinders beneath his clothes.

She squeezed him hard. "Don't give up," she whispered. "Keep trying. Please. For me."

Then she whirled away and into her car before he could see the tears standing in her eyes.

~*~

Tango watched her pull away, still feeling the energy of her body where it had pressed against his. Like his chest and arms were glowing, tingling, even. Like he'd hugged sunshine.

His steps grew heavier the higher he climbed up the iron staircase. The air seemed colder, stealing the warmth she'd given him. Likewise, the apartment had changed: full of shadows, the sunlight gone, the air chilly and thin.

His breath caught when he heard the knock on the door. Whitney was back. She'd forgotten something. She'd called out for the rest of the day. Something.

He spun, threw the locks, snatched the door open...

Not Whitney.

Ian.

The sight hit him with physical force. Not merely Ian's presence, but the harsh set of his features, the flare of rage in his eyes.

"Ian."

"Aren't you going to invite me in, lover?"

Tango stepped back. "Yeah. Of course."

Ian wore scarf and gloves – cream cashmere, red leather – and removed both as he crossed the threshold. "Charming." He set the gloves on the table alongside Tango's keys. Hung his scarf up on the peg beside Tango's cut. "This is a new acquirement."

Everything about the moment screamed *wrong*. Ian didn't belong here; neither did his anger.

With the sense that he entered a dreamscape, Tango shut the door and followed the man deeper into the apartment.

"Mercy used to live here before," he explained. "It was up for rent again." In a rush: "How did you know I was here?"

Ian pivoted, long wool coat swirling around his legs, hair slapping across his shoulders. His look said, *Don't insult me.* "Darling, I know everything about you." A smile flickered, and then was gone. "Well, most things. Except what you find so fascinating about that virginal schoolgirl who just left here."

So Ian knew Whitney had been here. Tango felt his hands curl to fists. A tremor of sudden violence rippled beneath his skin, fast as a shiver, sharp as a straight razor. Virginal schoolgirl. Said with dislike. Open hostility. The idea of either sentiment directed toward gentle, sweet, neck-hugging Whitney left him hot with emotion.

"Whitney's a friend," he said tightly. "I have lots of friends."

"Not like her, though." Ian moved toward him, steps deliberate, Ferragamo loafers clipping on the floorboards. "Not who you want to fuck." The obscenity became a bomb on his tongue, viler than the word itself, hinting at an intent that was ugly.

Tango stood his ground. "I fuck women. You know it. You've seen it." He flashed him a nasty, humorless smile. "Back in the day, you used to help me do it. But I haven't done anything with Whitney."

"Not yet."

"Why do you care?"

Ian closed the final distance, so they stood face-to-face, Ian's expensive scent filling his nose. "Because," he said, voice low, fierce, bristling, "you're not two steps out of the grave, and you pushed me away – over and over you've pushed me – and here was *Whitney*," he spat her name, "making you lunch. Putting that dreamy look in your eyes."

"You're jealous?" Tango asked, incredulous.

A flush came up along Ian's aristocratic cheekbones. "You need your whores. Your biker sluts. Them I understand. The itch needs scratching. The monster needs to be fed. But what could that *child* possibly give you? How could you turn to her now?"

Tango swallowed with some difficulty. "Because she cares."

"And I don't?!" Ian roared.

Wires tore loose in Tango's head. Barely-latched doors came open. He wasn't Tango, wasn't even Kev, but Loverboy again. Scared, self-loathing, hopeless.

"You weren't there!" he shouted back. "And the second the words were out, more followed. "You weren't there, when they shoved a broom handle in me! I wasn't holding your hand. You...you...you weren't there..."

He was going to cry, he realized. He was going to sob, and no matter how embarrassing, he could do nothing about it.

Ian's angry mask crumpled. "Darling." He took Tango's face in his hands, pulled him in close. "Darling, no, no, I wasn't. But I was there before. I was there the first time, remember? When it was just the two of us. I was there when–"

"She doesn't know," Tango said through clenched teeth. "She doesn't know what I am, or what I've done."

Ian's auburn brows crimped together. His eyes glittered with unshed tears. "Love, then how could she ever give you what you need?"

"I don't need it," he protested. "I don't."

"My beautiful boy, of course you do. It's in your DNA now. The craving."

Tango opened his mouth, and no sound came out. He couldn't breathe.

"It would only hurt her," Ian muttered. "Hiding yourself from someone like that. She doesn't have what you need," he repeated.

What would Whitney say, he wondered, if she knew all the dirty secrets of his past?

His eyes fluttered shut.

And Ian kissed him.

A beautiful, expert, involved kiss. Lips. Tongues. He allowed himself to open to it. Relished Ian's fingers sliding into his hair.

It was different with Ian; it always had been. So unlike anything he'd ever had with Jasmine or the club girls. The tender violence, the exquisite stirring of passion, and gentleness, and anger. Such anger. That sharp-edged kernel of self-hatred that turned the mating of lips and tongues to sweet red wine.

All his bitter resistance melted. Their intimate history wiped away all thought, all fear, all pain. This was the trap, the one he'd always entered willingly.

Hands pulling at fabric. Heavy wool and cheap cotton. The expensive weave of Ian's suit jacket, and the rough denim of Tango's jeans.

It was desperate.

You tried to kill yourself.

I don't want to live with it anymore.

Come to bed with me.

Yes.

The mattress dipped beneath their combined weight. Soft comforter against his back. Ian's face hovering above his own, his hair an auburn waterfall, his eyes liquid. "You're all skin and bones. I don't want to hurt you."

"You won't." He reached blindly toward the nightstand, managed to pull the drawer, curl his hand around what they would need. Offered the tube to his lover.

With incredible gentleness, expression soft, his touch tender, Ian settled over him, kissed his throat, joined them, that pressure Tango knew so well by now.

He closed his eyes, but the tears came anyway. This was the thing none of his brothers knew – what they could never know. Because they could never understand the magnitude of what Ian had given him. Two broken, ravaged, ruined boys, chained in basements, made to dance, made to whore themselves to sweating, disgusting, middle-aged men with sick fetishes. In the dark, they'd reached for one another through the horror and the pain, and in Ian's arms, Kev had learned, for the first time, what it meant to make love, what it meant to find physical pleasure with another person.

He loved Ian.

And he hated him for reminding him of all the horrors of the past.

But oh to feed the beast, and to feed it with pleasure and love.

And Whitney wondered why he'd slit his wrists in the bathtub.

~*~

No matter when, no matter why, no matter who, the sex was always necessary. The pressure in his head, the weight on his heart, could only be alleviated by a physical release. He craved that sense of being filled – being full. Complete. A part of something outside his own sick self.

That was an insult to Ian. Because…this was Ian.

But even so, the aftermath always came. The cooling of sweat, the slowing of heartbeats. The doubt. The wonder.

Ian lay stretched behind him, arm around his waist, fingers playing against his chest. "Why didn't you tell me you were thinking of it?" he whispered.

There were too many reasons to list, so Tango kept quiet.

"You know that you have to leave the club."

Again, he didn't answer.

"When they find out what you did," Ian pressed, "they'll never let you stay."

"I don't want to talk about it."

Ian's hand flexed, fingers stroking above his heart. "You know I'm right," he said, gently.

"I know Ghost isn't gonna say anything to anyone."

Ian snorted, his breath warm at the back of Tango's neck. "Maybe not now. Not until he needs leverage."

Tango rolled over, so they were face-to-face, pressed together, damp skin gluing them to one another. Ian's face was beautiful with afterglow. It felt wonderful to be in someone's arms, to be tangled like this. He should shut his eyes, fall to sleep, and not question it.

But he said, "You know," in a soft, defeated voice, "sometimes it's the most tempting thing in the word. The idea of walking away from everything."

"Then why don't you?"

"Because it won't solve anything."

"And slitting your wrists will?"

He didn't get to respond. There came the sound of the apartment door opening. Aidan's heavy, graceless footfalls; jangle of keys. The pause, when he saw the jackets on the floor. Deep inhale.

"Tango?"

Tango disentangled himself from Ian and sat up, reached for his jeans on the floor.

"Did Whitney leave?" Aidan asked. "Did…"

The bedroom door was open, and Aidan appeared between the jambs. His expression, hopeful, worried, curious, turned sour when he saw them. He turned away quickly. "Jesus. Put some fucking clothes on." And he moved out of sight.

"Shit," Tango muttered. His vision swam as he bent to step into his jeans. His head felt light, empty, a balloon on top of his neck.

Behind him, he heard Ian sit up in bed. Heard him sigh. "Kevin. Why are you shaking?"

He was, fingers fumbling as he tried to work the jeans up to his hips.

"He already knows," Ian continued. "Why should it matter that he sees?"

74

It seemed to take years to do the zipper, the button. Then he turned to Ian, shaking so badly now that if affected his voice. "It doesn't matter that it's you. It doesn't matter if I'm gay, straight, or bi. It matters that all I am, all I've ever been, all I'll ever be is something for people to fuck."

Ian leaned toward him, started to speak.

"Go. Please. Just go."

And for once, Ian didn't act lordly and superior. Sadly, he complied. Tango turned away as the man climbed from the bed and dressed.

He didn't rush, but he was efficient, and when he was finished, he placed a hand on Tango's shoulder. Brushed his hair aside and kissed the back of his neck. "Eat something, darling. You're much too thin."

Tango listened to him leave. Then he went to face Aidan.

His best friend stood at the kitchen sink, staring out the window above it, smoking, gray trails curling around his head.

Tango joined him. "I know what you're going to say."

"I doubt that."

"And you're right." Tango took a deep breath and let it out in a rush. "I need help," he admitted, for the very first time. "I think…I think I need therapy."

Seven

The sky was black beneath the veil of a new moon when Whitney pulled into the driveway. Lights glowed in the windows, beamed yellow rectangles out onto the brown winter grass of the lawn. It was easy to pretend, as she sat in her car, that this was a happy home, a place full of cheerful voices and delicious cooking smells.

But she knew better.

After leaving Kev, the rest of her day had seemed to drag. She was restless, preoccupied, too consumed with replaying their lunch together to pay much attention to the customer service calls she fielded. One woman grew flustered, cursed her, and vowed to call Whitney's manager before hanging up. Even that hadn't lifted the fog.

It was worry that had plagued her. That sense of drowning she'd felt when Jason was going from pills to heroin, and she'd had no way to break through to him. So she'd cooked a few hamburgers and hugged Kev. How could that possibly be helpful?

Inside, she encountered the stench of something burning. "Oh no!" She dumped her purse and keys on the floor and rushed to the smoking stove. A pot of rice had been allowed to boil over, clumps of rice blackening on the electric coils beneath it. The bubbling and hissing was awful. How had anyone missed the noise? Much less the smoke!

She snatched up a dish towel and shoved the pot off the eye, clicked the unit off.

"Madelyn?" she called. "Are you here?"

In the living room, Ashley and Charlotte were in front of the TV, somber, not arguing for once.

"Where's your mother?"

"In her room," Ashley said, chewing her lip. "She's mad."

"About what?"

"Everything."

Out of the mouths of babes...

"You two stay here," Whitney said, "and I'll make dinner in just a bit."

They nodded.

The house, she couldn't help but notice, was even more of a sty than normal. The laundry she'd folded and left in a basket just inside the linen closet was strewn across the hallway floor. She stepped over an upturned glass, its liquid contents already soaked into the carpet.

"Madelyn?"

Her sister-in-law was in her room, face-down on the bed, snoring softly.

It struck Whitney as repulsive, suddenly. All of it. The clothes spilling from the hamper, the drawn curtains, the unmade bed. Madelyn was greasy, disheveled, and reeked of alcohol.

Was everyone in her life going to come unglued?

She felt a small inner snap, and the confrontation Kev had suggested came boiling to the surface, same as the rice that was now baked onto the stovetop.

"Madelyn," she repeated, voice hard, and stepped up to the bed, gave the woman's shoulder a hard shove. "Wake up."

"Wha…" Madelyn pushed up on her arms, groggy, swaying. She blinked a few times, smacked her dry lips.

"I'm making coffee," Whitney informed her. "And you're going to clean yourself up and come spend some time with your girls."

With seemingly great effort, Madelyn sat up, pushed her hair from her eyes, and yawned.

Whitney found jeans and a reasonably clean sweatshirt on the piled-up dresser. "Here." She tossed them onto the bed. "Why don't you grab a shower while I make the coffee? You'll feel better."

Madelyn blinked a few times, then turned glassy eyes on Whitney, finally. She scowled. Her voice came out a rough croak. "Why're you back so late?"

For a year she'd been patient. She'd picked up the slack, overlooked the mess, pretended things would go back to normal. But seeing Kev today, touching him, however briefly, had begun a launch sequence of sorts. And so her patience and kindness wavered.

"I always get home at the same time," she said. "Come on, get up. Maybe we can get some of this mess picked up before bedtime."

Madelyn drew herself upright. Her face – puffy, flushed, bleary-eyed – pinched up with anger. "Are you telling me what to do right now?"

"Yes. And high time, too. You're letting this house, and yourself, and this family go to hell."

"This family?" Her lips peeled back in a nasty sneer. "This isn't a family anymore, dumbass."

Whitney took a deep breath. She wanted to scream. She wanted to track down every vodka bottle in the house and pitch them against the wall. The idea of the shattering glass, the satisfying smash, was infinitely appealing.

Instead, she said, "Madelyn, Jason's gone because he was a junkie. How is you turning into a drunk going to help the situation?"

With an angry snarl, Madelyn heaved forward off the bed. Her legs buckled and she fell, catching herself against the dresser.

Whitney watched in horror. Her once-merry, always-smiling sister-in-law was well and truly gone. Same as Jason. "Look at yourself," she said. "You can't even stand up at six-thirty in the evening."

"Shut the hell up!"

"Look at this house," Whitney continued. "God, Madelyn, look at your daughters! They lost their father; do you want them to lose you too?"

"Shut up!" she shouted. "This isn't your goddamn business!"

Tears stung her eyes. "Yes, it is," Whitney shot back. "It was my brother who got hooked on the needle. My brother who got me locked up in a drug lord's basement. You're my family, you and the girls. This is completely my business."

Madelyn tried to slap her. She lost her balance and had to clutch at the edge of the dresser. "Don't talk to me about Jason!" Tears flooded her eyes. "Don't you dare!"

"My brother," Whitney repeated. "I can talk about him."

"Not here you can't. Not in front of me."

~*~

It was shaping up to be a cold night, the frost already sparkling on the grass, the stars already winking to life overhead, the sky clear and windswept. Mercy's breath plumed like smoke as he went up the back sidewalk. He felt the air testing the hem and sleeves of his jacket, looking for a way to his skin, trying to make him shiver.

A few long strides carried him to the back door, and then he was inside, shutting it against the night, locking it.

Home.

He was assaulted, always, by the ordinary beauty of it. His and her jackets and helmets hung up in the mud room. Scent of dinner cooking – tonight he smelled homemade chicken noodle soup, and knew it came with sourdough croutons for dunking, roast veggies, maybe even a cake for dessert; he smelled something sweet. His Ava Rose knew he needed more than regular-man portions at the end of the day. He strained for the sound of her voice, the boys', sweet with innocence and childhood. Their house, so full of their things, their conversations, their love.

He passed through the kitchen, saw the soup simmering on the stove, the cake cooling on the counter. Ava and the kids were in the living room, Remy and Cal on the floor with blocks and trucks, Ava holding Camille and peering at the screen of her laptop, all set up at the writing station Mercy had installed for her in the window.

"Hi, baby," she called.

"Daddy!" Remy exclaimed.

Cal said, "Di-deee!"

Home.

Greeting them all was the usual joyous circus. He loved swinging his boys up into the air, hearing them shout with delight. Loved the clean, fragile smell of baby when he kissed Camille. Love the press of Ava's hand over his heart when he finally got to kiss her sweet mouth.

His family. The people who were his.

He'd be dead or incarcerated if not for them.

They traded news of their days. Ava was nervously awaiting an email about a magazine article. He told her about one of the day's customers that made her laugh until she was breathless.

It was when they were finally at the dinner table that he brought up the heavy stuff.

"I had lunch with your dad today."

She drew upright in her chair, spoon frozen above her bowl, instantly alert. "Just the two of you?"

"No, Aidan too. He wanted to talk about Tango."

She nodded.

"Tango?" Remy asked, and Mercy locked eyes with his wife. They weren't going to be able to discuss adult things around the kids much longer.

"Yes, sweetie, Uncle Tango," Ava said, turning a smile to their oldest.

It would be better to wait, he decided; better to stick to benign topics for now. "If your story gets accepted, have you got another ready to send out?"

"Uh-huh. I'm working on something serialized right now…" She spoke enthusiastically about her projects, and the plan she was hatching for her career, but he could see her wild curiosity about Tango, simmering just under the surface.

The boys were in bed and Mercy was just getting out of the shower when Ava finally pounced on him. Well, figuratively. Not literally, because she was sitting up against the headboard of their bed, nursing Camille.

"Lunch with my dad," she prompted, dark eyes serious.

He wanted to smile, watching her go from bedtime story mama to motorcycle mama in a matter of seconds. Instead, he sighed and went to sit next to her.

"Aidan stayed with him last night."

"Right."

"And Kev woke up from a bad nightmare. He wanted to call Whitney; he said that's what he usually does when he can't sleep."

"He wakes her up?"

"Apparently she stays up most nights painting."

"God," Ava said softly, expression sad. "They're really attached to each other."

He nodded. "I know he's the one with the demons, but I think she's just as manic about it as he is."

"Hmm. You know, a professional would say they need to learn to stand on their own, come to terms with their problems separately."

He sensed she wasn't finished. "But what would you say?"

She smiled. "I'd say sometimes you need help from the person you love. It's always easier fighting demons together." And he knew, the way she looked at him, that she was talking about him, them.

He smiled back. A little. "Whitney went to have lunch with him today. Aidan left them together, and that was when the three of us had lunch. We don't disagree with you. If Whitney can help, then we ought to let her. He won't ever forget what happened to him, but we've got to get him to a place where he can live with it, and can maybe be happy moving forward."

"Agreed."

He sighed. "But Aidan called, right before I clocked out for the night. When he got back to the apartment, Whitney was gone, and Ian was there."

"Oh."

"That guy…"

"You can't say he doesn't love Kev, though."

"He loves who he used to be. Or he loves the idea of keeping him as a pet."

"I don't think it's that simple."

"*None* of it is simple. Not any of it." But even so, there had been a sort of breakthrough. "Kev told Aidan, though, that he needed help. He actually said 'therapy.'"

"Really?" Her brows shot up. "He's open to it?"

He nodded. "And that's where it gets tricky. Any doctor would gladly listen to him. Hell, they'd probably want to make a case study of him."

"A doctor could listen," she agreed. "But even if you get past the idea of an outlaw with a very illegal track record talking to someone outside the club–"

He snorted.

"–Kev...Kev's not looking for just ears, I don't think. He's drowning, Felix," she said, quietly. "And he needs someone to pull him back to the surface."

Not just someone who could offer professional advice, but someone who'd walked this outlaw path; who'd made dark decisions; who knew well the taste of self-loathing.

"Whitney can be his soft place," Mercy said. "And your folks can be his folks, and Aidan can be his best friend and his brother. I'm nominating myself to keep his secrets."

Her eyes filled with tears, glittering in the lamplight. He imagined her silent *Oh, Mercy.*

"Who better to help someone sort through his dirt than a guy who's already as filthy as they come?"

She leaned sideways into him, and he put his arm around her, her and the baby, his precious girls.

~*~

It was the very last thing she should do, but after an hour of driving around the city, no doubt smearing her mascara every time she wiped her eyes, she had no idea what to do. She seriously considered parking in front of a gas station, flopping her seat back, and sleeping in her car. All her clothes were in the back seat; she could use them as pillows and blankets. But one look at the sketchy-looking guy propped against the side of the Citgo station had her rethinking the idea.

So at nine p.m., she parked in the alley behind the bakery and trudged up the iron stairs to Kev's door. She sniffed hard, tried to mop her face with her sleeve, and knocked.

It was Aidan who answered the door, and her first thought was that she was so glad he was still here, and hadn't left Kev alone. The relief brought fresh tears to her eyes, and, ashamedly, she felt her face crumpling.

"Whitney?" He sounded surprised. "What's wrong? What are you...Here, come in."

"I'm sorry," she mumbled, dabbing furiously at her eyes with her fingertips. "I hate to do this. I mean, I shouldn't be bothering you."

Kev was on the couch and shot to his feet. "Whitney?" Narrow face creased with worry, he came to her, and to her surprise, pulled her into his arms.

Which only made the crying worse.

But how wonderful it felt to press her face against his shirt and feel his arms around her. It wasn't just about being held; there was something magic in being held by him. With his bony ribs digging into her breasts and his backbone jagged beneath her hand. More comforting than any touch of recent memory.

~*~

It took her an embarrassing amount of time to pull herself together, but finally managed. Kev sat her down on the couch beside him, and Aidan opened the wine she'd bought that afternoon and brought her a glass. Kev's arm behind her, across the back of the couch, was a comfort. As was the kind way he asked, "What happened?"

Aidan was sitting on the arm of the recliner, arms folded, watching her with a sharp cynicism that somehow seemed brotherly and protective.

She took a bracing sip of wine and told them about the fight she'd had with Madelyn. Madelyn had refused to calm, and by the end, had been sobbing and screaming incoherently. The girls had walked in, and they'd burst into tears. Finally, with nothing left to do, Whitney had made to leave. Madelyn had threatened to "throw" her "shit out in the yard." So she'd packed her things, paints included, and now here she was.

"I know I should have gone to a hotel," she said. "In fact, I should go to one now. I don't know what I'm thinking bothering you…"

"No, don't waste your money on a hotel, you were right to come here," Kev said.

"I just needed to get myself together," she said, "but I'll go to a hotel. I'll–"

"No," he said, more firmly, and his arm dropped off the sofa and settled, tentatively, almost as if he were afraid to touch her too boldly, across her shoulders. "You can stay here. I want you to," he added. "Just stay here tonight."

Overcome with both gratitude and guilt, she nodded, and pressed the back of her hand to her trembling mouth.

His arm was light as a matchstick around her, careful and precise in its placement. Respectful. Platonic.

So why did it send shivers down her back?

~*~

When Whitney had stopped crying and excused herself to the bathroom to, quote, "clean up," Aidan slid off the arm of the chair and dropped onto the couch beside Tango, gaze direct, and uncharacteristically knowing. He hadn't been kidding about Sam adding some much-needed culture to his life. Marriage, or fatherhood, or both had sharpened him. In a polite voice, he said, "Um, excuse me, what the fuck are you doing?"

"What?"

"Okay, you might be all sad, and hate yourself, or whatever, but you're not brain-damaged, that I know about. So what are you doing inviting that girl to spend the night?" It was said so sweetly, almost supportively, so against the words themselves, that Tango almost smiled. Aidan, his very best friend, loved people aggressively.

"Am I supposed to kick her out?" he countered.

"You probably should, yeah."

The idea was appalling. "This isn't some random woman, Aidan. This is Whitney."

"Who means a lot to you, right?"

"Well, obviously."

"Right. Which is why you can't see that she's, like, stupid in love with you."

A sensation like cold fingers clamped against the back of his neck. A quick shock. And then a bolt of warmth, shafting right through the center of him. "*What?* No, she's just…"

"Making you lunch, sitting with you, running to you when she gets into trouble. Bro, she sits up at night and takes your sad phone calls. That is not friendly. That isn't sweet. It's love. People do a lot of things for a lot of reasons, but love's the thing that makes them available."

"I…" He couldn't take his next breath, much less form a cohesive sentence.

"Maybe it's friend love," Aidan went on. "Maybe that's all it is, and she doesn't want to have your long-haired babies. But I don't think so."

For some reason, it had never entered his thoughts. He'd only been grateful for her presence, and leaned on her, and been afraid of tainting her in any way.

"She can't be with me," Tango said, suddenly, finding his voice. "That would…no, that would ruin her."

But what a sweet fantasy it was. A soap bubble of fragile possibilities, a shiny, warm glimpse of waking up beside her. Those long-haired babies Aidan mentioned.

He clamped a lid on it fast, before it could rip him in half.

Aidan sighed and flopped back against the couch. "Of course you'd say that."

"What's that supposed to mean? Aren't you trying to warn me off of her?"

"No, you dork. I'm pointing out what you're being too thick to see, so you can freaking do something about it."

Tango blinked. "Um…"

"She's sweet, and she's cute, and she worships you." His brows lifted, and the implied line was, *And she hasn't ever stripped and hooked before.* "I think, if you want to, you should go for it."

"Why are you even saying this?"

"Because trust me when I tell you this: the very best thing in the world is having sex with someone who knows every bad thing about you, and loves you anyway."

~*~

Tonight, when Tango told Aidan that he ought to go home and be with his girls, he agreed. "If you're alright…?" Pointed look to Whitney, who was reheating leftover burgers for their dinner, her narrow back to them.

Tango sighed and nodded. Sighed, because now, with Aidan's prediction of long-haired baby-having love, he wasn't sure he trusted himself with her.

Because the beast hadn't been satisfied with the fast, heartbreaking tumble he'd taken with Ian earlier.

Listen to him, thinking about sex with someone else while his sheets smelled like man in the next room.

God, he was awful.

Aidan knocked him on the shoulder. "Call if you need something, okay?"

"Okay." But he wouldn't, because Aidan deserved to hold his daughter, unwind over dinner and beer, and then hold his wife.

The sound of the door closing was like a casket lid; self-restraint was going to be the death of him.

He took a deep breath, braced himself, and walked into the kitchen.

"Aidan couldn't stay?" Whitney asked as she laid patties out on a plate.

"Nah. He needs to spend some time with the fam."

"I'm sure Sam and Lainie miss him," she said, and sent him a quick smile that made his pulse jump. "He's been a good friend to stay here with you."

How…lovely she was. That was the word. Lovely. Because she was a pretty girl in an objective sense, with all that dark hair, and those big pale eyes, and her tiny snip of a nose. The distinct shape of her upper lip. But there was an energy in her, a soft, delicate femininity that was built of kindness and steel clothed in softness that called to something deep and shriveled inside of him. Maybe everyone wouldn't think her lovely, but he did. And he wanted to bury his face in her hair and feel the strands get caught in his lashes. Wanted to slide his hands down inside her tight jeans and find the warm smooth curve of her ass.

Standing beside her at the kitchen counter as she pulled the cling film off leftovers, he could close his eyes and imagine laying her down on his bed, breaking her in slowly: lingering kisses, petting, grinding against her, letting her feel the way he wanted her.

Disgusting. Why did he always have to go there?

He realized she was saying something, and shook off the fog. "What?"

Her expression was patient. "Do you want it like you had it his afternoon?"

This afternoon? Ian's teeth sunk in his shoulder, sunlight slanting between them, playing against sweat-slick skin.

"Uh…"

"Your burger. Lettuce, ketchup, mustard, and red onion?"

"Yes," he said with a little gasp, ashamed once again of his thought process. "The burger. Right. Yeah. That'd be good."

~*~

"I can sleep on the couch," she offered, and that made him feel like a douche.

"No, I will. You can have the bed." The bed which he'd fucked someone in not hours ago. "Just let me change the sheets for you," he added, hoping he didn't sound desperate. "I think Mags left some clean ones…"

But Whitney shook her head. "No, really. I won't be able to sleep and I brought my painting stuff. I'll probably spend most the night at the table, so please, I refuse to kick you out of your bed."

"Or," he said, starting to feel frustrated, "we could just stand here and be super polite to each other for another half hour."

A beat passed.

Then they both laughed. The tension eased, and he could breathe again.

"You're such a gentleman," she said – which, ha! – "and it's so sweet that you want to give me your bed. But honestly, I'm not just being polite. I don't sleep much anymore, and no doubt I'll want to paint. So if you've got an extra pillow, I'll crash out here." She gave him a gentle smile. "And hey, if you wake up tonight, you won't have to call me."

He smiled back. "There's that."

~*~

Sex dreams were the worst. They always started one place, and ended up another. When he was with Jasmine, his stirring usually roused her from sleep, and then she would wake him, nails trailing down his stomach, and she would take him in her mouth and finish what some errant scrap of memory had started. Before things went dark, there was Jazz, and her magic tongue…which was a sort of darkness all its own.

But he hadn't been with Jazz since Don Ellison's basement. And the dreams were more distinct, and more disturbing than ever.

Tonight it was The Nest. That pink-on-black, black-lighted room in the back where he and Ian worked together. Everything smelled like chemical flowers. His heart pounded, and his fingers itched, and the carpet was plush against his knees as he worked on their client.

So many clients. He'd lost count. He was better at this than he was at tying his own shoes. He had, in Ian's words, a beautiful mouth that knew everything there was to know about cocks.

What an accomplishment.

He glanced up through his lashes, and a jolt of acknowledgment moved through him. The man above him was Daniel. Oh, sweet Daniel. When was the last time he'd thought of him?

Ian was behind him, watching Tango over Daniel's shoulder, those kohl-ringed eyes bright and liquid with excitement. "He's very good at this," he whispered in Daniel's ear. And Daniel moaned, and his neck went limp, and he let Ian support his weight.

And then everything blurred. And then it was a woman, Daniel's bored blonde housewife who'd put on thigh-highs and a garter belt and come to the club looking for something young and thin and thrilling. She had fallen back across the mattress like a sacrificial offering. Ian's smile, sharp as a wolf's, hair falling over his shoulders. "Shall we?"

And then it blurred again. And it was Carla. And he screamed.

He woke with an awful start, same as always, yanked out of the dream and tossed back into his bed. He was on his side, curled up in the fetal position, sporting a raging hard-on.

This was the danger of Whitney. This. Waking scared, shaking, alone, turned on, and wanting her comfort. The perfect cocktail: he wanted to be with her, and he wanted to fuck something, so he in turn wanted to fuck her.

Dangerous.

There was a strip of light beneath his closed bedroom door. She was in fact awake.

"Fuck," he muttered, and climbed from bed to search for clothes.

~*~

The sound of the bedroom door opening should have startled her, but she'd been waiting for it for almost an hour now. She paused mid-stroke and glanced over. Kev was in a baggy white t-shirt two sizes too big for him and thick gray sweatpants with cuffs at the ankles. His hair was all over the place, and she couldn't help but smile.

"Nightmare?"

He rubbed at his eyes, his hair, the back of his neck. He looked strung-out. "Yeah." He headed for the kitchen and she turned back to her work.

It was flowers again, white roses this time. The color was a challenge, because she was painting highlights and shadows, rather than filling in with white. On her palette, she had blends of blue, and green, and gray, and hints of yellow. It was a complex piece, and it had been soothing the past two hours, her easel set up in front of Kev's sofa, listening to the occasional car pass on the street below.

Kev returned and sat down beside her, glass of wine in each hand. "Here." He passed one to her. "Best sleep aide in the world."

"Thanks." She set her brush down and took the glass in both hands, took a small sip. She wasn't really much of a drinker, and swore she felt the effects after just one swallow. When she lifted her head, Kev was staring at her canvas, and his expression was awed.

"You're very good."

That made her blush. Or maybe that was just the wine.

"I mean, you could be in galleries."

"Oh, no, it's just a hobby."

He grinned. "So's everything until it starts to pay the bills."

She took another sip of wine.

He continued to stare at the half-finished painting.

"Are you interested in art?"

"For me? Nah." A notch formed between his brows. "But I know someone who is...Was. I dunno if..." His gaze dropped to the glass in his hands.

"Are you going to tell me what the nightmare was about this time?"

She assumed that, like always, he would decline. He made that face she always had to imagine him making over the phone: mouth tucking up in one corner, brows lowering, a sad, concentrated sort of face. But then he took a deep breath and said, "I always dream about the same thing lately." His eyes flicked to her, and then darted away again. "The place where I used to work."

A chill moved through her. "The Cuckoo's Nest?" In the time since she'd first heard it, she'd come to think of that as a sinister name.

"Yeah."

"What sort of place was it, Kev?" she asked, softly.

"A terrible one."

"Why did you work there?"

"I didn't. Not willingly. I was a slave." His voice grew reedy and distant with memory. "And then, after so long, it started to feel almost normal."

"God," she whispered. "What..." She had to dampen her lips. "What did you do?" But a part of her already knew. Her stomach clenched, and she felt sweat bead up on the back of her neck, under her hair. In this day and age, "slave" could mean a lot of things. But somehow...somehow...she knew.

"I was used for men's entertainment."

She tried to swallow. "Kev—"

She didn't realize how close they were sitting until he turned to face her, his eyes huge and haunted, pale cheeks framed by his bedraggled hair, just two narrow blades of white beneath the sharp edges of bone. He swallowed, and she watched his throat move.

"The Nest," he said, voice a strained whisper, "is a place where men go to watch boys dance. And they pay for private time with them in the back. Do you understand what I'm telling you?"

Her eyes filled with tears and he became blurry.

"I'm nothing but a sex toy."

"Stop. Don't say that, because it isn't true."

She couldn't tell because of the tears, but she thought his eyes grew shiny, reflecting the lamplight. "They started breaking me in when I was ten. And when I was twelve–"

"Stop!"

"That's what I'm good at. Fucking. Being fucked." The curses were tiny explosions between them, as ugly as the acts they conjured. "I'm not interested in art. I'm not interested in anything. I just learned to do what they told me."

"You *are* interested in things. Whatever happened, whatever they...You're your own person now. You can–"

"I just told you I used to be a goddamn hooker, and you're *still* trying to play the bright side act?"

"I'll play it as long as it takes."

"You're un-fucking-believable," he muttered, shaking his head, turning his face away from her. But it didn't sound like an insult.

Or perhaps she'd lost all perspective.

"Do you want me to leave?" she asked.

His eyes came back to her, gaze unfathomable. He swallowed, Adam's apple jacking in his throat. "Trust me. Of all the things I want right now, you leaving is *not* one of them."

"What do you want then?" She swallowed, too. "What's...what's one of those – those things you want?"

His eyes widened, darkened, and unworldly though she was, she felt that tug in her gut, the answering response. She needn't have asked; she knew what he wanted. She'd been wanting it herself for a while now, trying to pawn it off as something else in her subconscious.

"What..." she started.

"Don't ask again. Please."

She didn't think she was leaning, and she didn't think he was either. But slowly, through some inexorable force, they drew closer, and closer, and closer together.

It startled her when Tango's long, delicate fingers brushed her hair back behind her ear, but she settled. He picked out a single strand and wound it around his index finger.

"I love your hair," he whispered, eyes on what he was doing, distant, unfocused. "I love most everything about you."

"Kev."

His gaze slid to hers. "I can't believe you're letting me touch it."

"Why wouldn't I?"

And again, he glanced away.

It was an actual, physical pain in her chest to watch him, to feel the hurt that burned just beneath his skin. Terrible, terrible things had been done to him, and he in turn was doing terrible things to himself. The cutting. Denying himself everything.

He was never going to do it, was going to push himself beyond with toying with her hair, so she did it for him. She leaned forward and kissed him.

She was a bad kisser. The last boy she'd made out with had told her so. He'd wiped his mouth on the back of his hand, made a face, and said, "Don't you know how to do this?" Like eighteen year-old girls without any experience were supposed to just *know* how to kiss well. Like they'd practiced, or watched movies or something. Studied up on it.

So she knew, when she pressed her lips to Kev's, that it would be the most stupid and underwhelming kiss of all time. That he would probably hate it, and wish she hadn't done it. But she just *had* to. She...yes, she had to.

It shocked her, the feel of lips against her lips, and the knowledge that this was Kev, finally, after all her wondering. Kev's mouth against her own. It sent a thrill chasing over her skin. The kind of shiver that started in her spine and ended up deep in the pit of her belly.

He didn't react.

Guess she was so bad he couldn't even muster a response.

Oh well. She pulled back a fraction, disappointed...

His hands clamped onto the sides of her head. His mouth fell open and he dragged in a ragged breath. He gasped. "Shit. Christ...shit." And his fingers curled into her hair, and he brought her back in again. And this time, *he* kissed *her*.

Maybe it didn't matter that she wasn't any good. Maybe it was fine to shut her eyes, and gasp right along with him, and let him show her the way.

His tongue swept across her lower lip, and she opened her mouth on instinct. He fit his lips against hers, and again, again, a new angle each time, a fresh taste, going deeper, pressing for more. And then his tongue slipped into her mouth.

His hands held her face, and it became savage, and desperate, but somehow delicate, the erotic precision of his tongue, and lips, and teeth, playing against her mouth.

Whitney's head throbbed, and her breath stirred faintly in her chest, and her heart thundered. It was like melting, and she loved it. Wanted to touch him with her hands.

She reached out and found his chest. She could feel the hard ridges of his sternum and ribs. His heart, pounding away same as hers.

The contact seemed to kick off another reaction, because his hands moved down to her hips, and then his arms were around her waist and he dragged her in close, so she was in his lap. A new angle. A new, deeper kiss. It was drugging, intoxicating as wine. She speared her fingers through his long hair; it was silky and light as down in her hands.

He broke the kiss, and she murmured a protest. Her lips felt swollen and slick, and she wanted more. It had never been like this before. She'd never felt *good*, kissing someone.

But he wasn't done, only migrating. Pressing wet, open-mouthed kissed down her throat. To her collarbone. She felt the fast nip of his teeth.

It was all so much more urgent and reckless than she'd thought. She'd envisioned him being so gentle and careful with her, but wasn't disappointed with the reality. This was amazing. This was...

She wriggled and felt something hard against the inside of her thigh. His cock, hard and straining, ready for more.

Warm wetness welled between her legs. She was ready too.

He toppled her back onto the couch cushions and braced himself above her. One hand eased her t-shirt off her shoulder, so he could kiss her there. And the other hand slipped between her legs, touched her through her leggings.

It was too much, and she wanted it to stop.

But it felt too rushed. Too much too fast, without talking, without any of those cautious looks she'd expected from him.

He was tugging her shirt, tugging…She heard threads snap.

Too much.

She pulled at his hair. "Kev."

He came up like a drowning man, dragging in a huge breath and then struggling for another. He pushed up on his arms and stared down at her face, his eyes huge, his mouth open.

"Kev," she repeated. "It's okay, it's just…"

"Oh *shit*." He vaulted off the couch and to his feet as if she'd burned him. "Shit, shit, shit!" He shoved both hands through his hair, eyes squeezed shut.

"Wait." She struggled to sit up. "It's okay, I just…"

"No. No, no, no it's not okay. I'm sorry. Shit, Whitney, I'm so sorry. I shouldn't have."

"Kev…"

But he walked back into the bedroom, shut the door, and she heard the lock click.

The apartment was achingly silent in the aftermath. She thought this must be what a bombed out city sounded like: the low buzzing of violence and the washing-out of sensation.

Whitney dragged a hand through her hair and exhaled. "Well. Shit."

Eight

Session 1

Mercy arrived at noon on the dot. He knocked, and like a nervous kid going for a job interview, Tango slicked his hair down in the mirror one last time before he went to the door. He looked like shit, but what else was new. Mercy wasn't here to pick him up for the prom, so it didn't matter.

He took a last look at the apartment on his way through.

Last night, after he'd locked himself away like a horny girl-eating mountain lion, he'd paced around the narrow bedroom until it became obvious that wasn't helping. He'd laid down on the bed, too hard to even stretch out properly. He lay in the dark, concentrating on his breathing, wondering how badly he'd hurt Whitney, afraid she'd never speak to him again, thinking that would probably be the best thing, in reality. Eventually, he'd slipped his hand down inside his sweatpants and taken care of the situation, ashamed, blushing furiously in the dark, as thoughts of Whitney, and what he'd wanted to do to her, filled his mind.

He'd fallen asleep with a sticky hand and tears burning his eyes.

This morning, he'd crept out of his room, wondering what he'd find, not expecting what awaited him. The couch was tidy, pillows plumped, Whitney's painting supplies stowed in their case, it and the easel over against the bookshelves. Fresh coffee was brewing in the machine and there was a note by it.

Hope you're feeling better. Made you a sandwich; top shelf of fridge. See you tonight.

There was a smiley face.

He'd already inspected the sandwich and found that it was turkey on rye, no tomatoes, because they would make it soggy.

God, she was wonderful. He felt doubly shitty for pouncing on her the night before.

But today was the first day toward not doing that again, hopefully. He wasn't too optimistic – when had he ever been? – but he was going to go through the motions. For the people who loved him. For his own safety.

He took another huge breath, reached the door, and opened it.

It was a cold afternoon, the kind that still felt crisp as morning, the air sharp against the skin. Mercy was bundled up in his heavy Black Watch jacket, beanie pulled down over his ears. His breath plumed like smoke in the pale wash of sunlight, and for a moment, he looked exactly like the kind of guy you sent to collect fingers for trophies – which he was – and nothing like the therapist he'd offered to be – which he wasn't.

Tango's stomach cramped. Damn, this was a bad idea.

But Mercy didn't give him a chance to voice that. "Shit, it's cold," he said, and stepped into the apartment, smelling of frost, chafing his hands together.

Heart thumping like he had stage fright, Tango closed and locked the door. "Yeah." His voice felt distant, disconnected from him somehow. "It smells like it might snow."

"Remy would love that. Every morning, when he sees the frost on the grass, he thinks it's snow, and it's like his whole world comes crashing down when we explain that it's just frost." He laughed as he shrugged out of his jacket and hung it up.

Tango could envision Remy at the front window of the Lécuyer house, hands pressed to the glass, squealing with delight. A mental image that made him smile.

"You want coffee?" he offered. "I made a second pot."

"Yeah, sure."

This was going to be weird, wasn't it? His pulse was migrating up into his throat as he went to the kitchen and poured two mugs. Whitney's note was still there, where she'd left it, and he scanned it again, not reading the words, but lingering over the lines she'd made with the pen. Marks she'd left for him. He closed his eyes, a hand wrapped around each mug, absorbing the warmth.

Please don't be too weird, he thought, and turned back for the living room.

Mercy, in what had to be an intentional move, had stretched out full-length on the couch, which meant his feet were kicked up on the arm and overhanging by about a foot-and-a-half. This left the recliner for Tango. A flip on the old patient-on-the-sofa stereotype.

All his fear of weirdness evaporated. Mercy wasn't a licensed therapist, and probably had no idea how to act like one. But he was kindhearted, and he was a sharp, thoughtful guy. And he was Tango's friend. Tango's friend who, once upon a time, had pulled his barely-dressed, heroin-ravaged body off a stage in The Cuckoo's Nest and carried him out to the car like a baby.

"Thanks," he said when Tango handed over the mug. "Smells good."

"It's something fancy Mags bought."

"She tends to buy nice things."

"Yeah."

Mundane small talk. A shield for what was to come.

Tango settled into the recliner and took the mug between both hands. If he could have, he would have crawled inside it. But perhaps baths weren't such a great idea anymore…

Mercy sat up in an unhurried way and smoothed a hand along the crown of his head, pushing his hair back. When he'd first come back to Knoxville a few years ago, it had been shaggy and chin-length. Now it was down past his shoulders, and Tango had secret suspicions that Ava played with it like he was a My Little Pony, and that Merc liked it. In any event, the longer hair always made his face look narrower, more sinister, his eyes darker.

But today he just looked like himself. Not scary. Not in any rush. The dichotomy of the man would never cease to amaze. Full of wrath and vengeance. And full of sweetness and sympathy. *Complicated* was too delicate a word.

The knowledge eased him further. This wasn't going to be that weird at all.

"Okay. So," Mercy said, sending him a friendly look. "I gotta say I don't really know shit about therapizing."

Tango smiled. "I figured you didn't."

"But I'm a good listener. And I think, really, it's more about talking and having someone listen than it is about any kind of doctorate."

Tango stared at him.

"And..." Mercy looked almost nervous. "I think, sometimes, talking to someone who cares about you might be better than talking to a stranger. Sometimes," he stressed.

"I hope so."

The nervousness went away. "And, listen. That poison you got up here?" He tapped the side of his own head. "That's not healthy. All that's gotta come out. And I'm not Ghost, and I'm not Aidan, and you don't gotta worry about freaking me out, or making me look at you different. I'll still feel exactly the same about you when all this is said and done."

A lump formed in Tango's throat, so he nodded again.

"And I promise you, there's not one thing you could say that I can't handle. My mama was a hooker and I castrated her boyfriend before I fed him to the gators," he said without inflection, as if he were stating the weather. "So don't worry about me. Whatever you say stays between us. I'll never tell. So you just go on and say whatever you want to say. Walk me through it. Fight it out with the old ghosts." He gave him an encouraging smile. "Okay?"

Another nod. "Yeah...yeah, okay." It was hard to swallow. "Where do you think I ought to start?"

Mercy considered. "Start at the start," he suggested. "*All* of the poison, remember? Go back to where your life first went off the rails, and tell me about that."

"Okay." He took a sip of coffee, fingers shaking against the mug. "I was seven..."

~*~

It was a single-wide trailer, no bigger than a motor home. White with green shutters. A green door. The screen door had a rusted spring that groaned when you pushed it open, and that never held, so it slapped shut every time, usually right into Kev's little backside. It sent him sprawling across the carpet, until he was big and quick enough to outrun it. Mama would pick him up, dust off the seat of his pants, and say, "My, Kevin, you've got to get quicker." And she'd smile and kiss the top of his white-blonde head.

A small trailer, yes, but clean. The yard full of hard-packed red dirt was always free of weeds. Mama plucked them up by hand, in her flower-printed garden gloves, and dropped them in the pail Kev carried as he followed her, helping. "Mama's little helper." A massive pecan tree stood at the edge of the yard, just inside the chain link fence, its oblong leaves tossing and rustling in the breeze, its dappled shadows falling across the plastic army men he lined up one-by-one, like Robert Ferguson had showed him at school. Robert had plastic tanks, and trucks, and even an army base, but Kev only had the soldiers, and so he made trips to the small stagnant pond in Mr. Willis's back yard with his pail, trudged it back, slopping droplets all down his skinny legs and into his sneakers; he made thick mud patties and then shaped them into little huts, and forts, and barracks for his army men. They baked in the slanting morning sun and hardened, a whole little earthen village. A place where he retreated every afternoon when school let out, alone with his imagination, fighting brave wars for freedom, while Mama folded laundry in front of Oprah.

It was not a bad life. For a seven-year-old boy, with a best friend, and a bucket of green army men, and a mama who loved him, it seemed all the life anyone could ask for. He was teased for being scrawny, for having such pale hair, for being so delicate in the face. But some of the girls said his eyes were "real nice," and he'd felt this funny sort of fizzing in his chest.

It was Daddy's friend, Miss Carla, who told him he was pretty for the first time.

Daddy didn't live with them, and never had in Kev's memory. "He has problems," Mama always said when asked. Most of the time, when he stopped by, he and Mama argued viciously, and she was in tears by the time he left. There was always talk of "money." And of "lies."

The day Daddy brought Miss Carla was a Saturday. Cloudless, warm, bursting with the sounds of summer: buzzing flies, droning bees, tossing tree limbs, rustling grass, the hiss of tires as cars went past on the highway. A hot morning; Kev was already pushing a damp forelock of hair back off his face as he knelt in the yard, red dirt coating his knees.

A car on the highway slowed, and then turned in at the gate, red dust pluming up beneath the tires. Kev didn't know what kind of car it was – he thought it was a Cadillac – but it was long, and white, and shiny, even as the dust boiled up over it. It was a strange car, one he'd never seen before, and it dipped and swayed on the uneven pack of the yard, finally coming to a halt beside him.

The driver door opened, and out stepped Daddy.

Kev took after his mother, fair, and dainty, and blue-eyed. His father was spare, but broad-shouldered, dark-haired, dark-eyed as a shark. Today he wore a pale blue suit and a skinny red tie that the breeze tugged over his shoulder. His hair was starting to get thin at the temples, a little further back off his forehead than it had been the year before.

He looked at Kev over the top of the car. "Hey, boy."

"Dad." Kev got to his feet, dusted off his knees. Just a year ago, he might have rushed around the car to hug the man. But he was beginning to grow wary of unsteady affection. He might be hugged, or he might be slapped. There was no telling.

The passenger door opened, and a woman climbed out, right in front of Kev. She was thin as a pencil, in a black dress splashed with big white flowers. Her hair shone bright red in the sun, piled up on top of her head and secured there somehow. Her face – angular, harsh – was dramatized with lots of makeup, much more than Mama wore. She had a rough voice, when she spoke, like old Mrs. Hawkins who smoked two packs a day.

101

"Well, hi there, sweetheart." She squatted down a little, so they were on eye level. Her smile struck him funny, made him want to take a step backward. "Aren't you just pretty as a picture." Her head tilted, like some sort of bird, and her eyes went all the way down to the scuffed toes of his sneakers, and then back up again. "What's your name?"

"Kev." He had an army man in one hand, and squeezed it tight.

"Cute." She smiled again, and again he wanted to retreat. "I'm a friend of your daddy's. You can call me Miss Carla."

He didn't say anything.

The screen door opened with a groan, shut with a slap, and Mama stood on the porch, hand shading her eyes from the sun, mouth twisted to the side with unhappiness. The breeze caught her flyway pale hair, streamed it out behind her.

"David?" she called. "What're you doing here?"

"Ah, Jesus, Judy, can I not even get a decent hello?" Daddy called back to her, face screwed up in a scowl.

"I haven't got any money this time," she said, sounding defiant. "I'm not setting any aside for you anymore."

Miss Carla straightened, and turned toward Mama. "Oh, don't worry, ma'am, we're not here for money. David's doing real good for himself these days."

Mama's frown deepened.

Daddy walked toward her, tie still flipped over his shoulder, flapping against the back of his neck. "I came to see my boy. Is that a crime? Can't I see my own son?"

Kev didn't hear what Mama said because Miss Carla was in his face again. "How'd you like to see the inside of a real Cadillac, Kev? Wouldn't that be fun?"

He shrugged. He didn't really care, he just knew that when adults said things like "wouldn't that be fun" that he was supposed to do what they said, that it wasn't a suggestion at all.

Miss Carla led him to the back door of the Cadillac, opened it up, and ushered him inside. "Isn't it nice? Smell that real leather!"

He slid across the cool leather seat, wide as a public park bench, cushioned and new-smelling. The inside of the car was still cold from the AC, and goosebumps chased across his skin. This was nice. Nicer than anything inside or outside of his house.

He heard footsteps crunch in the dirt, and then Daddy's voice, real low, talking to Miss Carla.

"What'd I tell you?" he said.

"He's heaven," Miss Carla said. "Just beautiful, pretty as a little girl. Those eyelashes! And the hair! And thin as a reed."

"He's a little fucking fairy alright."

"Don't make fun of my fairies. They're responsible for this car you're driving." She laughed and it turned into a rattling cough.

"So you want him?" Daddy asked.

Miss Carla caught her breath. "Absolutely."

What were they talking about? Kev slid toward the door…

And it slammed in his face.

Daddy and Miss Carla popped into their seats, shut their doors, and the locks engaged with a thump.

Daddy tossed Kev a small smile. "We're gonna go for a little ride, Kev. How about that?"

"Okay…"

The Cadillac started with a roar and Daddy slammed it in reverse, sped backward. The big car swung around and nearly threw Kev into the floor.

He twisted around to look out the back window as they headed for the highway. He saw Mama running toward them, mouth working, eyes wide with alarm. Reaching toward him.

Then the car turned onto the street and she was gone.

~*~

They drove, and drove, until Kev was exhausted and starving by turns. He asked once where they were going, and when would they get there, and Miss Carla had turned around, patted his leg, smiled, and said nothing.

Finally, they turned in at a McDonald's. It was dark now, and when Daddy opened the back door for him, he heard the sawing of crickets, and smelled unfamiliar smells beneath the typical grease and frying-meat smell of the restaurant.

"Where are we?" he asked, as he slipped from the car. His legs were like jelly and it was hard to stand upright, soles of his feet on pins and needles from sitting for so long.

"We're at McDonald's," Daddy said with a grin, and ruffled his hair.

Inside, Miss Carla gave their order to a pimple-faced, sour teenage employee who slapped their cups across the counter without making eye contact. Miss Carla paid for the food, and handed a cup down to Kev with a smile – still that smile that left him feeling funny.

"Get your drink, sugar. You can have whatever you want."

He got a suicide, because he'd never had one, and because Robert wore they were great. Coke, and Sprite, and root beer, and orange soda, all mixed together. The tickle of bubbles under his nose made him laugh. The drink tasted strange, but he sort of liked it.

Daddy found them a table by the window, so he could watch the passing traffic, headlights coming at them in neat rows.

Miss Carla brought the food on a tray and sat down on the plastic booth beside Kev. "There. Isn't this cozy?"

She gave him yet another smile.

The first bite of cheeseburger was perfection, because he was so hungry. But after a few more bites, once the hunger was dulled, he began to worry, and to grow homesick, and slowly he set the burger down.

"When am I going home?"

"Sweetie, aren't you having fun?" Miss Carla asked. She had a fleck of salad dressing at the corner of her mouth.

"Yeah, but…"

"Just don't worry about it," Daddy muttered, face growing dark. "Always like your damn mother. Worrying about shit."

"David."

"What? He is."

"Eat your food," Miss Carla told him.

But Kev didn't want to anymore.

~*~

Another car ride – a shorter one this time – took them to a one-story motel with ice and vending machines right outside the door. Their room had two double beds with flowered spreads, carpet dark with stains, a TV Daddy couldn't get to work, and a faucet that dripped...dripped...dripped in the bathroom.

"I don't have any pajamas," Kev said. He was tired, and still a little hungry, and his tummy hurt, and he wanted to cry.

"You don't need them, sweetie," Miss Carla said. "You can just sleep in your underwear."

"This fucking thing," Daddy said to the TV, and whacked the side of it with his hand. "I just want to know the damn score. Jesus. Shitty-ass place."

"Can we call Mama on the phone?" Kev asked.

"No."

"Maybe in the morning," Miss Carla said. "Come on, sweetie, you can share the bed with me."

The sheets smelled like wet dirt, and were scratchy against his skin. He curled up on his side, and Carla curled up right behind him, an arm across him, like Mama used to do sometimes. But it didn't make him feel safe and warm, like when Mama did it. Miss Carla had bad breath that whistled in his ear, and she snored. It was too dark, and he imagined creepy, crawling things coming across the carpet toward the bed, climbing up its edges.

He wanted to go home. He closed his eyes, and chanted like Dorothy in *The Wizard of Oz*.

But the next morning, he was still in the motel, and he didn't know it, but he'd never go home again.

~*~

105

"Your old man kidnapped you?" Mercy asked, brows lifting.

Kev was on his third mug of coffee, and starting to shake a little. "Yeah, more or less." He took another sip, and damn the shakes. "I found out later he sold me to...to...Carla." It was still hard to say her name, after all this time. The images it conjured, the way it felt like a spell that would summon her here. "I found out later he was a shopper for her. He found little boys. She liked them to have a certain look, and to be young, so they could be trained and molded. Less defiant that way."

"Jesus," Mercy whispered.

The shaking intensified. Tango slopped coffee out of the mug and onto his hand.

"You wanna stop for the day? Pick back up tomorrow? Or the next day?"

He felt like a total puss, but he nodded. "Yeah. Maybe that would be better."

"Whatever you want. You just tell me."

He sighed and looked down at his trembling fingers. The dominoes inked into the backs of them. "We didn't get very far."

"Who says we have to get far?"

Tango sent him a smile, feeling shy and stupid. "Thanks."

Mercy nodded. He leaned back against the couch and spread his arms across the top. Throughout the story, he'd leaned more and more forward, until his elbows were braced on his knees, chin cupped in his hand.

Tango felt terrible about that; felt bad that his life was affecting anyone in any way.

"I talked to Aidan at the shop before I came over," Mercy said. "He said Whitney spent the night with you last night."

Tango fidgeted. "Not like you think."

"What happened?"

"Her sister-in-law kicked her out, and she doesn't have any other family. She doesn't have anywhere else to go. So I told her she could crash here for a little while."

Mercy smirked. "That's not the kind of happening I was talking about."

Tango wanted badly to bury his face in his hands. Instead, he sighed and let his head flop back. "I sort of…jumped on her. But," he added, in a rush, "I stopped. I didn't actually *jump her bones* or anything. Only tried." He grimaced. "Shit, I can't believe I did that."

"Why not?"

"Because she's a nice girl! And because she's, like, twelve, or whatever."

"Bro, you're talking to a guy who got a very nice seventeen-year-old girl pregnant once. Don't overthink the numbers."

"How about the part where I used to take it up the ass for money, and God knows if I've got HIV or something?" he blurted, shocked by his own bluntness. Mercy had said he couldn't he shocked, after all.

And to his extreme credit, he didn't look shocked now. He shrugged. "So go get tested. All I'm saying is, you really like this girl, and she really likes you, and from what I can tell she's sweet. You need sweet. Hell, you deserve sweet."

He swallowed. "I don't deserve anything."

"Not true. What have you ever done that was evil? Nothing," he said before Tango could answer. "You got the real shit end of the stick, my friend. So finally, destiny's handing you something worth a damn. Take it. Just…maybe buy it dinner first, yeah?"

Tango couldn't help but smile. "You know what?"

"What?"

"I think you're probably an awesome therapist."

Mercy made a self-congratulatory face and tossed his hair. "Totally nailing it, right?"

Nine

About three o'clock, Whitney's stomach began to grind with nerves. She set down her bag of pretzels half-eaten and tried to concentrate on answering each and every customer service call with gusto and helpful redirection.

She did a decent job, she thought, but still the churning continued. When the clock struck five, she was actually sweating a little, sweater clinging in her armpits and to her back.

What awaited her back at the apartment? She didn't know if Kev would be hiding in his room, still, too mortified to face her. Or if he'd be awkwardly trying to apologize, or, worse, pretending it hadn't happened. She'd never been in this situation before, and the unknown was driving her nuts.

At five-fifteen, she sat in her car in the parking lot and texted him. *Should I pick up dinner?*

He texted her back in about ten seconds: *Already taken care of. :-)*

A smiley face. That was good, right? That meant they'd be able to actually look at one another and speak, right?

She didn't know. And so her legs were quivering with stupid nerves by the time she parked in the alley behind the bakery and hiked up the stairs to the apartment door. It was unlocked, and when she let herself in, she was assaulted by savory smells.

"Kev?" she called as she hung up her purse and jacket. "It smells nice."

"I'm in here." And that was in front of the oven, the door of the old-fashioned unit cracked open as he peered inside, frowning professionally. "Come see what you think. Does this look done?"

"What is it?" she asked, joining him.

"It's supposed to be mac & cheese." His nose wrinkled and it was adorable.

Her nerves melted. "Well, let me see." She stepped up beside him, shoulder-to-shoulder, close enough to hear their clothes brushing together; his hair tickled against hers.

A big rectangular casserole dish bubbled inside the oven, the edges golden brown, the center a lovely cheddar color, cheese sauce hissing and popping.

"Wow," she said, truly impressed. "It smells and looks amazing. Is that bacon on top?"

"And potato chips," he said, a note of pride in his voice.

She elbowed him, smiling. "You've been holding out on me. I didn't know you could cook."

"I can't, actually. But I called Mags and had her give me very careful instructions and a shopping list."

She stepped back from the oven and looked up at him, chest swelling with hope. "You went shopping? And you cooked?"

He dragged a hand through his hair and became self-conscious. "Some accomplishment. Two things everyone else in the world does every day." He sent her a fleeting, skittery look, eyes hooded and nervous.

"Progress is progress," she said. "And I think it's ready." She wasn't going to let him get stuck in his head, feeling down on himself, she decided. "I'll get us something to drink while you take your masterpiece out of the oven."

He nodded. "Yeah."

She liked the way they moved around the kitchen, crossing each other's paths, but never colliding. It felt easy, this sharing of space, the completion of the all-important evening meal, and she marveled at the way it wasn't strange, despite what had happened last night.

They sat down across from one another at the table, steaming plates of mac & cheese in front of them, Coke instead of wine, because that had so not been a good idea last night.

Kev stared at his plate a moment. Gave the noodles an experimental poke with his fork. "I hope it tastes alright. There's cut up hot dogs in it. For protein, Mags said. I need more protein."

"You do." She took a bite, decided it needed more pepper, but she wasn't going to tell him that. "It's delicious."

His brows lifted. "You're not just saying that?"

"Would I do that?"

"Yeah, you would."

She grinned. "Try it. You'll like it."

He took a deep breath – she tried not to laugh – and took a tiny bite. Then his brows jumped. "It doesn't suck."

"Definitely not."

He ate with real appetite, bigger and bigger bites, fork already loaded before he'd swallowed. So Whitney kept quiet, tending to her own dinner, stealing glimpses of him that made her heart warm with gladness. He was shopping, and cooking, and eating. This was progress. This gave her hope.

Finally, he set his fork down, plate clean save a lonely hot dog round and a smear of cheese sauce. He exhaled like his belly was too full and that made him uncomfortable, but God bless him, he'd eaten all of it.

Whitney set down her own fork, unable to keep quiet any longer. "You're better today," she observed.

He took another deep breath, and met her gaze with an open and vulnerable one of his own. A sharing sort of gaze, like he hoped she wasn't going to think poorly of him. "I started therapy today."

"Kev, that's wonderful."

His eyes flicked away, and he picked up his fork again, dragged the tines through the cheese sauce smear on the plate. "Yeah, well…It was good. I think. I hope. I don't know how it's gonna go…"

"Kev," she said, cautious, "things were bad for you for a long time, right?"

He nodded.

"So it will take a long time to get better. There's nothing wrong with that. The important thing is that you're taking the right steps."

Another nod.

"I'm really proud of you."

He smirked a little. "Be proud when I don't attack you like a rabid dog."

She had to swallow. Remembered sensation chased across her skin. "That's...that's not what you did."

He sent her a wry glance from beneath his lashes.

"You were...a little...excited, yeah—"

"Don't try to make it sound better than it was."

She bit her lip. Tough love, or kid gloves in this situation? She said, "Do you like me?"

He blinked. "What?"

"Do you like me?"

"Of course I like you. Why would you even ask that?"

"Did you...last night. Was that because you like...what we were about to do? Or because you like me?"

He didn't hesitate. "Both."

"Oh." She wasn't sure how that made her feel.

He sat back a little in his chair, and reached into the pocket of the hoodie hooked onto the laddered back of it, coming out with a pack of smokes and a lighter. He fetched his saucer ashtray off the counter where she'd left it clean and shiny last night, lit up, settled at the table again.

"Okay," he said after he'd had his first drag. "Here's the thing. I'm a fucking pervert."

"Kev!"

"No, just listen." Another drag. Tapping of ash. "I really am. After what happened to me...what I did..." He shook his head and forced smoke through his nostrils. "I think about sex all the time, even when I don't want it. I fixate on it." Another head shake. "And the first time I saw you, a very big part of me was thinking about what I wanted to do to you."

Her mouth went dry.

"And the longer I know you, the worse that feeling gets. Because I do like you. I more than like you."

She tried to swallow.

"But because I'm a sick pervert, I would only hurt you, or scare you, or ruin everything." His eyes, up 'til now flicking across the table, lifted to her face, expression earnest. "So I'm not going to touch you again. Not like that."

Why was that disappointing? "You weren't hurting me," she said. "You were just going a little fast."

"Fast is my only setting. I'm a goddamn sex toy. I'm not even a person."

"Don't say that."

He ignored her. "But part of getting better is learning how not to be a toy. And that means no sex. That means having some self-control."

"Is that what your therapist told you?"

An inexplicable smile tweaked one corner of his mouth. "No. This is something I've decided for myself."

"You're not a sex toy," she insisted.

He made a disagreeing face and looked away again, dragging on his cigarette.

"Wanting to be with somebody doesn't mean there's anything *wrong* with you."

He grinned, a nasty grin, like he was mocking himself. "Sure."

"Kev—"

"You're a good person," he said, making eye contact again. "You are. One of the best people I know. I'm not gonna let my bullshit bleed all over you. I'm just not, Whitney. I want you to stay here as long as you need to. And I don't want you to have to worry about what I might do."

This conversation was giving her a headache. She dropped her forehead into her cupped palm and fought the lump in her throat, the burn of tears. "I can move out, if that's what you really want."

"No," he said, at once. "That's not what I want at all. I mean." She heard him fidget. "Unless that's what you want."

"No. Eventually, yes, but not at the moment. I'll have to find a place."

"Oh. Well, you can stay here while you look for one."

"Thanks."

Her other hand was on the table, and she felt his cover it, his skin smooth save the years-old calluses he'd earned working on bikes at the Dartmoor garage.

"Whit," he said, quietly, urgently. "I'm trying to do the right thing here."

She nodded. "I know."

They sat there for a long moment, before he finally pulled back. "I'm gonna wash the dishes."

"I'll help you." When she picked her head up, he was giving her a crooked, hopeful smile, like he so badly didn't want her to hate him.

She couldn't help but return it.

~*~

Ian dreamed of home all the time now. Tonight, he went back to his old room, flopped down on the bed on his stomach, flipped open his sketch pad to a new page, and began to draw. Vague, light strokes at first, and then more detailed, getting darker, defining shapes and adding shading so that the figure looked more of a human and less of a mannequin. It was the man who'd showed up at the back of dance class tonight.

Ian had had one foot up at the barre, stretching alongside his classmates, enjoying the deep sense of pulling in his hamstring, when in the mirror he had seen a man standing against the far wall. He'd looked like a dancer: lithe, tall, narrow in the right places with just enough wideness in his shoulders to suggest strength. He had been older, perhaps forty, his face lined, though still handsome.

Handsome. Something Ian had started to associate with men. He'd begun to look at them, seeing features and finding them attractive. A dusting of hair on a wrist; a cleft in the chin; a nose sharp as a blade. He noticed things, so he noticed that this man was well-groomed, and nicely-formed, and that his eyes were sharp and glittering in his fine-featured face.

The man had spoken to Madame Clarice for a long time, so long that their warmup had ended and all the students had

113

plopped gracefully down onto the floor to await further instructions.

When their meeting was over, the man walked away and Madame Clarice turned to the assemblage with unusually bright eyes. She clapped her hands too sharply and said, in a voice high with excitement, "First position!"

Ian had never seen her so exuberant.

After class, she had asked him to stay late; had called him into her office. It was an office as exacting as its mistress. Small wooden desk that she had sanded and refinished regularly; tidy file cabinets full of student information; spotless blotter; chrome cup full of pens and pencils; framed photos of her students, and of herself as a young student, done in tasteful black-and-white and framed in black on the walls. A pair of faded shoes hung behind the desk, tied to a decorative hook by their ribbons. It smelled like cedar and lemon. Because it was summer, the window was cracked and street-scented air slipped in, fragrant currents that stirred the pointe shoes.

"Have a seat, please," Madame Clarice said, and Ian folded quickly into the chair opposite her desk. "You saw the man who was here?"

He nodded. "Yes, ma'am."

She pressed her lips together, face coloring as if she was pleased, but not wanting to demonstrate as such. "He's a representative for a very prestigious ballet school." A school that sent a representative to look at him, specifically.

Ian thought he might faint right off the chair. "They did?"

Madame Clarice nodded. "Yes, of course. You're my best student."

She told him, in her crisp, no-nonsense voice, that the man's name was Mr. Brigg, and that he'd once been a dancer himself, and now worked as an instructor at the aforementioned prestigious academy. He was looking for new "raw talent" to add to the roster and he'd heard that there was "a very fine young dancer" at Madame Clarice's he ought to observe.

"He wants to take you for an audition there," Madame Clarice had said, a smile breaking through the cracks of her stern façade. "Isn't it wonderful?"

"But…I like dancing here."

"Of course you do, my pet, and I would miss you terribly in my class. But you mustn't waste such an opportunity."

An opportunity. Would Mum and Dad see it as such? he wondered. It would mean driving him farther, weekend practices, a possibility of missed dinners.

He set his pencil aside and reached for the stick of charcoal at his elbow, for the darkest shadows, loving the powdery feel of it.

Two days later, Mr. Brigg was back at Madame Clarice's, and Ian buzzed with excitement all through class, missing marks again and again, fumbling in his nervousness. Afterward, after Madame Clarice had told him to "pay better attention next time," Mr. Brigg stepped forward and asked if he might walk home with Ian.

Ian was delighted. He spent an extra five minutes in the changing room, running his fingers under the tap and adjusting his hair with water, wishing he didn't look so flushed and warm and floppy-haired. His cheeks glowed pink, and his eyes seemed too wide, too bright, too caught between blue and green to be any real color. He was just so *nervous*.

If Mr. Brigg thought he was floppy-haired or strange, he didn't let on. He greeted Ian with a warm smile. "Ready to go?" He had a faint touch of Irishman in his voice. A nice voice, deep and resonant.

"Yes!" Ian said with too much enthusiasm, and they set off.

Mr. Brigg told Ian to call him Sean, and he said that Ian shouldn't be nervous, that being approached was as good as acceptance. If you were special enough to draw attention, it usually meant you were special enough to get into the school.

Ian wanted to talk about the school, but Mr. Brigg – Sean – wanted to know more about Ian. Where he went to real school, how many siblings he had, what were his mother and father like.

"They must be so proud of you," he said.

Ian shrugged. "Maybe." But he wasn't sure of that at all. Dad thought he was some sort of fairy for wanting to do ballet. And Mum was too caught up in the social whirl to pay much attention to any of her three children. "My sister is," he said, smiling as he thought of little Janie, grinning her gap-toothed smile at him, insisting he must be "the handsomest ballerina" in all of London. He loved her for that, and had told her so, often when she'd had a nightmare and crept down the hall to his room, rooting under his covers like a frightened little pug.

"She'll miss you, then," Sean said, warm smile shifting, growing almost somber. "All the time you'll be spending away from home, dancing."

Ian didn't think much of that; he was too excited to worry about consequences.

Two days later, he was walking to Madame Clarice's when a black bag dropped over his head, and he felt the sharp prick of a needle in the side of his neck.

He slept.

When he woke, he was surrounded by strangers. And Sean was there.

The dream that wasn't a dream, that was really a memory, ended there, Sean's deadened face fading to mist as Ian opened his eyes and gasped.

Darkness. Faint slatted patterns on the ceiling: ambient city light filtering through the vertical blinds. Gentle rush of breathing beside him. Alec. Perfect pink lower lip, little cleft in his chin, expressive, vulnerable brown eyes, taste of rose water in the hollow of his throat, beneath his collar, hidden, unless your tongue was searching for it.

"I've never been with a man before," he'd whispered, hours ago, like a confession.

"Do you want to be with one?" Ian had asked, nipping at his ear, feeling his chest press against his own as Alec gasped. Shocked. Delighted. Afraid. Thrilled.

"Yes."

116

There had been something sweet about the awkward, virginal fumbling, the blushing, the uncertainty. Something delicious in showing someone what he wanted for the first time.

Almost as delicious as it had been with Kev, years before.

Ian reached out blindly and found the half-full crystal glass of Cabernet Sauvignon he'd left on the nightstand. He lifted his head as he brought it to his lips, not spilling a drop on his expensive steel-colored sheets. He'd had lots of practice with this.

He'd had lots of practice with so, so many things.

Beside him, Alec stirred, kicking through the sheets, murmuring something.

Ian passed his knuckles down the hard knobs of his spine. "Go back to sleep, darling. It's only a nightmare."

Ten

Session 2

Mercy brought brownies. "Not the fun kind," he explained with a grin, brows twitching. "Just the regular kind. But Ava put chocolate and peanut butter chips in them." She'd also put them on a white ceramic cake stand with little scalloped edges and wrapped it carefully in Christmas themed cling wrap. Mercy set them down in the center of the coffee table and took the wrap off with surprising dexterity – at least, Tango had once thought it was surprising. He was long since used to the incredible gentleness of the big man.

"They look good," Tango said.

"Yeah, I know. That's why you're going to eat one." He sent him a meaningful look.

Tango sighed and leaned forward to snag one. His stomach cramped at the idea of sweets that weren't alcohol, but he was serious, wasn't he? About getting better? He could eat a damn brownie.

He nibbled a corner – it was delicious, a hint of cinnamon in the mix – and earned a nod of approval, just before Mercy devoured one in two efficient bites.

"Okay," the Cajun said when he could. "You wanna pick up where we left off yesterday?"

Tango shrugged and nibbled a little more. Just two small bites, and he could already feel them solidifying in his stomach. "Seems as good a place as any."

~*~

They were no longer in Georgia, Miss Carla informed him around ten the next morning, as the Cadillac barreled down the interstate. She was in the same dress as the day before, hair limp from hotel shampoo, as she turned to look at him in the back seat. Kev was getting really tired of the smile she kept giving him.

The sight of it curled his little hands into fists and left him feeling energized...and violent. Like the urge to kick an anthill. Or cover his face during the scary parts of a movie.

"Where are we?" he asked. There was a dull, lifeless quality to his voice; his tongue felt heavy, his throat thick. He hadn't cried, but he wanted to.

"Tennessee," she said. "The great state of Tennessee."

Tennessee looked much the same as Georgia, open fields and pine forest flashing past the window. But the soil, the open patches of it he could see, were paler, not that red Georgia clay that he used to build bunkers for his army men.

He wanted to go home.

The sun was in the middle of the sky when the Cadillac turned into the driveway of a house and the engine went quiet. Daddy and Miss Carla opened their doors and climbed out. The safety locks had been engaged the entire ride, so Kev had to wait for Miss Carla to open his door and invite him outside with a wave of her arm.

It was a real house, and not a trailer like where he and Mama lived, but it didn't look fresh, and clean, and white like their trailer did. It didn't look like any sort of place he would want to live. It had a long, uneven porch in front, and rooms and extensions boiled out in all directions, like warts, the shape of it messy, displeasing to the eye. The paint peeled in thick strips, like sunburned skin, and there were bars over the windows, thick as Kev's wrist and crowded together.

Tall, shaggy trees shaded a yard that was mostly dirt, tufted with weeds. A high chain link fence surrounded the property, and in back, Kev glimpsed the wood boards of a privacy fence.

His gaze landed on small things: a Snickers bar wrapper caught in the links of the fence, a Styrofoam cup at the base of a tree, a crack in one window, just visible through the bars. He smelled...bad things. Dark, foul, frightening things. An odor he couldn't identify, but which tickled the back of his conscience, told him there was danger near.

A turn of his head in both directions showed that the whole street was full of un-homey houses like this one. Lots of trees. Lots of shadows, even in daytime. He heard dogs barking in anger and fear. Heard a radio, dimly, from somewhere, the kind of music Mama never let him listen to.

Miss Carla's hand clamped down on the back of his neck, her fingers cool, but damp. It was gross. It made him jump. "Come on, honey, don't just stand there. Let's go inside."

Kev sent a pleading look toward Daddy, but Daddy didn't seem to be coming, propping a hip against the window of the Cadillac and lighting a cigarette.

"Dad."

"Go on, sport." He didn't glance up.

Miss Carla's fingers tightened; he felt the sharp tips of her nails bite into his skin. "Come on," she said again, and propelled him forward to the door.

She pushed him up porch stairs that sounded like they might splinter, and unlocked the front door one-handed, hustling him through with the other.

His first impression was of darkness. A stale smell. Not enough sunlight.

The door closed and locked behind him with a resounding sequence of clicks.

His eyes adjusted to the light and he saw that the front door led into a narrow foyer, devoid of all furniture. A sequence of hooks on the left wall held jackets, hats, an umbrella.

"This way," Miss Carla said behind him, and urged him forward.

They stepped into a wide, shadowy living room: TV, sofas, chairs, all of it sad, dark, dusty. A stairwell with wooden spindles led to an upper story, but Miss Carla steered him past it, and into the kitchen.

Buckled, checkered linoleum, peeling up at its yellow edges against the bases of the cabinets. Cabinets that might have been white, once, but now were the color of handprints and splattered grease. A stained cooktop; a coffee maker; a table stacked with magazines, one corner reserved for a standing mirror and a large black plastic case. The bars over the windows striped the floor with shadows and sunlight. It smelled like ripe garbage.

"Over here." Miss Carla jangled her keys, selected several, and unlocked a door tucked beside the pantry with not one, but five deadbolt locks screwed into the wood.

Kev could smell it the second the door was open: a pit of humanity.

Miss Carla clicked on a light somewhere. Down they went, a narrow flight of wooden stairs, walls tight on either side. Click of her heels. Gentle sounds beyond the walls: voices, rustles, questions. Smell of people, of rats.

The basement was unfinished, concrete floor, block walls, exposed joists overhead, spangled with cobwebs that floated in air currents. Bedrooms, narrow bunks, pallets on the floor, boys. Lots of small, skinny boys, just like him, with girl-pretty faces. The walls of the bedrooms were bars. Cells. They were in cells. And Miss Carla had the keys.

Her clammy hand pinched the back of his neck until he whimpered. "Alright, Kev. Come meet your new brothers."

~*~

Mercy's eyes had gone that scary black color that accompanied the buzzing of power equipment. "She had a basement full of kids?"

Tango nodded and pulled a hard drag on his smoke, willing the tremors in his hands to fade. This couldn't be healthy, could it? Going back to that place, breathing in its scents and remembering its textures. But this was how therapy worked: the talking, the revisiting. The conquering.

"I didn't understand any of it for a long time. She put me in one of the cells and I..." His throat ached, and he took another drag. "I thought I musta done something wrong. Kid logic, you know? I thought Mama...Mom," he corrected, clearing his throat. He hadn't seen her during that period when "Mama" became "Mom" in boys' mouths, and so he slipped sometimes, on the rare occasions when he talked about her. "I thought she musta sent me away," he said, shrugging. "That it was something I did."

It helped immensely that Mercy nodded, staring at him. Whitney, he knew, would have chewed her lips, and fought tears, and told him how valuable he was. He couldn't have taken that right now; he would have crumbled.

Mercy said, "Kids always think it's their fault."

Tango reached for his coffee, asking silently with his eyes.

"I know I did. And I was twenty, so go figure."

He nodded, sat back, took a soothing sip. How odd, he thought, that the only things getting him through his new heroin-free life were cigs and coffee.

And Whitney.

"I can keep going," he said.

Mercy nodded. "Okay."

~*~

There were ten of them, including Kev. He was put in a cell with a bunk bed, a pallet of blankets on the floor, and boys named Lee and Simon. Simon and Lee were dark-haired, olive-skinned boys, not related, they told him. Lee had giant brown eyes the color of hard caramel candy, and Simon's arm was bandaged, because he'd called Miss Carla a slut, he informed Kev without reaction.

They crowded in close around him, curious, their gazes like those of interested foxes: wanting to know more, but wary, a little, of someone from the outside.

"Where are you from?"

"Where did she catch you?"

"*How* did she catch you?"

"How old are you?"

"Was anyone upstairs?"

"Are you gonna cry?"

He wanted to, he really did.

"You can have the top bunk," Lee offered, plunking down on the bottom one. "Simon likes it on the floor."

"More room," Simon said. "My legs hurt all the time."

They seemed so...so...*normal*. It didn't seem possible.

"What do you guys *do* here?" he asked, stomach squirming with unhappiness.

"Whadya mean?" Simon asked.

"Here." He flapped his arms, at a loss for the very grownup words he needed to describe this place. "What do you do?"

Lee considered, head tilting to the side; the overhead lights glinted off his eyes, turned them to caramel glass. "We do whatever Miss Carla tells us to do."

~*~

The first night was, in many ways, the worst. The new smells and sounds filtering through the dark. The utter insanity of it all, the idea that two days ago his mama had tucked him into Ninja Turtles sheets, and now he was in a bunk, in a cell, in a basement, and had no idea when or if he'd be let out.

Lee or Simon snored; the other one whimpered in his sleep, fidgeting like a dog with nightmares. From the other cells he heard sleepy gasps and small shouts. Night terrors ran rampant through the damp concrete prison.

Kev rolled onto his side and curled into a ball, little hands clasped tight between his knees, eyes staring into the darkness. He hated himself. Why hadn't he ducked away from Miss Carla's hand? Why hadn't he hit her? Kicked her? Fled? Fought? He'd just walked, pliant as a rag doll, and let himself get locked up behind these bars, with these strangers, away from home, and Mama, and Robert, and school, and his little green army men...

Did the boys here have toys? He didn't think so. He thought he might start crying if he asked.

Somewhere beyond the basement, the outdoor night sounds crept in to him: crickets, cicadas, the hoot of an owl, dogs barking. The same as back home in Georgia. The only thing that was the same.

Eleven

Alec wore glasses at work, when he was bringing Ian perfect cups of tea and delivering mail and messages. He pushed them up his nose with a knuckle and blushed a little, as Ian stared at him. But he kept reading, smooth, twenty-four-year-old cheeks suffused with a gentle pink, like the petals of fresh roses.

"...and then Mr. Thompson wanted to confirm your lunch meeting this afternoon. You said one-thirty?"

"I did."

Alec nodded and used the stylus to make a note on his iPad. "Right. Well. That should be all for now." He tucked the stylus away and looked up with adorable shyness, swallowing, throat pressing against the starched collar of his shirt.

Ian immediately thought of the rosewater, imagined one of Alec's manicured fingers dipping into the bottle and then slicking it there in the hollow of his throat.

Delicious.

"Well done, Alec. That will be all for now."

"Very good, sir." He turned smartly to return to the outer office, giving Ian a splendid view of the way his hipster skinny dress pants hugged his ass.

Alec was new, in Ian's employ for only three months. Ian had clocked him during the interview, the quiet, studious slant to his brows, the soft, sweet voice, the innate sensitivity. He'd been a little bit enraptured. A crush, he'd allowed himself. Yes, he could have crushes on sweet, beautiful boys. Vulnerable had always been his type.

But Kev's rejection had done something to him. Had snapped carefully-strung wires. He tried, always, to keep work professional, his personal life a total secret. Don't muddy the waters, he'd always said. But after Kev, he'd been howling inside. This terrible, dark vacuum, a blackness that ate itself...ate *him*...until he was all juiced nerves and restless craving. The sort of craving that left him longing for needles and razorblades.

He'd turned to Alec instead. And in soothing the craving, he'd discovered something unexpected, something he'd missed in his earlier preoccupation: Alec was wonderful.

Which of course meant he deserved better.

But Ian wasn't Kev. He could admit that he was a selfish bastard, that he wanted pleasurable things for himself.

His phone rang. His personal phone. The ID display told him it was Aidan Teague.

"Hello, beautiful," he answered, just to fuck with the man.

He earned an exasperated sound in response, which made him grin. "You're a sonovabitch," Aidan said.

"Yes, my mother was, in fact, a raving bitch. No argument there."

Aidan sighed. "Can you be serious for five seconds, Dr. Evil?"

"Of course."

"Have you talked to Kev recently?"

Hearing his name sent shivers skittering down the back of Ian's neck. He shuddered hard inside his Armani suit. "Not since the last time you saw me."

"Really?" Aidan sounded surprised.

"Really."

"Oh...okay. Well. I wanted to let you know that he's in therapy."

Ian said, "Excellent." But it was a shock to hear. Kev consented to have someone open up his poor head and look inside? It didn't seem possible. They'd opened up to each other, once upon a time, that had been the beginning of their bond, the enduring thread, that drew them together again and again. They were magnetized by disaster. But to talk to a professional? That sounded unlikely.

"Yeah, it's good," Aidan said. "And I think it's helping. I hope it is, anyway. He's not any worse, that's for sure."

"That's..." Ian swallowed. Hard. "That's wonderful."

"And." Aidan's voice became nervous. "I've been thinking."

"Heavens, don't strain anything."

"Ha. No. Seriously. I've been thinking…I know you…shit, I know you *care* about Kev." Now he was nervous and awkward to boot. "But I think you remind him of bad shit. You know?"

Ian sighed. "You're asking me to stay away from him until he's back on his feet properly, aren't you?"

"I am, yeah."

He should have been expecting as much. He and Kev together were a flammable cocktail. There was love, and tenderness, and remembrance; but the past echoed tragically in their bloodstream. The lows were as low as the highs were high.

But he hated Aidan for voicing it.

And yet…he had to give the man some credit. Aidan Teague belonged to a brotherhood of men who followed very strict, very old, very intolerant rules. The fact that Aidan kept him informed, and allowed for Kev's proclivities…there was goodness there. Of a sort.

Ian's head felt suddenly heavy, and he reclined in his chair. "Don't worry, darling. I won't pester him. Not until he wants me to."

A beat of silence, one fraught with biker tension. Then: "Thanks, man. That's good of you."

"Think nothing of it," Ian said, and hung up on him.

He sat very still in his ergonomic chair a moment, watching birds flit in the bare tree branches outside his window, breathing in the cold, faint fragrance of the unlit aromatherapy candle on his desk.

He leaned over and punched the intercom button on his phone.

Alec's voice said, "Yes, sir?"

"Pencil me an extra hour after lunch," he said. "And plan on accompanying me."

He swore he could hear Alec blushing. "Y-yes, sir."

~*~

"So Tango's still with his aunt?"

Aidan let out a womanish scream of surprise and whirled away from the bike on the rack, wrench clenched in his hand like a weapon.

Behind him, Michael stood with his hands in his pockets, undisturbed.

"Jesus!" Aidan exhaled in a rush, ashamed to admit he'd been so startled that his heartbeat was now fluttering behind his ears. "You can't just sneak up on people, damn!"

"I told him he should wear a little bell," Mercy called from the other side of the garage. "Like a kitty cat."

Michael stared at Aidan, non-responsive to the joke. Not apologizing. "He's with his aunt?" he repeated.

There was a crawling sensation down the back of Aidan's neck. He scowled at the guy. "Yeah. He is. What do you care?"

Without blinking, Michael said, "Holly saw him at Leroy's yesterday."

A knot of dread, hard and big as a melon, formed in his gut. He might have gasped a little, before he could catch himself. Then he gave Michael his hardest, most threatening glare – which was like a sunny smile compared to Michael's resting bitch face. "Holly didn't see him," he said, firmly. "She saw someone else, who looked like him, but she didn't see Kev. Understand?"

Michael's head kicked back. His mouth twitched. "What's he into? The smack again?"

A correct guess, but only a fraction of the bigger issue. "No." Aidan leaned in close, got in his face. "He's fucking not. Now back off about it."

With impeccable timing, Mercy loomed up behind Michael, making the man look small, which was no easy feat. "Drop it, Michael," he said quietly. "The boss man's in the loop. Just let it go."

Michael stepped back and swapped a look between the two of them, eyes narrowed. Finally, he shrugged. "Not my business anyway. Just thought someone should know."

"Go back to work," Aidan told him. It was the first time he'd told an officer to do anything. And, shockingly, it worked.

Michael wandered on silent cat feet back out into the winter sunshine, and turned in the direction of the auto garage.

When he was gone, Aidan released a deep breath and sagged back against the bike lift. "Shit. He's not the first one to get curious, and he isn't gonna be the last."

"No," Mercy agreed, expression grim. "Kid's gotta be more careful when he goes out."

"I'll talk to Whitney. See if she can do some of the shopping for him. I can do some of it. Something." He glanced over at his brother-in-law. "Talking to him. You think it's helping?"

"I do." Mercy nodded. "But we've just scratched the surface, you know? There's lots of ghosts left."

Twelve

Session 3

Miss Carla didn't live alone. She had four men who brought the boys their meals, who ushered them to the pitiful corner of the basement where they could use the toilet, wash themselves in a big laundry sink, and brush their teeth in front of a mirror. The tooth brushing was mandatory. "Pretty teeth," Miss Carla insisted. "My boys have to have pretty teeth."

The worst of the men was named Max. He was tall, and almost too wide to fit through the door. His black t-shirt stretched tight over layers of fat and muscle, and he had a thick roll on the back of his neck that hung out over his collar. Lee said he looked like a "movie gangster," but Kev didn't know what that meant, only that he had dark, slicked-back hair and mud-colored eyes that turned black and mean if any of them dared to talk back to him. Which wasn't often.

There were no windows in the basement, so days and nights were judged by the droning of the light bulbs overhead. On for day, and off for night. It had been eighteen days since his arrival when Max came to collect Kev.

He'd become fast friends with his bunk mates, and though they lacked toys of any sort, Lee and Simon had books that they took turns flipping through, all of them lined up and squashed together on Simon's pallet, Lee turning the pages, all of them murmuring in awe and appreciation. Their favorite was a book of full-color photos of ballet dancers. Most were women, but some were men, and all of them were suspended in impossible, graceful poses, limbs lifted above their heads, bodies balanced at impossible angles.

"We're learning to dance like this," Simon confided. "We have class."

The idea struck Kev as preposterous. Why would anyone who kept them locked in a basement send them to dance class?

Lee stood up to demonstrate, his posture becoming tall, shoulders thrown back, feet light and together at the heels on the floor. "First position." He held his arms lightly at his sides, tensed and ready for action, but fluid, too. A picture of delicacy, and of strength.

Kev wrinkled his nose. "You look like a girl."

"Boys do ballet too," Simon insisted, flipping to one of the photos of just such a thing in the book. "It isn't just for girls."

Kev didn't agree, but he wasn't going to argue with his new friends.

The sound of the door opening up at the top of the stairs was only a whisper, a shushing of air and a faint groan of the hinges, but it hit the basement like gunfire. Everyone went silent, still, breath held, waiting.

A heavy set of boots descended, and then Max appeared in front of their cell, a set of keys jangling in his hand.

Lee snapped the book shut. "Class?" he asked, equal parts hopeful and frightened.

"Bring your new friend," Max growled.

The neighboring cell was emptied – Jimmy, Eric, Carson – and the six of them were marched up the narrow stairs, Max behind them, another of the black-clad guards waiting for them at the top. Kev would forever remember the bite of the sharp edge of each step against the sole of his worn-out Converse All-Stars. The way their footfalls echoed his pulse, the fast drumming of his heart in his ears.

They were led out of the kitchen and down a hall, and into a room that he thought must be one of those ugly carbuncles jutting out of the house that he'd seen from the outside. A long rectangle of a room, the windows high and narrow, barred, light slipping in at an angle that struck a fire against the long wall of mirrors. Wooden floors, the smell of sweat, and BO, cubbies opposite the mirror, pair after pair after pair of scuffed white slippers hanging from little hooks. He'd seen slippers like that – on the ballet dancers in the book.

Beneath the hooks were plastic laundry hampers with folded clothes in them. The other boys walked toward them,

130

already reaching for the hems of their shirts and the fastenings of their grubby jeans.

Kev's heartbeat sped up another notch. "What are you doing?" he asked, voice a quick hiss that echoed in the empty room.

"We have to change," Simon explained. With a face like he thought Kev was stupid, he reached into one of the baskets and came out clutching a handful of fabric. "Here." He walked over and handed it to Kev. "Put this on. And then shoes."

"But..." He didn't want to. So badly that his stomach cramped, and he wondered if he'd be sick. They were just clothes, and shoes, but he so, so, so *didn't want to*.

"Hurry," Lee said from the hooks, now standing in his underwear, pale and gangly as a newborn foal. "She'll be mad if she sees."

As Max and the other man in black watched from the doorway, Kev shucked his clothes and pulled on a leotard and tights. And the soft white slippers, black on the bottom with dirt.

~*~

Miss Carla wore a long, floating skirt, and tights, and a clinging black shirt. It would have been a nice outfit, if it hadn't made her look so thin, and harsh, and if the edges of the shirt hadn't been so frayed, nor the shirt such a washed-out pretend-black. She entered the room wearing too much makeup, her mouth a crooked pink slash in her painted face, hair drawn up so tight on top of her head it pulled at the skin around her eyes. She carried a long black cane, thin as a whip, and she tapped it absently against the side of her calf as she walked down the line they'd formed in the center of the room. "We have to stand like this," Lee had said, and given Kev's shoulder a little encouraging squeeze. "For inspection."

She was indeed inspecting them. The same way Mama always turned over a week-old loaf of bread, frowning at it, searching for mold. Miss Carla tidied a lock of Simon's dark hair. Poked Eric lightly in the stomach with her cane and told him to "straighten." Tilted her head this way and that as she considered Lee. "Half-rations for dinner," she told him, and Lee's Caramel eyes fluttered down to the floor, his shoulders hitching.

And then she was in front of Kev, hands clasped together on her cane, expression softening. No, that wasn't true – her mouth softened, it slid into that same smile she'd been giving him from the first. But it never touched her eyes. Those tracked up and down him, the possibly-moldy piece of bread.

"Well, Kev." Her voice made him think of cold water trickling down the back of his neck. "Are you ready to learn how to dance?"

"No," he said, bluntly. "No, I don't want to dance."

Her arm moved, a fast flash, and the cane caught him in the side of the head.

He saw stars.

~*~

The teacup saucer overflowed with cigarette butts, his and Mercy's. They kept leaning in closer and closer over the coffee table to tap their ash, grind the nubs out, and then light new ones.

"I learned how to dance," Tango said. "I didn't want to be, but turns out I was really good at it. Took to it like that." He snapped the fingers of his free hand. "But I was built for it. That's why she wanted me – I had the look. Built like a dancer and pretty as a girl in the face."

He flashed his friend a smile he knew to be terrible and settled back in his chair, taking a deep drag, chasing it with coffee.

Mercy studied him, a close scrutiny, but Tango wasn't bothered by it; he could feel the way it was about love, and not some animal need to evaluate him for market. "Sometimes," he said, quietly, "even if you hate what you're doing, you find a little pride somewhere. It feels good to be good at something."

Tango snorted, and nodded. "Yeah. Exactly."

Thirteen

Session 4

At first, it had seemed like the hardest thing in the world to dig into his memory banks. They weren't the sorts of mental file drawers one opened at will to flip through. No, they were more like little explosions that occurred when anything traumatic happened: bursts of remembrance. They'd become a sequence of relentless detonations, right before the bathtub incident… And so Tango hadn't anticipated being able to carry any sort of narrative.

Now, though, his fourth session with Mercy, the apartment smelling of coffee and cigarettes, a plate of Ava's chocolate chip muffins on the table between them, it felt like the easiest thing in the world to open up the old scars, reach inside, and come out with fistfuls of blood.

It terrified him.

But no one had ever said therapy would be easy.

~*~

Ballet was incredibly difficult. What had looked so delicate and dainty in photos was actually an intense amount of strain, athleticism, and intense pain. In his toes, in his muscles, in his bones. Miss Carla delivered exacting commands during their hours' long classes, tapping at shoulders, shins, and ears with her cane if anyone wobbled, or slipped, or forgot a movement.

At first, Kev hated it.

Then he started to improve.

And then he realized in this hellish world of cells, and bunks, and bland meals brought to them in horse feed buckets twice a day, dancing was the only aspect of his life over which he had an ounce of control. He couldn't get out, couldn't slip past Max, couldn't get to a phone to call Mama, couldn't dictate when he slept, ate, bathed, or submitted to the *crack* of the cane. But he could stretch dramatically at the barre, and reach fluidly above his head, and dance until his feet were sore and blistered, never wavering once.

"You have to learn to dance as children," Miss Carla told them as they practiced before her. "Children are elastic. Children can make their bodies do anything."

His cellmates became his friends. Simon showed him how to massage his knotted calves and his poor abused feet after a particularly rough day in the studio – that's what it was, in all its insanity in this prison of theirs – a dance studio. They ended up sitting in a circle, legs extended, feet in one another's laps, working the awful tension from arches and bloodied toes with their small fingers.

"Do you like it?" Lee asked him, small face earnest, giant caramel eyes almost hopeful. Because that's what hope had become in this new world where they all lived: dance, and friendship, and surviving another day, finding something in it to like.

"I think so," Kev said.

~*~

He was a good dancer. After who knew how many weeks, and who knew how many whacks with the cane, it became apparent to Miss Carla, and everyone else, that Kev was a damn good dancer. He hated himself for taking pride in that, but he did so all the same. He couldn't choose when to bathe, when to eat, when to sleep – was he even a human anymore? He felt like one of his little plastic army men, taken out of the bucket every afternoon so someone could play with him.

So he resisted in the ways that he could. He chose things. He chose to lie awake in the dark, if only so he could feel defiant. And he chose to dance well. So well.

"You're better than me," Simon complained. "And it's not fair."

His reflection looked different in the big mirrors in the studio. He'd always been a thin and gawky child, but now he stood taller, and there was something elastic and graceful about his arms, the way they hung at his sides. He stepped differently. Dancing had changed his carriage so completely, his eyes met those of a stranger when he watched himself perform. Who was this blonde-haired boy who could leap, and twirl, and flex? He couldn't be Kevin Estes.

He was pretty sure his birthday must have come and gone – his clothes were too small, now, and his face had hollowed out – when Miss Carla sent Max for him. Only him.

A private lesson? He wondered.

But Lee and Simon sent him matching looks of dread.

"What?"

"No talking," Max said, and shoved him hard between the shoulder blades.

Max steered him to a new part of the house, one of so many undiscovered rooms in the ugly labyrinth of add-ons. It was a bedroom, crowded with heavy dark furniture. A towering dresser. A four-poster canopied bed flanked by nightstands. The canopy and the window drapes were a faded rose, and fuzzy with layer upon layer of dust. Dust everywhere: inches deep on the hard surfaces, puffing up in little clouds as they crossed the carpet.

Miss Carla sat on a dusty padded bench at the foot of the bed and she patted the space beside her, motes spilling upward into a shaft of sunlight. "Come sit down here by me," she said, and gave him The Smile.

He did as told. Resistance was something for the dark and quiet now, never something to be flashed right before her.

She smelled like sweat and too much perfume. Her dress was black, and fit poorly, and she had a bright red belt cinched too tight around her slim waist.

A scene flashed through his head, an imagining: turning and hitting her right in the nose with his little fist, cracking something in her face, hearing the bones break, seeing the blood spurt. A fantasy that excited him.

It frightened him, the urge, and he closed his eyes.

Miss Carla put her hand on the back of his neck like she always did. "You're my best little dancer, did you know that?"

He nodded, which pressed her fingernails deep into his skin.

"Oh-ho," she laughed. "Proud of yourself, are you?"

He didn't know what to say, so he didn't say anything.

"You should be," she said. "You're my *best*. I've never seen anyone take to it like you. There's no substitute for natural, God-given talent."

She squeezed his neck and leaned in to put her lips right beside his ear. "Let's see if you have other talents."

He felt invisible fingers tickle down the bumps of his spine.

"Max, come here, dear," Miss Carla said.

The big man shut the door and then came to stand in front of them. The sunlight struck him full force, and brought his more benign details into sharp focus: the way his shirt dipped down into his bellybutton. The way the zipper of his fly hadn't been pulled up all the way. The way crescent moons of dirt lingered beneath his fingernails. His arms were covered in hair, and it looked like white fleece as the sun passed through it.

"Listen carefully and follow instructions," Miss Carla said, pressing hard at the back of Kev's neck.

Max opened his pants, and at first Kev had no idea what he was...

And then he realized.

And then he started to cry.

~*~

"She slapped me about five times across the face," Tango said, finishing his cigarette. "I stopped crying. But I threw up afterward."

~*~

Safely alone, Mercy paused in the alley outside the apartment, steadied himself with a hand on his bike's headlamp, and tilted his head back so he could drink in the sharp cold air. Feel the weak December sun on his face. He closed his eyes and let the afternoon cleanse him a moment.

The air smelled like car exhaust and snow. The bakery was playing Christmas carols and he could just hear the tinny sound of "White Christmas" floating through the wall.

He wanted his Ava. No, scratch that, *needed* her. Needed to put his head in her lap and feel her skinny fingers comb through his hair. Needed to absorb her warmth, and goodness, and innocence through osmosis, smell her skin and listen to her quietly turn the pages of a book.

Ava and their babies were the only things in the world that kept him human. He wasn't a delusional man; he knew that without them, he'd be a wrecking ball on legs, some kind of berserker his club sent on idiot suicide missions.

Tango wasn't like that. No, instead of killing the world to stop the screaming in his head, Tango had tried to kill himself. Though the idea grieved Mercy, he understood it. It made sense to him. What that kid had been through…the things that had been done to him…

He wouldn't survive. No amount of "therapy" or brotherly support would do the trick. If he was going to trudge through the rest of his years on this earth, Tango would need antivenin. Something had to cancel out the poison. He needed his very own Ava.

And Mercy was pretty damn sure they'd already found her.

Fourteen

What sort of mood would he be in today? Whitney wondered, as she fitted her key into the apartment's lock and let herself in. Today had been Kev's fourth therapy session, and he'd seemed a little looser and more relaxed after the first three.

She hustled in and shut the door against the cold. "Hey," she called as she hung up her coat. "How was your..." She trailed off when she turned and saw him sitting on the edge of the couch, perched like a nervous kid at the principal's office.

But he looked wonderful.

Yes, he was still too thin, and too pale, and hollow-eyed, but he'd made an obvious effort. His hair had been washed, and then dried; it was brushed back off his face and carefully styled behind his ears, sleek and shiny down the back of his neck. He wore a black button-up shirt with the sleeves folded back, new and clean jeans. His sneakers where black with white soles, crisp and neat, not the battered Nikes or boots she usually saw him in. He looked like someone who cared about his appearance, like he cared about himself, and it warmed her faster than a shot of whiskey.

"Look at you," she said, smiling, and he blushed.

"I, um...I hope it's okay, but Mercy and Ava invited us to dinner at their house, and I told them we'd come."

Everything about that sentence sounded perfect. "We? As in you and me?"

"You and me," he verified, still blushing.

"Well, of course. But I don't have anything to take. I ought to bring a hostess gift or something."

He shook his head. "No. Mercy said just to come and not to worry about that."

She glanced down at her rumpled shirt and skinny slacks. "I should change."

"You look great."

It was a throwaway compliment, the sort of thing men said because they didn't want to have to wait around on a woman to try on alternate outfits. But his inflection caught her attention, and she glanced up to see him studying her, his gaze intense in a way she didn't quite understand.

"You're sure?" she asked, quietly.

He met her gaze and smiled. Her stomach somersaulted. "Yeah. I'm sure."

~*~

They took her car, and she drove. "I'm supposed to be out of town," he said, apologetically.

She said, "Don't worry. I like being in on your undercover mission."

He grinned. It was dark by the time they reached Mercy and Ava's house, but even so, Whitney could tell that it was small, clean, white and cute as something off a postcard out front. It struck her as funny to think of someone as monstrous as Mercy living in a postcard-worthy house.

Kev led her around behind the house to the back door, and Aidan let them in to a mudroom that fed into the kitchen. It was an eat-in kitchen, and she was immediately struck by old memories of Jason and Madelyn's house, when Jason was still alive, and they'd all prepared dinner together, laughing, the kids underfoot.

Samantha and Ava were working on meal prep. The fridge was cluttered with crayon drawings held up by cartoonish magnets.

Sam brought her a glass of wine.

Aidan said, "Merc and me have got the kids in front of the TV."

Kev sent her a look that asked if she was okay, and she smiled encouragingly, giving him a shooing gesture. He followed his friend, beer in hand, and then it was just the three girls.

Would it be strange? she wondered. Awkward at all? She wasn't part of the family. Was only the pathetic girl sleeping on Kev's couch whose unreciprocated feelings were probably going to break her in half one day.

But Ava sent her a warm look and said, "Tango says you're an awesome cook."

"Oh, well, I don't know about awesome, but I get by." Was she blushing? Shit, she was blushing. She wanted, for dumb girly reasons, to make a good impression on these people. They were Kev's family, after all.

"I could use some help with these carrots if you feel like it," Ava said.

"Absolutely. Point me to a knife."

Her worry had been unfounded. It wasn't going to be strange.

"How's it been going?" Ava asked in a conspiratorial tone as Whitney set to peeling the carrots.

"Ava's subtle," Sam explained, rolling her eyes and chuckling.

"I am my brother's sister, after all," Ava said. She looked over at Whitney as she measured rice. "But seriously."

The carrot peel unfurled in a long straight strip, landing with a thump in the bowl she was using. "He seems better," Whitney said, thoughtfully. "In the last week, though, I mean. At first, when he came home from the hospital, he was – I dunno. Disconnected. But he's more plugged in now. He actually smiles a little. Therapy's helping, I think."

"Hmm," Ava said. "That's good."

"He looks nice tonight," Sam said. "Less like…" A heroin addict who'd tried to kill himself. "…he did."

"Is he still waking you up with nightmares?" Ava asked.

"If he's having them, he doesn't come out of his room and tell me about them anymore." She'd been painting all by herself the last few nights, and if she was honest, that had been a little lonely. In the last year, she'd grown used to the sound of his voice, his frightened admissions and worries infecting her paintings with heavy shadows and bold strokes of color.

She lifted her head and both women were staring at her. Oh no. Had she sliced up the hem of her shirt by accident?

"What?"

The sisters-in-law shared a quick look. Ava, delicately, said, "You aren't sleeping in the same room?"

"No." Her face heated and she glanced back down at her work. "It's not like that between us."

When she dared another glance, Ava was still studying her. "There's nothing wrong with taking things slow. I'm sorry. We shouldn't have assumed."

"No, no. I mean, when a guy and a girl live together, it's only natural to think…" The blushing was terrible; she swore her eyes must be pink by now. "But Kev doesn't think of me like that."

"I'm pretty sure that's not true at all," Sam said, a smile in her voice.

Whitney felt foolish that such a simple sentence could make her heart flutter, but it happened all the same.

~*~

It was never going to stop looking ridiculous, Mercy holding a baby. It was a spectacle made all the stranger now, since the baby was a girl, bundled up in white fleece footie pajamas with little bunnies on them. Camille, though, was quite content to sleep in the crook of her daddy's elbow while her brothers played on the floor.

Lainie was similarly passed out in her swing, and Aidan's eyes darted to her every few minutes, just checking. Tango loved seeing that, his friend worried about something besides a good time. This version of Aidan wasn't new; he'd always been there, but he'd never been nurtured properly, not before Sam.

It was peaceful, sitting on the couch, listening to Remy and Cal talk excitedly to one another about their toy cars, football game on the tube. But he knew his brothers wouldn't leave him totally alone. And they didn't disappoint.

"How's Whitney?" Aidan asked, less casual than he probably thought.

"She's good."

"How's her apartment search going?"

"Uh…"

"She's looking for a place?" Mercy asked, all pretend-innocent and shit.

"As far as I know."

"She's not gonna stay with you? Indefinitely?"

"Merc, what are you getting at?"

The guy gave him a face that managed to be maternal, somehow. Too much time spent around Mags and Ava, most like. "I don't think you ought to live alone. And I think Whitney's good for you."

He shrugged, feeling a little itchy, a little angry, for reasons he didn't understand. "I'm not good for her, though. So she shouldn't stay."

Aidan and Mercy looked at each other, and then looked at him again. "No," Aidan said. "We're not going down that bullshit soap opera road."

"It's not bullshit."

"Yeah, it is," Aidan continued. "You are not bad for people. That's totally untrue that you're bad for her. So pushing her away hurts her, and it hurts you, and it's fucking stupid."

"Thanks, doc," Tango shot back. "Whit is *twenty—*"

"She bought wine," Aidan reminded.

"Twenty-one, then," Tango huffed. "Whatever. She's a kid. She's a kid who doesn't need to be saddled with a recovering drug addict ex-hooker who tried to kill himself."

He threw the words across the room at them, low, but heavy as stones. He swore he heard them hit the floor.

Neither of his friends looked shocked, and Tango realized, with a hot flush of shame, that he'd wanted to shock them. Say something dark and violent that had them backpedaling.

Mercy said, "If it was about being with someone we were good for, I'd still be alone."

Tango looked down at his lap.

"Sometimes," Mercy continued. "It's okay to be a little bit selfish, if it's for the right reason."

~*~

The girls made fried chicken – double batter, from Mags' recipe – with roasted veggies and rice dripping with butter. Tango put too much food on his plate, wanting to look like he was making an effort, and settled in with the idea that he would mostly just pick, and mostly just listen.

But he'd forgotten what family dinner was like. And God, he hated that, that he'd been so stuck inside himself he'd actually forgotten what it was like to be a part of this crazy bunch of brothers and sisters he had.

And tonight there was Whitney. And he felt guilty for bringing her, because she was sweet, and she was the sort of person who got attached to things, to other people, and she couldn't stay, not long term. He didn't want her heart to break when the split happened.

Such morose thoughts were interrupted by Ava saying, "Tango, none of my baked goods gave you food poisoning, did they?" She grinned at him across the table.

He knew what she was doing, and was actually grateful for it.

"None of them," he confirmed.

"I don't believe you," Aidan said.

"You're eating my food right now," Ava said.

"Yeah, but Sam and Whitney helped you. So…"

"So you think Sam didn't let me slip that laxative into your rice?"

"You didn't."

"Guess you'll find out in about fifteen minutes."

Aidan made a horrified face.

Tango snorted a laugh…and then another. And then he was laughing freely with everyone else at the table.

~*~

Aidan had not been dosed with laxative, a conclusion he reached a solid half-hour after dinner when the kids were asleep – Lainie tucked in with her cousins – and they were parked in front of the TV and a cable showing of *Inception*.

"This movie's fucked up," Aidan said.

"Yeah," Mercy agreed.

Tango sat on the end of the sofa, elbow braced on the arm, and Whitney had decided to sit on the floor in front of him, leaning back against his knees. The movie could have been fucked up, could have been wonderful, could have been hardcore porn for all that it registered on him, nothing but flashing colors and sounds. He was consumed by the physical connection of her back touching his shins. In a very, very unhealthy way.

Dinner had gone so well, and Whitney had seemed to be having a great time. It was still early, and a movie had sounded like a good way to have another beer, unwind a little more. But now he was in knots, without a prayer of unwinding.

He kept thinking of Jasmine. Not that he wanted her here, or wished it was her instead of Whitney. God no. But he kept imagining what Jasmine would do in this situation, if they were in the clubhouse.

She would twist around slowly, sliding a hand up the inside of his thigh, looking up at him from beneath her lashes. She would give him that smile that was an invitation. Would tease at his inseam with her nails until she finally reached the bulge of his cock behind his fly. Then she would laugh, a deep throaty chuckle, and tug down his zipper, take him in her hand...

He squeezed his eyes shut and pressed his head back against the sofa. *Don't get hard*, he begged his traitorous cock, that organ that had claimed his life. *Please, not here, not in front of everyone, not with* Whitney.

"Hey," Mercy said quietly, touching his shoulder. "You alright?"

That got Whitney's attention. She turned around, and between his legs, he saw her huge pale eyes, her perfect little mouth, and...

Yeah. He couldn't do this.

"Yeah," he gasped. "Yeah, just...ju...excuse me." He lurched to his feet, nearly kicking Whitney over in the process, and bolted for the guest bathroom. He locked himself in with shaking hands and slumped back against the door.

Fuck.

The walk to the bathroom hadn't helped. If anything, the friction from his jeans had only furthered the problem. Here he was at a friend's house, on a goddamn dinner and movie night, with a perfectly sweet girl for company, and he had a hard-on emergency.

Because he was nothing but a pleasure object, and always would be, no matter what he said to Mercy in his living room. Shit, like that was even real therapy? It was a joke, is what it was.

He took a deep breath and let his eyes track across the room, searching for a grounding point. It was the guest bathroom, after all, so there was a moss green shower curtain, matching towels, a few boxy candles and bars of decorative soap on the counter. But there was also a stool for Remy, and he knew there would be toys and bath sponges if he looked behind the shower curtain. Doubtless blue little boy toothbrushes and bubble gum toothpaste in the drawers. *Name brand* bubble gum toothpaste, probably, and not that gritty, awful stuff he'd scrubbed and scrubbed his tongue with when he was living in Miss Carla's basement, when his mouth tasted like…

He gagged before he could catch himself.

It was just a dry, useless heave, but he leaned forward and tucked his head between his knees. "God," he whispered. Or maybe he prayed. He didn't know; he was pretty sure God wouldn't want to talk to the likes of him, after all the things he'd done.

A knock sounded on the door, the vibrations moving through him. Mercy's voice: "Hey, tiny dancer, listen. The last thing I want is to be standing outside when somebody's in the bathroom, you know? But I think I need to make sure you're alright. You hurdled Whitney back there."

"Shit." He let his head fall back against the door. "Is she okay?"

"Fine. Just worried about you."

"I'm…I don't think I'm okay."

"That's what I was afraid of. Can you open up?"

Tango managed to get to his feet, holding himself upright against the wall, and unlocked the door. When Mercy opened it, he shuffled over to sit on the closed toilet lid, elbows resting on his knees.

Mercy propped a hip against the counter, and looked about as nonthreatening as a six-five Cajun pro-torturer could look. Which wasn't much. "What set you off?"

He bit his lip, face hot with shame. "Whitney."

Mercy's brows lifted. "Whitney?"

He nodded, miserable. "I...I started out just liking her there. Leaning against me. But then...shit, then I started thinking – and it wasn't that I wanted to, but it just happened – about what Jazz would do, if she were sitting like that."

"Oh," Mercy said.

"And then I started thinking that I wished *Whitney* would do that. And that's so...it's so...terrible of me to think. And I shouldn't. And she's not that type of girl," he started to rush, chest tight with panic. "So I came in here, and then...toothpaste," he said like an idiot. "And Carla, and..." He let out a defeated, trembling sigh and dropped his face into his hands. "It doesn't make any sense, I know. I'm sorry."

It was silent a long beat, long enough that Tango became convinced he'd just freaked the poor man out. He gapped his fingers and peeked through them.

Mercy looked thoughtful, though, and not freaked out. His dark eyes flicked across Tango's face. "Can I say something as your ghetto therapist and not as myself?"

"Okay..."

"Ask something, actually. And it's not gonna be comfortable."

He swallowed. "Okay."

"In our last session, you told me about...what you told me about."

Blowing someone for the first time when he was eight. He swallowed again, the imagined taste of salt on his tongue. "Yeah."

146

"Maybe that's what's causing this little panic attack," Mercy suggested. "Bringing the old shit back up. Maybe it had nothing to do with Jazz, or wanting Whitney to do what Jazz would do. Maybe it was just about the memories, and them getting you all turned around."

"Maybe," he said, unconvinced. "This isn't a panic attack, though."

"No?"

"No, I know what those feel like."

Mercy's expression became a little helpless, and it was almost sweet. "I've been reading up on therapy. On the types of things that therapists say to help victims of..."

He didn't say *sexual abuse*, and Tango was grateful for it.

"There's so much I don't know," Mercy continued. "If you wanted to see a professional—"

"No," Tango said, vehemently. "I don't. I can't."

"There's no shame in—"

"I'm a Lean Dog," Tango said, bristling. "I'm a member of one of the largest, most notorious, most well-respected MCs in the entire world. Members of *that club* don't cry on therapists' couches. They shove their shit down where it belongs, and they sure as shit don't freak out about it in people's bathrooms. Jesus Christ, why haven't you guys taken my patches yet? What's wrong with you that you'd let me stay?" He was stupidly, unreasonably, spitting mad all of a sudden.

Mercy scowled at him. "You're a member of this club. It isn't about us 'letting' you stay. You belong here."

A low, angry laugh bubbled in his throat. "Belong here? In what way, exactly? I'm an ex-junkie, ex-stripper, ex-hooker bisexual freak of nature who's tried to kill himself twice. I'm not even a man. I'm not even sure I'm human. In what alternate fucking universe do I *belong in this club*?"

He expected a number of responses. He didn't expect Mercy to hit him. Which he did. And he realized, the moment the loose fist connected with the side of his face, that he'd never been hit by Mercy before, and definitely, definitely didn't want it to happen again. Ever.

He flew off the toilet and landed with his torso in the tub, his feet sticking out of it, the shower curtain threatening to pull loose of its rod up top.

Before he could register shock, or the fact that his face was now on fire, Mercy hooked a hand in the crook of his elbow and hauled him upright, sitting him back on the toilet as if Tango were no more than a doll.

When he was steady, or mostly so, Mercy braced a hand on the top of his head, bending down to peer into his eyes. "Didn't rattle your brain, did I?"

It hurt to open his mouth, his jaw numb from the blow. "No."

"Shame. I wanted to." He straightened, sighed, propped his giant face-hitting hands on his hips. "Here's the thing. Since I'm trying to act like a real therapist, I'm not going to validate you – yeah, *validate*, that's a therapy word – when you say stupid shit like you're not a man, or not a human, or whatever other idiot things you're thinking. Because what happened to you – bro, it happened *to you*. Someone did awful, awful, illegal things to a kid, to a lot of kids, it sounds like, and that wasn't something you could control. And it doesn't make you not a man, or not a human. Do you understand me? Or do you need to meet Leftie too?" He held up his other fist for demonstration.

"I wasn't just a kid when I was sixteen," Tango whispered, and to his shame realized he was close to crying. "At The Nest…I could have left, then. Tried to."

"Except they had you hooked on heroin, and they still had a lock on the door, and you'd been conditioned for years and years by that bitch, and you weren't able to leave. You honest to God *couldn't* get up and walk away, Tango. That's the point. You were still imprisoned, your age had nothing to do with it."

"Or is that just the lie people tell themselves so they don't feel so guilty?"

"It's the truth," Mercy said, and Tango had no idea if this was research talking, or a bluff, or a desperate lie. Maybe all three at once. "What's happening now? This is a setback. I figured you'd have one. But it's just that, a setback, and it doesn't mean

148

you're stuck, or that we shouldn't keep going, 'cause I think we should. It's helping at least a little, right?"

Tango nodded, and Mercy grew nervous.

"I'm really starting to wish you'd go to a pro, though. I'm fucked up, but I'm not exactly versed in becoming un-fucked up."

"No. No pro."

Mercy sighed and dragged a hand through his long hair. "Look. Maybe you ought to get a good night's sleep and you'll feel better in the morning."

Yeah right. But he nodded. Then a thought struck him, froze him cold on the spot. "Whitney."

"What about her?"

"I'm not sure I should be alone with her tonight."

"Um, *what?*"

"What if I...what if..." He took a ragged breath and wet his lips; flexing his tongue hurt; he could already feel the bruising coloring his jaw. "What if I hurt her...or something?"

Mercy gave him a withering look. "Hurt her how? Kick her in the head when you go leaping out of the room?"

The answer was so unexpected, a grin touched his mouth before he could help it.

Mercy touched the top of his head again, gentle and paternal this time. His expression softened. "I won't say you aren't a lot of things, because I know you are. We all are. We're screwed up, all of us. But you have the capacity to love, too. And you would never hurt anyone you love. I trust you. Trust yourself a little too."

~*~

"God, what happened to your face?" Whitney asked, gasping, when they were home and standing under the living room lights. She started to reach for him, then winced sympathetically and thought better of it. "Kev?"

"Um..." He felt a blush adding layers of pink to the red blossoming on the left side of his jaw. "Little accident."

"When?"

"Right before we left. I kinda…fell into the bathtub."

Her brows plucked upward. "Fell into the bathtub?"

"I tripped."

"You only had two beers."

"A regular trip, not a drunk one."

"Okay." She took a step back, sliding her coat off her shoulders, suspicious. "You okay?"

"Fine." He gave her a sad attempt at a smile to demonstrate.

She didn't believe him, he could tell. Even her back seemed doubtful, when she turned to hang up her coat.

The problem was, though, that his gaze didn't stop with her back, that little knot of tension between the fragile wings of her shoulder blades. No, his traitorous, perverted eyes traveled downward, tracing the delicate inward curve of her waist – he could put both his hands there and his fingertips would almost touch on either side – and then farther, to the full round curve of her ass, the swell of her hips, slender legs.

Every single experience he'd ever had with a woman had involved some shoulder rolling, and ass shaking, and come-hither looks, Cheshire cat smiles. One of the groupies? Jazz? They would have wanted him to push them up against the wall and take them right there.

What would Whitney do if he tried that?

The thought, the pure speculation of it, got him half-hard. Because he was a sick freak.

When Whitney turned back around, he took a step back, and her face fell.

"What?" she asked.

He edged another step back. "I…"

Her gaze dropped to the front of his jeans. Shit.

"Oh," she whispered.

"I'm gonna take a shower." When he started to move away, she plucked at his sleeve.

"No, wait a second. Please."

"So you can stare at the tent in my jeans some more?" he asked, rude and too embarrassed to care. This must be why people wore skinny jeans; you didn't have enough circulation to properly get it up, so you never had this kind of situation.

Her eyes bored into his, small chin lifted at a brave angle. "Is this what happened during the movie? When you ran to the bathroom?"

He rubbed the back of his neck and didn't answer.

"Kev, it's okay."

"It is definitely not okay."

"Says who?"

"Says the sick creep who got hard watching you take your jacket off and wondering..." God, was he actually saying these things *out loud*? He clamped his mouth shut, teeth grinding together.

Her eyes widened a little. "Wondering what?"

"You really don't want to know."

"That's where you're wrong."

"Whit..."

"You used to let me help you," she said. "Calling me when you woke from a nightmare? That was asking for help. And sure, I don't have a clue what I'm talking about, but we at least *talked*. And I hope it helped. I..." She sighed. "So talk to me now. Tell me what you're wondering. Why you think this is wrong."

"I will not put my shit on you," he said, and started to shake. "I just won't."

"Kev." She was so steady, so certain, so poised. How could she be? Didn't she know she was in the room with a monster?

"I want to fuck you," he said through his teeth. "I look at you, and I think of...things. And I want to fuck you. Is that what you want to hear? It isn't like our nightmare talks. This is the truth, Whitney: my dick is very interested in getting better acquainted with you." He exhaled in a rush. *There, you happy?*

Her eyes went big as saucers. Big as the teacup saucer she'd gotten down for him to use as an ashtray; he had a saucer reference now. But she took a deep breath and said, "Okay."

151

"What the hell does 'okay' mean?" he growled.

"It means I hear you, and I believe you." She lifted her brows. "Okay?"

He took a deep breath, let it out. "Okay. Yeah." Then he pressed his palm over his eyes. "Shit, I'm sorry, I don't mean to…"

"Talk to me," she urged. She let out a low, uncertain laugh. "I think we've already gotten the worst of it out of the way, right?"

"Right," he echoed, not believing it.

"So…"

Another deep breath. "We've been bringing up a lot of stuff in therapy that's hard to talk about. A lot of…sex stuff. And tonight, I just…and you were leaning against me…"

"Oh, I'm sorry!" she exclaimed. "I didn't think. I should have—"

"But I liked it," he rushed to say. "Too much, actually. That's why…" He gestured to his crotch. "Sorry."

She looked at his erection for far longer than he would have thought, then licked her lips and glanced away. Cleared her throat. "Does – does your therapist have any ideas? Tactics to handle it?"

"Ha!" An explosive, mocking laugh burst out of his lungs. "Yeah, right. My therapist…" *Is maybe more fucked up than me*, he added in his head.

She frowned. "He ought to be helping you with coping strategies."

"Coping?" he echoed.

She nodded. "Jason was in therapy for a while." She rolled her eyes. "It didn't take, obviously. But they were working on his cravings. The doctor gave him some coping exercises to run through when he got too wound up. So maybe we can come up with some to help with your…" Her eyes flicked back to his crotch, an unconscious glance. "*Cravings*." The way she said the word made him want to drag her up on her toes and kiss her.

For starters.

He swallowed hard. "Strategies like what?"

"Strategies that…" Her eyes came to his face, full of doubt. "I don't really know. He didn't like to spell anything out for us. But I'm sure we could research something," she hurried to add. "We need to think of ways for you to get your mind away from the harmful thoughts, and onto positive things."

"Positive things," he echoed, numbly. Really, he wanted her to shut up, because he really needed to know if her bra opened in the front or the back at this point.

A small, logical part of his brain acknowledged that he was in that hazy sexed-up headspace that he'd never been able to talk himself out of. Heroin, sex, or, lacking either, his left hand were the only things that could shake the fog.

She was starting to look a little impatient with him, and it was cute as hell, the way it warmed her cheeks. "Yes. Even though you mope around all the time, you do have some positive things in your life."

He wanted to trace her eyebrows with a forefinger, a thought that startled him. Sex-fog or no, he didn't usually have those sorts of thoughts.

"Your friends for one," she said. "Your club. Your job, your bike—"

"You," he said, and her blush went from impatient to embarrassed.

She ducked her head. "I'm not—"

"You are. Which makes me really, *really* hate that this is happening." He gestured to himself, shame burning his face.

Face still downcast, she murmured, "Not that I'm an expert or anything, but I'm pretty sure it's called being turned on, and it's totally normal."

"Nothing that happens in my head is normal."

"False."

A grin tore at his mouth, sudden and painful. "You don't get to say 'false.' You don't know."

Unflinching, she met his gaze and said, "I know you let those men in Don Ellison's basement do awful things to you to protect me. Given that." She took a shaky breath, but her eyes never wavered. "Maybe 'normal' isn't what you should be trying for. You're too brave for normal."

She might as well have punched him, the way pain flared behind his ribs and all the air left his lungs. Such was the shock of such absolute support.

He wet his lips. "Just...just don't," he whispered. "Please."

"Why not?" she asked. Gently. Oh so gently. She didn't seem to move, but somehow eased into his personal space. Had she been anyone else, it would have been a practiced, subtly alluring movement. But on her it was just as if she was drawn to him, unable to help it.

God help him, she *cared* about him, in a way that she shouldn't. And she didn't even understand the threat of him, was so clueless, it made him ache in a way that was all bound up in the relentless *sex* of it all.

"Are you a virgin?" he asked.

She blinked and looked wounded.

"Are you?"

"Why does it matter?"

"You know why."

Her lips pressed together, paling. "Don't make me out to be some sort of good girl, Kev. That isn't fair and you know it."

"It's safer–"

"Shut up about safety!" Her voice went shrill, quavering with emotion. "Do you think I'm afraid for a second that you'll hurt me? The only way you can hurt me is if you get back in the bathtub and slit your wrists again!"

She spun away from him and hurried deeper into the apartment, hand pressed over her mouth.

Tango stood rooted, her words moving through his brain in a sequence of dark pulses. He watched her go to the kitchen sink and clutch at the counter, shoulders shaking, head bent so the incoming light from Bell Bar frosted the hair at the crown of her head.

He'd wanted to keep her out of reach, hadn't he? A little afraid of him, safe on the other side of awkward emotional barriers.

No. He didn't want her crying silently over the sink. He didn't want any of this.

"Whitney." He came up behind her and put a hand on her trembling shoulder. Even through her sweater, he could feel the faint warmth of her skin. The slick satin of her bra strap. "Whit, I'm sorry."

She wiped at her eyes with the back of her hand, jerky, furious movements. Dashed beneath her nose. She turned to look at him with blame in her gaze. And pain. And naked longing. "I just don't understand what you're doing."

"I don't either." And he pulled her into his arms.

Fifteen

Everything about her soothed and aroused him all at once. The conundrum that was Whitney: comforting as a warm blanket, intoxicating as quality cocaine. That was Tango's interpretation, anyway.

She pressed her face into his collarbone and clenched handfuls of his shirt in back, trembling in the circle of his arm.

He'd never had this before, an honest, vulnerable, emotional woman holding onto him. He held no ill feelings for Jazz – in so many ways she was the only thing that had turned him from the fractious, confused boy he'd been into the man who rode in Ghost Teague's phalanx of warriors. But Whitney was something new and precious to him. Something he'd never been within reach of before.

He knew good women – Maggie, Ava, Holly, Sam, Emmie…all the old ladies. Strong girls with fast draws, and flawless aim, and gentle smiles when he needed them. But they belonged to his brothers, they always had, and he'd never been jealous, or pined for any of them, or thought anything inappropriate. He just hadn't ever thought…hadn't begun to imagine…that there could be someone like that for him.

And having her in his arms, knowing she was real, and solid, and trying hard to get her emotions under control, stirred him in a dangerous way.

In his mind, it was impossible for her to want him. She could say she did, and she might even mean it. But there was a difference between idle wanting – that skin-deep curiosity, wondering what it might be like – and his brand of *want*. The kind of craving that made his bones ache, and set his teeth on edge. She didn't – couldn't – understand how deep the want ran, how nothing careful and chaste could satisfy it.

It was terrible. He wanted to push her a little and let her see why she ought to be frightened. And he wanted to love her platonically, like a brother, like the friend they both needed, because she deserved so much better than what he could give her.

In any event, as his brain whirred through its normal cycle of guilt and self-loathing, his hand moved of its own accord, sliding down the ridge of her spine. Pausing a second at her waistband, before it moved lower and cupped her ass.

She stiffened. "Oh." Only a second, then she pressed closer.

He breathed a humorless laugh against the top of her head. Shit, he needed to move his hand. He shouldn't touch her like this. But the command got lost somewhere between his brain and the nerves in his arm. "Just that makes you say 'oh'?" He'd meant it to be degrading, to scare her back a little, but it came out soft, and full of longing.

"I wasn't expecting it." No way was she expecting half the stuff that happened during sex. "But I like it."

"Shit," he muttered.

Whitney squeezed his waist and drew back, bringing her hands up to wipe away the last of her tears. She offered an unsteady smile, and he finally managed to let go of her. "Sometimes," she said, like an admission, "I wish you weren't such a good guy. But that's not fair, because it's one of the things I love most about you."

Love.

The word electrified him. Started up a rapid beating in his chest that rivaled the old reliable throb of desire.

"Can I make a suggestion?"

He nodded, afraid his voice would come out low, and husky, and betray him.

"Neither one of us can sleep. Let's share the bed together tonight."

"Um…" He didn't have the energy to rehash the conversation they'd just had, but apparently it needed to happen. "You know that's a terrible idea, right?"

"I trust you," she said, killing him with her wet, blue eyes.

"Well, you shouldn't." He had no doubt that the second he started to drift, he'd move toward her, reach for her through the sheets, and as vulnerable and idealistic as she was, she'd let him touch her, damn it.

"Kev." She put her hands on his chest, feather-light. "I'm not…" She sighed, and looked disappointed, for some reason. "I'm not coming onto you. I'm just talking about sleeping. We both need to sleep."

He shook his head, but he could already feel the deep, inner delight unfurling inside him. The idea of sleeping beside her, smelling her skin that close, hearing her breathe as she slept. Like when they were in the cells together, and she was holding his hand.

"No," he said, throat closing up. But he knew he would cave. He always caved.

~*~

He caved around midnight.

At bed time, when Whitney came to him in her loose, threadbare sleep shirt, thin pale legs bare, hair loose down her back, he took one sniff of his soap on her shower-warm skin and insisted she take the bed, and that she lock the door if she didn't feel comfortable.

Why the hell she didn't just pack up her shit and leave right then, he had no idea.

He stretched out on the couch and spent an inordinate amount of time trying to figure out how best to avoid the bad springs under the seats, hating himself for ever allowing Whitney to sleep on this thing. He was an asshole. He was an absolute monster. The second she turned up on his doorstep, he should have put her back in her car and offered to drive her to a hotel. He'd let her stay for completely selfish reasons.

Trust himself a little, Mercy had said. He should trust himself. That's what every addict had to do at some point, right? Trust that they could get within arm's reach and keep from touching what they wanted.

Oh, but he *wanted*…

At midnight, not at all sure he could, in fact, trust himself, he got up off the couch, crossed the room to the bedroom door, and tested the knob. It was unlocked. He took a deep breath and held it as he turned the knob, eased the door open…

And found Whitney awake and sitting up against the wall where a headboard would have been on a decent bed, pillows propped behind her, a notepad balanced on her upraised knees. She looked small, and worried, and so very sweet in his bed, that he couldn't linger at the doorway, instead let his feet propel him fully into the room, right up to the edge of the mattress.

He swallowed the dozen things he wanted to say and said, "What are you writing?"

She tapped her pencil against the pad. "Sketching, actually." Her smile was small and tired, but she softened her face in a way that told him, without any doubt, that she was glad to be talking to him. That was something she always did, he thought – made him feel like he wasn't bothering her. And if she wasn't sleeping, he guessed he really wasn't.

"Can I see?" he asked.

She patted the empty spot on the bed beside her.

Here went nothing. He exhaled – it felt like he'd been holding his breath for a full minute – and eased slowly, deliberately down onto the bed, giving her time to flinch away if she wanted to.

She didn't.

He mirrored her position, back to the wall, knees pulled up, and glanced over at her sketchbook. She had a photo taped into the top left corner, two smiling little girls, and she'd loosely sketched their faces on the paper. The pencil marks were faint, but he could already see the realism of the sketch, the way the girls were going to come to life in graphite.

"Wow," he said, and meant it.

She rolled her eyes in a self-deprecating way. "Faces aren't my specialty. But I'm trying to work more on my figure drawing. Nobody wants to be a one-trick artist."

"Pony," he corrected, smiling.

"Not that either." She smiled back.

They were sitting on the bed together. He knew that, and had known that's what he was doing when he climbed into bed, but the realization hit him hard, then, after she sent him that smile. He became all too aware of their closeness, the faint heat of her skin, the soft clean scents of her.

God, he was so *tired* of this. It was exhausting: wanting, and worrying, and berating himself, and fearing that he'd hurt her.

Shut up, he told his fevered brain. *Shut the hell up.*

"I was wondering," he said, and heard a note of shyness in his voice, "if we could try to get some sleep."

Her expression eased with relief, smile widening. "Yeah. That sounds good." She handed him the sketchpad. "Would you mind...?"

He took it carefully and set it and her pencil on the nightstand. "Ready?" he asked.

"Yeah, I'm good."

He clicked off the lamp and they booth scooted down so they were lying flat, heads on the pillows. Whitney was beneath the covers and he was on top of them, but he figured that was for the best. Less chance of inappropriate touching that way.

He lay flat on his back, hands linked on his stomach, shivering beneath his skin. Would he even relax enough to sleep? Probably not.

But he heard Whitney let out a deep sigh and heard her snuggling down into her pillow. So at least she was relaxed. At least this nearness was good for her. And that was more important than anything, really.

He closed his eyes, though he knew it was futile...and fell asleep before he had a chance to be surprised about drifting off.

~*~

Not a nightmare this time, no. Just a dream, but a solid one; he felt the tug of gravity beneath his boots.

He was at The Nest, its familiar black walls, pink neon, shining glass bar. He smelled the old smells: sweat, and cologne, and arousal. Heard the electronic music, a low bass thump through the hidden speakers.

This place had been his home for three years. His personal hell.

It was empty now, nothing but the music, and the vibrating lights along the edge of the stage.

He glanced down at himself, and saw that he was wearing his cut, a white t-shirt, jeans. He was covered with ink, all the tats he'd let Ziggy needle beneath his skin after he finally left this place for good.

He felt his voice welling in his throat; felt the urge to call out. But he didn't, just started walking instead, because he knew that, this being only a dream, he wouldn't find any demons tonight. At least not the kind he was afraid of.

The music dimmed as he headed down the back hall, replaced by a low sultry jazz that echoed softly beyond the closed doors that lined the walls.

It was room number eight, because it always had been. Ian's favorite.

Ian, a small voice chimed in the back of his mind, the sound mournful, full of longing, like he'd lost Ian somehow. None of it had ever been Ian's fault, not even what Ian had become.

He didn't knock, but let himself in, already knowing what he'd find. Ian knelt on the mattress, shirtless, his form pale and slender and perfect, wearing the black leather shorts that were his trademark, hair a straight shiny sheet over his shoulder, eyes ringed in kohl. He wasn't alone. Daniel knelt in front of him, and they had their hands on one another, kissing in that deep, thorough, relentless way that Ian always kissed.

Heat coiled tight in Tango's stomach.

Ian broke the kiss, hands still cradling Daniel's face – such elegant, long-fingered hands he had – and turned to Tango, eyes sleepy with lust.

Daniel was breathing hard, his mouth wet and red, eyes sparkling. He'd always been so beautiful in a natural way, not in the feminine, painted-up way that Ian and Tango had been made to look.

"Come here, darling," Ian said, and Tango went.

And then he felt the familiar lurch and slide as the dream became a nightmare. It was no longer Daniel on the mattress, but Miss Carla now, in that awful pink negligee she'd worn when…when…when she…

"Such a pretty little loverboy," she said, lips pursed around a cigarette. And there was a rope around Ian's neck, and she curled her hand around it. Tightened it until Ian's face began to purple.

Tango screamed…

And woke with a start, gasping. He was clinging to something, a pillow maybe, mashing his face into the side of it, holding on for dear life, and shaking.

Wait. Not a pillow.

He felt the sharp point of an elbow scrape across his stomach. Felt the regular rise and fall of breathing beneath his arm.

Definitely not a pillow, but a slender girl in an old white t-shirt, her small arm curled around the back of his head.

Whitney. Oh shit, he'd grabbed onto Whitney. Was pressing his face against the side of her breast. Had thrown a leg over her knees.

Oh *shit.*

"Sorry! Shit, I'm sorry." He tried to scramble away from her, still groggy and disoriented. He managed to grab her boob, in his efforts – soft, yielding, unmistakably feminine – and yanked his hand back as if he'd been burned.

"Hey, hey," she said, arm tightening behind his head. "It's okay. Don't get up."

Except he had to, because he was literally nuzzling her chest, and there was no way that was okay, or friendly, or appropriate in any way.

"Kev." Her lips brushed his forehead. "Just be still. It's okay. I'm here."

She *was* there. Small, but so very real; and she was holding him, raking her fingernails through his long hair, murmuring sweet things.

The fight washed out of him on a deep sigh. "I'm sorry," he repeated, quietly, and was grateful for the dark, so she couldn't see his shamed blush.

He was half-hard in his pajama pants, which meant the nightmare had killed his arousal, which meant that during the first part of the dream, he'd been very aroused. Oh God. And this time, he hadn't been alone in bed, humping the mattress without any witnesses.

He eased his hips back, leaning away from her. "Did I—" His tongue was dry and he had to swallow, wet his lips. "I wasn't…doing anything in my sleep…was I?"

She didn't answer.

"Fuck." His face flamed and he pulled it away from her breasts. "I'm sorry. Shit, I'm so sorry. That's why I knew we shouldn't do this."

She took a deep breath. "It didn't," she started, and paused. "It didn't bother me."

"Fuck," Tango breathed. "Don't *say* that."

"But it's true." Her voice grew defiant, a little sharper along its edges. "I liked it."

"You're killing me here, Whit."

"No, you're killing yourself."

She gasped the moment the words left her lips. A gasp that sounded like regret, and like bitter honesty; like she wanted to snatch the statement back, and was so afraid she'd hurt him.

He closed his eyes and breathed in deep the scents of the sheets, and of her, skin and soap, and laundry detergent. "No. You're right. That's all I ever do."

She shifted, slowly, until she was lying on her side and they were facing one another. His eyes were still closed, but he could feel her breasts against his chest, her leg sliding over his hip, her nose bumping into his. She pushed his hair back and clasped the back of his neck, and just held him.

It was the most intimate moment he'd ever shared with a woman.

He trembled, one hard shudder, and then couldn't stop, overwhelmed by the gentle, innocent closeness. No one had ever offered him this. No one had ever let him know without words that he could just be held, and not be expected to perform.

And then Whitney said, "I was having a nightmare too," so soft he thought he'd imagined it. But then she continued: "I knew it was a nightmare, but it was the kind you can't get out of. And everything's bloody, and dark, and there's all this screaming, and I just needed something to latch onto in the real world, so I could pull myself back. And then I felt you beside me."

Humping you, he thought.

"You brought me back," she whispered. "So don't be sorry for it. I wasn't sorry that I felt it."

Tears built up behind his lids, and he clamped his eyes tight, trying to keep them at bay. A few slid through, hot against the delicate skin up high on his cheeks.

Whitney rested her forehead against his, and he thought he felt her shivering too.

Sleep came on slowly, gently, and dreamless.

Sixteen

Morning. He became aware of its pale light the same moment he remembered the way he'd spent the night. And he felt…

He felt peaceful. He waited for crushing guilt and shame to descend, but when his eyes slitted open, he found that he was still wrapped up together with Whitney, and that they were clothed, and that the only things they'd shared had been nightmares, and fears, and careful touches, and a sense of comfort. Benign, good, innocent things. Things as precious as gold to him, always unattainable.

He'd slept beside a girl he wanted so badly he *ached*, and he hadn't crossed any boundaries. Hadn't betrayed her trust.

He wanted to cheer, but was too exhausted for that, so he smiled instead, and she sent him a sleepy smile back.

"Okay?" she asked.

"Better than okay."

Except for his morning wood situation that he wasn't going to let her see, feel, or acknowledge.

He was saved by her phone alarm, blaring and vibrating into the quiet.

Whitney sighed and rolled her eyes. "Yay, work."

Tango was relieved, in a way, that they could close this moment on a good note, before his sick, sex-craving side could ruin everything.

~*~

"You can have the first shower," he said. And she could read what else he wanted to say, self-deprecating things about not going to work, about staying home, about not being worthwhile. Things she might have slapped him for if he'd actually voiced them.

Now, hot water coursing down her back, she passed her soap-slick hands across her body, and shivered. She had goosebumps, and her nipples were hard, and it had nothing to do with the temperature.

Last night, she'd come awake from a nightmare with something hard grinding against her hip. Her nervous system had lit up like a Christmas tree; she'd flushed hot and then cold, skin prickling. She'd known what it was, that he was hard, that he was rocking his hips and thrusting against her in his sleep. And it had stirred deep, erotic longings in her, the kind that made her blush and bite her lip and avert her eyes when the women at work talked so openly and wantonly about their sex lives. She'd had crushes, and stared adoringly at actor posters when she was a girl, but she'd never felt like *this*: like she could come if he traced a fingernail down the outside of her arm.

It wasn't just the cock against her leg, wasn't just the dark, or the nightmare; wasn't anything but Tango. He electrified her, in some primal, physical way that other men didn't.

In the shower now, she let her soapy hands linger, and wanted him to touch her so badly it hurt.

~*~

Whitney was running late, so she rushed out of the apartment half-buttoned into her jacket at quarter 'til nine. She took the time, though, to flit toward him at the kitchen counter and put her arms around him in a quick but fierce huge. "Bye," she said, breathless, smiling at him, and was gone.

He stood alone in his kitchen, sunlight streaking the floors, the air smelling of coffee and the Toaster Strudel he had cooking. He lifted his mug to his lips and marveled at the normalness of it. He was awake, and clean, and sober, and already couldn't wait to see Whitney again. And he was…maybe he was happy. Maybe. At least a little bit.

Mercy arrived a few minutes later, box of doughnuts in hand, and he froze in the act of sitting down on the couch, box held out comically in front of him, hovering over the coffee table. His eyes were trained to the crumb-filled, icing-smeared plate beside Tango's mug. "You ate?" he asked, incredulous.

Tango shrugged. "Freezer food."

"Yeah, but it's calories." Mercy sat down, dropped the doughnuts, and almost looked proud. "Did you make it yourself?"

"Fuck you," Tango said without malice. "I can feed myself."

"Except you usually don't."

"Yeah." He sighed. "I know."

"So I'm guessing this means good things," Mercy said. He leaned back and folded his hands loosely over his stomach. "Care to tell me about it?"

Heat bloomed in his cheeks, and he knew, fair-skinned as he was, that Mercy would see him blushing. Shit. This was therapy, wasn't it? He had to talk; had to admit things. And what happened last night wasn't embarrassing – only special and private, and he didn't want to shatter the contentment it had given him by sharing it with someone.

Who knew, he thought, that cuddling could be more personal than any sex act.

"*Oh*," Mercy said, grin widening, if that was possible. A sharp smile – hell, an alligator smile. "*That* happened, huh?"

"No, not *that*. Just–" He huffed out a breath. "We slept. Really slept. In the bed together. And it was nice." If there had ever been a less adequate word than *nice*, he didn't know what it was.

He expected Mercy to laugh at him, but instead the big man's expression softened. "Yeah. I get that."

"She did try to get me to put the moves on her when we got home last night, though."

"Ha! Damn, I like this chick."

"You can't have her," Tango said, more bite to his voice than intended.

"I've already got my own." Mercy flipped the box open and pulled out a maple-frosted doughnut. "I'm just glad for you, man."

And the thing about Mercy was, when he said something like that, he always meant it.

~*~

"Well aren't you just all smiles this morning," Cathy said at her elbow, and Whitney started.

Coffee slopped out of the mug she was stirring and she jumped back before it could splatter against her white blouse.

"Oh, goodness," Cathy said, and handed over a wad of napkins from beside the sink.

"Thanks." Whitney blushed as she mopped up the mess. "I'm sorry. I didn't hear you walk up."

"*I'm* sorry," Cathy said. "I didn't realize you were lost in dreamland." When Whitney glanced at her, she smiled, and elbowed Whitney lightly in the ribs. "So what's his name, huh?"

Whitney knew she blushed. "Why does it have to be a boy?"

Cathy patted her shoulder. "Oh, honey. I have three daughters. That smile is always because of a boy." She lifted her brows for emphasis.

Whitney laughed, stomach full of butterflies. "Okay, so maybe there's a boy." When she turned away from the break room counter, Cathy fell into step beside her, and they headed back for the warren of cubicles.

"What's his name?" Cathy sounded so much like an excited, gossipy teenage girl that Whitney couldn't disappoint her.

"Kevin."

"Is he cute?"

"Cathy!"

"I'm just curious. I'm old and married; I need to live vicariously."

Whitney was very glad, suddenly, that she wasn't one of Cathy's three daughters.

"I think he's cute," she said, "but I'm a little biased because..."

Because he was wonderful. And because he was stepping off the elevator right now, and was turning and seeing her, and smiling.

If it was possible, he looked even better and more present than he had last night: clean flannel shirt under a leather jacket, jeans, sneakers, hair shiny and golden, tied back in a bun at the nape of his neck. His hands were in his pockets, and he looked shy and nervous, but he looked happy too, and that flooded her with warmth to see.

"Kev!" she said, and thought her smile might dislocate her jaw. "What are you doing here?" Cathy forgotten, she hurried toward him, managing to slop hot coffee down her hand. She had to pause and hiss. And crap, there wasn't anywhere to even set her mug down.

Kev closed the distance between them. "Here." He took the mug from her, and if its hot, wet edges burned his fingers, he didn't react to it.

"Careful," she cautioned. "I'm just kind of a mess this morning." She was still blushing, and still smiling, and he was *here*.

"I don't believe it." He smiled back. "Where can I put this?"

"Oh, back here. In the breakroom." She turned to lead him that way.

Cathy was still standing where Whitney had left her, staring in wide-eyed surprise, gaze fixed to the mug in Kev's hands.

No, Whitney realized with a lurch, not the mug, but at Kev's hands. The dark tattoos on his fingers and the backs of his hands.

She'd been set to introduce the two of them, and instead she had to clamp down on a sudden surge of anger. "Excuse us," she said, and took Kev by the sleeve, leading him around Cathy and into the break room.

"Ugh," she said when they were alone at the sink, and he was pouring out her twice-spilled coffee.

"What?"

"Nothing, just…nothing." She couldn't tell him what she'd noticed, not when he was in such a good mood. She couldn't ruin that with her petty anger over the prejudices of her coworkers.

"Run some cold water on that," he said, tapping the red patch on the back of her hand with one tatted index finger. He turned the tap on and she stuck her hand beneath it.

"I'm sure it's fine."

"Never hurts to treat it, though."

"My hero," she said, only half-joking, tipping another smile up to him.

Even in the awful fluorescent office lighting, he looked beautiful, the bags under his eyes less noticeable, his delicate features clean and sharp-edged, eyes clear, almost ice-colored indoors.

"Why are you here?" she asked again, softly, with all the warmth she felt. "I thought you had a session this morning."

"We pushed it back. I wanted to come see if you could take an early lunch with me."

A part of her worried that he was skipping a therapy session. She thought it was important to keep going, and not just quit the moment he felt a little better. But she wasn't going to ruin *this* moment, when all she wanted was to melt against him.

"Let me get my purse."

~*~

They took his bike just up the street to IHOP. When they were seated, and sipping water, waiting for their food, Kev rapped his fingers against the side of his glass and said, "She freaked out about my tats."

Whitney felt her stomach drop, but said, "Who?" She wanted to pretend he hadn't noticed Cathy's reaction.

His wry half-smile said he knew that she knew. "The woman at your office. I saw the way she was looking." His fingertips danced on the glass again, and the dominoes looked like they were knocking into one another.

"Kev," she said with a sigh. "Cathy's just one of *those people*. Don't worry about it."

"Those people?"

"The kind that think the way they do things is the best and only way. The small-minded kind." It made her angry all over again just saying it, thinking of Cathy's over-plucked eyebrows disappearing up into her hair in the kind of shock usually reserved for car accidents.

"I'm not worried," he said, and looked like he meant it. "I'm always an anomaly, everywhere. Nothing new." He shrugged and stared down into his glass. "I just don't want you to suffer for it."

"Suffer?" Her heart swelled with love for him, the way he was selfless to the point of self-flagellation. "Nothing anyone at work says could ever make me 'suffer.' I'm so glad you came to see me today."

Their food arrived: club sandwich for her, and cheeseburger for him. The waitress gave them a quick, warm smile like she thought they were cute, and Whitney felt some of her disquiet ease. There were people like Cathy in the world, sure, but there were also people who just liked to see others happy.

"Can I ask you something?" she asked, nibbling a fry. "And you don't have to answer if you don't want to."

He paused with his burger halfway to his mouth and his brows jumped. "That sounds kinda scary," he joked, but she saw the way his mouth trembled.

He really shouldn't have skipped his session.

"Your tattoos," she said, touching the back of her own index finger with her thumb. "The dominoes. Can I ask what they mean?"

He set his burger down and wiped his hands on a napkin, studying her. "Most people don't ever ask."

They just wrote him off as a guy who'd covered himself in tattoos, she thought, and her throat felt tight.

"I'm asking," she said, giving him a hopeful smile.

He smiled back, nerves showing in the way his nostrils flared. "Okay." He eased his plate to the side and laid his hands on the table between them, palms-down.

Whitney pushed her plate over too, and because it felt like he'd been offering his ink to her, she reached to trace the domino on his ring finger.

"When I was sixteen, my friend," he said, and paused, pain flickering across his face. "My *friend* said something to me. When I was…" He cleared his throat, and she hated herself a little for making him talk about something that brought up old hurts. "When I was trying to figure out who I was. *What* I was. He said, 'You always try to deny what you really are. You line up all these reasons. But then, it gets harder and harder to fight your nature. Your true nature.'" His pronunciation had become crisp as he quoted, and Whitney remembered a long black coat, and shining auburn hair under hospital lights. "'But it never fails. One-by-one, like dominoes they fall, all the reasons why *not*.'"

His head dropped lower, as he stared at the swirls of ink on his hands. "My reasons fell, and I had to face what I was."

"And that was?" she whispered.

"An addict."

She cupped both her hands over the backs of his. "You *became* addicted. What you *are* is a man. A *good* man."

He sent her a pitiful look from beneath his lashes.

"He wasn't just your friend, was he?" she asked.

"We were lovers," he said, and the plainspoken admission touched her deeply, had her hands tightening over his. This man – this broken boy – had never walked an easy path. He deserved all the love, and all the lovers who'd made him feel loved, that he could get. "I loved him."

"You still do," she guessed.

"In a way. But we're no good together." He finally lifted his head, and looked her square in the eyes. "I love you."

Her heart grabbed, and her breath caught.

Not "in love," but "love," and that was a pretty precious thing. She'd take it.

~*~

He walked her to the door of her office and caught her with an arm around her waist, pulled her in close to his chest. Pressed his face down into her hair. He smelled like soap, and cold winter wind, and old leather. Through his clothes, she felt the lean shape of his body, its quiet, beautiful strength.

"I love you too," she whispered into his collar.

He kissed the top of her head and let her go.

~*~

Tango rode aimlessly through town after he left Whitney, knowing he was playing with fire. Any of his brothers could hear his pipes, lift their heads and spot him on the road, when he was supposed to be out of town. Aidan and Mercy had been covering for him, fending off questions. And he had Ghost on his side – a staggering kind of knowledge he couldn't wrap his twisted head around – but he didn't know how Ghost could spin a lie to explain Tango riding down the streets of Knoxville and yet not returning to the clubhouse, and his brothers.

He pulled up to the balk line at the next red light and took a deep, shaky breath that had nothing to do with the vibrations of his bike. It was time to man up. He'd needed time alone, time indoors, time with Whitney all to himself. But he was a Lean Dog. He hadn't joined this club lightly, and he owed it his allegiance. He owed it his presence, among so many other things.

When the light turned green, he hung a right and headed for Dartmoor, December air stinging his face.

The familiar sight of the long stretch of industrial property sent a swooping sensation through his stomach, like the plummet at the top of a roller coaster. When he was away from it for long stretches, he forgot, for a while, just how impressive this concrete and steel monument to outlaw life was, lying like a sleeping beast at the edge of the Tennessee River.

The first time he'd ever come here, in the passenger seat of Maggie's car, nothing but elbows and long hair, he'd been gripped with cold terror. What was he doing, he'd wondered, just a nothing-special bisexual prostitute junkie, about to walk up to the rest of the Lean Dogs MC and introduce himself like he was worth an actual damn.

He felt the echoes of those old nerves now, as he turned in at the nursery and took the long route through the parking lot jungle to get to the bike shop.

He parked beside Aidan, Mercy, and Carter's bikes, stalled a moment as he took off his helmet and hung it on the handlebars.

Aidan stepped out of the garage, looking so shocked Tango wanted to laugh. His voice was overly calm when he said, "Hey, man. You just get back?"

"Yeah." Tango swung off his bike and walked toward the shop, itchy in his own skin, suddenly, shoulders heavy under the burden of lies his friends had been forced to tell on his behalf. He hated himself for that, making people tell falsities because he couldn't get his shit together.

Aidan studied his face a moment, gaze contemplative, then he broke into a grin and pulled Tango into a fast, masculine hug. He slapped his back and said, "Missed you, man. Glad you're back."

Tango let out a deep breath and felt himself tremble inside his clothes. He didn't know if he was back, only that he didn't know what he'd do without his best friend's love and acceptance.

Aidan pushed back and Tango saw Mercy coming toward them, doing a good job of hiding his surprise.

"Didn't expect to see you yet," he said, offering a crushing man-hug of his own.

"Yeah, well," Tango said when he pulled back. "Aunt Anne's not exactly *well*, so…"

"Don't worry about it." Mercy clapped him on the shoulder. "You can take short days if you need to."

Tango nodded, the grateful lump in his throat making it too hard to voice his thanks.

Then there was Carter, young and blonde and sporting a hickey on the side of his neck that Jasmine had doubtless given him. Tango thought he might feel jealous, but couldn't find that emotion in himself at the moment.

"Dude," Carter said. "How's your aunt?"

"Doing better," Tango said. "She was real sick."

"Yeah. Sorry about that."

Tango nodded again, and managed to swallow.

Aidan's arm went around his shoulders. "Oh, so hey, you gotta check out this Indian some guy brought in. So pretty it'll make you cry."

And just like that, he was one of the guys again.

~*~

The thing Whitney hated about winter was the way the sun went down so quickly. When she clocked out at five, the sky was already darkening beyond the windows, and the wind was already laden with frost.

Whitney tightened her scarf around her throat, hefted her purse, and prepared to dart across the parking lot, not liking the way the shadows of the surrounding buildings lay opaque and sinister on the pavement.

She gripped her keys a little harder and arrowed across the lot. Not running, but hustling. She wasn't afraid. She was...cautious.

She was ten feet from her car when she realized there was something low-slung and gleaming black parked on the far side of it. When she was five feet away, one of its doors opened and a man unfolded himself from the back seat, moving around the hood of her car with alarming speed.

She noticed the coat first, ankle-length black wool, expertly tailored to frame his lean build. Then his hair; she'd never seen such perfect, shiny long hair on a man. It hung in glimmering sheets behind his shoulders, and highlighted the dramatic bone structure and big, luminous eyes that made him, like Kev, more pretty than handsome.

Her panic eased – but only by a fraction. She ground to a halt, keys digging into her palm, breath pluming in the cold air.

He flicked a smile and walked toward her, leather soles of his expensive shoes grinding over the grit of the asphalt. "Hello, Whitney. Do you remember me from the hospital?"

"Y-yes." She hated herself for that little stutter, and clamped her lips together, took a deep breath, tried not to think about the way Ian's smile widened like the sudden slice from a knife. "Ian, right? Nice to see you again."

He kept coming, slowly, deliberately, stalking toward her. "Yes. How lovely."

Her stomach quivered, fear rippling down her nerves in sharp pulses. She told herself that this was someone Kev had loved – had been *in love with* – his lover. That there was some good in him if Kev could feel that way about him. But something about this man, with his cool British airs, frightened her.

He halted a foot from her, close enough that when the wind caught the end of his coat, it brushed forward across the toes of her boots. She shivered.

"I was just heading home," she said with a lame smile, gesturing to her car.

He tilted his head down and locked eyes with her. "And where is home?"

Telling him, she thought, would be a bad idea.

"You're living with Kevin, aren't you?" His expression told her he already knew the answer.

"Just temporarily, while I find a place of my own." She took a deep breath and willed her shaking not to become visual. Her teeth were on the verge of chattering, and it had nothing to do with the cold.

"Ah." He reached inside his coat, and for a moment, her panic spiked, and she envisioned a gun or a knife emerging. But when he withdrew his hand, he held a checkbook in his long fingers. "Allow me to insert myself into the problem." Small, self-deprecating smile.

"I'm sorry…what?"

He opened the checkbook and balanced it in the palm of one hand, fishing a pen from his pocket with the other. "I'd imagine a deposit might be a bit of a stretch at the moment.

176

Forgive me, dear" – he glanced at her car – "but you don't look all that financially independent at the moment. I'd like to help you. I know of an apartment, perfectly nice, that's just come available, and I'd like to put a–"

"Why would you do that?" she interrupted.

He gave her a patient look. "So you can get your own place. I like to donate to charitable causes." This time, the smile was nasty and condescending. "Listen, darling, it's never wise to question handouts. Just take them and be grateful."

And then she understood. "You don't want me to live with him," she said, softly, more afraid than ever, but unable to hold her tongue. "You're still in love with him."

The change in Ian was immediate and visceral. His mild expression turned into a snarl, lips skinning back off his teeth. He leaned low into her face, and he latched onto her arm lightning-fast before she could twist away. "You don't know shit about Kev, little girl. You are a *child*. You can't even hope to understand what he needs," he hissed, flecks of spit hitting her face. "Do us both a favor and stay the hell away from him."

He released her, a rough shove that sent her staggering. Then turned and strode back to his car, ducked into the backseat and slammed the door. It started with a low roar and the lights came on. As it accelerated forward, Whitney saw that it was a Jag, new and shiny and expensive.

She stood gasping, massaging her arm through her sleeve where he'd grabbed her, stunned. She didn't know how long she stood there, hair whipping across her face, before she unlocked her car, climbed inside it, locked herself in, and dug out her cellphone.

~*~

He needed to go see Ghost before he left, Tango decided. He owed his president more than a few favors after all this time he'd taken, and hiding from the man would be cowardly and rude...even if he was too self-conscious at the moment for words.

He found him in the main office. Maggie was just clocking out, jacket on and purse over her shoulder, straightening from the kiss she'd given her husband, thumb lingering to flick across Ghost's lower lip in a quiet gesture that felt too intimate for outside viewers. Her face lit up when she turned to the door and saw Tango.

"Hey, baby." She hurried to him and gave him a hug, one he was glad to return, her warmth seeping through their clothes to get to him. "You're back!" She was beaming when she withdrew. "How you feeling, huh? You sure you're ready to work again?" She reached to tidy a stray lock of hair that had slipped past his ear, face etched with motherly concern.

Behind her, seated at the desk, Ghost watched, frown critical and assessing. Tango was convinced he had X-ray vision, and was using it now, looking for gaps and flaws in the coils of Tango's brain.

"I'm okay," he told her, and managed a smile.

She didn't believe him, mouth twitching to the side. But she patted his cheek and said, "It's good to see you up and around."

Damn. Like he'd been ill or injured. Oh, he really hated himself a lot of the time.

"Thanks," he mumbled, as she let herself out.

Then he was alone with his president.

Ghost lifted his brows which somehow managed to clearly convey *you wanna sit?*

So Tango sat in the chair across from him, and didn't squirm under the scrutiny…though a large part of him wanted to.

"Are you back for real?" Ghost asked. "Or is this just a visit."

"I'm not sure, actually," Tango said with a wince.

Ghost lifted his hands a little off the desk, an open-palmed gesture. "Hey, I'm not pushing. If you need to take breaks, you can keep using your aunt as an excuse."

"Using." Tango snorted. "I'm real good at using things, aren't I?"

Ghost sighed and looked like he wanted to chastise him, but said, "How's therapy going? If you can call it that."

"It's going okay."

"Okay in general? Or okay considering who your *therapist* is?"

"Mercy's a good listener," Tango said in a small voice.

"Yeah, he is." Ghost became gentle, seeming to choose his words. "And he's, well, he loves hard. So his heart is in the right place. But there's snakes in his head. Big ones. Man-eating ones." His eyes widened for emphasis. "It kinda spooks me, thinking about the sort of advice he might give."

Tango sighed and slumped down in his chair. "I'm not sure I'm in a position to question anyone else's mental health."

Ghost looked at him for a moment, face thoughtful, then pulled out one of the desk drawers and rummaged around in it for a while. He came back out with a business card and handed it across to Tango. "Here."

Tango took it, and read aloud: "Dr. Tabitha Jones." There was a phone number, but nothing else. "What is this?"

"A few years ago, when Ava was in high school, after…" He gestured and Tango knew what he was talking about: after her assault and miscarriage, after Mercy broke her heart and left. "She wasn't doing so well. So we, um…Dr. Jones is nice. Just…I wanted you to have her number. If things with Merc get too weird or whatever." It was the most awkward Ghost had ever looked.

Tango stared at the card, passing his thumb across the embossed letters. "Thank you."

~*~

"He did *what?*" Aidan's hand spasmed with anger and the wrench slid out of his grip, clattering noisily on the concrete of the garage floor. "He threatened you?"

"Not exactly," Whitney said on the other end of the cellphone connection, voice shaking. "I mean, not at all, really. He just…" She let out a deep breath. "Shit. I'm sorry. I'm freaking out, and I shouldn't have called you. Everything is probably fine–"

"Yeah, okay. First off, you should have called. And second off, things are not fine. That guy is a grade A whackjob. And now he's apparently pulling crazy ex-girlfriend stunts. Jesus."

He'd been surprised to see Whitney's name on his ID display when his phone rang, even more surprised when she'd started telling him about Ian. Well, not *that* surprised, if he was honest.

"Where are you?" he asked her.

"Headed home." She sounded like she was trying not to dissolve into tears.

"Okay, don't go there by yourself. Sam's working…shit. Okay. Come to Dartmoor. Kev's still here, we're all here. Drive up to the bike shop, alright?"

She sniffed. "Are you sure? I don't want to blow his cover or anything."

"You won't. Just come, okay? I don't want you alone." Not while Ian was playing the title role in whatever Lifetime movie he was acting out at the moment.

"Okay, okay."

Aidan hung up and turned to find Mercy and Carter staring at him. Carter looked confused. Mercy looked worried.

"Ian tried to spook Whitney."

"Seriously? Shit," Mercy said, muscle jumping in his jaw.

"Who did what to who?" Carter asked.

Aidan waved for him to shut up, but turned out Pretty Boy Jockstrap had had enough of being in the dark.

"No," he said, drawing himself up, brows tucking low over his eyes. "Something's going on – something's *been* going on – and I'm not some goddamn prospect anymore, so tell me what it is. Damn it," he tacked on, chest heaving.

Mercy sent him a mild look. "How long you been waiting to let that loose?"

"A while," Carter bit out.

Aidan gave him a look, his best impersonation of Maggie's *look*.

Which of course didn't work.

"This is Tango's business," Aidan said. "It isn't club business, it's his personal business. And if you want to know what's going on, then you need to ask him about it. I won't go spreading his shit all over the clubhouse like some kinda teenage girl. If you wanna know, then ask him. But rest your pretty little head that it has nothing to do with you or the club."

Carter wanted to hold onto his anger, but nodded.

"Don't overthink it," Mercy told him, clapping him on the shoulder.

~*~

She'd never been to Dartmoor, only driven past it a time or two. She'd forgotten just how massive it was, all those buildings spread across all that asphalt. It was daunting, seeing it laid out before her, and knowing all of it was Lean Dogs property, an empire fit for a family of outlaws.

Not outlaws, she reminded herself. But friends.

She flicked on her blinker and turned in at the gate, the one with the running black dog sign for the bike shop, and immediately her heartrate slowed.

The last bit of light was just winking across the river, the sky plum-colored and velvety overhead as she pulled to a stop in front of the shop. Hers was the only car; the boys' bikes were lined up off to the side, black and sinister.

Aidan, Mercy, and Kev stood in front of the open roll top doors, and Kev walked to meet her, face a study in concern, a hand already on the top of her door when she opened it.

"Aidan told you?" she asked, feeling guilty. The last thing she wanted was to stir ill will between him and Ian, no matter what they meant to each other these days.

His answer was to pull her out of the car and into his arms, crushing her in a tight hug.

"I'm sorry," she said against his shoulder, the worn leather of his jacket cold against her lips.

"No, *I'm* sorry," he said. "You shouldn't have to deal with that. Ian–" He bit off whatever else he wanted to say with an audible click of his teeth. "I'm sorry," he repeated.

"Don't be."

"It's my fault–"

"Or it's nobody's fault 'cept Ian's, 'cause he's a giant creep-ass who needs to be punched in the mouth," Mercy suggested, suddenly standing right beside them.

Kev pulled back from her, but didn't let go, shooting a frown at Mercy.

Mercy shrugged. "I'm just saying."

Seventeen

The watchman in the lobby of Ian's building ducked his head and said, "Mr. Estes," in greeting, which was testament to all the nights Tango had spent here. His face was familiar, his presence expected.

His hand shook as he reached to press the UP button at the elevator.

What an idiot he'd been. How could he not have expected this? Beneath his veneer of British calm, Ian had never been able to control his sizable temper. Tango had always worn his trauma on his sleeve, a shivering, cutting mess. But Ian buried it deep, let it eat at him slowly, until he couldn't contain it and it all came boiling to the surface.

Right now, it didn't matter that they were years out of The Nest, and that they weren't promised to one another; all Ian could see was Tango finding someone new. Could see that he was being replaced, and of course, *of course* he would take that out on Whitney.

The elevator glided up to Ian's floor, silent and steady, and Tango tried – unsuccessfully – to get his anger under control. If anything, the shaking was worse when he stepped out of the car, and his breath came in sharp draws through flared nostrils.

Fuck it, he thought, and pounded on Ian's door with the side of his fist.

"Ian, I know you're here, your car was in the garage," he called through the sleek gray panel. "Open up." He was in the middle of pounding again when the door was snatched open, so quickly it lifted Ian's hair in the breeze it created.

Ian's narrow face was tight and flushed with anger, eyes over-large in his face. "Come in here and stop making a scene," he hissed, stepping aside and waving Tango in.

The second the door was shut, Tango rounded on him. "*I'm* making a scene? You wanna rethink that?"

Ian turned the latch and sent him a questioning look. "Whatever are you talking about, darling?"

"Don't 'darling' me," Tango snapped. He had too much nervous energy coursing through him; he stalked deeper into the apartment, and heard Ian's expensive shoes follow him. "And don't play innocent," Tango said as he reached the kitchen. "You—"

There was a man sitting at the kitchen island, glass of red wine in one hand, eyes wide and nervous behind the lenses of his glasses.

Tango stumbled to a halt. "Who are you?" he blurted, too wound up for politeness.

"Uh…" the guy said, face flushing. He was young, just pretty enough, with a little cupid's bow in the center of his upper lip. He looked guilty, and nervous, and Tango knew immediately why he was here.

He turned and glanced at Ian over his shoulder, noticed his appearance for the first time: suit jacket removed, shirt open an extra button at the throat, cuffs rolled and sleeves pushed up. His mouth was damp, and pink, the same as the boy's.

Tango took a deep breath and his voice came out a snarl. "Who is this?"

Ian's brows lifted, a look of mock disbelief crossing his face. "I have to say, this is really unbecoming of you, all this anger—"

"I asked you a goddamn question."

Ian sighed, expression that of the abused parent of a tantrum-throwing child. "Alec works for me. He's my assistant."

"Your boy toy you mean, right?" Tango seethed. He took a step toward Ian, leaning up into his face. "If you have him, why the hell were you bothering Whitney? Just for fun?"

"Who's Whitney? Honestly, Kevin, I have no idea—"

"Stop it!" Tango shouted, startling himself, startling Ian, if his face was anything to go by. "Stop playing stupid. You're a lot of things, *Shaman*, but stupid isn't one of them."

Ian grimaced at the sound of his alias. "We're not together anymore, darling," he said, voice tight. "So you don't get to come into my home and scream at me."

"Right. We're not together. Which means you had no *fucking right* to go scaring Whitney like you did."

Ian made a disgusted face and moved away, walking around the island to get to the bottle of wine airing on the counter. "It always comes back to that little cunt, doesn't it?" He plucked up the bottle and spun to put his back to the sink, facing Tango. "Honestly, what's so special about her?"

Alec looked like he was trying to disappear down inside his shirt collar.

"Say something like that about her again," Tango said, "and I'll break that bottle over your head."

"Violent, violent," Ian chided. "Is this her influence? This new bloodthirsty you?"

Tango gritted his teeth and swallowed down his retort. No, this wasn't him. He wasn't the kind who flew off the handle and started bashing heads – mainly because he wasn't capable of that sort of thing. But also because that just *wasn't him*.

"You followed her to work," he said instead. "You are *stalking* her. And you ambushed her, tried to buy her off to get her away from me, for God's sakes."

"She's just a girl," Ian said, and didn't bother to deny the allegations. "What could you possibly want with her?"

"I love her!"

Silence.

No one moved, no one breathed.

Slowly, Ian raised the wine bottle to his lips and took three long swallows, mouth red afterward, before his tongue flickered out to chase the droplets. The bottle landed on the counter with a loud *gong* sound, and Ian stalked toward him, gaze predatory. He got close enough for Tango to see the vein jumping in his throat, to smell the wine on his breath.

"You love the idea of her," he said in a razor-sharp whisper. "But she doesn't love the real you, the you that you are with me."

His hands came up to curl loosely around Tango's neck, hot and smooth. He didn't have to work anymore; didn't have calluses from the pole like he had when they were kids.

185

"You are lying to yourself, Kev," he murmured, tone softening. "And if it takes frightening a girl to show you that, then so be it."

His eyes glittered with moisture, soft and beautiful now. "Why are you doing this to us?" he whispered. "Kev, you could be free. We could be together, finally. We could be *happy*." His thumbs stroked up the back of Tango's neck, and Tango's pulse leapt in response. "I know you love me. I *know* you do."

Tango went back to the club in his mind, back to their shadowy dressing room, makeup palettes strewn across the tables, boas and scraps of satin and lace hooked on the corners of the lighted vanity mirrors. Ian's hands on his neck, face-to-face, Ian's beautiful eyes ringed with black liner, his lips trembling. *I know you love me. I know you do.*

Yes, he'd said then. *I do, I do.*

Now he brought his hands up and curled them gently around Ian's wrists. It would be easy as breathing to fall into him, press their foreheads together and cave. He would never have to explain himself with Ian, never have to hold back, or worry that what he wanted was too dark, too much, too wrong. Those phrases didn't exist in Ian's vocabulary.

Ian had all the power in the world to make him feel good – for a little while, at least, while they were both straining toward pleasure. But there always came the hollow comedown afterward, their joy tainted by old horrors no amount of love could erase. It was a reminder, every time, of Miss Carla, of The Nest, a reminder that they'd been *turned into* the men they were now, conditioned and carved and beaten into shape.

And when he looked at Whitney he *ached,* and it was the sweetest, most alarming sensation, and there were no ghosts behind her eyes, only love.

Tango wet his lips. "I have *always* loved you," he whispered back, fiercely. "But we make each other miserable, Ian. And you can't ask me to give up the club. They're my family. If you can't understand that..."

Ian looked wounded, turning his face away, fingers stilling against Tango's skin. "Family."

Tango leaned in a little closer, smoothing his fingertips down Ian's wrists to his forearms. "Ian, call your parents. Talk to them—"

Ian gave him a rough shove and stepped back, dragging his hands through his long, shiny hair. "Tell them what?" he snapped. "That their son isn't dead after all, they'll just wish he was when they find out what he's been doing?"

"They won't care, they'll just be so glad you're alive—"

"Shut up," Ian growled. "Shut your bloody mouth, you traitor."

Somehow, they'd reversed roles, and now it was Tango reaching out for Ian, something placating on the tip of his tongue.

"No." Ian sliced an arm through the air, blocking Tango's gesture. "You don't get to say those things to me and then *comfort* me."

"Isn't that what you always do to me?" Tango shot back, but his voice was kind.

The scrape of chair legs on the tile reminded Tango that they weren't alone, and he glanced over toward the island where Alec was getting uncertainly to his feet.

"Um…" he said, blushing. "I think maybe I should go."

"Stay," Ian ordered.

Tango shot the man an apologetic look. "You should stay," he said. "He shouldn't be alone."

To Ian, he said, "I'm serious about Whitney. You won't like what happens next time."

He paused when he reached the door, and glanced back. Ian stood with a hand over his eyes, head bent. Alec stood at his elbow, looking on helplessly.

~*~

Whitney hadn't known what to expect from an MC clubhouse, but she hadn't envisioned the tidy, clean-smelling bar/living room atmosphere she found herself in now. She sat on a leather sofa that had a view of the large flat-screen TV and the Lean

Dogs memorabilia decorating the walls on either side of it. There was a massive white flag with the running black dog emblem in its center. Pennants for various chapters. Framed photos. The Stars and Stripes, Stars and Bars, and the Union Jack, hung one atop the next. She was itching to get up, walk around, and inspect the photos up close, but she didn't want to overstep her welcome; instead sipped the tea a girl named Chanel had brought her.

The tea was warm, and too sweet, and slowly her nerves had settled, the shakes easing so she could hold the mug in one hand without slopping tea over the sides.

She heard a squeak of hinges and a tumble of voices as people entered through the front door. When she turned, she saw Mercy, Aidan, and, thankfully, Kev. She half-expected him to be bruised and roughed up, but he looked the same as when he left her, a few loose strands of hair falling free of his bun and framing his face.

She set the mug on a coaster and surged to her feet. "You're okay?" she asked as she walked toward him.

He looked tired, a little tight around the eyes, and he sighed, shoulders slumping. But he said, "I'm fine," and let her hug him.

This was becoming so frequent, so normal, so *right*, putting her arms around his waist and pressing her face into his shoulder. And it wasn't even about practicality anymore. She'd been worried, frightened even, but this right now, this was just because she wanted to. Because feeling his body pressed against hers was becoming necessary. How selfish, she knew, because he didn't want their relationship to become more complicated. But she couldn't help it at this point; she *needed* it. *Him*.

She pulled back reluctantly, but knew she had to. She couldn't just cling to him in front of his friends like some sort of sad lovestruck child.

"I'm sorry," she said, looking up into his perfect, beautiful face. "I didn't mean to make things weird with you and...him."

He smirked. "Things have always been weird, and trust me it's not your fault."

"The guy's got problems," Aidan said. "And he's a total drama queen about it. It's not your fault," he seconded, clapping Whitney on the shoulder as he headed for the bar.

She looked at Kev again and he gave her a lopsided smile. "You hungry?"

Her stomach *was* awfully empty, though she'd been too nervous to feel hunger pangs. "Maybe."

"The girls are on their way," Mercy said, his face lit up with happiness. "Why don't you hang around, Whit? You don't look like you eat much."

She smiled back at him, grateful for the invite. But she looked to Kev yet again; she wasn't going to insert herself into his club family if he didn't want her there. If he...

But he grinned. "Yeah. Stay."

"Okay."

~*~

"What can I do? Put me to work." Whitney rolled up the sleeves of her sweater in anticipation.

The clubhouse kitchen was surprisingly large and modern, with the air of a restaurant kitchen: stainless everywhere, huge pantry, glass-front industrial fridge. The kind of kitchen that saw a lot of cooks and fed a lot of hungry men.

Maggie Teague stood at the stove, managing the burners, and the sizzling pans on top of them. "You can come stir this," she said, and it was somewhere between a gentle request and a command.

Whitney hustled to comply, taking the queen's place at the stove.

Ava, mixing together salad dressing at the counter, leaned over and whispered. "Sorry. She's a little overbearing in these situations."

"It doesn't bother me," Whitney said. "You know where you stand with your mom. She's the boss, and doesn't make a fuss about it. I can deal with that."

Ava laughed under her breath. "And you were worried about fitting in."

The old ladies had arrived, kids in tow, about twenty minutes before. The guys were out having beers around the TV, babysitting, and Whitney had been swept in here with the women. She felt like one of them, and it was exhilarating, the thrill of being included. Of being around competent, contented women who weren't giving her passive-aggressive dark looks and wishing her dead.

Her heart squeezed for Madelyn, like always. And, like always, she had no idea how to go about making things right.

She picked up the wooden spoon on the edge of the skillet before her and gave the sautéing onions and peppers a stir, oil hissing.

"Here, honey," Maggie said at her shoulder, and a brimming glass of white wine was held beneath her nose.

Whitney took it with surprise. "Thank you."

Maggie winked at her. "Liquid courage."

"Mom, that makes us sound terrifying," Ava said.

"Well you are, a little bit," Sam said from the island, where she was breading chicken tenders.

Maggie laughed as she went to gather up the plate of chicken, all ready to slide into the Dutch oven of hot vegetable oil. "Way to give a woman a complex."

"I think you enjoy it, though," Sam said, blushing.

"Just a little bit."

A pretty brunette came bustling in, shopping bag held triumphantly in one hand. "Rice," she announced.

"There's a pot ready for it, Holly, thanks," Maggie said.

Holly came to the stove, orange Uncle Ben's box in hand, and smiled at Whitney in a warm, sweet way that made it impossible not to reciprocate. "Hi, I'm Holly. I'm Michael's wife. You're Whitney, right?"

"Yes, hi, nice to meet you." Whitney didn't know anything about Michael, only that he was the scariest looking guy she'd ever seen...and she'd spent time locked in a basement dungeon.

Holly beamed at her. "Tango is the sweetest. I'm so glad he found somebody." Her vivid green eyes widened and her smile slipped. "Oops, that was, well...sorry. I just meant...I'm glad you're here, is all." She shook her head. "Sorry, I'm always awkward."

"Me too," Whitney said. "I just don't think anyone's realized it yet."

Holly chuckled and tore the top off the box of rice. "I won't tell if you won't."

"Deal."

~*~

They had homemade sesame chicken over rice and veggies at the cobbled-together dining table composed of several round tables pushed together. The food was good, the wine was strong, and the company was lively – well, except for Michael, who maintained his scary status, but who would lean sideways to whisper things to Holly from time to time – and little by little, Whitney felt her anxiety melt completely away, until she was loose-limbed, relaxed, and sleepy.

Afterward, she helped with the dishes, and then went to find Tango.

He was in a black leather chair, beer in one hand, and he scooted over against one arm and patted the scant space beside him, shooting her a hopeful look.

How could she refuse?

She snuggled down into the little hollow beside him, and had to hook her knees across his thighs, settling into the crook of his arm. It was blissful.

For about ten seconds.

A young blonde man, handsome in an athletic sort of way, sat nearest them, and an overtly sexy, albeit older blonde woman sat tucked under his arm, fingers playing idly with the zipper of his cut. Both of them were staring at Whitney.

She squirmed a little deeper into her chair nook and said, "Um, hi. I'm Whitney."

The man gave her a little two-finger salute. "Carter."

The woman smiled at her, almost predatory beneath her playfulness. "Hi, Whitney, I'm Jasmine. Baby boy," she said to Tango, "did you finally go and get yourself a sweet little girlfriend?"

"Jazz," Carter said, shooting her a dark look.

"What?" She scowled and elbowed him in the ribs. Then turned back to Whitney, smiling again, her teeth bright like she'd had them whitened at the dentist. "I always knew Tango needed a nice, good girl in his life. Didn't figure he'd have to find you in a basement, though," she added, lifting her brows, smile slipping. "Jesus, you doing alright now? You over all that?"

"Jazz," Tango said, and Whitney felt tension steal through him, turn his lean frame to stone. "Leave it alone. We're just friends."

Whitney had been ready to say something, but the words died on her tongue. *Just friends.* He'd more or less said so already, but to hear it, so plain like this…

She surged up from the chair.

"Whit." Tango made a reach for her. "I–"

"I'll be back," she said, but she didn't want to be. She wanted to get far away from him so he couldn't see the mortified color in her cheeks, or the tears that had leapt to her eyes.

She moved quickly, head down, not making eye contact with any of the bikers and old ladies who were doubtless watching her with open curiosity. She ducked down a hallway, found a door ajar, and slipped inside, shutting and locking it behind her.

She was in some kind of bedroom, a sagging double bed with a plain blue coverlet across from her. A dresser. A mirror. A desk. An open door through which she could see a bathroom.

Whitney slumped back against the closed door and blinked furiously. She shouldn't be upset; should be grateful she had Kev in whatever capacity she had him, even as *just friends*.

But it hurt so badly, to hear him phrase it like that. Like there wasn't a chance for them, like he couldn't feel that way about her, while she was…she was…God, she *wanted* him, in ways her stupid virgin body couldn't begin to decipher. And she knew she shouldn't, because he was a wreck of a human being, and so was she, and what good could they do each other with their nightmares, and miscommunication, and obsessive worrying?

She focused on her breathing for a few minutes, venting the deep, shuddering exhalations into the quiet of the room, walking herself back from the edge of tears.

And then someone knocked on the door and she went to pieces again, gasping and dabbing at her eyes. She'd never thought she could be the kind of girl who locked herself away and refused to have a rational, adult conversation, but there was no way she could talk to Kev right now while she was this raw.

It was a female voice, though, that called through the door. "Whitney, you alright?" It was Ava. "Can I come in?"

Saying no would make her look like a brat. So she unlocked the door and opened it, inexplicably grateful to see Ava's sympathetic expression on the other side.

She slipped in and said, "Might want to lock it again, or RJ and one of the girls will be stumbling in here with us."

Whitney hurried to flick the lock on the knob.

Ava went to sit on the edge of the bed, posture relaxed. She was at home here, comfy in a dated old dorm room in an MC clubhouse. This was her domain.

Whitney tried and failed to imagine what it must have been like to grow up here.

Ava gave her a plain look that, though kind, wasn't going to tolerate any bullshit. "Jazz said something stupid to you, didn't she." It wasn't a question.

"*I'm* stupid," Whitney said, leaning against the door again, hands knotted together. "Jasmine asked if I was Kev's girlfriend –

a 'nice little girl,' she said – and Kev said that no, we were just friends. And." She took a deep breath. "I know that. I do. I think I just…" She gestured vaguely. "I'm sorry. Having a chick moment, I guess," she said with a forced smile.

Ava sighed, and looked queenly and wiser than her years. "I'm going to hit him. I swear. That moron."

So not the reaction Whitney had expected. "You're…what?"

"Kev, Kev, Kev," Ava said, rolling her eyes. "I'm sick to death of these stupid boys denying themselves out of some kind of nobility shtick – which, they're not noble, not a damn one of them – and accomplishing nothing but making everyone miserable. Idiots," she huffed.

Whitney could only stare, shocked.

Ava grinned. "Mercy broke up with me when I was seventeen and told me, 'It won't hurt forever.' The giant asshole. And then it did hurt forever, and what the hell did we gain by losing five years?"

Whitney felt oddly privileged to have been given that kind of insight on part of the MC royal family, as it were. But she shook her head. "I think this is different, though."

Ava's expression softened. "Whitney. I was seventeen, and I'd just miscarried our baby, and my dad threatened not to pay for college if Mercy didn't leave me. It wasn't your situation, no, but it was shitty."

"Oh God, I'm sorry," Whitney gasped. "I didn't mean–"

Ava waved off the apology. "Kev's bi, and Ian's possibly insane, and things are messy. Yeah. It's not enviable. These boys don't ever seem to get it right on the first try. You should talk to Sam about that," she said with a snort, shaking her head. "But they're worth it. If you care about him, and I know you do, then it's worth sticking out the stupid until their heads catch up to their hearts and they stop sticking their giant booted feet in their mouth." Her grin turned conspiratorial. "Hey, you're twenty-one and not pregnant yet, so you're doing better than me."

Whitney shook her head, but grinned. "How can you be so laid back about it?"

Ava's smile turned into a smirk. "Target practice. Hell of a stress reliever. The sex doesn't hurt either."

"I'll keep that in mind."

~*~

"How was I supposed to know?" Jasmine asked, looking both affronted and sorry, mouth at a harsh angle, eyes large and worried as she glanced between Carter and Tango. "I'm happy for you," she said to Tango. "You don't gotta get all prickly and ruin it for yourself, baby boy."

Tango sighed and got to his feet.

"Just leave him alone," he heard Carter say behind him. "He's...I dunno. Fucked up or something."

The remark, said so casually, stung worse than it should have. Carter didn't know about the razor blade and the bathtub, about Aidan dragging him out of the water and screaming at him not to be dead.

And probably no one knew that he was hanging by a thread, still, and that Whitney was his main motivation to get up in the morning, though he couldn't let himself touch her like he wanted, couldn't ruin everything that way.

Fuck.

Whitney hadn't bolted just now because of anything Jazz had said. But because of what had come out of his own stupid mouth. *Just friends.* He was an *idiot.*

He settled on a stool at the bar, grateful there were no hangarounds tending tonight, and reached across for a bottle of whatever was in reach. Macallan. Ugh. But he got down a glass and poured himself a slug.

Aidan climbed onto the stool beside him. "Shit, where'd that come from? Is that some shit Candy brought with him last time he was here?" He gestured to the bottle still held in Tango's hand.

Tango shrugged and poured another finger.

"Whoa," Aidan said, and leaned close, lowering his voice. "I'm not an expert–"

195

"On anything."

"–but I'm pretty sure getting blind drunk isn't the way to make you all warm and fuzzy inside. Also – dude, low blow."

Tango raised his glass. "I'm pretty sure getting drunk is the *best* way to get warm and fuzzy inside."

Aidan made a face that he would have laughed to see on himself only a year ago. It was a dad face.

Tango pushed the drink away, intact. "I'm fucking it up," he said. "I'm not trying to, but I am, and I can't stop, apparently."

"Have you talked about it in your whatever-you-call-them?"

"Sessions."

"Yeah, have you talked to Merc about it?" They were both whispering at this point.

"A little." Tango shrugged. "He said not to question it. To just go for it. But…"

"But you're guilt-tripping yourself, yeah, I figured." More dad-face. "Look, bro, I tried all that pushing-away, it's-for-your-own-good shit with Sam. And it didn't go over well. And it didn't help anything." When Tango continued to stare at him, his expression softened. "You aren't going to hurt her, or break her, or ruin her, man. Being with you isn't going to be bad for her, not the way you're thinking."

"You don't know what I'm thinking." But it was a weak protest.

"Yeah, I do. And it's stupid."

"Ugh." He reached for the Scotch, threw it down with a grimace, and moved off the stool.

Aidan clapped him on the shoulder on his way out. "You got this."

"I never thought I'd get tired of pep talks."

"Just wait. They're gonna get peppier."

He ran into Ava in the dorm hallway, and when her dark eyes flicked up to his, he knew he wasn't going to be able to pass her with a nod and keep going.

She came to a halt, hands on her hips, and he wondered when exactly she'd gone from Aidan's lanky little sister to this terrifying younger version of her mother.

"You fucked up," she said without malice.

He nodded.

"Fix it." She pointed to the first door on the left, and patted him on the shoulder as she walked off.

To be a boy who was snatched from his home at age seven, he somehow had this plethora of helpful mothers in his life now.

Mostly helpful.

With a sigh, he knocked once on the dorm door, said, "Whit, can I come in?" and tested the knob. It was unlocked, but he lingered in the threshold, waiting to get the okay from her.

Whitney sat on the end of the bed, hands in her lap, expression pensive. She nodded right away, though, and said, "Come in," in a quiet, distracted voice.

He eased the door shut behind him and came to sit beside her, slowly, so she had a chance to move away if she wanted to.

She didn't.

"Just friends," she said, staring at her fingers as she twisted them together. A lock of hair fell forward against her cheek, and Tango itched to tuck it back behind her ear. He wanted to see her face, its dainty profile, the way her dark lashes lay against her cheeks, the way she chewed at her lower lip.

He'd always been a sucker for a pretty girl, in a way that made him feel feverish and desperate. Like that time…

He slammed the lid on his memories, heard the resounding thump of it echo through his head.

And then caught himself.

She wanted honesty, didn't she? His whole biker family wanted him to open up, didn't they?

Fuck it. He'd open up. What else did he have to lose?

"Whitney," he said, and her eyes flicked toward him, a quick glimmer of blue. "When I say that you're my friend, I mean that you're really important to me." He swallowed a rising lump in his throat. "Really important. And it doesn't mean I don't want more than friendship. 'Cause I do. Trust me, I do."

Her head turned so she faced him fully. How lovely she was.

"Shit," he said, because he didn't want this to be complicated. He longed to dump all his problems at her feet, and just let himself have her, whatever she'd give him, no matter how selfish that was.

"Whit," he tried again. "We've talked about this – how sex is weird for me." Honesty it was going to be; here went nothing. "I can't call you my girlfriend if I can't be a good boyfriend. I won't do that to you." He dragged his hands through his hair, unable to look at her any longer.

"I know what you said, and I know it wouldn't be easy. But I think I deserve to have an opinion about it. It's not any fun feeling like the little kid you're trying to protect," she said, quietly.

He nodded down at his lap.

"Ian's still in love with you."

"That's what he says." It was hard to breathe.

"Are you still in love with him?"

He huffed a laugh. "I'm about to be one of those assholes who says there's a difference between loving and being *in love*. Ah, Jesus."

It was quiet a beat, and then Whitney said, "I think maybe I really should find my own apartment."

Pain sliced through his ribs, an acute physical reaction to the thought that he might lose her so quickly, so easily. "No," he blurted, gaze swinging back to her.

She gave him a patient, pained look. "If me being around makes it more difficult for you—"

"No, it doesn't. You *don't*." He *hated* himself for making all of this so muddy and difficult. "Last night was the best sleep of my life."

"But, Kev—"

Enough, a voice in the back of his head snapped. *Fucking enough already.* He'd pushed her away, and he'd denied both of them, and he just...he just...

He leaned into the space that separated them, captured her face in his hands and hauled her in close to kiss her.

It was soft at first, just a brushing of lips. Whitney froze in surprise, and he felt her sharp exhalation.

He swept his thumbs across her cheeks, warm and soft, and pressed in a little closer, asking for just a little more. Coaxing. He could *taste* the sweetness of her, the way she was nothing lascivious and calculating, only innocent and kind…and in love with him. Yes, he could taste that. And the sugar rush of it left him wondering why he'd ever thought he could hold out long-term.

Then Whitney sighed and melted. All the tension bled out of her in a gentle rush, and her hands landed on his chest. Her mouth opened beneath the easy flick of his tongue, and then he was inside it, hot and slick as blood.

She made a muffled little sound that sent pleased chills skittering across his skin. It felt good to her. It felt *good*. And even if he was good for absolutely nothing, he knew how to pleasure people.

He'd been looking at this the wrong way. It wasn't about ruining her. It was about taking the opportunity to make her first time spectacular. Because he couldn't talk about his past without breaking down, and he couldn't keep from stocking his medicine cabinet with razors, but he could do this for her, by God. He could give her the time of her life.

It's what The Nest had trained him for, after all.

He broke the kiss to trail his lips, feather-light, across her cheek. Pressed a wet kiss just under her ear, and felt her shiver. He let his hands ghost down her body, glancing pressure at her collarbones, her breasts, and finally her hips, where he latched on.

"Let's go home, baby," he whispered in her ear, and she nodded.

~*~

Maybe it was stupid (read: pathetic), but Tango was a little bit proud of himself for pumping the brakes at the clubhouse.

Restraint wasn't really his game, and yet he'd paused, pulled back from the brink, no matter how painful it had been to rearrange his jeans and walk back through the clubhouse, say his goodnights to everyone. Ava had given him a knowing and pleased little smile, like maybe she was proud of him too. And he figured that Whitney's blood would cool on the drive back to the apartment, and she wouldn't want to continue. But if that was the case, so be it. He owed her more than a dirty romp in a clubhouse dorm. He owed her some important information.

He caught her shooting him looks as they headed up the iron staircase, but it was too dark to get a good read on her.

He was almost afraid to flip on the lights when they got inside, afraid he'd see rejection on her face, but did so anyway, taking too long to hang up his jacket and cut, finally meeting her gaze when he offered to take her coat.

The emotion in her eyes brought him up short. It was trust. Complete and total, adoring trust.

Dear God, please let him be worthy of that.

He fumbled to get her coat on the rack without looking, clearing his throat. "Um, okay, well, it's okay if you...if you don't..."

She smiled like she thought it was cute that he couldn't string a sentence together. "Weren't we in the middle of something?"

Oh. Oh yes they were.

The idea that she still wanted to, that she wanted *him*, was potent as good brandy, the kind Ian kept in his office. His hand found her waist and he was kissing her again, gentle but warm, with the promise –

"No," he gasped, pulling back, forcing his hands off her.

Whitney looked devastated.

"No, I meant, just...hold on. For a sec. There's something I need to tell you. First. Shit, I'm..."

"Incredibly awkward? I picked up on that, believe it or not."

Tango sighed and tried to smile. "I don't usually have sex with people I care about."

Whitney, sweet little inexperienced Whitney, slid an arm around his waist and steered him toward the bedroom. Bless her.

They sat down on the end of the bed together, and he realized she was trying to recreate the moment back at the clubhouse. A good plan, especially considering they were now alone, and it was quiet, and the rumpled covers behind them smelled like them, and no one else.

Whitney rested her head on his shoulder and Tango put his arm around her, thankful for the chance to talk without looking at one another.

"Okay, so," he started. "If we're gonna...then I want us to go into it knowing all the facts. Or *you* knowing. I'm the one with all the skeletons."

"Kev," she said, gently.

"I've been with a lot of people," he said, rushing to get it over with. "Mostly men, and mostly safe, but some of it not." When the clients had been even bigger jackasses than normal. "But I went and got tested. And I'm clean. I wanted you to know that I'm totally clean. I wanted you to know that—" His voice cracked. "I wouldn't put you at risk like that. I couldn't live with myself if I got you sick."

There. He'd said it. The silence felt heavy and judgmental, and...

"Oh sweetie," she said, snuggling in deep beside him. "I trust you."

He finally turned his head to look at her, and couldn't believe how sweet and *wonderful* she was. "I don't know why," he said.

"Because I care about you, too." She leaned up to kiss him, tentative and careful, still so new to all this.

He cupped the back of her head and angled the kiss, adjusted the way their mouths fit, and felt all the awful tension start a slow bleed out of his body. He was clean. He could teach her, take care of her. He *could* – and for the first time, he didn't try to run from that realization.

"Come here, baby," he urged, and put his hands on her waist.

She shuffled forward on her knees and let him guide her so she straddled his lap, his hands anchoring her waist.

Tango pushed a smile across his face, that dreamy smile he'd used at the club, lewd at the edges with the promise of sex, but soft enough to melt grown men. "You're perfect, you know that?" he asked, and kissed her, nipped lightly at her lower lip.

When he pulled back her eyes were heavy-lidded, her breathing unsteady, her gaze full of the kind of inexperienced desire he'd never had a chance to understand.

"Kev," she said, voice shivering, and licked at her lips, leaned in for another kiss.

He was rock-hard in his jeans. Apparently, the whole sweet virgin thing really did it for him.

No, that wasn't fair to her. *Whitney* did it for him. In every way, all the time, simply by being her.

He kissed her until it grew sloppy; until their mouths were wet and tender; until she was whimpering and grinding lightly in his lap. When he kissed down the length of her pale throat, she tipped her head back to give him better access, breathing raggedly. He tracing her throbbing pulse with the tip of his tongue, sucked at the little hollow at the base.

"Kev," she said again, searchingly, her fingers tangling in his hair.

"Easy," he murmured. "We're gonna go real easy."

His fingers made quick work of the small pearl buttons down her shirt, and then he separated the halves, sliding his hands inside the fabric to get to her bare skin.

She made a little choked sound as he stroked her waist, and he pulled back from her throat to look at her.

Fine pale skin exposed between the open halves of her black shirt, black, lace-edged bra, her head tipped back, a beautiful line of temptation from the underside of her chin all the way down to the button of her jeans.

Tango leaned forward and pressed his lips to her sternum, stroked his hands across her back, and sides, and the flat of her belly in gentle, slow passes. "Is this good?" he asked against her skin, fingertips flirting along her ribs. "You okay?"

"Y-yes." Her voice came out high and breathless; he could hear the want in it, there was no mistaking that sound. "It's good. It's...Kev..."

"I know, baby." He ducked his head lower and let her feel the warmth of his breath in the shallow valley between her breasts. His hands migrated upward, slowly – achingly slow, his patience straining – bit by bit, until the pads of his fingers were brushing over her satin bra cups.

Whitney said, "Oh."

"More?"

"Yes, yes."

He cupped her breasts, and even through her bra he could feel her nipples drawing up, the perfect heaviness of the weight in his palms. He traced the hard buds with this thumbs, firm strokes, pressing a little, until he heard another of those sounds leave her lips.

"More?" he asked again.

And again: "Yes."

He kissed a path across tops of her breasts, first one and then the other, right along the lacy edge of the bra, letting her feel the heat and wetness of his tongue. Lingering a little, thinking about the shape and color of her nipples, wanting them in his mouth.

He shuddered, and dropped one hand to his lap, pressing down on his cock. He was too wound up, and the whole point of this was slow and lasting, making it good for her.

Whitney, though, must have had ideas of her own.

She lifted her hands from his shoulders and shrugged out of her shirt; the fabric whispered as it slid down to the floor.

Tango pulled back, searching out her face with his eyes.

She looked flushed, and hungry, and not at all freaked out. Nothing in her gaze said *stop*, only *more*.

He had to swallow before he could speak. "What do you want, baby? I only want to do what you want to."

She touched his face, her small warm hands framing his jaw with nothing short of reverence. "I want you to keep going."

He circled her throat with one loose hand and pulled her in for another kiss. Messy, wet, tongues sliding. She was getting bolder, more sure of herself, her tongue flexing shyly against his.

He groaned against her mouth.

"Good?" she asked against his lips, a touch of doubt in her voice.

"Fantastic."

And it was. It was better than fantastic – it was perfect, the way kissing her was more important than breathing, the way she arched her back and leaned into him.

Not stopping. No way was he stopping.

He wrapped his arms around her and laid back across the bed, her slight weight shifting on top of him, her breasts pressing into his chest.

The slick satin felt nice, but he wanted skin. Nothing but skin.

Whitney kissed him. When she pressed her damp lips to his, he let his hands slide around her ribs to meet at the clasp of her bra.

A tug of guilt in his gut froze him in place. Shit, she was so young, and she probably had no idea what she really wanted, and he shouldn't –

Whitney broke the kiss with a wet smack and sat up, smiling at him as her hands went back around and she undid the clasp herself. "I'm okay," she promised, running the straps down her arms, setting the bra off to the side. But she bit at her lip and her shoulders slumped in a show of nervousness, now that she was naked from the waist up.

Tango looked, because how could he help it? And because she wanted him to, he believed that.

Her breasts weren't large, just palm-sized, but they were real, and sweetly shaped, and seeing them bared like this, with her going pink in the cheeks with uncertainty, only confirmed all his theories that every single part of her was gorgeous.

He sat up, and spanned her narrow back with his hands, her skin satiny against his palms. Her face hovered above his; he heard the soft, desperate sound of her breathing, felt her peaked nipples up high against his chest. He slid one hand up the bumps of her spine, her neck, cupped the back of her head. With his other hand, he reached for her wrist, maneuvered her hand so it was curved around the back of his.

"Just show me where you want me," he said, their lips flirting together, the barest touch. "Show me, baby."

She gasped a little against his mouth, and her thighs tightened against the outsides of his. Slowly, so slowly, she shifted his hand up the silken stretch of her stomach, up the fretwork of her ribs, and then…there. The soft weight of her breast in his hand.

He'd always loved women's bodies, the incredible contrast with his own, the curves and soft places.

He cupped Whitney in his hand, flicked her nipple with his thumb, and she shivered.

He was hard to the point of madness. The control it took to touch her like this, to let her lead, was devastating. He could barely breathe and his fingers twitched and he couldn't imagine what his face looked like; his jaw ached from the tension.

Whitney leaned into his touch, and his hand tightened automatically. She whimpered again, and her fingers flexed against his, encouraging him.

It hit him then. He knew exactly what he needed to do.

"Whit, hold onto me," he said, and both her hands landed on his shoulders.

He reached down to the waistband of her jeans, careful to go slow and telegraph the movement so she knew where he was going, letting his knuckles skim down her stomach on the way. When he flicked a glance to her face, he saw that her eyes were on his hands, and that she had her lower lip caught between her teeth again in an unmistakable way. She was okay; she wanted this. Wanted him.

Tango unfastened her jeans. Eased the zipper down. He could see the waistband of her black panties, the same delicate lace as her bra.

He teased at the lace with his thumb, back and forth, until her hips shifted. And then he slid his hand inside the open V of her jeans, cupping her sex through the cotton.

She was damp already, and warm to the touch, even through the material. His brain fizzed and caught and shorted out for a moment, the intimate feel of her drawing on a dozen memories, and a hundred secret wishes.

"That feels…" she whispered, and brought him back to himself. "God, can you, Kev…"

"Yeah, baby." His voice was full of gravel. "I can do that."

He stroked her as well as he could within the confines of her jeans, gently, with his fingertips. A steady, light touch across her sex, until the panties were soaked and her hips were shifting forward and back.

Her fingers dug into his shoulders and she leaned on him, letting him support her weight as she lost herself in the sensation.

"Does it feel good?" he asked in a whisper.

"Yeah…yeah…it feels good…so good…it…*ah*."

He swept the wet fabric to the side and the first contact with her bare, slippery skin caused another brain meltdown.

Until he heard her say, "Oh, God," in this quiet, breathy, melted voice, and she surged forward, trying to get closer.

He put his free hand against the small of her back, encouraging the grinding of her hips, and stroked her. Teased her open, and probed at her entrance.

"God," she said again.

He slid the tip of one finger inside. In and then back out. Again. A teasing little penetration, stretching her the slightest bit, letting her get used to the idea.

She let her head tip forward, and he felt her chin against his forehead. "Kev, I've touched myself before, you know," she said in a ragged voice.

The image that put in his mind did dangerous things to his blood pressure. "Shit, you're gonna make me come in my pants like a teenager."

She breathed a strung-out laugh.

Loverboy

And he slipped his finger in to the hilt.

"Oh."

"Okay?"

"Oh, _please._"

He set up a steady tempo, thrusting into her with his finger, until they were both panting and damp with sweat. He urged her down onto his hand with the hand at her back, and thrust a little harder, twisting a little, getting her wetter, getting her ready. She was hot as blood, the wetness sliding down over his knuckles, collecting in his palm.

There wasn't a single drop of blood left in his head, but he was a professional, damn it. He could, he could…

He ducked his head and flicked his tongue across her nipple as he added a second finger down below.

He felt the bite of her nails through his shirt, felt her back bow as she offered her chest to him.

She had to be so close. It wouldn't take much more.

He suckled her nipple into his mouth, delicate teases from his tongue. And with his thumb he found her clit, and pressed.

She made a wordless sound, a quiet gasp, and she went still. He felt her walls squeeze around his fingers, impossibly tight. And then she was shivering, her hips churning, as she chased the bright sparks of orgasm through to the downward spiral.

He eased her through it, fingering her, murmuring praise against her breasts.

She finally slumped against him, spent, arms looped around his neck, her breath dancing through his hair.

Tango's immediate urge was to flip her onto her back on the bed, mount her, and fuck her through the mattress.

Instead, he carefully withdrew his hand from her jeans and brought it up to his face. Which was creepier, but somehow more civilized, by his own sick reasoning. He took his fingers in his mouth, sucked them clean, tasted the faint muskiness of her sex on his tongue.

"Did you just…?" she started.

"I'm gross."

"No." Her voice was dreamy, faraway. "You have *amazing* fingers." Her own fingers raked through his hair, scratching at his scalp in a way that felt incredible.

"What about you?" she asked against his temple. Her hand left his hair and moved to his lap.

He gritted his teeth against the very real prospect of coming the second she made contact through his jeans.

"I'm okay," he managed.

"Let me," she urged. "I'm not very – I don't really – you can show me." He heard the blush in her voice, felt the heat in her cheek as she pressed it to his. "Kev, I want to," she said when he didn't respond.

He shut his eyes, and tried not to think about the weight of her breasts against his arm, her legs still bracketing his hips, the way she'd been so hot inside, so wet for him.

Her hand closed over the shape of his rigid cock. She pressed at him, lightly, with the heel of her hand.

"Kev."

He let out a deep, defeated breath. "Yeah. Yes. Please. I'm sorry."

He hated himself as she leaned back a little, and reached for his fly, worked it open. Hated himself a little more as she reached into the slit of his boxers. Hated himself the most when she had his cock out, and both her small hands wrapped around it in a show of sweet, innocent boldness.

She sent him a pleading look from beneath her lashes. "Show me?"

"Here." He curved his hand around hers, fitted her fingers around his cock. "Like this."

He guided her thumb to the head, to the slit and the leaking pre-come there; urged her to spread it down the length of his shaft. Just enough slickness to smooth the way. Her hand was small, and soft, but strong for all that, and it only took a few pumps before she had the hang of it, jacking him steadily, with that little twist at the end he needed so desperately.

He wanted to hold her, to murmur sweet things in her ear, to be *present*. But it felt too good. He was too overwhelmed by the knowledge that this was *Whitney* touching him, finally, when he'd wanted it so much.

He leaned back on his hands before he collapsed and lifted his hips, rutting into her hand, totally helpless. She watched what she was doing, still a little sex-drunk, her gaze admiring, and reverent, and so many things he couldn't believe. She swiped her tongue across her bottom lip, and that did it. He came in hot spurts all over her hand, grunting deep in his throat.

~*~

Had that just happened?

Yeah. It had happened.

Shit.

They lay side-by-side on the bed. Whitney's head rested against his shoulder, her dark hair splayed across his chest.

He took a lock in-hand, rubbing it between his fingertips. He could have done that for hours, he knew: playing with her hair, listening to her catch her breath, breathing in the smell of her skin. Not just *could*, but *wanted to*. He wanted so much more. He wanted everything.

But…

"I'm sorry," he said.

She shifted onto her side, the covers rustling, and put her arm across his chest. He felt her breath on his skin, the faint flicker of her eyelashes as she tucked her face into his shoulder. "Don't be."

Eighteen

Ian's father had always belonged in a previous century, the sort of father who preferred for his children to be seen and not heard; who took the *Times* and a glass of brandy in the library every evening; who had a dressing gown; who pecked his wife solemnly on the cheek and eschewed passion, and love, and emotion of any kind. In the evenings, when Ian arrived home from school, he called him in to stand beside his favorite arm chair and report on what he'd learned that day. Father would never take his eyes from his paper, only nod afterward, and say, "Very good."

Disappointment had been his default setting. Only exceptionalism could earn his grudging approval. And complete disownment was always a possibility.

What would Father say, Ian's wine-addled brain wondered, if he could see his son now?

Alec was tender and sweet, half-melted in Ian's arms, clinging to him. His breathing hitched and his skin glowed, flushed pink with arousal. He was beautiful, and willing, and still so innocent, and Ian wanted to devour him.

It was a wet, sliding, desperate kiss. Ian traced the inner contours of Alec's mouth with his tongue, mapping all its dark, slippery secrets. He thrust in slowly with his tongue, and then again, fucking his mouth, drawing a low moan up out of his throat.

Ian cupped the smooth, sharp line of his jaw and pulled back from the kiss with a wet sound, pressing his thumb into the damp curve of Alec's lower lip. His *face*. Gorgeous pink cheeks and heavy eyelids, pupils blown.

After Kev left, it had been a blur of wine, and suppressed tears, and a terrible ache in his chest that made it hard to breathe. Alec had come to him, had slipped an arm around his waist and comforted him. And Ian had launched himself at him. And Alec, sweet Alec, had been a willing victim. Then it had been a matter of stripping clothes and fumbling to the bedroom, and now here they were, the covers turned down, naked and ravenous.

"Hands and knees," Ian told him.

A notch formed between Alec's brows. His expression, still hazy with want, tightened a little with doubt. "But…"

Ian slid a hand down the smooth plane of his belly and found his cock, curled his hand around it and gave it a stroke. "I want you on your hands and knees," he repeated, a command this time.

The notch between Alec's brows deepened. He wet his lips, needlessly, tip of his tongue passing across Ian's thumb. Ian chose to pretend he didn't shiver in reaction. He was seasoned, and he didn't even love this uncertain man-child. His assistant, for God's sakes. He wasn't affected. His gut *didn't* clench and his cock *didn't* twitch, and he didn't *care* about that flick of his tongue.

"No," Alec whispered.

Ian stilled; his breath caught. "What did you say to me?"

"No." His voice, incredibly, grew stronger. His gaze clearer, bolder than Ian could have imagined. He brought a hand up to push Ian's hair back, cradling the side of his throat in a gentle grip. "I want you to make love to me."

Something happened in Ian's bloodstream. Surges of cold and hot emotions. His chest tightened. "What did you say to me?" His voice came out raw, wounded, dangerous.

But it didn't put Alec off. He leaned in closer, gaze relentless. "I'm here, if you need me. I'm here for you. But I won't let you put my face in the pillow and pretend I'm him. I don't deserve that."

"Oh no?" Ian asked, his head spinning, his meticulous plans derailing. This wasn't supposed to happen.

"No," Alec said, and kissed him.

The role reversal hit Ian like a slap – in a good way. It was easy to think of Alec as virginal, but that wasn't true. He'd just been awkward, kind, passive, and still so new to being with men. But this kiss spoke of passion, and skill, and a latent dominance that had Ian's toes curling in the sheets.

This wasn't supposed to happen. His good little boy toy was supposed to roll over and put his ass in the air, and let Ian pretend that his world wasn't hanging by a thread. He wasn't

211

supposed to slide his tongue between Ian's lips, or scrape his fingernails across Ian's nipples, or melt his insides in a matter of seconds.

The moment narrowed down to the points where their bodies connected: wet mouths sliding together, hands roving over chests and stomachs.

Alec gripped Ian's cock and stroked it, firm and steady, with a boldness he'd never shown before now.

"Getting the hang of this, are we?" Ian asked, voice ragged.

"I'm falling in love with you."

Another wet, messy kiss.

"Oh, don't say that, darling," Ian said. "You don't want to do that."

"You're beautiful," Alec said. Another kiss. "And you make me feel...*amazing.*" Kiss. "Don't treat me like this." Kiss. "Please." Kiss. "I can be—"

Ian captured his head in his hands and pushed back into the kiss, surging against Alec's lips, as his hips bucked in helpless reaction to the tight grip on his cock.

"Don't plead," he said. "I can't take pleading."

He felt Alec smile against his lips. "Good to know."

If he kept stroking, Ian wasn't going to have the strength to push him away and make it last, carry out what he'd intended for them to do. There were sparks in his veins and the most pleasant fog rolling through his head. There were no worries, only the bed, and Alec, and the way he felt.

"What can you be?" Ian prompted, and he didn't recognize the breathless sound of his own voice. "What were you going to say?"

Alec nibbled at his chin, and then soothed the sting with a pass of his tongue. "I can be a good boy," he murmured. "I can be whatever you want."

"Oh, fuck," Ian breathed, hands tightening on Alec's waist, his cock kicking in Alec's hand.

Whatever he wanted.

And what did he want?

"Fuck me," he said, and his blood sang at the idea. "I want you to fuck me."

Alec's hand stilled, and when he pulled back, his expression was rapturous.

Ian slipped his arms around him, drew him in even closer, so he was straddling his lap. "Come on, darling." He nipped at his throat. "I showed you how before, remember?"

Alec shivered, voice raw and deep when he said, "Yeah. God, *yeah*."

~*~

"Okay, so I'm glad we came home for that," Whitney said as she smoothed her shirt down her front.

Tango – cock tucked away and zipped up, sitting up on the side of the bed with a smoke hanging off his lip – pushed his hands through his hair and said, "Yeah."

She made a face, but she was grinning underneath it, he could tell. He kept waiting for the bad feelings to hit; for what they'd done to become this awful poisonous thing that would claw its way between them. But it hadn't and it didn't, as Whitney tidied her hair with her fingers.

"Then again, since we came out of the back and then left right away, I figure everyone knows what was going on anyway." Her grin widened.

Something warm and content settled in his chest. "Shit, you're gonna have a reputation now," he said, grinning back.

She chuckled. "First time for everything, huh?"

Tango licked the ends of his fingers and pinched out his cig, tucking it behind his ear. "Baby, come here," he said quietly.

When she started to sit beside him, he caught her hand and steered her down so she was sideways on his lap. He loved the weight and feel of her there. All he wanted at the moment was to gather her close, tuck them under the covers, and go to sleep together. But he didn't want to pass out on her right away, not after what she'd shared with him. *Him*, of all people, for the first time.

"You're calling me baby," she said, eyes warm as she stared down into his face.

"Is that okay?"

"I like it."

He circled an arm around her waist, keeping her close. "What happened..." he started, awkwardly. "That wasn't just because I was horny. I need you to know that."

She smiled and reached to trace his eyebrow with her thumb. "I think I know that."

"Yeah?"

"Yeah."

He gave her a squeeze. "Let's get cleaned up."

~*~

Ian couldn't remember the last time someone had meticulously taken him apart. Couldn't remember the last time he'd *allowed* it. When he escaped The Nest, he'd been too determined to carve all traces of weakness from his life. No more getting fucked – he was going to be the one to do the fucking. And Kev had always taken it so sweetly; he'd never stopped being the victim, poor sweet boy. He hadn't taken his life in-hand the way Ian had.

But now...

Now.

It was the wine, and it was the heartache, and it was the strangely electrifying way Alec had defied him with sweetness and passion.

Ian kicked his head back against the pillow, awash with sensation. "More," he said, and now he was the one pleading. He should have felt panicked, the way his legs were drawn up, the way they were spread open, leaving him vulnerable. But all he felt was want. That dangerous, violent want, vibrating in every inch of his skin, melting him from the inside out.

Alec had two slicked-up fingers in him, stretching him open slow and gentle, the way Ian had taught him. He withdrew almost all the way, and added a third finger when he thrust in again.

214

Ian's nerve endings fired, a crackling energy he hadn't felt in so long. He'd loved this once upon a time. He loved it still, Alec palm-deep, twisting his fingers.

A high, keening sound slipped through Ian's lips. "There. Right there," he panted. "Fuck me. Come on. Now."

There was an acute emptiness as Alec's fingers withdrew. And then Alec's hand was on Ian's hip, and he was aligning them.

"*Yes*," Ian whispered, voice raw and trapped in the back of his throat. "*Now, now, yes, I want it.*"

The head of Alec's cock pushed in slowly, steadily, and though he'd been prepped, it was still an invasion. Ian closed his eyes and surrendered himself to it. The stretch, and the burn. The marvel of having someone *inside* him.

That was the secret, after all. He'd died inside a long time ago; he was only alive when he borrowed someone else's soul for a little while.

He forced his eyes open, just slits, so he could see Alec between his legs above him. See the lock of hair clinging to the sweat on his forehead; see the dazed way his eyes were trained where they were joined, his mouth open in awe.

Ian hooked his legs around Alec's waist and urged him closer.

"It's different, isn't it?" he managed to say. "What does it feel like, darling?"

Alec started to work in deeper, little rocking motions of his hips, in farther and farther on every forward nudge. "It…it feels…oh *God. Tight.* And…and *Jesus.*"

"You won't hurt me," Ian choked out. "I won't break."

Alec dropped his head and started to really move, withdrawing and plunging back in again, hissing through his gritted teeth. "Jesus *Christ*," he whispered, hands leaving bruises on Ian's hips.

He was beautiful, slender and almost-delicate, lost to the sensation. Lost *in* Ian.

Yes, *Jesus Christ.* Ian closed his eyes again and let everything go, let a beautiful boy fuck him until he forgot how to feel anything besides the drag and press of skin.

~*~

Tango didn't want to keep his hands to himself. He'd always felt that emptiness inside him after sex, the need for physical human comfort in the afterglow. It was more acute, now, with Whitney.

So he didn't try to deny himself. Not at this point.

Not in the shower, wrapped in the steam of hot water, and gentle soaped-up hands. There was nothing sexual in it, and Tango didn't want there to be. An unhurried and genuine care between them. He could almost shut his eyes and convince himself that she was washing him clean; the suds lifting the sins from his skin and rinsing them down the drain.

They dressed in pajamas and climbed into bed, warm, loose-limbed and content.

"You okay?" he asked, and heard the thickness in his voice.

She covered his hands with her small ones. "I'm good," she murmured. "Really good."

His heart gave a little bump, and his belly twisted with a sudden excitement, something between naughtiness and childlike joy. Could they do this? Maybe they could do this. Maybe it was okay to want it, and reach for it, and take hold of it.

He fell asleep with his face in her hair.

~*~

Ian lit a cigarette on his lip, took a single drag, and then passed it over to Alec. Alec's movements were languid and drowsy; his hand lifted as if too heavy to take the cigarette, finger sure and content around the filter, and against Ian's finger.

"I had no idea," he said, voice dreamy, and drew on the cigarette.

"Hmm."

They lay on their backs, staring up at the ceiling, the smell of cooling sweat and sex coiled around them. Ian had expected an immediate rush of regret, but so far, it hadn't come. He tingled pleasantly with aftershocks, and wasn't even bothered by the tacky mess cooling on his stomach. He'd wash up later: a nice long, hot shower. Maybe he'd invite Alec to join him. Maybe he'd drop to his knees on the slick tile floor. Maybe he'd chain Alec to the foot of the bed.

So many possibilities.

The sheets rustled as Alec turned onto his side, facing Ian, propped up on an elbow. He was careful to hold the cigarette clear of skin and bedding. He was beautiful, hair mussed, lips pink and swollen, face slack with exhaustion, eyes still full of glad sparks.

"Who are you thinking of right now?" he asked, voice low and secretive.

"You," Ian said, and it wasn't a lie. "Only you, love."

Alec tucked his face down onto Ian's shoulder and exhaled deeply, contentedly, sated and sleepy.

Ian took the cigarette back. "You'll set us on fire," he chided, but not unkindly.

"Already did that," Alec said into his shoulder.

Against all belief that it was possible at the moment, Ian smiled.

~*~

The nightmare rolled into his dreamscape as fog, low and dense around his ankles. Tango was dreaming of formless expanses, fields and creeks, and flowers bobbing in the breeze. And then suddenly he was back in the dorm room, on the bed. Whitney was under him, and he had a hand around her throat, tightening, tightening, tightening…

He came awake with a low shout, jackknifing upright in bed. He closed his eyes to stop the room from spinning, and became aware that he'd sweated through his shirt and boxers, and was slick all over with fresh sweat.

Whitney. Shit, had he…?

He glanced over and saw that she was safe, whole, stirring awake thanks to his yell, but unharmed. She pushed her hair back and eased up onto an elbow, blinking in the dim light. "Kev?"

He let out a deep breath and pressed his shaking hands to his knees. "I shouldn't have skipped my session."

Nineteen

Session 5

Kev learned to suppress his gag reflex. He learned how to use his hands. He learned how to wring gasps and sighs of pleasure from the men Miss Carla put in front of him.

When he was twelve, it was time for The Nest.

Miss Carla went with him the first night. He was marched up from the basement by Max, his hands cuffed together behind him; a normal occurrence at this point. He knew that it was nighttime when he saw the black sky through the barred windows. And he knew something was badly wrong when he saw Miss Carla leave her bedroom, dressed in a short, black dress dotted with sequins, her hair piled on top of her head, her makeup dark and almost unrecognizable.

"There he is," she said, clapping her hands together, smiling. "You're in for a treat tonight, my little Loverboy."

It was the first time he'd been outdoors in four years. He was assaulted by the crispness of the air, the sound of cicadas and night birds, the scent of car exhaust and rotting garbage, and a dozen other beautiful outside smells, all things from road kill to an early leaf fire. It was early autumn, he decided, judging the temperature and the state of the dry leaves rattling overhead.

If his hands had been free, he would have slit Max's throat just to have a few seconds more in this paradise of bad neighborhood hell.

But his hands were bound, and he was shoved into the backseat of a black van, and buckled in, wrists caught behind him in a way that made his shoulders ache.

Miss Carla slid into the passenger seat and turned to regard him over her shoulder. "This is a real honor, you know," she said. "The other boys aren't ready yet. You're special, though. I hope you appreciate that."

He wanted to spend the trip hating her, but instead spent it marveling at the city sliding past his window. Buildings with lights glowing behind the windows, yards with mown grass, businesses with parking lots full of cars: gas stations, Dollar Generals, and dry cleaners. The alleys they passed grew darker, the streets littered with half-dead cars and questionable pedestrians on the corners. A dark part of town.

Then Max turned into a parking lot behind a large, low, inscrutable building with pink neon flaring out from its sides into the night. Kev had one fleeting glimpse of a sign: The Cuckoo's Nest.

~*~

His cuffs were removed once they were inside a long, dark hallway. Max was behind him, and Miss Carla in front.

He didn't even consider trying to escape.

"This is where you change," Miss Carla said, stopping outside a door that read *Dressing*. "With the others. Go on in, and Ian will get you set up. He knows what you're wearing." She opened the door, shoved him through, and then shut it behind him; he heard a lock click into place.

He froze.

He stood just inside a long, narrow, dark room, illuminated by the round light bulbs affixed around mirror after mirror, set above tables flanking one wall. Dressing tables, loaded with vials, and pots, and compacts, makeup, like Mama had worn, like Miss Carla inexpertly smeared across her papery face.

And at each table, peering into the mirrors, applying paint and eyeliner, boys. Boys just like him. Some young, some older, all thin, and lithe, and pretty to the point of pain.

They didn't seem to notice him at first, and he had a chance to lean against the locked door and catch his breath, try and slow his galloping heart. But then the nearest boy lifted his head, his black-ringed eyes alighting on Kev, and his mouth pursed in an interested O of surprise.

"Ooh, fresh meat," he said, and moved toward Kev, snapping his fingers to get the attention of the boy next to him.

220

Two of them advanced on the door, dressed in little shorts that might as well have been underwear, bare-chested, done up as artfully as women with kohl and lip gloss, their long hair slicked back behind their shoulders. They were older than him, though he couldn't tell by how much, going by their slim figures and flawless faces. He only knew they had broad shoulders, and that their ribs stood out from lack of feeding – as his did. They moved with a quiet grace, quick, unexpected, fluid movements, nothing like the telegraphed violence of Max and his cohorts back at the house.

"Look at you, sweetheart," the first one said, bracing a shoulder against the door and leaning over Kev. "What's your name, baby?"

The endearments made Kev cringe, because Miss Carla always used them so freely, but they didn't hold any malice in this young man's mouth. They seemed…kind. Maybe. It had been so long since kindness, it was hard to tell.

"K-kev," he stuttered, trying to shrink down into the collar of his ratty t-shirt.

"Hi, Kev," the second one said, his tone and his smile warm. "I'm Andy."

"And I'm Jared," the first one said. "Did Carla just drop you off?"

"Y-yeah. She said – she said Ian knew what I–" He had to dampen his lips; they were so dry they were sticking together. "What I had to w-wear?"

"Oh sweetie." Jared slid his arm across Kev's narrow shoulders. "He's down here, come on."

Kev let himself be towed along the hall of dressing mirrors, down to one at the end.

"Queen Vicki," Jared called in a sing-song voice, maneuvering Kev at his side, so he had a view.

The young man leaning over the table was as thin as the others, each bump of his bare spine prominent beneath his porcelain skin as he bent low and fitted what looked like a cut-off drink straw to one nostril. A neat line of white powder marked the wood, and as Kev watched, the young man covered his exposed nostril with a finger, inhaled deeply, and sucked all the white powder up through the straw, head moving to the side as he followed the line. He lifted his head, wiped his nose, shook his head, and sniffed loudly. Then checked his reflection in the mirror. He had long reddish hair that fell down past his shoulders, slick and shiny as oil poured from a bottle, and wide blue-green eyes ringed in careful strokes of black kohl.

He was the most beautiful person, man or woman, that Kev had ever seen.

Those blue-green eyes met Kev's gaze via the mirror. His voice, when he spoke, sounded like something from a movie, his English accent with its crisp pronunciation. "Fresh meat, I see."

"Carla wants you to dress him," Jared said, gave Kev's shoulders a squeeze, and slipped away.

Kev took a deep breath, resolved to be brave, and then couldn't form any words. He wasn't brave. He was terrified, and a little bit enthralled, and he had no idea what was going on.

The young man studied him a moment, head cocked, and then his expression softened, beneath his perfectly applied makeup. "What's your name, darling?"

"K-kev."

He smiled, flashing straight white teeth, the kind of smile that belonged between the pages of a magazine. "Hello, Kev. Let's get you dressed."

~*~

Kev had no idea what to make of Ian Byron. Never before had a man used endearments like "darling," and "love," and "baby," with him. He'd thought – incorrectly, he supposed – that tender pet names were women's things. He'd only ever been "champ," or "sport," or "buddy," around adult men. If asked right then, he would have said he preferred the sweet names. But Ian didn't ask, only used them, and pushed through a rack of clothes, occasionally glancing over his shoulder to give Kev a thorough scrutiny, head tilted, eyes narrowed.

"Hmm," he said, finally pulling something off the rack – a pair of pants – and holding them up to Kev, one eye closed. "Yes." He nodded. "These will do." He reached and caught Kev's hand in his own. His fingers were long, smooth, and warm. "This way, love."

There were a half dozen clothes racks, and behind them, a large three-way mirror, flanked by lamps that cast warm, buttery puddles of light across the floor. Two waifish boys stood studying their reflections, primping and pouting at themselves, reaching to adjust an eyelash, a smudge of clear lip gloss.

The scene hit Kev somewhere low in his belly. A place that made him warm and short of breath. How strange it should have seemed, to see boys not much older than him at the mirror this way, like ladies. But there was an undeniable masculine grace to their movements; there was no mistaking their gender. Only a forbidden, subtle eroticism about the tableau.

"Give us a minute?" Ian asked, and the boys withdrew.

One of them gave Kev a long look as they passed, but said nothing.

"Alright, my little love," Ian said when they were alone, urging Kev up to the mirror with a hand on his shoulder. "Take everything off, and get into these."

He'd long since stopped being modest about undressing in front of others; there was no privacy amongst the boys in the basement. He shimmied out of his threadbare clothes and left them folded neatly over against the wall. The pants Ian had picked out were some fake approximation of leather, tight, and hard to slide his legs inside. He wriggled, and struggled, and finally got them in place and fastened. They were cut much lower than his jeans, sitting just beneath his hip bones.

What the hell was going on?

When he lifted his head to search for Ian, Kev saw that he'd carried over a stool and a little tray loaded with colored wells, brushes, and pencils. Like an art kit, but the smell told him it was makeup; he thought of the scent of powder on Miss Carla's cheek when she tapped her face and told him to give her a kiss, and he had to swallow sudden nausea.

Ian looked at him with gentle eyes, and patted the stool. "Come here, baby. I promise it won't hurt."

Once upon a time, Kev might have dug in his heels and refused. But he was a good little loverboy these days, and he always did as he was told.

He settled on the stool and Ian crept in close, kneeling between his open legs, close enough for Kev to see the vivid striations of his irises, to smell the light, almost floral scent he'd dabbed onto his skin.

Ian took Kev's chin in one hand, fingertips light against his jaw, and eased his head first to one side, then the other, examining his features. "A light touch, I think. Bring out your eyes. They're beautiful." He gave Kev a fleeting smile, then let go of him and reached for a brush on the tray. "Close your eyes."

He did. The brush touched his eyelid, a faint kiss of pressure, fleeting, like butterfly wings. And in that moment, with his eyes shut, with the warmth of Ian so close to him, he allowed the reality of the moment to fall away. He let himself pretend that this small show of kindness was but one of many, that he was loved, that there was someone in his life who would look out for him, and treat him tenderly. Tenderness – some nights, staring at the ceiling rafters above him, he thought he might kill for a little tenderness.

"All done," Ian said, and his voice was so close, Kev swore he could feel it against his face.

He opened his eyes, and yes, there was Ian, close enough to…

To what? What was it he wanted to do?

Ian touched his thumb to the corner of Kev's mouth, and he smiled, soft and slow. "Perfect."

Kev took a breath that shivered in his lungs. "Ian," he said, quietly, just a whisper, "what am I supposed to do?"

"Oh, love." Ian's expression grew heavy; he stroked Kev's hair. "In just a few minutes, Carla will come for you, and she'll walk with you out into the club, and she's going to introduce you to some gentlemen." His hand slid down Kev's neck, out to his shoulder. "They're going to exclaim over you, and they're going to want you to sit in their laps, and sip their drinks." His face spasmed, almost crumpled, then smoothed again, that mask of tender sadness. His hand slid down Kev's arm, cupped the inward curve of his waist. "And then one of them, or maybe even two," he continued, "will take you into one of the back rooms. And there will be a bed without pillows, and soft pink lights along the walls. And they're going to touch you."

At this, his hand moved to Kev's thigh, and then shifted inward, and he palmed the soft shape of Kev's cock through the leather pants.

Kev huffed out a startled breath.

"They'll touch you here, and…other places. They'll tell you to do things, and they'll expect you to mind them."

Kev's eyes pricked with tears, even as he felt a not-uncomfortable tightness in his pants. A sharp, tingling, acute awareness of his sex he hadn't felt before.

Ian continued to touch him, massaging him with the heel of his hand. "Listen to them, do what they say, and they won't hurt you."

Kev blinked hard.

"Kev, Kevin, listen to me." Ian leaned close, hand cupped almost protectively over his cock. "You must listen to them. You have to be a good boy, okay? When Carla takes you out, I want you to look at the stage. I'll be up there – look at me. I want you to look at me. I've been where you are, and I got through it, okay? Just like you're going to get through it. Just remember, no matter how terrible it is, it only lasts a little while."

~*~

The club was called The Cuckoo's Nest, and Kev could have never conceived of such a place, in his world of the basement and Miss Carla's dusty bedroom. It was a marvel: black walls and carpet, and low, multi-colored lights that cast all the chairs and couches in an otherworldly glow. The room seemed cavernous, the bar glittering and jewel-toned against one long wall, the stages lit from beneath in bright flares of pale blue and pink. Men lounged on the furniture, the smell of cigarette and cigar smoke heavy on the air.

The boys from backstage, in pants like Kev's, some of them in shorts, one of them with a sequined tank top, danced on two of the three circular stages, limbs fluid, hips gyrating in a way that Kev had never imagined, and couldn't seem to look away from.

His eyes were snatched, though, almost against their will, by a thin beam of bright blue light that sprouted up from the Lucite floor of the very center stage, right in front of him, a solid bar of light that went all the way up to the ceiling, hugging the silver pole mounted there, so the metal seemed pure energy.

Anticipation moved through the crowd; conversations skittered and broke off. The music cut out, and then started again, something sinuous and exotic, the low baseline a thump through the floor that tickled at the base of Kev's throat.

A figure materialized from the shadows, in the center of the main stage. A spot of bone-white skin, striking through the blue. A foot, an ankle, a long slender leg. Slender hips and a narrow ribcage, etched with deep shadows. Shoulders, lean arms. And a face carved from glass, long sleek auburn hair.

Ian wore nothing but a pair of boxer-briefs made from some unknown shimmery fabric, and a white feather boa draped across his shoulders. In the blue light, his makeup lent his face an ethereal glow, his eyes huge and luminous, lips dark, as though bloodied.

He gripped the pole with one hand, hooked his lower leg around it, and began a slow, artistic sweep across the stage, pivoting around the pole, seeming to float, his thin body flashing lean planes of muscle, and the hard curves of bone. At once delicate, beautiful, and powerful, the contrast of the masculine and the feminine working in breathtaking harmony.

Kev couldn't look away.

And then the man on whose lap he was sitting breathed in his ear. "Gets ya all hot and bothered, don't it?" he asked with a wheezing, smoke-flavored laugh. His fat hand dropped down into Kev's lap. "Let's find us a quiet spot, sweetheart."

~*~

He couldn't stop shivering. Kev cupped his pointed elbows in his hands and hugged himself hard, trying to ease the tremors that wracked him. But it was no use – the chill had nothing to do with the temperature; it was rooted somewhere inside him, somewhere small, broken, and screaming, that smelled like fear sweat and the fluid the fat man had left to leak from his small, violated body.

He staggered into the changing area, legs weak, stomach churning, teeth chattering. What did he do now? Where did he go? Was Carla pleased?

He wished he was dead. He wanted to lie down on the floor, close his eyes, and cease to exist.

In the rush of boys moving back and forth, trailing boas, jackets, and sharp-smelling cologne, one cut through the crush and knelt down in front of Kev.

Ian.

He reached to smooth his hair back, fine-featured face creased with worry. "Oh darling," he murmured. "It was terrible, wasn't it?"

Kev bit his lip, nodded, and couldn't speak for fear of bursting into noisy, wet tears.

"I know, I know." Ian looped his long, dancer's arms around Kev and pulled him into a tender hug. "I'm so sorry, my love. The first night is always the worst."

In that moment, the promise of more nights, of more fat men, and deeper violations was crowded into insignificance by the simple kindness of Ian's arms, and the steady strong beating of his heart against Kev's face.

~*~

Sitting on his sofa, chain-smoking, one of Ava's peanut butter chocolate chip cookies untouched in his free hand, he recalled the exact terror of his first night at The Nest. And the smell of the scent dabbed along Ian's throat. The way the unnatural light had hit his eyes. The weight and shape of his hands against his painfully innocent skin.

"I fell in love with him that first night," he said, exhaling smoke. "I just didn't know it then."

Over on the couch, Mercy watched him with a strained expression, gaze heavy with sympathy, and something like doubt.

Tango rolled the hand with the cookie, so his wrist was exposed, the two white scars glimmering in the sun. "I would have done this a long time ago, if it wasn't for Ian."

Mercy took a deep breath and let it out in a rush. "Kev. I want you to call that doctor Ghost told you about."

The scars flared and dimmed as he rotated his arm, lighting strikes across his skin. "Yeah. I think maybe that's a good idea."

Twenty

She only had an hour for lunch, Whitney reminded herself, and took another bite of her sandwich. Peanut butter and raspberry preserves on whole wheat from the bakery below the apartment. Kev's apartment. Her temporary apartment.

She couldn't drag her thoughts away from the session he'd been scheduled to have that morning. She kept wondering if last night had been a help to him; if the simmering heat of post-coital peace had sustained him through their few stolen hours of sleep, the way it had for her. Even now she felt heavy-limbed, languid, unworried by the dirty look her supervisor had given her earlier.

She took another bite and checked her phone where it rested on the table at her elbow. No new messages. One-ten. Fifteen minutes left of her lunch break.

The childish simplicity of her PB&J and Coke comforted her in the way all things comforted in the wake of sex and good sleep.

Please let it have helped him, she thought, and then her phone rang.

She nearly dropped it in her haste to answer; the screen told her it was Kev, so she greeted him with a warm, somewhat-lovestruck, "Hi."

The reciprocated warmth in his tone was unmistakable. "Hi, baby."

A beat of silence passed, and it wasn't awkward, and didn't beg to be filled. A quiet acknowledgement that things had been forever changed between them, and that it had been a *good* change. She felt the goodness glowing with great certainty deep beneath her skin; imagined she saw it pulsing through the veins on the white inside of her wrist.

"How was your session?" she asked at last.

"It was good. Really good. That's why I called you. There's something I think I have to do."

Her pulse quickened. "Okay."

"I got us another invitation to dinner. Emmie said it'd be great if you could bring dessert."

~*~

He'd heard it said before, but he hadn't believed it until now: sometimes making a firm decision about what to do next was as emotionally beneficial as taking physical action. The answer had come to him in the living room, while he contemplated the scars of his self-loathing, and Mercy watched him with a fascinated sort of pity and terror over what he might do.

"I think you were right at first," he'd said. "I do think I have to get all the poison out. But I think I need to do something more, too. I think I need to *make things better.*" For himself, for Whitney, and for Ian.

After Mercy left, he spent fifteen minutes scratching out feverish notes on scrap paper, listing the things he wanted to accomplish. This was it, he knew; this was the path to getting past it all.

He'd made a phone call to Walsh, and another to Emmie, and then he went to work. He threw himself back into the swing of the shop, smoking cigs when his hands shook, ribbing Carter back when the young member tried to crack a few hesitant jokes.

He texted the Briar Hall address to Whitney and headed off to meet her there at ten after five, night falling with relentless force, the sky dark and star-studded.

The farm driveway was illuminated by real gas lamps, flickering in the dusk; the barn windows glowed with warm light, the hulking building somehow cozy in its nest of landscaping shrubs and established trees. The sand of the arenas glowed like the surface of the moon.

He parked his bike up at the house, behind Emmie's truck, and beside Whitney's car. She was standing by her driver door, covered cake plate in her arms. She couldn't wave, but she smiled at him; he caught a glimpse of it in his headlamp before he switched it off.

"Hi."

"Hi."

An effervescence like champagne tumbled between them in the cold evening, and for the first time Tango didn't hesitate to do what he wanted. He swung off the bike and dumped his helmet in one fluid motion; caught Whitney around the waist with one arm and drew her in for a fast, warm kiss. Even brief contact with her lips sent sparks darting along his nerve endings. The rabid, animal part of his brain urged him to crack her mouth open and dive inside with his tongue, put his hands under her clothes, push her back against her car and –

He pulled back and clamped his lips together so she wouldn't hear the desperate sound climbing up the back of his throat.

Whitney's eyes sparkled in the darkness, gathering stray flecks of light like bright magnets. "This place," she breathed with a little laugh, "is incredible."

Tango lifted his head and cast a glance across the shadowy driveway, the looming stone house, the view of the illuminated barn down the hill, and the sprawling tapestry of pastures beyond. He'd been stuck in his head for so long, he wasn't sure he'd ever stood back and taken a proper look at the farm, really absorbed how stunning it was.

"Yeah," he agreed, "it is."

"So this is where Walsh lives."

Tango wasn't sure if they'd ever met, and he knew Emmie hadn't been at dinner last night. "Yeah." He didn't say "you'll like him," because he had no idea if she would. It seemed like a good possibility, because Whitney was the sort of person who liked people. But Walsh was quiet, and serious, and women sometimes didn't take to him straight off.

"Is he rich?" Whitney asked in a stage whisper.

"Not with money, no." He put his arm around her waist and steered her up the front walk. "The club bought this place. And Emmie used to be the barn manager. Still is, I guess, she just lives in the big house now."

Whitney chuckled. "Good for her."

"Right?"

Shane answered the door when they rang the bell, in jeans and a UT sweatshirt.

"Feeling local?" Tango asked him.

Shane shrugged. "It's not so bad, your Tennessee."

No. He guessed it wasn't.

~*~

Five-twenty. Ian needed to make three phone calls: one to New York, one to LA, one to El Paso, Texas. Three delicate clients who wanted to speak to him personally, hear him smooth their feathers and assure them they were important to his business. Another endless day in the life of a mogul who dabbled in all things illegal.

Around him, his office loomed silent and beautiful, full of furniture and knick-knacks he'd paid too much for, but which held no emotional significance for him. He'd wanted to build an empire – and he had; a giant fuck-you to the world that had so royally fucked him.

He sat up and reached for the decanter on the corner of his desk. Poured himself a finger of Scotch.

An empire, and what did he have to show for it? Manipulating the world brought only an empty sort of satisfaction.

A soft knock sounded at the door and then it eased open. Alec poked his head through, hair perfectly styled, glasses sitting square on his nose, the picture of professionalism.

"Sir? I have New York on the line for you."

"Tell them I'll call them back tomorrow."

Alec's brows jumped above the rims of his glasses. He pushed the door a little wider and said, "Sir?"

"Go tell them. And then come back."

Alec withdrew, wide-eyed and confused.

Ian swallowed the Scotch down, one long burn in his throat.

Alec was back a moment later, hands held at a nervous angle in front of him.

"Shut the door, please."

He did, and came to stand in front of Ian's desk, delicious in his skinny black pants and gray sweater.

"Do you know who the client in New York is?" Ian asked him.

"Marco Mancini."

"Yes, but do you know *what he is?*"

Face pale with uncertainty, Alec said, "Your...client?"

"He's a mafia don. I sell him cocaine and marijuana."

Poor sweet Alec; his face went from pale to bleached-bone white. His lower lip trembled as he sucked in a fast breath. "No," he protested weakly. "You...you..."

"I'm a drug dealer, darling, yes. I also own several porn studios, which, while not illegal, is admittedly unsavory. Oh, and a handful of strip clubs. A fairly successful escort business – it's New York-based, of course. There's not a market for that here in Hicksville." His heart thundered against his ribs; his hands were clammy and he wrapped them both around his cool glass so Alec couldn't see them shaking.

He sent a mocking smile to his young lover. "There you have it. I sell drugs and sex. All I need now is to sponsor a band, and we can add rock 'n' roll to the mix."

Alec's blue eyes seemed huge through the lenses of his glasses.

Softly, Ian said, "This is the part where you hate me."

Alec stood blinking at him for a long moment, then drew in a deep breath that jacked up his shoulders. "No." His voice wobbled. Then, firmer: "No. No, Ian, I don't hate you."

Ian was...dumbfounded. "Why not?"

Alec shook his head, a small rueful smile breaking across his face. "I just can't."

Ian sucked in a breath. "Feel like dinner?"

~*~

Walsh's wife Emmie was very small, very blonde, and very pregnant, her belly not at all hidden by her loose cream sweater.

"I have a whole new respect for mares," she joked as she and Whitney sliced and arranged chocolate cake onto dessert plates. "And they do it for eleven months instead of nine."

"Well that sounds terrible."

"Eleven months, and no epidural."

Whitney made an "ouch" face and set a fork on each plate. "Makes a girl glad she's not a horse."

"Hmm." Emmie licked a spot of frosting off her thumb and slanted a look at Whitney that was suddenly assessing. Not in a cruel way, but in a shrewd one. Horsewoman look, Whitney guessed. "You doing okay?" she asked, and it wasn't the rote "hi, how are you" of their meeting an hour ago. A real question, one between girls, meant for the snatched moments when the boys did their biker thing. Another of those small moments that meant so much to Whitney, being included in the sisterhood.

Whitney took a deep breath. "Yeah, I'm good, actually. This is all a little–" She gestured to indicate the moment, the club.

"Weird, and different, and scary?" Emmie guessed.

"Kinda. Yeah."

"Trust me, there are still mornings I wake up and wonder how the hell I ended up married to an outlaw biker. I'm not sure it's ever going to seem logical in the context of the world." She shrugged. "But we're happy, and it makes sense to me. So. Whatever. You'll get there."

Whitney smiled. "Thanks."

~*~

"I need to get in touch with someone in London," Tango said.

He sat with Walsh and Shane at the three chairs at the head of the long dining table, drinking vodka on the rocks.

Shane's brows gave a little jump of interest, face staying impassive. "What sort of someone?"

"Someone's parents. Or siblings. Whatever family he's got left."

Walsh sent him one of his flat, unnerving, calculating looks. "Just a stab in the dark here, but I'm thinking you don't have that many English friends."

Tango felt his face heat, but he shook his head. "A mutual friend of ours, actually."

Walsh and Shane shared a glance. "Ghost wouldn't like it," Walsh said. "You understand that?"

"Yeah, and I don't care. I'm not asking for club reasons. This is personal. I know Shaman from..." It frightened him, if he thought about it, that his brothers had no idea what sort of past he shared with Ian. They'd cut the black dog off his back and throw him to the wolves in a heartbeat. "From before," he finished. "I want to find his family. Let them know he's still alive."

"In hopes his daddy will come drag him back home by the ear?" Shane asked, ghost of a smile playing across his lip.

"Because he needs them," Tango said, making firm eye contact with both half-brothers.

Walsh swirled the contents of his glass, ice cubes clacking together. Thinking. "Albie could help, I'm sure."

Tango released a breath he didn't know he'd been holding.

"You have anything for us to go on?"

"No, just a last name. Byron."

Walsh nodded; he looked like his mind was made up, and when that happened, he wasn't usually dissuaded. "That's enough."

"Thanks," Tango said, and felt a surge of lightness in his chest. It was a start. It wasn't much, but God, it was a start, and that was more than he'd had in a long time.

~*~

Ian's favorite restaurant in the city was a tiny wedge of space snugged in behind a larger, flashier steakhouse. He took people he wanted to rattle into the steakhouse. He'd only ever gone into the nameless, impossibly chic little restaurant in back by himself.

Well, and with Bruce, because he was always lingering in the shadows with his gun and his ham fists.

The place had no name that he'd ever seen – not above the door, nor printed on the menus, the menus themselves changing between each visit. It was multi-national and gourmet, but all the ingredients that didn't need to be imported were locally grown, organic, farm to table. The interior was simple, unadorned, but incredibly elegant in its clean lines and low lighting.

They were shown to a table in the deep corner, where it was dark save the three flickering candles in glass lamps on the table, and the hidden can lights above that had filters that turned the floors and tabletops into galaxies of pinprick stars. The hostess was to be their waitress too, and she carried a bottle of wine as she escorted them to the table, uncorked it, and filled the two waiting glasses before melting into the dark and stars and leaving them to their menus.

Alec glanced around in obvious wonderment. "Oh wow," he breathed. "This place is…" His gaze came to Ian's, glasses painted with tiny stars. "What's it called?"

"I don't know, and I imagine that's the point." Ian had to smile, a soft brush of warmth teasing at his belly as he watched Alec examine his wineglass like it was magic.

"Do you come here a lot?"

"Only ever by myself," Ian admitted, and was surprised when his voice caught, a betraying snag of emotion he would have rather kept hidden.

Alec studied him a moment, the glamour effect of his glasses hiding his expression. Finally, he said, "So what do you recommend?" and lifted his menu.

Ian let his eyes trail down the list of offerings, and realized he hadn't thought about Kev all day.

~*~

"You want to walk down and see the horses?" Kev asked when they were standing beside her car, the cold night tugging at their hair and jackets.

Whitney's heart gave a girlish flutter at the idea. She wasn't convinced there had ever been a little girl in the world who hadn't longed for a pony. But she said, "Would that be okay with Emmie, you think?"

He snorted. "I'm pretty sure Camille was conceived in that barn. She won't mind us just looking. And her working student lives up above. Becca. She hasn't turned the lights out yet, so I say it's fair game."

She blushed a little, thinking about Mercy and Ava entangled and pressed up against the front of a horse stall. "Conceived? Really?"

"I think Becca kinda walked in on them."

"Oh God." She laughed.

"So yes?" He reached into his jacket pocket and came out with three carrots. "I have treats."

"Then yes."

She slipped her arm through his and together they walked down the gently sloping driveway, listening to the calls of whippoorwills and the bone-dry rattling of bare limbs overhead. Their breath misted, white clouds visible in the ambient light cast by the glowing barn windows.

Whitney wrapped the moment up in silk and laid it in a special place in her memory, a little chest dedicated to perfect, peaceful, important moments.

The double barn doors stood open a crack, warm champagne-colored light spilling between them, and Kev hooked a hand around the edge of one and pushed it wider. A horse whickered, welcoming treat-bearing visitors.

"Wow," Whitney said, not knowing how else to describe the long aisle stretched out before her. Rich, golden brown tongue-and-groove paneling. Black iron grillwork. Sleek, well-groomed heads of all colors bobbing over stall doors. She spotted several open-fronted, empty stalls with black mat floors and hose racks she thought must be for bathing. A partially-open door through which she could see saddles and riding paraphernalia. The aisle itself was brick, and as she started down it, footfalls ringing, she glanced up and spotted a chandelier housed in the cupola.

"Okay," she said. "The house was gorgeous, but I think the barn might be even nicer. Talk about luxury horse living." She let out a low whistle, and several horses pricked their ears in interest. One, a shiny chestnut with a white face, bobbed his head, and she smiled.

"It's pretty unbelievable," Kev agreed. He broke a carrot into pieces and handed them to her; they were cold and damp from the fridge, fresh-smelling. "Here, hold your hand like this." He demonstrated with a carrot wedge balanced on a flat palm.

"Horse Whisperer over here," she said, smiling.

He blushed. "No. Em just showed me once. I kinda…I like being here. It's peaceful, with the animals…" He trailed off, high cheekbones going scarlet, staring down at his toes.

"I get it," Whitney said, touching his shoulder, drawing a smile out of him.

The vulnerability in his eyes was almost too much to look at. Almost. She couldn't have looked away if she wanted to.

She hauled her gaze toward the row of stalls. "We don't have enough for everyone," she lamented, and approached the inquisitive chestnut, who'd stopped bobbing his head in favor of staring fixedly at the carrots in her hands, nostrils flared as he caught their scent.

"Hiya, handsome," she said as she approached, carrot held as demonstrated. "Well, I'm assuming you're handsome and not pretty. I can't see the hardware," she said, snorting.

His name plate, shiny brass, read *Prince*. "Okay, so handsome it is."

He took the treat off her palm with a quick movement, the brush of his whiskers and damp velvet of his lips a surprise. She laughed in quiet shock. "For some reason I didn't think it would feel like that."

"Weird, huh?" Kev fed a carrot to the horse next to Prince, an obscenely large black one whose name plate read

Apollo. "This is Emmie's horse," he explained. "She's says he's Widowmaker, but I haven't seen it yet."

The horse nudged Kev's empty hand, ears flicking back and forth, thick, muscled neck shining under the barn lights.

"I wouldn't want to," Whitney said, shivering a little.

They moved down the line, handing out all the carrots they'd brought, stroking chestnut, and bay, and black, and gray noses. By the time they were done, and wiping the dampness of horse slobber off their hands onto their jeans, Whitney swore she could *feel* that her blood pressure was lower. It put her in a warm, fuzzy headspace, where the truth didn't seem so scary, and obstacles seemed surmountable. This, she realized, was why Emmie put up with the stall-mucking and the early mornings and the blazing afternoons on the arena sand. The way being around these animals made you feel like life was something you could take hold of by both hands, rather than a mere survival test.

"You ready to head home?" Kev asked.

"Yeah."

~*~

"Can I ask why?" Alec said, and his tone lacked all traces of accusation; he was only curious. He'd taken his glasses off and folded them away in his pocket, eyes pale and bright and a little unfocused, full of candlelight, lovely as the London summer sky Ian thought he'd forgotten how to miss.

Ian didn't need the question clarified. He sighed and pushed fingerling potatoes around his plate with his fork. They were drizzled in truffle butter and tasted like indulgence. His stomach cramped at the idea of another bite.

"I decided, years ago, that I wanted to be a wealthy man. And I knew that wasn't going to happen through normal channels." He sighed again. "I also wanted to be a powerful man. And no one has more power over people than the provider of their favorite vices."

Alec speared a fry on his fork tines, but made no move to eat it. His gaze grew raw, almost wounded. "Why did you want it? Money and power?"

Ian shrugged. "Every man wants it."

"But you're not every man," Alec returned, softly, dampening his lip with a slow swipe of his tongue that made Ian's knees tremble beneath the table.

"That's what you think," he tried to joke, but it fell flat.

"What happened to you that made you so angry?"

"Oh darling," Ian said on a broken breath. "That's not a story you tell the person you're sleeping with."

~*~

Whitney's fingers started to flicker against the steering wheel on the drive home: that familiar urge to pick up a paintbrush. The horses had inspired her in a visceral, artistic way, the kind of mania that hit hard and demanded she paint the moment she was within reach of her palette.

"I need to paint," she said as she climbed out of her car in the alley behind the bakery. "Like, right now."

"Is this an emergency?" Kev asked, and she saw the glint of his smile in the security light.

"Absolutely!"

He laughed and waved for her to lead the way up the iron staircase.

Whitney went straight to her art supplies, stacked neatly on the bookshelf beneath the window, and Kev headed for the kitchen.

"Nightcap?" he asked. And then, like he anticipated a protest, "Just a small one."

"Sure, why not."

Setting up her easel was a matter of a few brisk movements; a little push from the heel of her hand when one leg wanted to stick. She propped up a fresh canvas, no sketching, no planning, nothing, and slid her paint tubes from their case.

Kev was setting a small glass of wine on the coffee table for her by the time she had her browns and whites and a deep coal black selected.

"Thanks. I need to get—"

A paper cup of clean water landed beside the wine, and she sent him a grateful smile.

He smiled back. "Just don't get the two mixed up."

"That would be bad."

He sat down beside her on the couch and settled in to watch her work. She was self-conscious about her work, and normally the close observation would have left her twitchy. But Kev didn't feel like "observation." If anything, his warm, steady presence beside her had a grounding effect; she tended to drift at times, while painting.

The horse took shape in rough, bold strokes. She realized she couldn't get the anatomy – all the delicate angles of legs, shoulders, and hindquarters – accurate, so she went for an intentionally unrealistic look. Thick layers of color, lots of shadow, shaggy green grass covering the hooves she couldn't hope to capture.

"Wow," Kev said, and he sounded awed.

She glanced at him over her shoulder, vision blurry-edged from staring at the paper. His expression hit her in a vulnerable place: the softness in his eyes, the warm half-smile lifting one corner of his mouth.

"What?"

"I wish you'd take classes or be part of an art show or something," he said, tone wistful.

Whitney laughed, but it stuck a little in her throat, caught on uncertainty. "Why do you wish that?"

"Because you deserve some credit."

"I don't do it for credit."

"What if you could do something artistic for a living?"

"That's a nice dream, but not the sort of thing that ever happens."

"Look at Ava," he countered. "And Sam. Their art makes their living."

241

Whitney set her paintbrush down on the tray of her easel, careful not to smudge the tip against the paper. "You almost sound like you're trying to talk me into something."

"Yeah. I think I am." He pitched forward at the waist, elbows braced on his knees, gaze sparkling with some hopeful emotion she'd never seen in him before. "I've been thinking about some things. About me getting better. And I think I've been doing it all wrong."

"Okaaaaay."

"I'm fucked up. I get that. My brain broke a long time ago—"

"Kev."

"—And it's like I – we – have been trying to put it back together and fix it. Like all of a sudden I'm supposed to teach myself to not be depressed, and not want to shoot up, and to feel good about myself or something."

She couldn't argue that they hadn't been hoping for that, and hearing it put in blunt terms made her feel horrible and guilty. They *were* trying to fix him. Hearing him say it aloud made it seem more hopeless than ever. People weren't cracked china; you couldn't line up their pieces and adhere them with a little super glue.

"Kev, nobody thinks you're broken."

He gave her a look. "That's sweet – you're sweet – but don't lie. You all think that."

She bit her lip, unable to argue.

"So far," he continued, "I've been shit at working on me. And I'm just a giant waste of space."

"Please don't say that."

"But I can do good things for the people I care about. I can help them. I want to *do something*, Whit. I can't just sit on the couch and talk about what happened to me and expect that to do anything."

She took a deep breath and tried to stem her kneejerk defensive reaction – her defense *of him* because he seemed unwilling to defend himself in this situation – and tried to look at what he'd said objectively.

242

"That's really sweet of you," she started.

"Don't say 'no' yet." He reached into his back pocket and pulled out a crumpled section of newspaper. He smoothed it against his thigh and then held it out to her. "Read this."

It was a call for submissions at a small art show being held at the university, highlighting local, amateur artists. All mediums welcome, including crafts and sculpture.

"You're scouting art shows for me?"

He shrugged, and though a blush crept into his cheeks, he refused to get bashful and look away from her. "Someone has to. If you can get onto my case, then I can get onto yours."

It took her a second, blinking at him, to register the emotion building in her chest. It was...delight.

She grinned. "On your case?"

"Like all the time. It's getting kind of old." He grinned.

She wanted to throw her fist in the air and cheer, because Kev was actually mocking himself, making a joke out of his recovery. And maybe a professional would tell her that was unhealthy, but she didn't think it was. She thought, after all his moping, and hyperventilating, Kev grinning and sniping was a *huge* sign of progress.

"Okay." She settled back against the couch. "Who else is on the Kevin Estes Recovery To-Do List?"

He lifted his brows.

"You know what I mean. Who else are you wanting to help?"

His expression caught, a fast flicker of pain. "Ian, for starters."

Whitney felt her smile slip. She swallowed. "You can always talk about him, if you want. If that's something you need to do. I can handle that."

The smile he gave her was tight. "No offense, but I don't really think you're ready for the whole story."

She sighed. "You never know until you try to tell me."

"Yeah, but...I kinda don't want you to stop looking at me the way you do."

Her stomach clenched, down low, the way it had last night, when his hand was between her legs. Heat rippled beneath her skin, raising goosebumps. "What way do I look at you?" she asked.

"Like you want me."

The blue of his eyes, the loose hair framing his face – devastating.

She dampened her lips. "That's because I do."

~*~

He knew he was going to kiss her. He wasn't going to lunge across the couch and tackle her, wasn't going to fumble in his haste to initiate. The craving that hit him, as he stared at her across the couch – the want – was low, deep, and slow-burning. It felt...*sustainable*. It felt like the hot coals at the base of the fire, full of potential and patience.

He got up from the couch, and it was a revelation. He didn't have to rut mindlessly against her in the middle of the living room. He could *wait*.

"Gonna grab a shower," he said.

"Okay. I want to work a little more."

He took his time under the jets, working a good lather of soap, cleaning himself with extra care, actually using conditioner on his hair. The hot water felt heavenly in a way he didn't normally pause to enjoy, beating the tension out of his shoulders. When he got hard, he ignored it; he wasn't going to jerk off to guilty visions of Whitney when she was in the next room...and about to be in bed with him.

He tugged on an old pair of pajama pants and a tank top, and climbed under the covers, leaving the light on.

He had no idea he would fall asleep; so used to being tight and tense all the time, he'd assumed he would stay awake, and suddenly forced his eyes open as Whitney slid in beside him, wearing that stupid white sleep shirt he could see through.

Though, he'd done more than peer through her shirt last night.

Whitney stretched out on her side, head propped on her fist, facing him. "I didn't mean to wake you."

"I'm glad you did, though." He shifted closer to her, and felt her knee touch his beneath the covers, the skin-to-skin contact quietly electric. "What time is it?"

"A little after one."

"You shouldn't stay up so late."

"Thanks, Mom."

The kiss would be *now*, he knew, the pleasant anticipation reaching a hot high point in his belly. But it would be sweet, and slow, and none of the desperate things kissing had always been for him.

Telegraphing his movement, so she could roll away if she wanted to, he reached out and cupped the side of her head. When he urged her in, she came willingly, and the kiss was soft, and careful, almost chaste.

He hesitated a moment, their lips just brushing, and let Whitney decide.

Her hands curled into the front of his tank top. Her mouth pressed into his, warm, and open, her tongue flirting along his lower lip.

Tango let his mind go blank. Blocked out all his old trauma, his worries, his preconceived notions, and just listened to what Whitney was telling him with her body.

She wanted him. She wanted *this*.

He cradled the back of her skull in his hand, and kissed her again.

He'd always thought, for some reason, that finally being with her would be like a discordant shriek of violins; a mad rush, pawing, mouths smacking together and then apart. He'd thought the guilt would bite into him, and he'd have to drill her fast, furiously, before he could let himself hate what he was doing.

But this was…this was so easy. And so perfect. The way he drew her in even closer, let his tongue dance against hers.

"Say no if you want to," he whispered against her lips as he eased her onto her back, mounting her in one smooth, long-practiced move.

No, he wouldn't let his *practice* intrude. He would only use it to make her feel good; channeling the talent in his fingers, and mouth, and hips.

"I don't want to say no," she whispered back.

He smoothed his hands up and down her sides, long, slow strokes, bunching up her sleep shirt just a little more with each pass. Her skin was so delicate and warm beneath his fingers, the simple feel of her going straight to his cock, getting him hard. He plunged his tongue gently, almost sweetly into her mouth, again and again, sloppy, unhurried kisses, catching their breath between them. He nipped at her lip and she murmured a wordless sound of pleasure against the corner of his mouth.

Her thin fingers speared through his hair and she urged his head down onto her shoulder. Her lips brushed his ear when she said, "Kev, I want you inside me."

And just like that he was fully-hard and more ready than he'd ever been in his life.

"Okay, baby." He kissed her clothed shoulder, gasping a little. "Okay, we can do that."

He skimmed her shirt up, and she lifted her arms to help him free it. Even though he'd seen her last night, it was no less stirring to see the smooth planes of her flat stomach, the rosy blush of her peaked nipples.

"You too," she urged, and he sat up to jerk his own shirt off and toss it somewhere behind him.

Whitney giggled at his haste, and then sighed when he settled over her again, arching her neck to meet his kiss.

God, her mouth was sweet. He could have drowned kissing her.

But he migrated across her jaw, down her throat, across the gentle ivory slopes of her breasts. Her breath hitched as he pressed kisses down her sternum to her belly. He curled his hands around the points of her hips, anchoring her, and spent long moments ghosting his lips around her navel, and along the waistband of her panties.

She wriggled and said, "Kev," in a low, foreign voice full of want.

There was still a voice in the back of his head telling him it shouldn't be this simple, this easy. The way should be laden with obstacles, and doubts, and a thousand little hurts. But it was easy as breathing when he slipped her panties down the length of her legs, and off her feet, and then she was totally bare to him.

"I wanna try something." He sent a smile up to her face, looking up the length of her body. "It'll feel good, I promise. I'm really good at this."

She nodded, and her thighs parted beneath his hands, like she already knew what he was suggesting. A quiver of tension in her stomach belied her nerves, though, and Tango spent long moments stroking her legs with slow sweeps of his hands, working slowly, slowly upward. He met her gaze one more time, hoping his smile was as reassuring as it felt, and bent to put his mouth on her.

It was overwhelming – for her, yes, going by the high, breathy "oh" that left her lips – but for him, too. To be doing this intimate act with someone who he actually cared for, who he *loved*, to want nothing but pleasure for her, to use every brush of his lips and flick of his tongue to wring sensation from the woman he wanted more than anything – it lit him up. Every nerve alive, as if he was the one being touched. He threw himself full-focus into the task, testing and teasing and listening for each whimper, each breath, pushing her harder when he heard the noises of acute pleasure.

She fell to pieces beautifully, with a strangled little moan, lifting toward his tongue.

Tango felt ten feet tall and invincible. His veins fizzed with warm champagne; it was better than if *he'd* come.

He crawled up her trembling body until he was braced above her on hands and knees, taking in the gorgeous sight of her sex-glazed eyes and the damp little tendrils of hair clinging to her temples.

She licked her lips, pulled in a deep breath, and smiled up at him. "Wow."

"Good wow?"

"*Amazing* wow." She breathed a laugh. "You *are* very good at that." Her little hands ran up his arms, nails teasing. "Now can we please have sex for real?"

He laughed, which was a total first. He'd never laughed while he was in bed with someone before. "Was that not real?"

"You know what I mean."

"Hmm…not sure I do. You might have to explain it to me."

Her answer was to wrap her arms and legs around him and pull him down flush with her sweat-damp skin, her nipples hard little pebbles against his chest, her mouth plump and red where she'd been biting her lips while he went down on her.

"Kev," she said, kissing the corner of his mouth. "Be with me."

His heart squeezed. "Of course, baby, whatever you want."

"And what do you want?"

"I want you." He could figure the rest out later.

~*~

She was a virgin, but she wasn't a prude. She understood the mechanics; she'd read enough novels to know that it was supposed to be rapturous. She also knew it was supposed to hurt.

And now she knew Kev was so careful, and so gentle, and so slow. Until the stinging stopped; until the pain faded and all she felt was the length of him pressed against the length of her, warm salty skin, ragged breath, skimming lips, and the incredible intimacy of having him inside her.

"Are you okay?" he asked against her neck, low and worried, still breathing hard, his chest heaving beneath her cheek.

She trailed her fingers between his prominent ribs, tracing the shadows of tattoos in the dark. "I'm okay."

"Promise?"

"Promise."

Twenty-One

Ian could be honest with himself. Tonight, at least. He didn't try to convince himself that it was Kev shifting toward him under the sheets; Kev's arm sliding across his chest; Kev's lips pressing against his shoulder; Kev's breath tickling his neck. He knew it was Alec, and it was a comfort.

He raked his fingers through Alec's short hair, marveling at its rich, slippery texture, pressing at his scalp with his fingertips.

"Not to knock your favorite restaurant," Alec said, making a pleased noise in his throat in response to the petting. "But I'm kind of starving again."

"Well. That's what fucking does for you."

Alec snorted and pressed his face into Ian's arm.

They'd turned the lights off before, and in the dark, warm beneath the covers, cold night air frosting the windows, Ian felt…peaceful, he supposed. Limp, and sated, and boneless, yes, but in a way that ran deeper than the simple aftereffects of sex.

It was almost like he was…

Well, he couldn't be *happy*…could he?

"I'll tell you a secret," he said, cupping the back of Alec's head.

"Hmm?"

"I have mint Milanos. But I have to hide them, or Bruce will eat them all when I'm not looking."

Alec breathed a laugh across his skin. "I don't believe you."

"Oh, I have them."

"No, I don't believe Bruce eats them."

"He's incredibly crafty for a man that large, you know. And he has a sweet tooth."

"Okay, so Bruce is banned. What about me? Did I earn a cookie tonight?" Alec's tone was so playful, and young, and devoid of all insidious intent, Ian couldn't help but smile. He kept waiting for the traps, the little verbal minefields men would use to make someone like him feel like he was still an expensive hooker. But Alec was just Alec; transparent, devoid of ulterior motives, earnest and straightforward.

If not exactly as straight as he'd originally thought himself to be. But even that change he was handling with remarkable aplomb.

"Yes." Ian slipped his hand down the slender, silken line of Alec's back and swatted his ass. "You can have biscuits."

"Oh God," Alec said, laughing as they disentangled and kicked off the covers. "Biscuits?"

"That's how we say it in civilized countries."

"In prehistoric countries."

As Ian shrugged into his robe and belted it, he reflected that he'd never had this, not with any lover – banter. The gentle back and forth jibes, tinged with laughter and knowing little smiles. Warmth curled through his stomach.

Alec stepped into his boxers and they walked to the kitchen together, shoulders bumping, arms overlapping, unhurried and content in one another's company.

"Come look at this," Ian said, stepping up to the counter and the row of stair-stepped ceramic canisters set up against the backsplash. He pulled the lid off the largest and revealed shiny brown flax seed. Then he lifted out the false bottom and revealed–

"Mint Milanos," Alec said, hooking his chin on Ian's shoulder, staring down into the canister with an astonished laugh. "You weren't kidding."

"Darling, I never kid."

Ian plated the cookies and set them at the island, on the edge between two stools. "Do you need milk?" he asked, and he tried not to sound too mocking.

"Water's fine."

When they were settled, the quiet of his expensive kitchen broken only by the sounds of chewing, Ian allowed himself another small revelation. Alec seemed glad to be with him.

Kev was the closest thing he'd ever had to a true romance, and their nights together had been fraught with sighs, and furtive glances, and the tension of guilt and regret, and shared memories of horror. They hadn't laughed. Hadn't teased. Hadn't been light with each other. It had always been heavy, tinged with emotion, desperate.

But that was *love*, wasn't it? Love was heavy, and hurtful, and it chafed you in all the wrong ways. Didn't it? His life had been a shitshow, so it only stood to reason that anything worthwhile, anything he really wanted, would be difficult. Like trying to hold onto barbed wire.

Then…what was sitting barefoot in his kitchen eating cookies with his lover? When nothing was wrong, and nothing hurt, and the only glances were sly and flirtatious?

Alec swallowed, flicked crumbs off his fingers, and took a sip of water. "Ian?"

"What?"

"You can talk about it, you know."

Bristling, Ian darted a sideways glance toward Alec, but eased a little when he saw Alec watching him with curiosity, and an open, honest sympathy that managed not to be pitying.

Ian couldn't take pity.

He took an unsteady breath. "Talk about what?"

Alec shrugged, but his gaze didn't waver. "If this is weird for you." He gestured between them.

Ian cracked his next Milano in half between his fingers, but didn't eat it. "Why would it be weird?"

Alec gave him a look that said *come on.*

"Having second thoughts?"

"No." Alec looked frustrated. "But you were really broken up about that other guy. I know I'm the rebound." He sounded hurt.

"Kev and I–" Ian started, shocked that the words had come so easily. He pressed his lips together and drew in a deep breath through his nose. Could he do this? Was it right? Or healthy, even? "Kev and I are a volatile combination," he said, finally, scrubbing at his face with both hands. A few stray cookie crumbs prickled against his skin. "We have too much history, I suppose. Too many bad memories."

"And I'm the distraction," Alec said, voice wooden.

"No," Ian said, faster than he expected. He turned to the boy beside him, took in the way he chewed at his lower lip, eyes wide with poorly veiled hurt. "You are not a distraction, darling."

Alec glanced away, blinking.

Ian moved to cover one of his pretty, pale hands with his own on the counter. "What I'd like to know is your reason for bringing this up."

Alec shrugged, but he kept blinking, eyes wet in profile. "It makes sense, I think. Wanting to know if you and your partner are on the same page."

A slow warmth shifted beneath Ian's skin. He'd underestimated this one.

"Sweet boy."

Alec sniffed and glanced down at their stacked hands. "It's…it's never been like this before for me. I didn't…" He exhaled. "I liked sex okay. With…with…"

"Women," Ian supplied.

Alec nodded. "But I never – I didn't know–" He sent a look of appeal to Ian, face raw with emotion. "I care about you. And I don't think I can stick around if you're just playing with me, or trying to make him jealous."

In truth, Ian *had* intended to use Alec. Not to make Kev jealous, because Kev wasn't a part of his daily circle, but to assuage the deep ache inside himself. That empty, clenching loneliness. He'd wanted to dull the sting of Whitney Howard. If Kev could find solace in a stranger, then so could he, by God. He'd liked the look of Alec – absolutely mouth-watering – and the easy access was a perk.

But then he'd taken the boy to bed, and watched his pupils dilate, and melted into the soft sweetness of his kiss. Somewhere in the midst of his Egyptian cotton sheets, he'd found trust, and satisfaction, and the kind of affection he hadn't felt in a long, long time.

"Baby." He brushed Alec's hair back and settled his hand on the back of his neck. "I promise you. I'm not just playing."

Not anymore.

Alec gave him a small, uncertain smile, eyes still glimmering. "That's good, 'cause I'm sort of...um...a little bit hopeless at this point."

Ian pulled him close and kissed his forehead. "I'm glad you are."

And maybe soon, hopefully, he could return the sentiment.

Twenty-Two

Session 6

"How's Whitney?" Mercy asked over the rim of his coffee cup.

"At work." Tango kept his tone light, but he could feel his smile threatening to break through.

Mercy's dark eyes danced. "Uh huh."

"I'm trying to get her to submit some of her work to this art show they're having over at the college."

"She's an artist?"

Tango rose to go fetch the canvas she'd left tucked alongside the TV last night, the horse in the green field.

Mercy whistled. "Damn. Why is she working customer service?"

"That's one of my goals," Tango said as he resumed his seat. "Get Whitney an art job."

"Hmm."

"What?"

"Nothing. You're in a good mood. Just…don't want you biting off more than you can chew with these goals."

Tango scowled to himself. "It's not like it's a long list."

Mercy sipped his coffee, face sliding into neutral. He wasn't going to push; either because he was a good friend, or because he didn't know what he ought to say. Or maybe both.

Tango really needed to make an appointment with the doctor Ghost had suggested.

"Okay," Mercy said. "More demons?"

Tango took a deep breath and nodded. He knew what he needed to talk about. Amid the blanketing horror of his past, there were moments that stood out from the rest. That defined him.

There were people, too. There was Ian.

~*~

The Cuckoo's Nest became Kev's world. The basement, the car (windows and doors locked, armed guard in the front), and the club. He felt like a nocturnal creature. A subterranean one. When he dreamed, he dreamed in neon pinks and blues. And when he had nightmares, there were always customers.

That was a nightmare consistent while both asleep and awake.

He was thirteen, and he'd been "working" for a solid year now. Every week, Miss Carla presented him with a bundle of cash, his tips from the week, and then told him she'd hold it for him. Sometimes she bought new outfits for him, tight, sparkly, feminine things the clients would enjoy peeling off of him. She bought him floral-scented shampoos, and lotions, and body oils. Condoms and lube for keeping in the room where he "entertained."

Most mornings, he hoped he wouldn't wake. He thought, again and again, how wonderful it would be if he'd never been born. Or if he could die now.

He started fantasizing. If only the doors of the car weren't locked, he could fling open the door on the highway and fall out, let himself splatter on the pavement. If only the cord of the hair dryer would stretch all the way to the bathroom sink. If only one of his customers would become overwrought and keep squeezing his throat until he stopped breathing.

Whatever happened to Mama? Their old house? His friends from school? All questions that passed through his mind less and less, and then only in an ephemeral way that made them feel as if they'd never really happened, and that he'd dreamed his boyhood in a weak moment of wanting to escape.

The only thing that made it at all bearable was Ian.

The door of the private room shut, too loudly, yanked by the heavy touch of the overweight customer who'd just thrown Kev face-down on the bed and panted and huffed behind him for all of two minutes. The really disgusting ones never lasted very long, and then they seemed ashamed and fumbling afterward, getting out of the room with haste. Leaving Kev to clean himself up in relative peace, the music a low thump on the other side of the padded door.

Movements unsteady, he tugged on the robe hanging in the corner and belted it tight, the worn terry cloth warm against his chilled skin. He leaned against the wall, because it would hurt too much to sit down, and because his legs were about to give out.

He needed another shot.

A light knock sounded at the door, barely heard through the padding, and then it eased open, a few inches at a time, which told Kev exactly who was entering the room. Ian slipped in, soft-footed as a shadow, alabaster face, and hands, and feet the only things visible beneath his own robe. His hair looked sweaty, and messy, and he'd tied it back in a bun to keep it away from his face.

"Hello, little darling." His voice came out rough, and tired; he'd just come from a client appointment of his own. "What do you say we go clean up?"

He offered a long, slender hand, and Kev took it, the skin-to-skin contact the motivation he had for moving away from the wall.

The hallway, dim and pink-tinged, made hump-backed shadows of the spent customers who tumbled out of doors still righting their clothes, heads whipping back and forth as they tried to remember which way the exist was.

"Hey, nice stems," one called out to Ian.

"Not on the clock, asshole," Ian hissed back, grip tightening on Kev's hand, towing him down the hall in a rush.

There were several wolf whistles.

"Listen to that smart mouth!" the first guy crowed. "Might have to put it to work soon. Miss Carla know you talk to customers that way?"

Kev felt Ian shudder as he walked, the movement traveling through their joined hands.

"I like the little one," someone else said.

"Had him last week," another man chimed in. "Tightest little hole you ever—"

Ian shoved through the door into the changing area, and Kev leapt in behind him. The voices cut off mid-sentence, and then they were blessedly separate from the men who paid to use their bodies.

Ian pulled Kev around into a crushing hug, his thin arms surprisingly strong. His strength was a refined, self-contained thing, one that enabled him to dance like a dream, suspended upside-down by one hand from the pole at the center stage. And so it always came as a shock to feel it up close like this – but a good one.

Kev tucked his face beneath the man's chin and let out the deep, shivering breath he'd been holding since the fat man with the sticky hundred-dollar bills first grinned at him across the room. He started to shake, and knew part of it was stress, and fear, and disgust – but part of it was his need of another injection.

"Are you okay?" Ian asked right against his ear, his lips soft against Kev's skin. "Did he hurt you?"

"N-no," Kev managed through chattering teeth.

"You beautiful little liar. I know he did. I…" His hands tightened in Kev's robe, at the small of his back. "It isn't supposed to hurt. I'm so sorry."

But Kev couldn't imagine a way in which it didn't hurt.

"Come on." Ian pulled back, hands lingering at Kev's back. His blue-green eyes shimmered with moisture. "Let's get clean."

There were showers in the dressing room, a bathroom with several toilet stalls and a communal shower with six showerheads poised at intervals down the white tiled length of the room. Usually, the space was roiling with steam and bustling with dancing boys intent on washing off the tacky sin of the night. But Ian and Kev were a little early, and the bathroom was empty. The knowledge brought an immeasurable comfort Kev didn't quite understand, but didn't bother to question. It was quiet, and it was warm, and soon there would be hot water…and there was Ian. That was all that mattered.

They left their robes on hooks and walked naked to one of the showerheads. Ian cranked it on and stepped back, testing the temperature with his fingertips, cringing against the initial coldness.

Kev let his eyes wander over the older boy, enjoying the simple pleasure of looking at someone slim and beautiful. The wide shoulders, the narrow hips, the glowing pale skin – a few dark mouth-shaped bruises lingering along the stark lines of his clavicles. Nudity had become so commonplace in Kev's life, he didn't avert his gaze as he moved down Ian's body, but instead followed the fine, tapering muscles of his belly down to the length of his soft cock. His slender, strong thighs, toned from dancing. All the way to his pale, narrow feet.

Ian tugged the elastic from his hair, slipped it onto his wrist, and reached for Kev, expression tender. "The water's hot now."

It was only much later, when he was an adult, and a Lean Dog, and part of a somewhat more normal society, that Kev would learn that showering sweat and semen off his body in the company of a seventeen-year-old was the sort of thing that would horrify the middle class of Knoxville. In the eyes of the gentle public, some lines should never be crossed, no matter the circumstances.

But to a thirteen-year-old sex worker – *sex slave*, he would finally acknowledge, when he was a man – the highlight of his night, his week, his month, maybe even his life was stepping beneath the fall of hot water with Ian Byron.

The soap was industrial, chemical-smelling stuff, strong enough to strip the night off their skin. Ian took it into his hands, worked up a good lather, and then smoothed the suds gently across Kev's back, and chest, and down his arms. He curled one arm around him, murmuring endearments, and washed him intimately. His hand came away pink with blood, and he cupped it beneath the water, washing the evidence of violence away.

Where the customer had been impatient and rough, Ian was slow and careful. He bathed him, and nothing else, no errant touches, no invasions.

Kev tipped his head back to stare up at him, the water droplets caught in his auburn lashes, the flush in his cheeks, his hair dark and slicked back off his face, and he thought of angels, and prayers answered, and every faceless beautiful thing that hovered at the edges of his imagination.

Ian brought his hand up to cup the side of Kev's face, thumb sweeping slowly along the ridge of his cheekbone. He dampened his already-wet lips, a slow flick of his tongue that mesmerized Kev.

"I want to show you," he whispered, and then he kissed Kev.

Kev had been kissed by clients, and he hadn't understood why it was something they wanted to do. Slapping their lips against his had tickled the back of his throat, made him want to throw up. But *this*. This was as gentle and sweet as all of Ian's attention.

He flattened his hands against Ian's shower-slick chest, and he leaned deep into the warmth of his body, neck feeling weak as the kiss continued...and continued. Slow, drugging sweeps of lips and tongues, until his mouth was open and he was gasping, his heart leaping against his ribs.

"See," Ian whispered against his lips. "It's supposed to feel good."

~*~

The shots came at the end of the night, all the boys damp and fresh from the shower, lined up along the bench in the dressing room, sleeves rolled up past their elbows.

Kev leaned into Ian's side, the warmth and comfort of the shower – of kissing Ian – fading in the face of the growing chills and shivers that racked his small body. When Big John appeared with his black bag full of syringes and tourniquets, Kev wanted to sob with relief.

Ian's hand found his, and their fingers slotted together, thin against thin, pale against pale, the pulses in their wrists thumping against one another.

"Him first," Ian insisted when Big John got to them. "He's shaking."

Conditioning. He would learn that word later. The way the tightness of the tourniquet, the plumping of his arm, brought an instant relief; there was a joy in the pressure. And then came the prick of the needle. Then the warmth. The acute, mind-wiping pleasure.

He squeezed Ian's hand, and he drifted, and he was happy.

~*~

"There were two things I cared about," Tango said from the kitchen counter as he topped off his coffee. "Ian, and the heroin."

"That's how they kept you from running off when you got older," Mercy said. "Got you all hooked, so you couldn't stray from home."

"Or defy them. They'd let you start to detox if you did, and it was…" He shuddered. "I only ever did that once."

He returned to the chair and tried not to feel too guilty about the disgust writ large on Mercy's face. Mercy himself had said he could handle whatever horrors Tango's brain needed to dish out.

Silence reigned for a bit, then, looking down into his mug, Mercy said, "Look. I'm not saying I like the guy. I think he's weird and he wants to be a Bond villain or something." His dark eyes flicked up over the mug. "But I get why Ian's important to you. Why you…love him."

Tango smiled, wryly. "You don't have to be comfortable with it."

Mercy shrugged. "I'm not comfortable with the fact that after he came back into your life, you tried to kill yourself. But I get the love part."

The old scars on his wrist gave a little throb of remembrance, calling softly to the razors he no longer had. He had a fancy electric shaver now, a gift and a safety precaution from Mags.

"Ian's the only reason I can even think about sex without going insane," he said. "The *only* reason."

~*~

All the boys in the basement kept track of their birthdays. It seemed a strange habit, because marking the passage of time could only cause depression. Later in life, when the ones who'd made it out alive attended therapy, their therapists would ask if it made their "confinement" more difficult. When at the time, all they'd known was that they had to know when they were older. They had to think that time passed, and life marched on beyond the walls of their basement, and their club.

On Kev's fourteenth birthday, he received no presents. There was no cake, no streamers. He had only the vaguest memory of a cake with candles and a bouquet of helium balloons from his life before, with Mama, but he had no expectations of delight. He was a year older; he'd survived that long.

The day was a normal one. Ballet. His meager lunch. More ballet. Then it was the car, and the bustling dressing room.

Familiar, long-fingered hands caught at his waist and spun him away from his dressing table mirror. He was already grinning before he caught sight of Ian's beloved, smiling face.

Ian stepped in close, and stole a kiss, a fast but warm press of lips. "Happy Birthday," he said when he pulled back.

"You remembered?"

"Of course, darling." He kissed him again. "And I have a surprise for later."

"Kevin!" The brief flicker of happiness was dispelled by Miss Carla, as she sailed into the room in a purple velvet dress, her hair teased to an impossible volume, lipstick a shocking orange slice across her face. "Kevin, come here, little boy, I have special news for you."

Said special treat ended up being a new pair of sequined blue shorts and the news that he was going to dance tonight.

Cold dread coiled in his stomach, but he said, "Yes, ma'am," and went to change.

How different could it be? he reasoned. He would still be out in the main part of the club, would still be expected to go back to a private room with the clients.

When Miss Carla was gone, Ian slipped an arm around Kev's waist and kissed his temple. "I'll be with you the whole time," he said, and it helped. A little.

~*~

It never occurred to him then, sheltered inside his dark cocoon, that the city was studded with legal strip clubs, where women with kids, and day jobs, and bills to pay danced for paychecks and went home at the end of their shifts. He would later learn the stigma attached to them, and he would speak to a few in his Lean Dogs career who expressed an intense displeasure in their craft, even shame. Still others enjoyed what they did. He would listen to the old ladies mutter about them under his breath, and all he would think was: but they had a choice. Even if that choice was between dancing and groceries, it was still a *conscious decision they made themselves*.

On his fourteenth birthday, all he knew was that he was expected to dance, and if he didn't, he'd be whipped to within an inch of his life and denied food for two days.

~*~

"Slowly," Ian told him. "You want to move slowly."

Under the lights, he couldn't see the crowd waiting below him in the dark. He couldn't hear the music above the thunder of his heartbeat. He couldn't tell where the baby oil ended and his sweat began.

But then Ian kissed him, on the stage, to a chorus of whistles, and catcalls, and cheers. And then he remembered all his ballet training, and he remembered *slowly*. And they danced.

~*~

Dancing, Kev decided, beat wandering around the club floor looking for customers by a mile. He couldn't see anyone, and between the music and his pulse, he couldn't hear them. He faded into a world that was his and Ian's alone, and for a little while, the horror faded to a low roar at the back of his conscious.

But then, after...

The clients were two brothers, athletic, suit-wearing, business sector types. They weren't unattractive, but the feral gleam in their eyes frightened Kev. Later, Ian would explain guys like these to him: "straight" men with wives, girlfriends, a truckload of prejudices about masculinity, and jobs that paid them well enough to enable their secret fantasies. "They'll never admit what they are," Ian would say, "and they hurt us to justify their own shame, to cover up the dark empty places in their hearts."

In the private room, one of the brothers shoved both his hands in Kev's shoulder-length hair and tugged his face in close. His pupils were dilated, and Kev could feel the strength in his arms, the dangerous tension vibrating through him.

"No kissing," Ian snapped from the other side of the room, and the brother with his hands in Kev's hair froze. It was the first thing Ian had said in his real voice, commanding and sharp, rather than the breathy, put-on moan he used with clients.

"What?"

Ian broke away from the other brother; his shorts were pushed nearly off his hips, and his shiny, straight hair was mussed, but his expression was wrathful. "There are rules in the private room. You'll obey them, or you'll be kicked out. No kissing."

"Yeah?" the first brother huffed, fingers digging into Kev's scalp as he shot Ian a dark look. "And who's gonna kick us out? You, fairy boy?"

Oh no, Kev thought. *Don't say anything.* He'd rather just kiss the man than risk Ian getting backhanded.

Ian took a step toward the first brother, his smile nasty. "No, that would be Big John's job."

The other brother caught Ian's wrist in a grip so tight Kev could see Ian's bones shift beneath his skin; his face contorted with pain. "Yeah?" the man asked. "And how're you gonna call Big John in here with your mouth full?"

Later, Kev would remember that there wasn't a "no kissing" rule. Ian had made it up on the spot.

~*~

"Loverboy," Miss Carla said. "Congratulations. You get to go home with the dancing boys tonight."

Kev didn't respond, attention focused on the split in Ian's eyebrow. He dabbed it carefully with the alcohol-soaked rag, and Ian didn't make a sound, the occasional facial twitch the only tell that it hurt like a son of a bitch. The skin around the split was red and puffy; the swelling would get worse. He might have a black eye. Makeup might not cover the bruising.

Kev swallowed and tried to pretend his tongue didn't taste bitter. He and Ian had chewed a handful of mints each, but the taste wouldn't go away.

"Did you hear me?" Miss Carla asked, voice edging toward anger.

"Yes, ma'am."

"I'll look after him," Ian said.

Miss Carla made a disgruntled sound, but moved on.

It didn't seem possible, given the sore, exhausted state of his body and spirit, but a small wisp of interest curled through Kev's stomach. "I get to go home with you?"

Ian gave him a fleeting smile, but his eyes sparked. That blend of sadness and excitement that always marked his face in Kev's presence. "It's not much, but it's better than the basement."

After their shots – the pleasure surging in tides, making his head heavy, fuzzing his eyesight – they shuffled to the garage in the back of the club; they never saw the light of day or night here, only the club and the cars. Drunk off his injection, the pain fading to the periphery, Kev gladly climbed into a backseat and slumped down against Ian. Together. It didn't matter where they were going, because they were together.

~*~

Ian lived in an apartment with the other dancers. Run-down, sad-fronted building, five deadbolts on the door, bars over the windows. Bunkbeds in the bedroom, futons and sleeping bags in the living room. Fridge full of protein shakes and questionable fruit. Whole wheat bread; diet food. TV, radio, racks of dancing clothes and laundry baskets of threadbare street clothes.

They were locked in. Some of Big John's boys lived across the hall. Guards.

As the prize dancer, Ian had the best spot: a futon snugged up against the window in the living room. It was draped with a ratty plaid blanket, two rumpled pillows at one end, the corners of a few cardboard boxes peeking out from underneath.

"Here." Ian stretched out on his stomach and patted the space beside him; the futon was just big enough for two and Kev settled in, mirroring the other boy's position, on his stomach, braced up on his elbows. The window was open a crack, cool night air slipping in through the bars and caressing their faces.

Ian leaned over the side, rummaged in one of the boxes, and came out with a crumpled pack of Kools and a lighter. He waggled his eyebrows at Kev. "Mentholated."

Kev had no idea what that meant, but he nodded like he was eager and accepted the cigarette Ian handed him. Leaned forward when the lighter sparked and mirrored Ian's inhale.

He choked, and thought he might throw up. Ian pounded him on the back a few times and the smoke found a place to settle inside his lungs. A strange numbness swept through him, a touch of calm, a faint tickle of the pleasure the injections brought.

Ian exhaled a long stream of smoke toward the crack in the window; Kev watched it strike the glass and purl upward, diffusing in the air around them, choking and sweet.

~*~

When Ian kissed him, his tongue tasted like the cigarettes they'd smoked. The other boys had bedded down, breathing deep, some of them snoring. Moonlight fell in through the window, shadow-stripes from the bars masking the full effect of Ian's expression, the heat and despair in his eyes.

"Let me make you feel good," he whispered against Kev's lips. "Let me show you."

He urged Kev onto his back, oh so gently, braced above him on his arms, his kiss deep and wet, searching until Kev felt a helpless pulse in his stomach and arched upward, trying to lean into the dance of their tongues. Ian's fingertips started a slow, incendiary trail across his skin: along the lines of his collarbones, down his chest, teasing lightly at his nipples until they tightened and ached; his ribs, his stomach, a brief dip into his navel. A crawling, delicate sort of pleasure. A kind touch; he'd never had that. No one ever teased him like this, feather-soft, tender fingers on his tender skin.

The kiss turned dark, exquisitely demanding, Ian's tongue flickering deep. He palmed the sensitive skin below Kev's navel, and then pushed his old frayed boxers down, baring his narrow hips and his rapidly-thickening sex. Ian's touch seemed to go straight to his cock, and he was breathless, and hard, and his hips wanted to move in the way all his clients' hips moved. That old primal urge the body knew without the mind's input.

Ian wrapped his hand around his cock, stroked him light and steady, pad of his thumb tracing along the head until Kev gasped.

"That's it, love," Ian said, voice low and rough. "Just like that."

His hand found a rhythm, a pressure, a pace, thumb flicking over the head each time, spreading the drops of wetness that beaded there, until Kev's cock was slick and hard, Ian's hand moving faster and faster.

He breathed in unsteady gasps, hands clutching at Ian's shoulders, stunned by the reverence in Ian's bruised face as it hung suspended over his.

"Have you ever come before?" Ian asked, growling now, eyes fire-bright in the shadows. "Come now. Come for me."

The pressure in his spine built and built…and then he was melting and flying apart all at once. Spinning. Hips stuttering. Wordless sounds catching in his throat.

Was this why men paid to take him into back rooms? Was this what they were chasing?

Ian ducked his head, crawled down Kev's body, and licked him clean.

~*~

He was always hungry, and he always hated the dancing, and what came after, in private rooms with handsy clients who treated him like a doll. But then came the shot, the spreading pleasure, and then after, in the dark of the apartment, there was Ian, and another kind of pleasure.

They lay in the dark, rutting together, hands tight against hips and ribs, the futon creaking beneath them. Ian held both their cocks in one long-fingered hand and the sensation whitened Kev's vision at the edges. He'd had no idea friction could feel like this. Before Ian. So many horrible things had happened Before Ian. Good hadn't exited Before Ian.

"I want to try something," Ian murmured, and Kev could only hum in response.

Then Ian pulled his hand away and Kev whined low in his throat.

Ian chuckled. "Just a minute, darling." He leaned over the side of the futon to dig something from the boxes beneath.

The crackle of the foil packet was like cold water across Kev's flushed skin. He pushed up on his elbows, sucking a breath. "What…?"

"Shh. It's okay. I promise." Ian knelt in front of him, between his legs, condom in one hand, small bottle of lube in the

267

other. "Hey." He dropped both onto the blankets and put his hands on Kev's thighs, a warm, familiar, grounding touch.

Kev struggled to breathe past the tight ball of panic swelling in his chest.

Ian dipped down low to kiss him. Familiar heat of lips and tongue, gentle nibble of teeth. "It's okay," he promised. "I've got you. I won't let anything hurt you."

It was, as all of the ones passed between them this far, an empty promise. Because they couldn't be together always. But for this moment, and the moments between them, Ian wouldn't let him get hurt. Kev believed that.

He closed his eyes and pressed his face into Ian's neck. "Okay," he whispered, shaky. "I trust you."

With the clients, sex was about force. It was all rushed and angry. Though it never was with Ian, Kev tightened anyway, his entire body a coil of tense fear beneath his lover.

But then he felt the pads of Ian's fingers, cool and slick, and gentle as a whisper. Just a hint. A question.

Kev released a breath and willed the tension from his limbs. It ebbed by slow degrees, as Ian stroked him, whispering endearments, touching him in a way no client ever had. With such care and patience.

When Ian finally eased the tip of one finger inside him, he felt the stretch and the pressure, but no pain.

"Okay?" Ian asked.

"Okay." And now Kev's voice was shaky for a different reason.

Time spun out, warm and slow, as Ian worked him open, his hair falling off his shoulders, his gaze reverent, like wringing quiet whimpers of awe and pleasure from Kev's throat was a religious experience.

"Yes, yes, love. Like that," he murmured as Kev's hips sought a rhythm. "You're beautiful."

Ian found a place inside him that shot sparks up his spine. Kev gasped, and Ian's fingers withdrew. "No," he said, hands reaching, half-limp and useless. "No, I want–"

"Shh. Just wait. I'll take care of you."

The foil crinkled; soft sounds of the condom. Then Ian was pressing in closer between his legs, and then he was easing inside, inch by inch.

And it was good. *Sex was good.*

Afterward, tears filled Kev's eyes, and Ian held him.

~*~

He grew more docile. Not that he'd been resistant before, but he felt the last vestiges of fear, shame, and confusion leave him. He didn't realize how tense and timid he'd been on the stage or in the back with the clients until he stopped caring. It didn't feel like giving up; it felt like resignation. This was his life. He gave his body over to the men at The Nest every night, just as Ian did. And after closing time, when they were cuddled up on the futon by the window, they took possession of their skin again; they gave and received affection, pleasure, and tenderness. They took the control back. They allowed themselves the luxury of knowing what it was like to feel good.

The tips got bigger, and the customers were happy, and Miss Carla noticed.

She turned up at the apartment one morning, and her long wool coat confirmed what Kev had guessed from peering through the barred windows: it was wintertime outside.

"We're going shopping, Kevin," she said. When Ian reached for his shoes, she said, "Just the two of us," with a pointed look.

Since Kev danced on a pole, got fucked up the ass most nights, and lived under lock and key, he figured there wasn't much danger in going with her alone.

Not alone, it turned out, because Max was waiting in the car. But it was daylight, and they were going for a drive somewhere, and the air was cold and stinging against his cheeks when they stepped out of the sedan in the parking lot of a department store.

She held a thin stack of bills. "You may spend all of this. On whatever you want." Then slipped the money back into her coat pocket.

Was he dreaming? He could buy things? New things? Things for himself?

And for Ian, he decided. He had to take a gift to Ian.

Except…except Kev couldn't remember going shopping. He didn't know how, he didn't…

He was hyperventilating.

"Hush, hush, baby," Miss Carla said, wrapping a thin, strong arm around him, taking his weight as he slumped against her, suddenly weak with anxiety. "I'll be with you every step. Come on, Max." And they walked up to the big glass front of the store.

It was all too much: the soft whoosh of the doors springing open automatically. The sudden swell of noise: voices bouncing off tile, the clatter of the wheels on a rolling rack of clothes, the squawk of employees' radios, the high strains of tinny music floating from unseen speakers.

Kev couldn't breathe. His legs would barely hold him. Look at all the people, all the light, all the colors. It was…it was…it was…

"Let's go look for some things," Miss Carla said in a sweet voice, her arm still around him, steering him toward menswear.

In his mad panic, Kev retreated to a place deep inside his head, watching the shopping trip as if he was viewing it through a TV, like he wasn't there at all. He was afraid he'd throw up if he opened his mouth. It was total sensory overload, and he could only nod and whimper as Miss Carla picked up item after item and held them up to him.

She showed him silk ties, microfiber shirts, and heavy wool sweaters. Told him he was a size small and that he looked pretty in blue.

Plastic garland, tinsel, and oversized ornaments decorated the displays: it must be coming up on Christmas time.

A woman walked past them, gaze landing heavy on the tableau of Max holding Kev by the shoulders while Miss Carla held the heavy blue sweater up beside his face. Kev looked down at the floor; he could already feel the phantom strike of Max's belt across his back, envision the pain he'd earn if he dared to make eye contact with anyone.

Finally, finally, though, he found his voice. "I…can I…please," he whispered. "I want to get one for Ian."

Miss Carla's smile froze. "What did you say?"

Kev closed his eyes and shivered. "I want to get a sweater for Ian, please. He gets cold."

For a long moment, all he heard was the Christmas music coming through the speakers, Max's heavy breathing behind him.

"I don't know," Miss Carla said, voice a low hiss. "You'd have to be an awful good boy to earn something like that."

"I will be. I promise."

Her face was tight with anger.

He picked out the dark gray sweater for Ian, a medium, one size up from him.

~*~

It didn't matter that the cashier looked at Kev for a long, unsure moment, like she wanted to say something. Kev didn't say anything, didn't correct Miss Carla when she told the cashier that they were mother and son.

It didn't once occur to him to run away. To make a scene and cry out to anyone for help.

Conditioning at its finest.

~*~

Ian's blue-green eyes widened, bright with shock when Kev handed him the present. They filled with tears when he saw the sweater, passed his hand down the front of it.

"Thank you, darling." He pulled Kev into a tight hug, kissing his temple, his forehead, his lips. "I love it."

~*~

Dancing was an athletic endeavor. It was all repetition, muscle memory, balance, and sheer strength, moving your own weight in elegant, graceful, gravity-defying arcs and dips. When Kev thought about it as entertainment – about the eyes on him, and the way certain movements of his hips drew cheers and fluttering dollar bills, the way they called for "Loverboy" – it overwhelmed him, heavy on his chest and shoulders, and his feet faltered. So he parsed it down to what it was: exercise. And he didn't think about the men watching him.

~*~

Sex was an exercise too, and practice made perfect. Kev learned all the movements, all the little tricks. He moved his body accordingly, and he grit his teeth through the pain, and he allowed his body to be used as the tool it was.

~*~

But what about when sex wasn't exercise? When it was with Ian. What was that?

~*~

He had food, and shelter, and Miss Carla took him shopping more and more. He was one of the favorite dancers, and the highest-paid boy after Ian. And then Ian – he had Ian, and the cigarettes they shared by the window, and their tumbled nights in the dark on the futon.

He didn't know what it was, only that it was his life.

~*~

He'd been fourteen for three months when Miss Carla called him into her office one night. It was the wee hours, and out in the main part of the club, chairs were being stacked on tables and the cleaning crew passed mops across the tacky floor.

"Sit down," she told Kev without looking away from her computer, glasses on a rhinestone-studded chain perched on her nose as she scanned the screen.

He did, squirming a little. He hadn't had a chance to shower yet, and inside his sweatpants, his ass was still slick and damp with lube, drying now and getting itchy.

"Kevin." Carla's fingers flew across the keyboard, little clicks and clacks. "You like your job, don't you? You're real good at it."

"Yes, ma'am."

She stopped and turned to him, her eyes strained and too large over the rims of her glasses, mouth pinched up. "You like being Loverboy, don't you? My good, pretty little boy, the one who all my customers want to treat special. Right?"

The stickiness in his pants itched in earnest. He tried not to squirm and said, "Yes, ma'am."

"You know how much I need you, right?"

He nodded, a strange swelling of emotion creeping up his throat. He wanted to cry. He wanted to throw up. He wanted her to stroke the top of his head and call him a good boy some more.

He did none of those things.

"Now, Kevin." She leaned toward him, elbows on the desk, voice dropping to a conspiratorial level. "I need you to do something really important for me, my special Loverboy. Can you do that?"

He'd just been bounced back and forth between two men like an inflatable doll. He nodded again, because what could she ask that was worse than that?

A smile he hated tugged at one corner of her tight mouth. "Good boy. One of our best customers wants to take a boy home for the night tomorrow, and he picked you."

The urge to vomit intensified. Thankfully, he hadn't been fed yet tonight. His bread and peanut butter would come after his injection, later, when his appetite was dull. But now, hungry, right on the razor's edge of panic, his empty stomach squeezed and his mouth fell open, breath heaving in and out of him as he fought to control his body's visceral reaction to her words.

"Kevin," she said, sharply. "Don't barf on my desk."

He closed his mouth and swallowed desperately, fighting the bile that wanted to rise.

"You be a good boy now," Miss Carla snapped. "You behave. You do what I say or Max'll take his belt to you."

He swallowed again, shuddered, and managed to nod. "Yes, ma'am."

"Now. You're going to go home with this client, and he'll bring you back the next afternoon when he's done with you. This is important for all of us. You hear me? Be a good boy and do as you're told."

"Yes, ma'am."

"Now go shower. You smell."

~*~

Ian's hands curled into white-knuckled fists in his lap. "She can't do that," he hissed through his teeth, expression taut with fury. "She can't!"

Kev shrugged and tried not to let his stomach fall out through his feet. "It's not any different than what I always do."

"Yes it is!" Ian turned away from him, spine bowed, its knobs straining the threadbare fabric of his t-shirt. "It is."

Feeling cold and bereft, Kev snuggled up behind him, his shins pressing into Ian's back. "Are you mad?"

Ian shook his head, and took a long time answering. "I'm scared, darling," he whispered. "I'm afraid for you."

Kev draped his skinny arms across Ian's shoulders, leaned forward and plastered his chest to his back. Ian's hair tickled at his face as he nosed against his ear. "It'll be okay," he said.

He didn't believe it, but he had to say it, for both of them.

~*~

274

The man who purchased him for the night lived in a sprawling brick two-story house illuminated by soft flood lights placed at artistic angles in the garden. Kev glimpsed pruned trees, topiaries, and brick paths flanked by hedges. Steep roof angles, dormers, many-paned windows. A tall wrought-iron fence circled the property, a gate sliding into place once they passed through it.

Locked in.

Max hauled Kev from the backseat with one meaty hand on Kev's upper arm. It didn't seem to matter that Kev walked along willingly; Max marched him up to a side door, through it, and into a warm library with walls and walls of books, and a fire snapping beneath a heavy fieldstone mantle. Max let go of him, shoving him toward the man poised beside the fireplace, brandy snifter in hand.

"Behave," Max ordered.

Kev nodded, swallowing his nerves.

The man by the fireplace was tall and thin, and auburn-haired. Like Ian, Kev thought, faintly. But as he drew closer, he saw that the comparison wasn't a good one. This man's hair was cut close to his head, and thinning, bits of shiny scalp showing through. His face, though thin and aristocratic, was haggard, weathered heavily, his skin rough. He wore an immaculate suit and shined shoes; his tie was sewn with thread so shiny it reflected the firelight.

Kev immediately disliked the gleam in his eyes.

"Well aren't you just delicious?" he asked, reaching to cup Kev's chin in his free hand. He smiled and it made Kev's stomach clench unhappily. "We're going to have some fun tonight."

~*~

Kev swallowed a mouthful of blood and felt around his molars with the tip of his tongue. One of the back ones was loose, but not overly so. If he left it alone, it would probably stay in.

Right now, he had to keep moving.

He couldn't believe what he'd done.

Couldn't believe.

He hadn't meant to escape. Not at first. It had been an involuntary, instinctual reaction to the things the client had wanted to do to him. The mistake the client had made, though, was not taking into account the thinness of Kev's wrists.

The cuffs had cut into his skin, blood trickling down his forearms in dark pearls, but then his slick wrists had slipped free. The man's back had been turned as he slowly, methodically removed his cufflinks, his watch, his rings, telling Kev in a low voice what he meant to do once he was undressed.

Kev had panicked. It was one thing to service customers in the back rooms of The Nest, where there were time limits, and Big John's people, and even Miss Carla, ready to praise him and tip him with the cash he'd earned. And then Ian. Riding home in the car snuggled up to Ian, going to bed with him, being made to feel like a human again. But here, trapped 'til morning, the danger of his situation wrapped around his lungs in a vise grip.

He couldn't stay. He just couldn't.

He'd rolled off the high four-poster bed, hitting the carpet with a muffled thud, knees and elbows stinging from the impact. The man made an inquiring, confused sound, and Kev kept rolling, wedging himself beneath the bed. And then out the other side, bolting for the bedroom door.

"Hey!" the man shouted. "You little shit! Get back here! I paid for you!"

The door was shut, and it would take valuable seconds to open it. Long enough for the man to catch him, grab him, restrain him…punish him.

Kev tasted bile in the back of his throat, heard the kettledrum throb of his pulse in his ears.

"You fucking—" The man's hand snagged a handful of Kev's hair, gripping tight. His fingers were strong.

But Kev was fourteen. And he had a little strength of his own now too.

He threw his meager weight backward, against the hold on his hair, and the man grunted in surprise.

"Shit."

The fingers slid out of his hair, and Kev whirled. He felt his heart pounding straight through his chest. Felt a desperation like he'd never known. And launched himself at the man who'd bought him for the night.

He'd never used his body as a weapon, and he was clumsy. They fell to the carpet in a tangle of limbs, Kev on top, the air rushing out of their lungs. Kev reached for the man's face, hooking his fingers into claws.

The client heaved him off, rolled over on top of him, and punched him in the mouth. The blow snapped his head to the side; he felt the instant, cottony pressure of swelling as the pain whited out, too overwhelming to be felt in full yet. Then the client hit him in the jaw.

Kev heard the soft sound of his tooth knocking loose inside his skull.

His next thought, though the man was still on top of him, was that soon he'd be made to take this client's cock into his throbbing, bloody mouth. He'd be choked and held down, and the pain was going to be…

No. No, he couldn't. No way.

He stilled, pliant and limp beneath his customer. Waited. Waited.

"Now," the man said, leaning over him, breath ragged. He was straddling Kev's hips, pinning him down. "Are you going to behave?"

"Yes, sir," Kev said, and head-butted him.

Head-butting was, no surprise, a terrible way to attack someone. But he did manage to crack his forehead right into the man's nose, and the guy then reeled back in surprise, shouting. Kev felt the hot wetness of blood against his face, and he pushed past the pain in his head – he was well-used to fighting past pain at this point in his life – and levered the client off of him.

The man scrambled to grab for him, but Kev was too quick, on his feet and aiming a sharp kick at his client's head. He was barefoot, but it sent the man sprawling across the carpet, which gave Kev the window he needed. There was a robe thrown across the end of the bed, and he snagged it on his way out the door.

Because he'd been nothing but compliant on the way up, the client hadn't tried to blindfold him. Kev knew exactly which direction to run down the hall, where to turn to go down the rear staircase, the one the hired help used to access the kitchen. He shrugged into the robe as he ran. The client pursued; he could hear his clumsy lurching and cursing, but Kev was much too quick.

He hit the kitchen, whirled out a side door, and shut it silently behind him. He was in a small garden, herbs going by the scents sent spiraling into the air by his bare feet as he dashed through low clumps of greenery. It was dark, and he dodged the landscape lighting like a thief, robe fluttering around his legs.

He got away. Somehow, he reached the fence, scaled it in a few awkward, long-limbed movements, and was loose in the night. On his own and out in the open for the first time since he was shut into the backseat of his daddy's Cadillac all those years ago.

He ran, not caring where he was going, gulping down cold night air and ignoring the way the ground cut into the tender soles of his feet.

That was how he'd ended up here in the indigo hours just before dawn, collapsed on a metal picnic table beside a large, flat-roofed brick building with a massive parking lot and not enough windows. Exhausted, bleeding, sore, and almost delirious with anger and the withdrawal that always accompanied delaying his injection, he laid his head down on the cool surface of the table and watched the sun bloom to life along the horizon.

He must have dozed, because a din of voices woke him. He pushed himself up on weak arms, unfocused eyes tracking across his surroundings. The parking lot was packed with cars, crowds of talking, laughing kids with jeans and backpacks pouring in through the main doors of the building.

A school. He was at a school. It had been so long since he'd attended one himself that he hadn't even recognized one when he saw it.

Hot tears filled his eyes, and he wiped at them with shaky hands. What was his life? Why wouldn't it just *end*?

"Hey," a voice said behind him, and he whirled. Pulse pounding, vision swimming, mind already conjuring an image of the customer, bruised and furious and come to claim him for his punishment. But it was only a boy. Maybe his age. Shiny black hair in messy curls cropped close to his head, expression nothing like the veiled fear of the other dancers at The Nest. He was dressed in destroyed jeans, a black Metallica t-shirt, leather jacket, and heavy motorcycle boots. He had a belt studded with silver, and a wallet chain. A little on the skinny side, but tall, and trying to look tough. "What are you doing out here in your goddamn PJs?" he asked without any heat, nodding toward the striped robe.

"I..." Kev had to clear his throat and wet his lips. The shakes were getting worse, trembling in his throat, making it hard to hold his head up. "It's...it's not mine," he said, stupidly. Because he hadn't interacted with a single person who wasn't a bodyguard, dancer, customer, or Miss Carla in God knew how long.

The boy snorted. "Good, 'cause it's damn ugly." His eyes flicked down to Kev's bare feet, and back up to his long, snarled hair. "You homeless or something?"

"No."

"You go to school here?"

"No."

"Why don't you have any shoes on?"

"I..." His hands squirmed and he pressed them down on the tabletop, breath hitching. He felt sweat gathering beneath his hair, sliding down the back of his neck, slicking the skin behind his knees and between the sharp bumps of his backbone. "I can't...I don't..."

The boy stepped up and sat down on the bench beside Kev, his expression hardening into something older and world-weary, sharp with concern. "What are you on?"

Kev swallowed a knot of shame; he couldn't bear to meet the boy's gaze dead-on. He stared at his leather-clad shoulder. "I don't know. It's just…it's a shot. I missed one. And I…" He held up his shaking hands to demonstrate. They leapt like they were on puppet strings.

The boy nodded, sighing through his nose. "Right. H'll do that to you." He frowned. "Wait, you were taking it and didn't know what it was?"

"They…they give it to all of us," he said, and bit his lip, knowing he shouldn't have said anything.

The boy's dark eyes flew wide. "They? Shit, did you…" He glanced back down at Kev's feet. "Holy shit, do you…did you escape from somewhere?" He was breathing a little hard himself now.

Kev should have lied. Should have said he was fine and stood up on his newborn foal legs, tried to find his way back home. Only he had no idea where he was, or which direction home lay, and he was too weak to even move at this point.

He started to cry. "Y-yes."

The boy said, "Fuck. Shit. Okay. Okay, okay, just hold on a sec." He dug a cellphone from his pocket, pressed and held one, and put it to his ear. "Mags?" he said into the phone. "Hey, yeah, I'm fine, no. But look. I need you to come to the school. There's this kid…"

Kev let his head fall back to the table, listening to the dire, sad description of himself the boy gave into the phone.

He must have dozed again. He jerked awake, and it was lighter, the sun all the way up, and it was quiet, all the kids inside the school now, class in session.

"What…" he said, trying to push up onto his elbows. It took him three tries, the shaking so terrible.

The boy was still there beside him, and across from him, one hand covering Kev's on top of the table, was a pretty blonde woman in a leather jacket of her own, hair windswept, expression soft and careful.

"Hey there," she said, and he liked her voice. Smooth and gentle. "Not feeling so good, huh?"

"No," he croaked. In fact, he felt too awful to care if these strangers were safe to be around. He just wanted to stop feeling like shit. He wanted to die, more than a little bit.

"I'm sorry," she said, sincerely. "Let's see if we can do something about that. I'm Maggie. This is Aidan." She gestured to the boy. "We're taking you home with us."

~*~

He knew he shouldn't, that he would be in so much trouble, but Kev was too weak to keep from sliding into Maggie Teague's Cadillac and flopping his head back onto the leather seat.

He existed in a buzzing pocket of pain and unsteadiness; the voices from the front seat seemed miles away.

"I left Ava next door with Mrs. Schneider," Maggie said as she pulled out of the parking lot.

"Okay," Aidan said. "What are we going to do with him?"

"Get some food in him. Clean him up. Call the police."

Aidan snorted. "Dad won't like that."

"Dad won't like the idea of some poor strung-out barefoot kid being alone and defenseless in the world."

Said world flashed past the window, a blur of brown winter grass and blue sky. He shut his eyes when the nausea started to encroach. Sweat misted his face, slicked his skin beneath the robe. He wanted to throw up. He wanted to lie down flat. He itched, and fidgeted, and wanted to sleep, but couldn't. Maggie and Aidan's voices turned to white noise in the background.

He wondered, dimly, how furious Miss Carla was. If she was searching for him now. If Ian was worried.

Shit. Of course Ian was worried. And Kev had no way to contact him and let him know he was alright. *I'm fine, Ian,* he thought. *I'm better than fine. I'm gone...*

Twenty-Three

The bleak truth? Ian Byron was a selfish asshole. Because Kev escaped from a client's home when he was fourteen, went totally off the grid, and Ian *wanted him to come back*.

Miss Carla dragged him into her office at the club and slapped him across the face. "Where did he go?" She was livid.

He refused to cower in front of her; some clients were twice his size and folded him in half – literally and figuratively – and he had no choice. But he'd be damned if he gave this bitch the satisfaction.

He gave her an insolent shrug. "No idea."

She cracked him across the other cheek. "Don't fuck around with me, you little shit! Did you two plan this? Did you talk him into it?" Before he could answer, she advanced on him, leaning up into his face with stale coffee breath and blazing, red-rimmed eyes. "He was sweet as sugar before I let you put your queer fucking hands on him. What the hell was I thinking? Letting you two fraternize like this. I'm fucking stupid."

"You are, but not for that reason."

This time, the blow came from behind, a cane across the backs of his knees courtesy of one of Big John's thugs.

"Where did he go?" Miss Carla hissed.

Ian tasted blood on his tongue; he'd bitten the inside of his cheek. "I don't know."

The cane landed again, and his knees buckled. He crashed to the floor.

~*~

The thing was, Ian had never gone a night without dreaming of London – of his bland-faced, English gentrified family, the beautiful townhouse in Mayfair, his dancing lessons, and the chafing wool of his school uniform jumper – not until Kev. Every night he closed his eyes and went home, clawing desperately away from the lumpy futon in this locked and guarded apartment full of too many boys. And then every night, just as he was walking across the library to greet his unsmiling mother, the word shifted beneath his feet and he was back on the ship plowing across the Atlantic, headed for America, and slavery.

But then there was Kev.

There was no rescue, no rehab, no savior strong enough to help these other boys – they were already dead. The glassy compliance in their eyes evidenced killed souls. They were permanently stained, just like Ian. But then Kev. Sweet, shaking, innocent, *alive* Kev. He still had a soul, hidden in the dark spaces between his ribs, and Ian loved it like freedom, craved it like air. Kev could be saved, and goddamn it, Ian was going to be the one to save him.

At night, as the sweat cooled their bodies and they huddled beneath the thin blankets on the futon, Ian traced the lines of Kev's delicate face with his eyes and fantasized about their escape. Lately, fantasy had begun to feel a lot like planning.

In his mind, he worked successfully through a dozen elaborate escapes, Kev tucked beneath his arm, clinging to him with relief, and awe, and…

Okay. So Kev was definitely the damsel in distress in those scenarios.

Which he basically was anyway.

Ian was going to do this. *He was.* He spent months psyching himself up. He'd lived in the real world – before being snatched – longer than Kev. He would be able to find them clothes, and food, and shelter.

He nicked a cellphone from a client's pocket one night, hiding it down the front of his shorts until he was finally in the showers and able to pull it out. He used the phone's GPS to figure out where the club was on the map, and then later the apartment, when he was back home. He looked up nearby gas stations, homeless shelters, fast food stops, the Goodwill. They were in Knoxville, Tennessee. Fucking Tennessee. All the way from Mayfair to Hicktown – someone should make a novel of his life.

Soon, he told himself. He would pull the trigger very soon.

And then Kev was sent to that rich asshole for the night. Ian had been to him before, when he'd still looked more like a little boy. Sick fucker.

And now…now…

Kev was gone.

Without him.

~*~

Kev wasn't aware of falling asleep, only of coming awake, teeth chattering, cold down to his bones, shaking uncontrollably. His skin *crawled*; he imagined it rippling in little waves down his arms and legs and chest, covered in ants, in welts. His muscles ached and his lugs caught as he dragged in a deep breath and opened his eyes.

He was on a bed.

Oh God, a bed, were there cuffs? His client? Was he…?

He screamed and heaved himself upright.

"Jesus!" someone swore, and Kev had to *get the hell out of this place.*

Except his traitorous body wouldn't cooperate. It shriveled and caved in on itself as the room tilted and blurred.

"Whoa, son," the same someone said, and a man stepped up to the side of the bed, hands held out in a *take it easy* gesture. "You're okay. Calm down, alright?"

Kev blinked furiously, trying to clear his eyes. He wasn't strong enough to stand, or even sit up all the way, hands thrown out for balance against the mattress.

"Hey, dude," another voice said, and it was the voice of the boy from before – Aidan. "Dad," Aidan said, "back up, you're freaking him out."

The man snorted. "Heroin's freaking him out."

Heroin. His injection? God, there was so much he didn't know about the world.

But he knew he needed to get up and leave.

To his horror, the bed dipped beneath the man's weight as he sat down next to Kev. Up close, he had a handsome, aggressive face, dark eyes, his relation to Aidan obvious. In his rattled state, it took Kev a few seconds, heart pounding in his throat, ears ringing, to realize the man wasn't looking at him the way all the clients looked at him. There were no traces of lascivious intent in the man's gaze, no sneering smile of anticipation.

"Look, kid, you're detoxing, so I'm not gonna spare your virgin ears or anything," the man said. "I've seen some weird shit in my time, and trust me, you fall in that category."

"Smooth, Dad," Aidan said from the desk chair across the room. "You should be a guidance counselor."

"Can it. Okay." He turned back to Kev. "Where did you come from? You didn't just drop outta the sky beside the school. Who was holding you?"

Kev closed his eyes and pulled his knees up to his chest, dropped his forehead onto them. Too late he realized someone had put clothes on him: a pair of plaid pajama pants and a t-shirt. He smelled a hint of soap beneath the tang of his own poisoned sweat, and thought someone must have washed his face. Maybe more than that. He shivered.

"You a call boy?" the man asked. "Or just a regular junkie?"

"Dad!"

"I can't help him if he doesn't tell me what's going on," the man said. "How 'bout a simpler question. What's your name?"

"K-kev," he stammered into his knees. The pajama pants brushed against his face, soft and worn, smelling of clean linen.

These people...they were real people, weren't they? People like Mama, who he only remembered in rare snatches.

"Alright, Kev. Let's try this again. Are you a junkie?"

"What's that?"

"Shit. Where did you get the smack? Did you buy it? Steal it off your old man?"

Kev lifted his head, chin perched on the very top of one knee, and drew in a trembling breath. He felt like he was in a self-contained earthquake. His voice trembled from the shaking. "They just...they just give it to us. Our shots."

The man's composure slipped a fraction, something sparking in his eyes before he covered it up again, wiping a hand down his jaw. "Shit," he said.

"Shit," Aidan echoed.

Soft footsteps sounded beyond the open door, muffled by the carpet, and then Maggie poked her head around the doorjamb. "You're awake?" she asked Kev, eyes coming right to him.

He nodded.

"Feel like shit, though, huh?"

Another nod.

"I brought you something to eat." She stepped into the room balancing a tray of food and set it down on the end of the bed. Chicken noodle soup, a sleeve of crackers, bottled water and Gatorade. "See if you can get some of this down, sweetie."

The man got up from the bed, making Kev feel marginally better. "Can I talk to you?" he asked Maggie, dark brows raised meaningfully.

She nodded and they slipped out of the room, voices low murmurs.

Kev stared at the tray.

Aidan said, "I've never shot up, but some of the guys have. They're totally wrecked after."

"Yeah," Kev said.

"The soup's homemade. Mags is a really good cook."

Kev's hand was shaking so badly it took three tries to pick up the spoon. He dragged the tray closer with clumsy movements, and managed to lift a bit of broth to his lips after a struggle.

Aidan was right; Mags was a good cook.

Aidan climbed off the chair and came to sit on the chest at the foot of the bed while Kev continued to sip broth. "Look, my dad's a total asshole, but he's not a bad guy." He made a face. "Okay, so maybe half the city would disagree with that. He's just, well…" Another face. "What I'm trying to say is, whatever you're running from, whatever kind of shit you're in, we can help. Nothing goes down in this town without the club knowing about it. And wherever you've been, that counts as something we want to know about."

"The club?"

Aidan smiled and looked proud. "The Lean Dogs. That's us." He ducked his head. "Well, it'll be me someday. Real soon. My dad's VP now, and I'm gonna patch in soon as I've got my own bike."

Aidan got up and went back to the desk, returned with a framed photo that he held out for Kev's inspection, holding it himself so Kev didn't have to go through the arduous process of setting down his spoon and reaching.

In the photo, scruffy men in jeans and lots of leather were lined up in front of a low gray building. Behind them, he caught a glimpse of a white sign with a black dog on it, and black lettering. *Lean Dogs Motorcycle Club.*

~*~

Kev managed to choke down half the bowl of soup and a handful of crackers, Aidan chatting happy and oblivious in the background, talking about what kind of bike he wanted when he turned sixteen, about how he assumed he'd follow in his father's footsteps and become an officer in the club. His father's name was Ghost, which didn't seem all that strange to Kev, seeing as how he danced as Loverboy. He wondered vaguely if Ghost was a dancer name too, but he doubted it. The man didn't have that look about him.

He was sipping Gatorade when the nausea hit, and Aidan lifted up a plastic wastebasket just in time.

Whoever these people were, these Lean Dogs, Kev had no choice but to trust them. And truly, no matter what they intend to do with him, it couldn't be much worse than a regular work day at the club. Right?

The first day passed in fits of stolen sleep, sweating, shaking, nibbling at bits of food, and lurching to the bathroom. He was sick, so sick, his body raw and damaged in the wake of the poison he'd been given every day for he forgot how long. *Detoxing*, Ghost called it.

The sickness moved through his GI tract late into the night. He fell asleep on the bathroom floor, half-curled around the toilet.

Sometime the next day, when bright sunlight filled the bedroom, he managed to keep down a granola bar and really take stock of his surroundings. He was in a bedroom – Aidan's bedroom, he knew – and he'd been lying on a comfortable double bed with white sheets and blue blankets. A desk occupied the wall opposite him, topped with a bulletin board full of magazine cut-outs of pretty girls and sleek motorcycles. To the left was a mirrored dresser. A few punk rock black leather belts were draped over the closet door handle. And to his right was a window. No bars. Soft white drapes. A view of a green yard full of flowers and trees, and a street beyond, slow neighborhood traffic sliding past.

A real boy's room, lived in by a real boy, who had parents, and went to school, and talked about what he *wanted* to do. He was allowed to *want* things.

The door was ajar, and eased open softly as Maggie peeked in. "Doing okay, sweetie?"

He nodded, not trusting his voice. Every time she said something kind to him, his throat tightened and his eyes burned, because he just didn't understand her. What was she getting from this? How did treating him as if he were her own child benefit her? Everything a person did, they did because they wanted something.

She stepped into the room, a box of Entenmann's chocolate doughnuts in one hand, tall glass of milk in the other.

"I brought a treat," she said. "I know when my boys feel like crap, this is their favorite guilty pleasure." She sat on the end of the bed, flipped the box open and set it down near Kev's feet. "I offer to get them fresh bakery doughnuts, but the uncultured cavemen like the boxed kind," she said with a laugh. "Go figure."

Kev stared at the waxy chocolate circles with total fixation. He hadn't had anything sweet to eat since the day he met Miss Carla. Sweets would make him chubby; sweets would detract from his Loverboy grace; sweets were forbidden.

"Go on, honey," Maggie said. "Have as many as you want. Your stomach still upset?"

"No, I..." He licked his lips. He couldn't even remember what chocolate tasted like; the faint scent coming from the box teased along his tongue, made his mouth water. "I can't have sugar," he admitted, face heating with shame.

"You diabetic?"

"I...I'm not *allowed*."

She pressed her lips together, hazel eyes going wide, soft...and a little murderous in the corners, a quiet inward aggression. Her hand was kind, though, as she reached to touch his ankle. "Kev. Sweetie. Eat all the doughnuts you want. There's no one here to tell you what's allowed." Her fingers squeezed, and for some reason, he believed her.

Slowly, as if there was a snake in the box, he leaned forward and picked up a doughnut between thumb and forefinger. The texture was as waxy as it appeared, and when he brought it up to his face, breathed in deep the scent, his stomach growled.

He started to say something, some last protest, and Maggie gave him a stern look.

He opened his mouth and took a bite.

And almost fainted.

She smiled. "Pretty good stuff, huh?"

He nodded and kept eating.

"Whoa, don't go too fast, you don't want to bring it back up."

He nodded again; that was smart. He slowed down, measured, careful bites, the flaking layer of chocolate and spongy yellow center. It was the best thing he'd ever tasted.

"Okay," she said, "you keep eating – eat all you want, baby – and I'm going to talk a little bit. I have some questions, and all you have to do is nod or shake your head, okay?"

He nodded and reached for the next doughnut.

"Ghost says you didn't inject yourself with the heroin," she said.

He shook his head.

"Was it a friend?"

Another head shake.

"Your mom or dad?"

No.

"So someone bad, then."

He nodded.

"Do you live with your family?"

No.

"You don't want to tell me where you came from, do you?"

No.

"Because you're afraid you'll get in trouble? Because you're not allowed to say?"

A hesitant nod.

She took a deep breath. "Kev, have you heard of a place called The Cuckoo's Nest?"

A lump of doughnut got stuck in his throat.

She patted his foot. "It's okay, baby, it's okay."

~*~

An explosive sound echoed through the dressing room. Eyeliner pencils were dropped, boys gasped. Big John barged in, scowling. "Get your shit, you buncha queers. We're leaving in five."

"What?" several voices chorused.

Several boys scrambled to comply without question, the little ones, scared shitless at all times.

Ian set down his brush slowly, his freshly-rouged face pale and perfect in the mirror before him. He turned away from his flawless reflection, and pushed through frantic boys to get to Big John.

"What's going on?"

"Get your shit," Big John said, dismissively.

"What's happening?" Ian pressed, and grabbed the man's sleeve.

The back of Big John's hand impacted his cheek with a loud smack. Ian bit his tongue and tasted blood.

"What part of shut up don't you fucking understand?" Big John asked. But he was distracted; none of his usual pointed looks and threats of personal violence. Through his glaze of pain-tears, Ian saw unmistakable fear caught in the fleshy width of Big John's face.

A raid, then.

"Move it, ladies!" Big John bellowed to the room at large.

Everyone hustled to comply, dragging robes and hoodies and track pants on over their shorts, cramming expensive makeup compacts into duffels. The dressing room fluttered with quiet sounds of panic and hurry.

Ian went back to his station, holding his face in one hand, unhurried. When he looked in the mirror, he saw that his mascara and kohl were dribbling down his cheeks, little black rivers, and he smiled at himself.

A raid. Thank Jesus, *a raid.*

~*~

"Hey. Hey, Kev, wake up." Someone shook his shoulder, and his eyes flipped open. In the dark bedroom, he could just make out another pair of eyes, their sheen from the ambient light filtering in at the window.

Ian, he thought at first. But these eyes were brown. It was Aidan, kneeling beside the bed.

"Come on," he said. "Dad wants to talk to you."

Heavy and disoriented, Kev pushed up onto an elbow, the room spinning around him, a whirl of shadows. His mouth felt full of cotton. "Is it morning?"

"Like four a.m. Sorry, dude, he says it's important."

Kev nodded and climbed out of bed. He could keep food down now, and the terrible shaking had eased, but he was still unsteady and weak. He didn't argue when Aidan handed him a borrowed robe to wear over his borrowed pajamas, just belted it on and followed the boy down the hall to the kitchen.

The house between the two rooms lay black with shadow, the night an even darker shade beyond the windows. That deep point between night and morning, when the world seemed to be underwater. The kitchen seemed too bright, the overhead light cold and unforgiving. Kev squinted when he stepped into the room.

Ghost sat at the table, nursing an amber drink in a low glass, wearing a black hoodie and the leather vest-thing with all the patches that Aidan had called a "cut," identifying his status as a Lean Dog.

Kev froze in the threshold, because in that moment, a smudge of soot on his forehead, face hard and lined, Aidan's father was the most frightening man he'd ever seen.

Ghost's voice was almost gentle, though, when he said, "Take a seat. Both of you – you might as well hear this," he added to Aidan.

They both slumped down into chairs, and from this angle, the overhead light seemed conical and threatening. At first, anyway. But Ghost's strained, tired expression wasn't something he was sending to them intentionally. He wasn't angry with them, but with something – some*one* – else.

"The boys and I," he started, "paid a little visit to Carla Burgess over at The Cuckoo's Nest."

That was as far as he got before Kev's brain imploded. A hard burst of static in his head, the closing of his throat all that prevented his abortive stomach from leaping out onto the floor. His knees did hit the floor, though, as he slid off his chair and curled around himself, gasping.

"Kev?"

He heard his name, dim through the roaring of blood in his ears.

"Kev." A set of denim-clad knees appeared in front of his own. He managed to jerk his head back, gulping air, clutching his heaving sides, and saw Aidan kneeling opposite him, his expression worried, brows tucked together over his eyes. "Kev, what's wrong?"

Ghost's voice floated down from above. "You were there, weren't you? At The Nest?"

Kev could only nod, voice too tight to speak.

"How long were you there?" Ghost pressed.

Kev couldn't answer, trying to breathe, trying not to pass out.

"Where are your parents?"

"Dad," Aidan protested.

The sound of heavy boots echoed against the linoleum as Ghost moved around the table to get to them. When Kev tipped his head back, his airway closed, and he saw the man's harsh frown, the darkness of his eyes.

"Dad," Aidan said again.

And Kev passed out.

~*~

He was in bed when he came to. Which meant someone had carried him back to the bedroom, handled him while he was unconscious. He wondered if he'd been touched. He clenched his thighs together, searching for tenderness, the telltale burn of post-penetration – but didn't find it.

Early sunlight filtered through the window blinds, slanted stripes of shadow across the covers on the bed.

Kev rolled onto his side and saw the desk chair pulled up beside the bed, Ghost sitting on it, arms folded, still dark and menacing as before. Aidan wasn't there; it was just the two of them.

But Ghost's voice was gentle when he said, "You're one of her dancing boys, aren't you?"

Kev swallowed hard and nodded, pillow rustling beneath his cheek.

Ghost sighed. Long, and deep, and weary. "Shit," he muttered. "For how long?"

The truth sat like a tight ball of sickness high in his gut. If he let it come up his throat, let it out into the room, then Ghost would know about the cancer of the spirit that lay deep in his bones. He would know about the clients, about the dancing, about the man whose house he'd fled. And worse yet, he might turn him back over to Miss Carla, and she would punish him for spilling her secrets. That he knew without question.

"Kev. Kiddo." Ghost leaned forward and placed one of his large, rough hands gently on top of Kev's head, cupped carefully over the dome of his skull. Kev shuddered. "I burned that goddamn place to the ground. You will *never* go back there again. She can't touch you anymore, I promise you that."

The awful ball rolled in his stomach, and he gasped, all the air forced out of his lungs. "Never?" he asked, weakly.

"Never. Hand to God."

And finally, finally, for the first time, the soul-quenching tears of relief came, pouring silently down his face.

And tears of grief, too, because what about Ian? *What about Ian?*

~*~

Ghost Teague was a hard-working, sharp-tongued, matter-of-fact blue collar man, but there was a certain rough poetry to the way he spun a tale.

Miss Carla's real name, as Ghost told it, was Carla Burgess, and she was – again, in his words – a notorious bitch of a madam. That's what you called a woman who held the leashes of prostitutes: a madam. Ghost called her other things, obscenities laced with truths Kev knew all too well, chiefly that Miss Carla's boys weren't prostitutes, but property. Stolen boys

294

made to dance and perform, because she liked the money…and because she liked the spectacle. And what she did was very, *very* illegal.

She'd never been arrested, though, because apparently she had a PD connection, and because the club kept moving around. Sometimes it stayed in place for only a few weeks, but Kev knew the latest location had been in place for at least two years, as long as he'd been there.

What surprised him was Ghost's apology. "We always knew she had to be somewhere, and that she wasn't getting picked up by PD anytime soon, but we should have pursued her. I'm sorry, kid. I should have taken her out a long time ago, then this wouldn't have happened to you."

What were the Lean Dogs, then? That they could "take someone out"?

"What happened to them?" he asked, voice a croak.

Ghost didn't seem to need any clarification on "them." "We burned the place to the ground. The FD's gonna have a field day with it. Took out a few of her thugs." He shrugged. No big deal; like he killed people all the time. "Made it look like an accident. But" – and here he looked regretful – "Carla and her boys were already gone. They're on the run."

Oh God. Ian. *Ian, Ian, Ian.*

"All of them?"

Ghost's expression softened. "You have friends there, yeah?"

He nodded, throat constricting too hard to speak.

"We'll find them," Ghost said, and it sounded like a promise.

~*~

"You know the story after that." Tango sipped from his fourth cup of coffee – he was going to regret this later – and tapped ash off his third cigarette. "Ghost found my aunt – Mom was already dead. She killed herself," he said, without inflection.

Sure she'd never find him, exhausted, unemployed, Mama filled the bathtub and drew a razor across both wrists. Like mother like son. It ran in the family, the urge to end oneself.

Mama's sister, Anne, had taken him in; she'd moved to Knoxville and they'd settled into a modest duplex near the high school, where he was enrolled and went to class with Aidan.

A small part of him marveled that he could sit in a chair like this, calmly smoking, and talk about the total reversal of his young, fucked-up life without shaking apart at his many fault lines. That must be the Lean Dog in him taking over, the hardened biker riding out the ice floes of doubt and heartbreak that his real self couldn't handle.

Mercy drew a massive breath into his massive chest and said, "You're still thinking about that real therapist, right?"

"Yeah. I am."

Twenty-Four

There were of course parts of his story that he didn't have to tell Mercy. Parts that he already knew, and had even been involved in, to an extent.

His recapture. The second act of his personal Shakespearean tragedy.

He knew who needed to hear that story.

~*~

Being back at work helped in a different, but just as important way. It was the same job, the same steady stream of Harleys and imports, the same old tools, and greasy rags, and low wooden benches, and big heaters they used to keep the shop warm in the winter months. But after his stint in the basement, back on heroin, he'd lost sight of the magic of having a job – having *this job*. Ghost Teague had trained him, mostly raised him, and gifted him with this mechanic position, which he'd never dreamed of and never thought he could deserve.

He'd lost sight of his blessings. He hated himself for that.

Evening was settling in quick and dark, and he was just finishing up for the day, stowing his tools in the large red Craftsman chests between the bays, when he heard a female voice call, "Hey, Handsome."

He turned and saw that it was Jazz, her too-thin denim jacket buttoned tight against the cold, the strategic rips in her jeans revealing tan skin pebbled with goosebumps. She looked sexy, because she always did, but she also looked cold, and she had on too much makeup, and she looked tired to Tango. Maybe it was all the time he'd spent in Whitney's young presence…but mostly he thought it was Jasmine's lifestyle catching up to her, finally. She'd spent her entire adult life partying as hard as she could, and it had dimmed her inner light.

"Looking for Carter?" he asked. "I think he went to talk to Mags."

"No, looking for you, actually." She climbed up onto the picnic table and patted the wood beside her. "Come sit with me."

He hesitated, and both of them realized that he did at once, Jazz's smile freezing, his stomach dropping. It was the first time he'd ever hesitated in their history together. Things had changed. They didn't have a claim on each other anymore.

Tango felt a brief pang of sadness as he walked out and climbed up beside her, there and gone again. They had both moved on; there was nothing close to heartbreak between them.

Jazz cupped the top of his knee with one hand. "How you doin', baby boy?"

He took a deep breath and let it out in a rush, enjoying the scrape of cold air in his lungs, eyes spotting the faint ghosts of stars along the purpling horizon, waiting to come fully into view. "I'm doing okay," he said, and it didn't feel like an empty statement this time.

"Yeah?" She sent him a soft, sad smile. "No more bad thoughts in there?" She reached and tapped his temple with a fingertip.

"Only manageable ones."

She knocked her shoulder sideways into his. "You're not funny."

"Never have been."

"I'm serious, though, Tango."

He took another deep breath; it felt cleansing. Healing. It felt *good*. "I'm better. I'm working through it."

"I'm glad." She relaxed against his side, head resting on his shoulder. "You finally found a sweet little good girl to settle down with."

"I'm not settled down, Jazz. It's still early."

"Whatever. She's exactly what you always needed. I can tell."

"Jazz the Mystic and Powerful."

"Shut up." She shifted a little closer as the sun swept out of sight below the trees, and the wind tightened its chill grip around them. She had something on her mind; he could feel its weight, pressed up tight to the edge of his shoulder, filling her head. She shivered and said, "Carter said I was his old lady yesterday."

"Yeah?"

Her voice came out almost shy, which he could safely say he'd never heard before. "He tried to give me some money. Shit, I told him no, that I wouldn't take his charity. But he said he was going to take care of his old lady." She let out a breath that was part-surprised, part-worried. "I've been hanging around here almost twenty-five years, and ain't nobody ever wanted me to be his old lady."

He turned his head a fraction so he could kiss the top of her head. She smelled like hair spray. "You deserve it."

"Said one whore to another."

"Yep." He slid an arm around her shoulders and squeezed. "Absolutely."

"I'm sorry."

"For what?"

"Letting go of you. That was a shitty thing to do. All of a sudden, the way I did it."

He rubbed her arm, and for the first time, touching her felt platonic. "Nah," he assured. "I'm not sure you ever really had me."

~*~

It was full dark by the time he headed home, the Christmas lights in the shop windows along Main Street shining happily, the illuminated swags on the lampposts reflecting along dark upper stories, dazzling in stray puddles. The air smelled of snow, and Frasier fir as he passed the tree lot set up on the corner.

Would Whitney like a tree? The thought flickered through his mind and found soft places to take root. Yes, Whitney ought to have a tree.

By the time he pulled up behind her car in the alley, he was smiling to himself. A strange lightness echoed in his chest.

He was happy, he realized. Right now, in this moment, he was happy. Happy for Jazz, happy to have laid his demons out in the light. He was thinking about Christmas trees and the pretty girl waiting for him upstairs, and he was *happy*. Imagine that.

He took the iron stairs two at a time and let himself into the apartment to find Whitney standing in his kitchen, peering out at the Christmas lights on the street, smiling to herself, the smell of sautéed onions curling around her in visible wisps of steam.

"Hi," she greeted, turning away from the window to give him one of her guileless, beautiful smiles. She had the sleeves of her sweater pushed up, a wooden spoon in her hand; her socks were a thick gray wool with little snowflakes on them.

The sight of her hit him hard, a fierce shove against his breastbone. He was in love with her.

He didn't return her greeting. He crossed the small apartment in a few strides, captured her face in both hands, and kissed her, long and deep.

Her breath hitched when he pulled back, a little puff of surprise against his lips. "Hi," she repeated, warm and melty this time.

He smiled so wide it actually hurt. "Hi." Then he had to let go of her, or risk setting her up on the counter and ruining his plans for the evening. "What are you making?"

"Uh…" she said, pink-cheeked and flustered, and Tango grinned to himself. "Spaghetti."

"Sounds good." And it did; his bachelor life's version of spaghetti came in a can. "How long 'til it's ready?"

"Well, I was about to put the tomato sauce in, and then the sauce needs to simmer about thirty minutes. Hungry?"

"No. Well, yeah, I am. But I want to do something first, before we eat."

She gave him a knowing look, smile turning sultry at the edges. Shit, when had she learned how to do that? "Okay."

"Oh! No, not that. Well, um, yes that, but later." He scrubbed the back of his neck, suddenly nervous. "I wondered if maybe you wanted to walk over and get a tree."

Whitney abandoned all pretenses of seduction and gasped. "Really? You would do that?"

300

"Yeah, what do you say?"

"I say yes! Hold on, let me…and then I'll just get my coat…"

He went to fetch her jacket for her, that lightness in his chest somehow expanding.

They left the sauce simmering, vowed to be quick, called themselves idiots for leaving the stove on purposefully, and made the short walk down the sidewalk to the tree lot. They picked out a small tree ("Look at you two cuties," the woman working the till said), and Tango lugged it back home while Whitney carried the stand they'd bought to put it in.

"I've never actually set one of these up," he admitted when they got back to the apartment and he stood with the fir propped against the front wall, hands sticky with sap.

"It's easy," Whitney assured. "If you've got the muscle, I've got the know-how."

With minimal cursing, and only a few near-disasters, they got the tree all set up in the corner, its stand full of fresh cold water, its branches slowly relaxing now that the plastic mesh had been cut away.

Tango admired their handiwork and said, "Well, shit, we don't have lights or ornaments."

"We could go get some after we eat," Whitney offered, coming to lean up against his side. His arm slipped around her automatically. "Home Depot will still be open."

"Hmm," he said, noncommittally. It was cold, and dark, and the prospect of fighting through the crowded Home Depot garden center didn't appeal to him all that much right now.

Whitney leaned in a little closer, her small body warm against his, through their clothes. "Or we could just stay in."

"Yeah." Something sharp and painful turned over inside him, something he knew had to come out. "Yeah, I…Whit, I need to tell you something." He glanced down at her and saw that her face was tipped up, her expression concerned. "I need to explain it to you. Why I…why I am the way that I am."

He hated himself already, but he knew he needed this one last test. One more chance to push her away with the horrible truth of his past. If she could survive this story, then she could survive all of it. He was in love with her, and he couldn't turn her loose at this point, not even to spare her. But he could share his dark secrets with her, and let her walk away on her own, if she wanted. He owed her that, at least.

One last chance to save her from himself, the Dogs, all of it.

She swallowed, eyes already a little wet, and said, "Okay. I'll fix our plates and then okay, you can tell me whatever you need to, sweetie."

Holy shit, here went nothing…

~*~

It was probably a good thing Tango had no idea what a regular sixteen-year-old's life was like, because he was pretty sure being a sixteen-year-old Lean Dog would have broken a regular kid's brain.

A fist pounded on the door, and Ghost's voice echoed through: "Five minutes! Get your asses out here!"

In the mirror above the dorm room dresser, Tango buttoned his gray flannel shirt and checked that his eyes weren't too bloodshot.

Beside him, Aidan raked his hair into shape and flashed a pretend smirk at his reflection, image-conscious as ever.

Behind them on the bed, Misty took her cigarette from her mouth. "Boys," she whined, "do you have to go? Really?"

"Really, doll, sorry," Aidan said, grinning in a smug, self-satisfied way as he turned around to face her.

Tango turned too, and he was too tired and spent to take much interest in the naked, disheveled state of the groupie lounging back on the bed, plumping her breasts together with her arms and pouting at them. She wrapped her lips around the cigarette filter in an unmistakable way.

She sighed dramatically, chest heaving. "I'll miss you." A mischievous grin cut across her mouth. "Later, then."

"Absolutely," Aidan said, and leaned forward to tweak her nipple, earning a squeal of a laugh, as they headed for the door.

In the hallway, the door shut behind them, Aidan clapped Tango on the shoulder and kept his hand there, squeezing. "You okay?"

Tango pulled in a deep breath and could smell sex on both of them, the scent of the woman they'd just shared. He always wondered, secretly, if Aidan thought it was weird to do it that way. Personally, after nothing but sex with men, he found it a little comforting having his best friend with him.

"Yeah, I'm fine."

Aidan's hand squeezed again. "You've been kinda quiet."

He snorted. "I'm always kinda quiet."

The hallway emptied and spilled them out into the crowded common room, preventing further discussion.

"Finally," Ghost said, shooting them an exasperated look. "Get laid on your own time."

Up by the bar, James held court, explaining their next run.

Tango tuned him out. He knew he shouldn't; what he did with the club was dangerous. But Ghost would repeat it to him and Aidan later, whether he listened or not. And it sounded like it was just a regular run, escorting a truck full of hidden guns. Unless they were pulled over by the cops – and even then they had protocols in play and good camo to keep their wares from being found – or ambushed by a rival club, the run would handle itself. All he had to do was fall in formation, and make sure Maggie wrote him a note excusing him from school.

"We leave at eight tomorrow morning," James said, wrapping up the impromptu meet. "Don't be late."

When the group dispelled, Tango slid onto a bar stool and folded his arms over the bar. He didn't want to drink. He didn't really know what he wanted. He felt the old restless buzzing inside him that had become such a part of his life with Miss Carla. He hadn't thought it would catch up to him here, not after he'd spent the last two years shaking off the horrors of the sex club, settling in with his aunt, prospecting and then joining *this* club, finding his own place within the brotherhood.

Maybe he'd been too busy to let this sensation catch up to him. Maybe now that he was finally stable, now that he had school, and work, and his bike, and more sex than any boy his age should have been exposed to…maybe the peace couldn't last. He felt it slinking up behind him, its hot breath against his neck: the craving.

Stupid, stupid, stupid. He'd thought he'd outrun it. That it was something he could leave behind. But his addiction lived in the marrow of his bones. He craved the bite of the needle. And if he was honest…sometimes…sometimes he craved the rough touch of a man, someone impersonal and brutal.

"Dude," Aidan said, startling him, sliding onto the neighboring stool. "Okay, for real now. What's up?"

Tango shrugged and refused to make eye contact, afraid Aidan would see the craving in his gaze. "Just feeling kinda out of it lately, I guess."

"You getting sick? Shit, you don't think Misty…"

Tango had to crack a grin. "You always wear a rubber."

"Yeah. Shit, I do." Aidan sighed and scrubbed at the back of his neck. How easily his panic came and went, sliding over him in transient little waves that really never touched him. "Damn, don't scare me like that," he said with a laugh, bumping his shoulder into Tango's.

Aidan stretched across the bar and plucked a bottle of Jack from the stash on the counter beyond, twirled it idly in his hands, like he was trying to decide if he wanted a slug of it. Yesterday, he'd taken a mighty sip and promptly coughed it all back out, dribbling it down his white t-shirt until their brothers were rolling with laughter, and the groupies were trying to hide little titters behind their hands.

He set the bottle back. "You wanna come to dinner tonight? Mags said she was frying chicken." He waggled his eyebrows, and Tango wanted to smile, because the guy always looked like an idiot when he did that.

"Nah, I should get back. Anne's expecting me," he said of his aunt. He didn't know if she really was. She'd mentioned something about going to the grocery store earlier. She always said she liked cooking for him, but she felt so needlessly guilty about what had happened to him she still had trouble not crying across the dinner table from him. He ate a lot of dinners with the Teagues, where he could get lost in Maggie's happy conversation, Ava's complaining about school, Aidan's dumb jokes and Ghost's stern but obvious affection for them all.

The craving didn't much want fried chicken and happy family times tonight, though.

"You sure?" Aidan asked, doubtful.

"Yeah. Thanks though."

"Sure. Always."

The sun rode low above the tree line when he walked out to his bike. It was a '91 Superglide that had seen much, much better days. But the engine thrummed happily when he cranked it, and he and Aidan had mapped out plans for new pipes, and paint, and maybe a little custom work on the tank – though Ghost had given them a withering look about that. Ghost liked black on black on black, without exception.

The craving eased as he pulled out of the Dartmoor lot and headed for home. The rumble of the engine beneath him, and the slap of the wind in his face, the drowning rush of passing traffic – he'd never imagined this. That he would go to school, have friends, have brothers, have sex that didn't involve money, have his own bike, and his own cut, and a few tattoos that seemed to keep multiplying. He had earrings now, too, just one in each ear, but he was thinking of adding more.

Because he could do that now – he could *think*. Make decisions. He was his own man.

Why the hell would he let heroin and a strange sex drive jeopardize any of that? He was a coward, an idiot, or both.

Tango coasted up to a red light and heard another bike pull up alongside him, felt its rumble through his own bike. Mercy halted next to him, big, tattooed arms bare under his cut, looking like the scariest thing on two wheels.

"Hey," he shouted, "you wanna grab a drink?"

Tango chuckled. The big monster's perpetual good mood was infectious. "Dude, I'm underage!"

"Ah, shit! I forgot!" Mercy reached to tuck a stray lock of hair up beneath his helmet, adjusted his glasses. "I gotta get to Ghost's anyway."

Because Tango knew for a fact that a lot of his protection detail involved helping Ava with school art projects. There was something about the sight of the big Cajun bent over a table with a delighted eight-year-old that warmed even the coldest of hearts.

Tango nodded. The light changed. "See you tomorrow!"

"Yeah!"

Mercy turned left and Tango went straight. He wondered, not for the first time, what his brothers would think of him if they knew the truth of his past. Aidan and Ghost knew, and they hadn't cared; they'd saved him. But the rest? Even someone as warm-hearted as Mercy? He didn't want to test their acceptance, not anytime soon.

At the next light, he checked his phone and saw a text from Aunt Anne: *grab some bread on your way home pls.*

Ok. He'd already passed Leroy's, so he pulled into the drug store up ahead and found a spot in the front for his bike, thankful he had his backpack and wouldn't have to balance groceries in front of him on the tank – he could still remember the sight of all those cracked eggs on the pavement, and the shout of laughter from the convertible in the next lane. Assholes.

"Hi, how are you?" a disinterested teenage clerk called when he entered.

"Good," Tango said, shyly, and headed for the small grocery section in the store, wending his way through displays of flip-flops, sunscreen, and big wire cages of beach balls. He grabbed a loaf of bread, then, on impulse, stretched up on his toes to reach for a box of chocolate mini doughnuts on the top shelf.

And froze.

In the big round mirror above him, he spotted three men in black t-shirts coming up behind him. Three *large* men. Not Mercy-size, but big enough.

Tango dropped and whirled, bread crushed to his chest. The man closest to him…was Max. Max, who'd cuffed him every time he took too long in the bathroom. Who'd put his cock in Tango's mouth when he was still just Kev. And he had a knife in his hand.

"Don't make a sound," he said.

And Tango didn't.

~*~

"Don't call me that," he seethed, straining against the duct tape that bound his hands together at the small of his back. As expected, it didn't give an inch.

Behind the desk, Miss Carla made a show of looking surprised. She pressed a hand to her chest, where a diamond pendant hung above the scoop neckline of her dress. How many lap dances and backroom visits had she needed to pay for that diamond? "Well. You're just full of piss and vinegar these days, ain't ya? Alright, sweetness." She gave him a wicked smile. "What do you want me to call you? What do your little biker friends call you, huh?"

He ground his teeth, realizing belatedly that he didn't want her to know his club name. That was for him; something connected to his new life and his brothers, and she didn't deserve to know it.

When he didn't answer, she said, "Just plain ol' Kev, then? Hmm. Not real sexy there, Loverboy."

He grunted in annoyance.

"How about this? How about I call you whatever I damn well please? Sound good?"

He pressed his lips together and didn't answer.

"Good," Carla purred, turning back to her computer. "Let's see here…hmm. You've been a busy boy since we talked to each other last. A B student at Knoxville High. Known patched member of the Lean Dogs MC – that puts you on a list with the PD, you know. They've got a list of all members and known associates." A quick, delighted smile. "You've got a nice little room with your aunt. And that family you stay with all the time. The Teagues. Lots of sleepovers there."

"How do you know all that?"

Miss Carla raised her eyes somewhere above his head and nodded.

Max's slap caught him in the back of the head, fast and hard.

"I hired a detective to find you," Miss Carla said.

"Why?"

This time, the slap sent him sliding out of the chair to his knees, colored spots dancing in front of his eyes.

"Because you're my favorite," he heard her say, before he blacked out.

~*~

He had no idea where this new club was located; he'd worn a hood in the van on the way over, after Max had bound his hands and kicked him in the ribs so hard he'd thought he'd puke inside the hood. The office had looked much the same, with a desk, and chairs, and a computer. And when Tango came to, he found himself on a cot in a shadowy, cold room with exposed floor joists in the ceiling overhead.

Panic seized his lungs and he lurched upright, head spinning, stomach grabbing, thinking he was back in the basement of Miss Carla's ugly patchwork house.

It wasn't the same basement, though. A different one. More cots like the one he was on marched across the concrete floor in an orderly line. But there were also a few couches and chairs, an open door through which he could see a large bathroom with several locker room-style showers and sinks. He didn't spot any iron bars, only a stairwell leading upward, and he had no doubt the door at the top was triple-padlocked against escape.

"Fuck," he muttered to himself. "Just fuck."

Several thin, pretty boys sat cross-legged on the rug in the center of the room, playing some sort of card game. They all turned to look over their shoulders when they heard his voice, and Tango caught a flash of bright coppery hair.

Ian stood up slowly, as slender and straight-backed and beautiful as a fairytale creature, expression unreadable, blue-green eyes luminous in the dim basement light.

Oh, Ian. He was alive, and whole, and safe, and he hadn't died in the fire Ghost had set to the old club.

Tango swallowed a sudden lump in his throat, unable to speak.

Ian's façade slipped, a brief flicker of deep, complex emotion, but he schooled his features and came to sit on the end of Tango's cot.

Tango wanted to say so many things, beginning with *sorry*, ending with some sort of declaration of love.

Ian leaned forward, a deliberate reach, and laid his hand on Tango's knee, stared down at the place where they were connected. His eyelashes danced as he blinked. "They found you," he said in a quiet, broken voice.

"Yeah. They did."

~*~

"Where have you been? It's been *two years*."

One of the goons had brought down dinner, a bland meal had been consumed by all, evening ablutions were completed, and the lights were cut off. All the cots were full but two, because Ian and Tango lay stretched out together on the couch, arms and legs tangled together, Ian breathing unevenly against Tango's throat.

Tango raked his fingers through Ian's long, slick hair. "A boy found me, after I got away from the client. A nice boy. My friend." He didn't say *best friend* because he didn't figure Ian was ready to hear something like that yet. "I stayed with them for a while, and then they helped me find my aunt. I'm living with her now."

Or, well, he had been. But he had a sick feeling he was living in this basement from now on.

"Really?" Ian asked, incredulous. "They just…they let you go home with them? They took care of you?"

"They're good people."

Ian made a disagreeing sound.

"They are, I promise. They helped me buy clothes, got me enrolled at school. Ghost gave me a job, let me patch into the club."

Ian pushed at his chest, propping up on an elbow and giving him a look mostly obscured by shadow. His voice came out mocking. "Ghost? Patch? Club? What the hell are you talking about?"

Tango sighed and traced his thumb down Ian's smooth cheek. "It's a biker club."

"Are you serious?"

He ignored Ian's mocking laugh and continued: "The Lean Dogs. Ghost is the vice president, and he's also the one who took me in. He doesn't…Ian, he doesn't care what I used to do. He let me into the club anyway. They're my *brothers*. They say so. They…" He trailed off as his chest tightened. It was still amazingly painful, the idea that such regular, masculine men called him *brother*.

"Oh, so that's what you wanted." Ian's teeth flashed white as his lip skinned back off of them. "Brothers? What am I then?"

Taken aback, Tango pressed his head behind him into the couch cushion, trying to read Ian's expression through the dark. "I thought…I thought you'd be happy for me."

Ian snorted.

"Ian…I got to be real for a little bit."

"Real?" Ian surged forward, their chests pressing together, their noses bumping. "What are we, then?" he hissed. "Pretend?"

"No. No, that's not what I—"

"Do you let them fuck you? Your *brothers?*" He said the word like it tasted foul. "Did they shove your face into the mattress and enjoy you?"

"What? No!" Tango squirmed beneath Ian's arm where it was clamped tight around his waist.

"Do they know what you taste like? Did you share with them?"

"No, dude," he said, and definitely saw Ian's brows jump over his use of the moniker. "It isn't like that. We fuck around with women." He wanted to take it back the moment he said it.

Ian's hand landed at the base of his throat. Not squeezing, just resting there. "You've been with a woman?"

Tango swallowed, hard, Adam's apple jumping against Ian's palm. "Yeah. A few."

Ian's grip slid down his chest, pressed over his heart, some of the anger bleeding out of his voice. "What was it like?"

~*~

Ian wasn't okay. Tango knew on the couch, when the guy fell asleep with his face pressed to Tango's chest, that Ian was upset, overcome with emotion after their sudden reunion. But he hadn't realized then – only now – that Ian was viciously jealous, seconds away from an emotional eruption at all times. He could see it in the dark flash of Ian's eyes every morning, in the way his hand trembled as he brushed his hair back. And Tango had no idea how to handle it.

They didn't let him dance, not at first. He was confined to the basement, left behind when the heavy-shouldered security thugs came to round them up each evening. Tango didn't spot Big John, and hoped the man had died in the fire Ghost and the Dogs had set in the old club.

Then they started denying him food. For three days, he wasn't brought a meal. The security guard who brought breakfast and dinner – already sparse offerings of boiled chicken, canned tuna, and a few wilted veggies – told Tango that, "She says you can eat when you learn how to behave." Tango knew what that meant, but he'd be damned before he grew as submissive and weak as he'd been before.

Ian snuck him a handful of shredded chicken one night, and they both earned a thrashing with a guard's belt for it. Sitting on his raw backside, Tango sucked the inside of his cheek and let the hunger gnaw at him. He sipped bottled water and imagined it filling his gut, pretended it could nourish him.

He passed out on the fourth day.

He came to in Miss Carla's office, one of the goons holding him upright in the chair across from her desk, the scent of cooked meat sharp in his nose.

"Ah, there he is," Miss Carla's voice floated to him through the haze. "You awake, Loverboy?"

He mumbled something that didn't sound like words, blurry eyes latching onto the plate of grilled chicken and vegetables in front of him.

"Hungry?" she asked innocently. "Dennis, help Kev with his plate, please."

The goon leaned forward and picked up the steaming, fragrant plate, held it just beneath Tango's nose. A fork and knife were balanced on the edge of the plate; someone had already draped a napkin in his lap.

"Go ahead, sweet pea," Miss Carla said. "Eat up."

His hands shook and he almost dropped the silverware when he picked it up. But he managed to stab the chicken breast and saw off a chunk. Bring it, quavering, to his lips.

Dennis hit him in the back of his head. The silverware flew from his grip. The plate jerked in Dennis's other hand, veggies tumbling down to the floor. His already dizzy head throbbed from the blow, his vision doubling and swimming.

"Hm, hm, hm," Miss Carla *tsk*ed. "What've you done to deserve dinner, hm? Why do you deserve to eat?"

A hard shudder moved through him, and then another. The hunger shakes, almost as violent as the detox tremors that had wracked him two years ago, when he was coming down off the heroin. "I…" What could he say?

He'd spent two years finding the strong voice that dwelled in his chest, so silent for so long, honing it and nurturing it. Until he could almost pass for human, almost pass for a man.

But that voice couldn't help him here. That voice hadn't been able to break the locks on the door, or overpower his guards, or even earn him a goddamn meal. Miss Carla held all the cards, the way she always had, and he was too hungry to fight her now.

"Please," he said, and felt the traitorous burn of tears in his eyes.

She flashed a smug smile. "Please what?"

"Please." He had to swallow down a choking a lump in his throat, breath stalling out in his lungs. He hated this. Hated *her*. And even as he thought that, the weakness overcame him and he slid down deeper into his chair, whimpering. "Please, I wanna eat."

"That's an awful big want, pretty boy. I dunno if I can make that happen for you, not after you've been so bad."

"Please," he said again, as his stomach folded over itself. He felt like he needed to throw up, but his gut was empty. He closed his eyes, tears pushing at his lids. "I'll be good."

"Oh, you will?" she purred with mock-surprise. "And how will you be good? What will you do for me?"

There was only one answer she wanted, and he gave it: "I'll dance."

~*~

The light beamed down from the ceiling, a soft blue. Always blue, his color, with his blonde hair and pale skin. Blue shorts. Deep blue mascara defining his lashes, blue veins stark beneath the thin white skin of his wrists and ankles. He was fragile-looking, and the clients loved it, their shouts and catcalls swirling around him as he took the pole in one hand and dipped backward, bending at the waist until his spine was a tidy arch.

The two years away didn't matter; his body remembered the routine, dipping and spinning, and bending in all the ways men wanted to see. The singles in the waistband of his shorts rustled against his skin, greasy from being held. The music pounded, something electronic and rhythmic. Cigarette smoke curled through the haze of the lights.

This new club was much smaller than the old one, and it gave off the impression of a converted family restaurant, with booths on the walls, and round tables arranged around the hastily-constructed stages.

Tango lifted again, swinging one long leg around the pole, hugging it close to the sound of wolf whistles.

A week ago he was a Lean Dog. Part of a traveling phalanx of mounted warriors feared and respected by the city.

Now he was a bitch on a pole.

~*~

"Mm. Shit." The customer's hands passed up the delicate shape of Tango's ribcage, fondling and pinching, sliding forward to cover his chest, tease at his nipples. The man looked like a high school athlete gone soft, his stomach doughy through the opened halves of his shirt, his dress slacks unfastened, erection pushing at the zipper. His face was red with excitement, sweat beading at his temples, dampening his hair. "What's your name, pretty thing?"

Tango closed his eyes and swallowed, and hoped it looked like he was overcome by the man's touch, rather than fighting nausea. He'd only had a few bites of dinner; he would have more if he behaved.

"Loverboy," he said. "You can call me Loverboy."

~*~

It was so easy to slip back into his old pattern. To be Loverboy again. So easy that he questioned if his time on the outside had ever happened. Maybe it had all been a dream.

~*~

Ian's clinginess and jealousy were the only things that proved he'd been gone for a time. Maybe Ian had always behaved that way, and Tango hadn't noticed before. Either way, it was a shock when Ian sidled up to Tango in the dark back hall one night and said, "Come with me. I've got a surprise for you." His breath was hot in Tango's ear, his smile wild and frantic, a white slice in the dark.

"We're working."

"This *is* work. Come on." He tugged at Tango's hand. "Carla knows about it. She wants us to work this one together; the client asked."

"Ian…" he started, but was dragged down the hall.

Ian took him to the last room on the left, the largest one, the one with the surreal pink filters over the lights so the whole room looked like cotton candy. It was always a shock, that bubblegum light, and that was why it took Tango a moment to realize what he was looking at.

A woman.

There was a woman in the club, sitting on the bed, waiting for them.

"What?" Tango asked, too shocked to put together a coherent sentence.

Ian slid an arm around his waist and squeezed, leaned in to whisper in his ear. "Mrs. Scott wants to play with us. And her husband wants to watch."

That was when Tango noticed the man sitting in a chair in the corner, a little pale-faced (or maybe that was the light), handsome, well-dressed, eyes flicking back and forth between the two boys and the woman on the bed.

Mrs. Scott lifted a manicured hand and gave them a little wave, her smile coquettish and excited.

Tango swallowed. His heart thumped wildly, nerves crackling through his limbs like static. It wasn't supposed to be like this. In the back rooms, the boys were the ones being penetrated, the ones face-down on the mattresses with the pink sheets. Now he would have to be the one performing.

And Ian, too.

He glanced over at his friend, his lover, and saw the mingling fear and wonder in the other boy's eyes. Ian *wanted* this, he realized. Tango had been with women, and now Ian wanted a turn. He wanted Tango to help him, show him how.

And the Scotts were paying clients, after all.

There was nothing to do but slide into his work-head and let knowledge and numbness take over.

"Watch me," he whispered to Ian. "Do what I do." And he ducked away from his arm and headed toward the client.

Mrs. Scott wore a dark minidress with a plunging neckline; Tango had been around Dartmoor long enough to recognize an expensive pair of fake breasts when he saw them, in this case mounding up above the tight weave of the dress's bodice. The woman wore her pale hair long and loose, expertly twisted with a curling iron; her eyelids flashed black and heavy with shadow every time she blinked. She was beautiful, a very expensive version of a club groupie, and when he drew close, Tango could smell her perfume.

A woman like this had no business paying two boys to service her, not when she could have had any man of her choice for free. But some people, Tango had learned in his short life, just had to try everything once.

When he was close enough, she reached out and hooked two fingers in the waistband of his shorts, drew him in close between her spread legs. He could see that she wasn't wearing panties.

"Hello, beautiful," she purred. "Are you as good as they say you are?"

"Better." He leaned in and kissed her. It wasn't encouraged, but that meant it was up to the dancer's discretion. Normally, Tango couldn't stomach the idea, but he had no idea how to initiate anything with a woman without a kiss. And also because…he didn't feel threatened right now. Didn't have that usual hard lump of dread in his belly. He breathed in her perfume and tasted her lipstick, and his cock twitched in response.

He was a good kisser; he knew that objectively. When he drew back, the woman was panting a little. She licked at her lips and her eyes stayed pinned on his mouth.

"What about your friend?" she asked, voice huskier than before.

Tango glanced back at Ian over his shoulder, and saw his lover watching him with an obvious mix of lust and jealousy. Ian's erection tented his shorts, but he held back and waited.

The realization hit Tango suddenly, and hard. He was the one in control in this situation. He would be the one to set the pace and give the orders. He'd never been in that position, and the headrush was blinding.

Mrs. Scott's nails teased down his bare sternum and he pulled in a deep breath, willed himself to calm down and focus. "Ian, come here sweetheart."

He'd never been the one to use a pet name before, that had always been Ian's thing, but Ian came now, obedient and wide-eyed, and knelt down on the floor beside Tango, Mrs. Scott's legs opening wider to accommodate both of them.

Tango passed a soothing hand down the back of Ian's head, fingers playing through his hair, rubbing all the way down his back. "Kiss her," he instructed, gently. "It's okay, I'm right here."

Ian leaned forward, as fluid and graceful as always, lashes dark against his cheeks, pulling in one last nervous breath. Mrs. Scott leaned to meet him, and the kiss was soft, and slow, and beautiful to watch.

He would make this so good for him, Tango decided. He would be slow, and thorough, and hold Ian's hand if he had to, but he would show him the pleasure to be found in a woman's arms. He would show Ian all the sweetness they'd never been allowed save with each other. This was a gift, this client, a chance to prove to his friend that sex didn't have to hurt.

Mrs. Scott's hand slid into Tango's hair, and then she turned from Ian and kissed Tango again, slipped her tongue into his mouth, nibbled at the fullness of his lower lip. Then back to Ian, this kiss deeper, messier, until Ian was leaning into it, his hand on the woman's thigh. She covered his hand with her own and urged it higher, up beneath the skirt of her dress, all the way up until Ian broke the kiss with a startled gasp.

Tango knew what his friend was feeling, knew what the surprise and awe on Ian's face felt like on his own.

"Hey," Tango said, smoothing his hand up the woman's other thigh. "Take the top of your dress down, okay?"

She grinned like that sounded like a great idea. She used both hands to reach behind her; the zipper made a soft sound and the front of the dress loosened. She pushed the straps down, pulled her arms through them, and wedged the bodice of the dress down beneath her naked breasts.

Her plastic surgeon was talented; her breasts thrust toward them, full and pale, defying gravity, her nipples already hard.

Tango snuck a glance at Ian and saw his friend goggle-eyed with surprise. He still had a tent pitched in the front of his shorts, though, so he definitely liked what he saw.

"Here." Tango touched Ian's arm to get his attention. "Like this." With his other hand he cupped the woman's right breast, testing its weight in his palm, passing his thumb across her pebbled nipple. The sensation of warm, smooth, feminine curves sent all his blood flooding south, engorging his already stiff cock.

Ian mirrored the touch on her other breast, and the woman hummed her approval, pushing her chest forward into their hands.

"Here," Tango said again, and reached up beneath the woman's skirt with his other hand, found her already-wet sex with his fingertips.

Ian followed suit and they spent long moments petting her together, Tango urging Ian's fingers to the right places, until the woman was visibly squirming.

"You boys sure like to move slow," Mrs. Scott said, finally, and Tango knew it was time to speed things along. She and her husband hadn't paid for a little petting.

Tango stood, Ian again following his lead, and stepped out of his shorts, rolled on a condom. "I'll go first," he whispered to Ian. "You can watch and see what it's like."

Mrs. Scott stood, slithered out of her dress, and laid back across the mattress in nothing but her spike heels and a wicked, almost-taunting smile. (It wouldn't be until Whitney that Tango learned not all women smiled like that in the bedroom.) She spread her legs and reached down to touch herself, biting her lip, eyes flicking to the corner to check and see if her husband was watching. "Mm. Hurry."

Tango mounted her, reached down to align himself, and entered her with one sure thrust.

She tipped her head back, neck arching prettily. "Ahhh," she murmured deep in her throat, hips rolling up to meet Tango's. "That's what I need."

She was warm and tight around his cock, and beautiful beneath him, and Tango's hips kicked without him having to tell them to. He could do this; he could fuck this woman for money. He *wanted* to, suddenly.

"You get up here too," Mrs. Scott called to Ian, biting her lip again as Tango fell into a slow rhythm. "Shit, yeah, come here sweetie, come touch me until it's your turn."

Ian forgot a little of his usual grace as he scrambled up onto the bed, kneeling beside Mrs. Scott, eyes wide and rapturous as he watched the proceedings.

She took one of his hands and pressed it to her belly. "Touch me. Touch me everywhere."

Tango never enjoyed his sessions with clients. He got hard sometimes, but he never came. He stayed painfully rooted in the moment and his own head; he never lost himself. But that's exactly what happened, now that the tables were turned.

The sex pounded through him, an accelerating pulse of *want* and *need* and *urgency*. It had nothing to do with Mrs. Scott – it could have been anyone. But the idea of fucking a woman and enjoying it here, at the club, where it had always been torture…that was heady, heady stuff.

Ian played with the woman's breasts, and eventually her clit, and Tango was barely aware of her shout of climax right before he came with a triumphant inner scream. He swallowed the sound, felt it burn bright in his veins. This wasn't for her, or Ian, or the creepy husband in the corner. This was only for him. This was his private victory.

When he could get his legs under himself, he stood and walked to throw his condom in the wastebasket, switching places with Ian. And Ian, quick study that he was, didn't need any instructions. In a matter of moments, he was sinking down into the woman's slick sex and gasping at the feel of it.

Tango braced a knee on the edge of the mattress, steadying himself, and settled in to watch with a mechanical sort of disinterest.

He felt the warmth of a body behind him a second before a strong male arm curled around his waist, and he jerked.

It was Mr. Scott, his white shirt rolled up at the cuffs to reveal tan, lightly-furred forearms, his hands dark from the sun and beautiful as Tango's own. Tango had no idea what was happening, but he kept very still, heart pounding as he felt Scott's warm breath fan across his ear.

"Did you like it?" the man asked. The words were no less than expected. The typical sick bravado of all the customers. But the tone – the hesitancy, the note of fear, the vulnerable little quiver – sent a shiver down Tango's spine.

"Yes," he said, honestly.

On the bed, Ian sat up so he was kneeling on the mattress, never losing contact with Mrs. Scott, bringing her with him so she was straddling his lap. The woman shouted with delight, hands landing on Ian's shoulders as she worked herself down on his cock.

Her husband flattened his hand against Tango's stomach, down low, teasing at the thin trail of hair. "I can't keep her happy," he whispered in Tango's ear. "She doesn't want me."

He was sixteen, and he wasn't made of plastic, and the visual display paired with the touch on his belly was starting to excite him all over again. He was still in that drowsy post-coital state, and all of it felt like a soft dream.

"I...I don't..." Scott's hand slid lower, and found Tango's cock. A gentle, almost reverent touch, but sure in its grip.

Tango sucked in a breath.

"God," Mrs. Scott murmured. "Oh God, *yes*."

Tango closed his eyes. He didn't need to watch anymore; the hand around his cock was *perfect*.

Never had a client touched him this way, breathed against the back of his neck so sweetly, been all muscle and sinew, hot-skinned and beautiful through his expensive business clothes.

The world turned sparkly, and Tango thought he and Mrs. Scott came at the same time.

~*~

The Scotts came back every week for a while. The second time, Mrs. Scott pulled Ian into one room, and Mr. Scott towed Tango into another. Tango was good with that arrangement.

Mr. Scott's name was Daniel, and upon close inspection, he was beautiful. He had a sharp-featured, refined face, tan like the rest of him, his dark hair styled carefully away from his face, his throat and shoulders strong, his stomach hard and lean.

"It might as well have been an arranged marriage," Daniel said, sitting opposite Tango on the mattress of their private room, both of them cross-legged, elbows braced on their thighs, leaning toward one another. "My dad walked her into the room and said, 'Daniel, this is Rebecca. You're going to marry her.'"

It didn't seem possible, given his own situation, but Tango felt sympathy for the man. "You don't love her?"

"No. I'd never met her before, not until two weeks before the wedding."

"Damn."

Daniel ducked his head, his smile charming and embarrassed. "I was...I made the mistake of telling my father I was questioning my sexuality."

Tango wasn't surprised. A man didn't just touch another man like that without having thought about it first.

"There was…there was someone," Daniel said, staring at his hands. "He worked for my father. I think Dad found out, and, well." He shrugged, and glanced up at Tango through his lashes. "Dad fired him. And then there was Rebecca."

Tango nodded along, though he couldn't conceive of such an arrangement. A father with that kind of influence? That kind of wealth? Unimaginable.

Daniel leaned forward, cupped Tango's cheek in his hand, his expression earnest and full of longing. "You look like him. You're beautiful, you know?"

Tango did know, so he kissed him.

~*~

Rebecca Scott stopped coming. One night Daniel materialized at the edge of the stage, looking up at Tango with nothing short of adoration stamped across his handsome face. For the first time in his history with the club, Tango smiled, and meant it.

~*~

"What are you doing?" Ian hissed.

It was three a.m. and the club was closed. Only Ian and Tango remained in the communal showers in the basement. The water was edging toward cold, the steam dissipating, and when Tango met his friend's gaze, he saw an angry snarl on Ian's face.

"What?"

"What are you doing with that fucking rich boy?" Ian leaned in close, until their noses almost touched. "Are you *falling for* him?"

"What? No!" Tango scrubbed the shampoo out of his hair, titling his head back beneath the spray. "Besides, you're banging the wife."

"That was *work*." Ian sounded a little too defensive. It was no coincidence this anger was coming out after Mrs. Scott's absence from the club.

"So's what I'm doing with Daniel."

"Oh, it's *Daniel* now?"

"That's his name, Ian."

"And when was the last fucking time a client gave his name?"

Tango ducked from beneath the water and sent Ian a level look. "This is really upsetting you."

Ian's expression was unrecognizable. "Are you in love with him?"

"No."

"Will you stop seeing him?"

"He's a client, and you know we don't get to choose our clients."

"Bullshit!" Ian shoved him, hard, crowding him back against the tiled wall. He got in his face. Water dripped off his nose, off the ends of his long hair, beaded in his lashes. His breathing stuttered, chest pressing into Tango's. "You *can't* love him. *Don't*. Don't you *dare*."

"I don't."

Ian kissed him, the touch of their mouths violent and suffocating. Ian bit his lip and Tango tasted blood.

~*~

The heroin injections started again, and Tango couldn't deny the peace each chemical rush of pleasure brought. He slept deep, and he lived in a daze, and more and more Dartmoor seemed like someone else's fantasy he'd only heard of in passing.

~*~

A horrible thing happened one night, two months into Daniel's patronage of the club.

In the warm, cotton candy light of his preferred back room, on sweat damp sheets, Tango was out of his head again, lost in the slick slide of skin and the quiet sounds of passion. He didn't even try to pretend anymore that this was about work, that he was capable of staying above the tide when it came to Daniel. The man was his lover, now, and Tango shut his eyes and gave himself over to it.

Which was why he didn't hear the door open. Why he didn't see Ian walk up to them on the bed. Didn't see the broken chair leg Ian raised like a club.

~*~

"Did he kill him?" Whitney asked, a terrified whisper.

"No. Knocked him out, though. Security came in and carried him out. I don't know what happened to him after that," he said to his untouched plate. "I never saw him again."

Across the table, Whitney pushed away her own plate and reached across the wood to lay both her hands over one of his. "Kev–"

"Don't pity me. I can't handle that right now."

"Okay." She didn't move her hands. "Can I just love you?"

How did he deserve her? It wasn't possible.

His throat tightened, and he realized he couldn't tell her the rest. The vicious argument he'd had with Ian after lights-out, the scratches they'd left in each other's skin with their nails. The heroin-addled haze of his last few weeks. Ian's kisses of apology, his vow that he had an escape plan, that he would get them out of The Nest once and for all.

It was all a blur; he didn't feel alive anymore.

And then Ghost, and Mercy, and Aidan had come striding through the dim light of the club one night. Mercy had swung a sledgehammer in an arc, breaking noses in dark showers of blood, and Ghost had pulled Tango's mostly-naked body down off the stage and into his arms.

"I've got you," he'd said. "It's okay, we found you. You're safe. We're going home."

Tango turned his hand over beneath Whitney's so he could lace their fingers together and squeeze. He hoped his touch said all the things he couldn't right now.

Her squeeze back said it probably did.

Twenty-Five

That night, when the Lean Dogs happened upon the eleven o'clock news broadcast, a story would catch their attention: *Fourteen-year-old boy missing, presumed abducted.* His name was Jamie Long, and he was slight, beautiful in the face, long-limbed and graceful in the gymnastics photo his family shared with the news station. He'd been walking – with his mother's permission – from his gym to the ice cream parlor on the corner, there to work on his homework, have a snack, and wait for his mom to pick him up. But there was no trace of her son when Mrs. Long arrived. He was just gone, vanished. Not at the gym, not at the parlor, not at home. None of his friends knew where he'd gone.

Ghost watched the story with Mags, who whispered, "Jesus." And he knew exactly where that poor child had gone. And what would be done to him.

Somewhere in the city, The Cuckoo's Nest was preparing a new crop of dancing boys.

~*~

Had anyone asked Ghost about the year they got Tango back from Carla Burgess, he wouldn't have wanted to tell the story. He'd only told it once, and that was to Maggie, in the warm safety of their bed, in the dark, while she combed his hair with her fingers and didn't comment on the way his shoulders shook. But had someone else asked, and he'd felt like telling it, he would have told them this:

Walgreens called the bike shop to ask if they could come pick up an abandoned bike. "Looks like one of yours anyway," the clerk said over the phone.

It was Tango's, parked right up in front, like Tango had just run in to grab a few things. They were putting it on the flatbed and Walsh was inside asking about security camera feeds when Tango's aunt called Ghost, tearful and insensible.

326

"He never came home last night," she cried. "I thought he was just out having fun, you know how boys are, but he wouldn't do that to me. He would answer his phone."

"He would," Ghost agreed, a grim ball of dread forming in his gut. "I'm looking into it, and I'll let you know when I hear something, okay? We're gonna find him."

"O-o-okay."

Shit.

Walsh came out of the store and waved for him. "Manager's got tapes, and he says he wants to turn them over to the cops, but he'll let us see them first." Walsh lifted a meaningful brow as they walked. "If we smooth the way a little."

"Fucker," Ghost muttered. But he pulled a crisp fifty out of his wallet and handed it to the manager when they reached the office. "What've you got?"

"This is from last night," the manager said, starting the grainy black and white video. "This your guy?"

Tango's leggy, long-haired delicacy was easy to spot, even with poor film quality. "Yeah."

"Do you know those guys?" The manager tapped the mouse and three heavy men in black came onscreen.

Ghost gripped the back of the manager's chair until his knuckles cracked. "No." But he would find out.

~*~

There weren't many enemies brave enough to kidnap a member of the Lean Dogs. Once Ghost realized none of said few had snatched Tango in the middle of Walgreen's, his suspicions were confirmed: Carla had taken Tango. Taken him *back*, as it were.

Ghost's first instinct was to sic all of the club's considerable resources on the bitch. With the help of his brothers, Ghost could find the poor kid in a day or so. But bikers couldn't be gay – one of those stupid-ass, archaic old MC rules that suppressed every one-percenter club in the world. How would the rest of the boys react when they knew what Tango had done for so many years? Would he be lucky enough to leave without his patches? Or would he be another grave dug into the side of a hill on his dad's old cattle property?

Fuck, he couldn't tell the club.

Not all of them anyway. There was one person he trusted with precious things.

He rapped once on the kitchen doorframe. "Merc."

At the table, Mercy and Ava made a strange portrait: the tall, big-shouldered, long-haired young man, sinister and weapon-like, now all smiles and softness as he helped Ava with her homework. Ava looked so tiny and fragile beside his big frame, a little bird between the paws of a massive attack dog. The affection between them was a palpable thing.

Hmm. Ghost made a mental note to question this tableau in a few years, when he had the time and energy to feel threatened by it.

Mercy's head lifted, smile dimming from the wide delight over Ava to something quieter and more professional. "What's up, boss?"

Ghost nodded his head back toward the living room. "Need to talk to you for a minute. Ava, keep working on your homework, okay?"

"Okay, Daddy." Her eyes followed Mercy as he stood and moved around the table to join Ghost.

Making another mental note to think about *that* later, Ghost led Mercy over to the couch, but didn't sit, standing with his arms folded tight.

He realized his chest was tight too, his head light, and he had to take a deep breath.

Picking up on the seriousness of the moment, Mercy mirrored his stance, black brows snapping up toward his hairline. "I'm starting to worry, boss."

"It's about Tango."

Mercy leaned in a fraction, and Ghost could sense the anger and protectiveness vibrating off the man. Yes, he'd made the right choice in trusting Mercy. He just had to make himself say the words.

Quietly, barely trusting the security of his own home's walls, Ghost told Mercy about the long-haired boy Aidan had found sitting at a picnic table outside the high school two years ago, about what went on in Carla Burgess's rotating club of delinquency.

"Shit," Mercy breathed, scrubbing at the back of his neck. "Fuck. Are you serious?"

"Wish I wasn't."

Mercy met his gaze, dark eyes flinty. "Whose head do I gotta put a hammer through, boss?"

Ghost felt a smile tug at his mouth. "Help me find him, and then all of them."

~*~

It took two months. Ghost wasn't sure he ate a full meal in that time, his stomach taut and lean, always growling, always hurting. Maggie looked at the bruises the sharp points of his hips had left on the insides of her thighs and said, "Not that I'm complaining, baby, you look fantastic, but I'm starting to think you don't like my cooking anymore."

He nuzzled into her perfumed throat and admitted all his fears, that they wouldn't find Tango, that he might have already been killed by some overzealous client, that he wouldn't be able to recover from that hell a second time even if they found him.

She wiped the pads of her thumbs under his eyes and didn't tell him his worries were unfounded; she knew what was at stake.

Mercy finally found the club. Without his cut, tats covered, baseball cap pulled low over his face, fairly new to town, he managed to ask the right questions at the right bar, and was slid a folded Post-It note with a handwritten address on it.

"How do you wanna work this?" he asked in the Teague garage the next day.

In the weeks since Tango had been snatched, Ghost had cycled through a whole list of ideas. He'd intended to tip off PD and get Carla finally busted. He'd seriously considered killing her.

But in the end, all he really cared about was getting Tango back. He felt like a shit heel for it, but he was too desperate to be anything less than honest. Tango was the priority. Involving the cops, setting up some kind of massive raid, would increase the club staff's chances of getting tipped off and moving the boys ahead of time. And he couldn't involve his brothers, for reasons he'd already explained to himself and Mercy.

"I just want to walk right in and take him," he said. "Simple plan. Merc, you're on point."

Mercy nodded, eyes already bright with the idea of violence.

"And what am I gonna do?" Aidan asked, skinny, petulant, and angry as any sixteen-year-old had ever been.

"You're gonna stay home with Ma–"

"Fuck that," Aidan said. "I'm going. He's my best friend, and you need an extra set of hands." He stood up, reminding Ghost that though he was thin, they were the same height these days. His little boy was growing up. "I'm a member of this club. I'm coming," he repeated.

Ghost sighed. "Fine." Secretly, he was proud.

~*~

A part of him hadn't believed they could pull it off; that they could get Tango back. But there he'd been on the center stage, lit up like Christmas, eyes glassy and mouth slack as he danced for the lechers below.

That image was burned in his brain, staining the backs of his eyelids when he blinked.

But again, that was before he'd seen the worst of it.

After Tango was home, after the detoxing, when he'd decided he couldn't live with what he'd been made to do.

Twice in one lifetime, Aidan had found his best friend's body in a bathtub full of blood.

It was too much. All of it was just too much.

Staring up at the ceiling of his bedroom, his wife warm and asleep against his side, a grounding presence, Ghost made one of those sober, middle-of-the-night decisions. The dinosaurs of the past were dead, and it was high time his club made another step out of the Stone Age.

Friday, at church, he was going to say the things he should have said a long time ago. And if they voted him out of office, so be it. It was high time Tango was made to feel like he really, truly belonged with them all. That he was family, no matter what.

Twenty-Six

Tango woke to the unobtrusive beeping of the alarm, cool winter sunlight toying with the curtains, Whitney's small warm shape pressed against his side beneath the weight of the covers. Whitney muttered something about not wanting to get up and tucked her face under his arm, into the worn cotton of his t-shirt. He slapped the alarm and lay still for a moment, soaking up the last few moments of peace before they had to crawl out of bed and start their respective days.

He listened to the hum of the fridge out in the kitchen, the low shush of traffic out on the street, the faint threads of music downstairs in the bakery.

It took him a second to realize what he felt: *calm*. Calm, and warm, and light, and content. Only good things. No ball of anxiety in his gut, no guilt that he was tainting Whitney, no fear, his craving only the faintest of voices, an echo of memory at the back of his mind.

"Hey," he said, quietly, not wanting to break the spell.

"Hmm?"

He rubbed little circles against her back with his fingertips, her sleep shirt soft, knobs of her spine prominent beneath. "Thank you."

That got her attention. She pushed up onto her elbow, so her face hovered over his, expression sleepy, but concerned. "For what?" She tucked her hair back behind her ear, and he thought she was beautiful, rumpled and makeup-free, seam of the pillow imprinted on her cheek.

"For listening last night." It took every ounce of self-control not to tell her he was sorry for unburdening on her. It seemed like something Mercy would tell him, to stop apologizing all the time. "It – it really helped, I think. So thank you."

She blinked a few times, and nodded. "Of course. Whatever you need."

His first instinct was to duck his head. But that was cowardly, not to mention bad boyfriend behavior. When she said

332

something supportive, he needed to show how much that meant to him. How much *she* meant to him.

So he cupped the back of her head and pulled her down for a kiss.

She wrinkled her nose as she pulled back. "I haven't brushed my teeth yet."

"Don't care. Me neither." And kissed her again, smiling.

~*~

Talking about what he'd been through had helped Kev – something had actually helped him that wasn't chemical or sexual – and Whitney was immensely glad for that. *Listening*, though…listening had fucked *her* up.

She sat at her desk in her cubicle, staring down at the candy bar Mark had brought her a few minutes ago, thinking about the way Kev had been denied food until he'd agreed to dance again. The only times in her life in which she'd ever been hungry was because she'd forgotten to eat lunch, or been running too late to grab a bagel on the way to work. Normal, comforting hunger, easily assuaged with a snack, tided over with a few sips of Coke.

No one had ever struck her.

She'd never been raped…because of Kev. Because Kev had offered himself up instead of her, as a sacrifice, because what was a little roughing-up from Ellison's men after the things he'd endured as a child?

She barely managed to grab the wastebasket under her desk before she curled over it and vomited. There was nothing in her stomach – she hadn't been able to eat breakfast – but the bile burned her throat; the dry heaves hurt her stomach.

"Whitney?" Mark asked, voice worried, popping up over the divider between their cubicles. "Oh crap! Are you okay?" She heard the squeak of his chair wheels as he got up and came around to see her.

She pushed her hair off her clammy forehead and managed to straighten, nausea still rolling through her. "Fine," she croaked. "Just upset stomach or something."

Mark stood at the entrance of her cubicle, frowning with concern, looking unsure how to help. "You need anything? Ginger ale?"

She nodded, just to get rid of him. "Yeah, that might help."

"Be right back."

Whitney laid her head down on the desk, the cool plastic a relief to her clammy skin.

Things that were not okay: throwing up after her boyfriend relied on her for support.

As it turned out, Whitney's boss didn't think a puking employee was good for office morale, so he turned her loose. Stepping outside into the crisp winter air helped a little. By the time she reached her car, she knew the danger had passed, and that she wasn't going to have to pull over. Stupid stomach. Kev had *lived* through all that, and she couldn't even handle hearing it? Pathetic.

She had most of the day left at her disposal, and she sat behind the wheel a long moment, thinking about her options. She could pick up lunch and take it to Kev at work. But that would involve food. And also smiling at Kev and pretending his story hadn't made her ill.

Some girlfriend she was.

Without much conscious thought, she ended up in front of Mercy and Ava's house, turning into the driveway and parking behind Ava's black truck.

Guilt needled her – Ava didn't need to be bothered by some sad sack girl-child who couldn't control her gag reflex when she thought about her boyfriend's sordid history.

But the idea of going home alone, to the apartment she had *no right* to call home, made her sick all over again.

So she climbed out and walked up to the door. The back door – she remembered from the last time she was here. She knocked and waited, wondering if it was too late to retreat. But a curtain twitched at the window and then the door unlocked and opened, Ava appearing on the other side, little Cal lurking behind her, peeking around her leg.

"Whitney, hi." Ava sounded surprised, but not unhappy to see her. "Is everything alright?"

"Oh, yes, fine," Whitney rushed to assure her. Her hands knotted together in front of her, nervous energy. "I wanted to see if I could talk to you for a minute. If you're not busy, I mean. I'm sorry, I should have called ahead—"

"It's fine," Ava said, smiling and stepping to the side, guiding Cal out of the way with a deft touch on his small shoulder. "Come on in."

"Thanks. Sorry, again, I should have—"

"No more apologizing."

"Okay."

Unlike the last time she'd been here, the kitchen was full of cool daylight and not issuing forth any delicious food smells, but it was far from quiet. A small TV was on in the corner, playing a national news station; Remy sat at the table, legs hooked up beneath his bottom, coloring in big bold strokes on sheets of white craft paper.

Whitney wondered if any of the people in Knoxville who hated the Dogs had ever seen one of their children coloring at a kitchen table.

"Camille's down for her afternoon nap," Ava said, pointing to the baby monitor set up on the counter, "so we'll have to be kind of quiet." She picked up Cal – a serious armful of little blonde boy – and plopped him into the chair beside his brother. "You want something to drink?"

"Maybe just some water if you don't mind."

"Sure."

Ava got them two glasses and then tilted her head toward the row of stools lined up beneath the breakfast bar.

They got settled – a good view of the boys without being close enough to distract them from their art – and Whitney took a bracing sip of water, wincing as the cold stung her sore throat.

"I'm guessing something's wrong," Ava said in a gentle voice. Not accusatory, just observant.

Whitney sighed and let her shoulders sag. She felt small and droopy, beneath the weight of what she now knew. "A little bit wrong," she admitted. "And I feel really terrible about it, because things are finally starting to go *right* for Kev."

"Oh," Ava said, and the word had a wealth of understanding behind it. "I don't know all the details, but I know that what happened to Kev is a lot to take in. For anyone, club-raised or not."

The words were such a relief – the simple acceptance of what she'd said – that Whitney found herself blinking back tears. "Crap. I'm sorry." She dabbed at her eyes. "This is exactly why my boss sent me home."

"Wait, what?"

Whitney gave her the brief rundown of her whole barf situation, and didn't betray Kev's trust, but said he'd shared a dark story of his past with her, that it was haunting her today.

"Okay," Ava said, stopping her babbling with a nod. "I get it. Okay." She took a deep breath and gave Whitney a kind smile.

It was an immeasurable comfort, just the sound of "okay."

"I'm being stupid."

"No," Ava countered. "Definitely not. You can't control how it feels to know something like that about someone."

"But it isn't like I'm disgusted by him," Whitney rushed to say. "I don't feel any differently about him. Well, maybe *more* sympathetic, if that's possible." She shrugged. "I'm glad he told me. I'm glad he trusts me like that, and I'm so, so glad he's feeling better. I just…" She made a helpless motion with her hands, feeling like an idiot, and maybe a child, for not being able to articulate her feelings any better than this.

"It's one hell of an awful story," Ava supplied.

"Yeah."

"Whitney." Ava leaned in close, a comforting hand on Whitney's forearm. "Most people would puke after hearing that. Hell, pretty much everyone would."

Whitney offered a bare smile. "Why doesn't that make me feel any better?"

Ava shook her head, smile rueful. "In my experience, it doesn't feel better. It just quits stinging so bad all the time."

~*~

"How you doing?" Aidan asked behind him, and Tango was proud of the way he didn't jump in reaction. He heard the footsteps approaching, recognized Aidan's voice, and his hands never slipped on the wrench he was using.

He set his tool aside and stood from his crouch, wiping his palms on his jeans as he turned to face his best friend. "Doing good." The words came easily; they didn't catch in his throat or taste like a lie.

"Yeah?" Aidan clasped his shoulder and gave him a hopeful, assessing look.

Tango smiled. "Yeah."

Aidan gave him a little shove, smile widening. "Dude. That's great."

And for all the things he doubted in life, all the ways in which he mistrusted people, Tango knew for a fact that Aidan was glad for him. That he wanted him to be alive and well. Not because he wanted to use him, control him, or own him. But because he loved him like a brother.

A simple given; a fact he always understood. But on this bright morning, feeling clean and easy on the inside for the first time, it hit Tango all over again.

He flung his arms around Aidan's neck and hugged him tight.

"Oh," Aidan said, surprised. Then his arms circled Tango and he squeezed back, just as hard. "That's great," he repeated, voice low and soft, full of a dozen things he didn't have to say.

"Boys," Ghost called, breaking them apart. He stood just beyond the roll top door, in the bright winter sun, face a strange blend of dread and tenderness beneath his sunglasses. "I wanna talk to you both about something."

~*~

"You have to decide if you can live with it." Ava's parting words as Whitney left the Lécuyer house after a mug of tea and a few nibbles on some homemade cookies.

Strange advice, in Whitney's opinion. Kev was the one who hadn't been able to live with what happened to him. Literally. And at this point, Whitney couldn't imagine walking away from him. It was unthinkable. Maybe someone else would call that obsession, but it felt like love to her.

In any event, her stomach was better, and she knew they needed stuff for dinner. She decided to forgo Leroy's in favor of the big grocery store, and headed that way to shoulder her way through the senior citizen discount crowd.

There was something peaceful about the retirees and mothers with small children ambling through the store in the middle of the day. No rush, no long lines. The music floating down from the speakers was louder than anyone's conversation. Whitney fell into a pleasant headspace and pushed her cart down the aisles, picking up what she needed for salad, garlic bread, chicken, and a few staples.

She was picking out a few yogurt cups when she heard, "Aunt Whitney!"

It killed her a little bit that the sound of her niece's voice sent fear trembling down her back. Not joy, not surprise, but flat-out terror. Because where there was Ashley, there was…

Except, no. Madelyn wasn't there. A harried-looking woman accompanied Charlotte, Ashley, and three other children, two of which were currently arguing over which brand of chocolate milk they wanted.

Charlotte and Ashely rushed Whitney, and she pasted a confused smile to her face and opened her arms to catch them

338

both together in a hug. "Hey, guys!" She sniffed the tops of their heads and smelled skin, and hair, and not a fresh wave of shampoo. They hadn't bathed last night, then. "Where's your mom?"

They wriggled backward out of her grip, swiping their messy hair behind their ears and chewing at their lips, unsure of their answer.

"Mommy doesn't feel good," Charlotte said. "Mrs. Patterson picked us up from school."

Whitney tried to keep her anger and disappointment hidden. Sure Madelyn felt bad; she was probably neck-deep in a fresh bottle and seeing double too badly to drive in and pick up the girls.

Mrs. Patterson joined them, her loaded cart sporting a bad wheel and squealing like mad. "Girls," she said, voice tired and long-suffering. "It's not polite to bother other people in the store."

"But this is Aunt Whitney!" Ashley said.

Mrs. Patterson's eyes widened.

"Hi, I'm Whitney."

"Madelyn's sister?" Mrs. Patterson asked, a strange, disgruntled look in her eyes.

"Sister-in-law. Um. The girls said she wasn't feeling well?"

Mrs. Patterson rolled her eyes. "Yeah. That's one word for it."

Whitney sighed. "I'm sorry."

Mrs. Patterson snorted. "You probably should be." She heaved herself against the heavy cart. "Come on, girls, time to go."

~*~

Maggie had left to run errands during a late lunch, so the central office was empty and that was where Ghost led them. The president sat behind the desk, and Tango settled in beside Aidan in the visitor chairs. The back of his neck crawled with invisible insects, nerves creeping down his limbs. He'd been having such a positive, such a *good* day, and he had the feeling it was about to go to shit. That was the story of his life – good things went to shit. Probably he'd shoot up later, and Whitney would leave him, and…

He closed his eyes and took a deep breath. He was sabotaging himself with thoughts like these; they avalanched one atop the next until he started looking desperately for a way out of his own life.

"Kev," Aidan said, touch warm on Tango's arm, even through his sleeve. "Hey, it's alright. Whatever it is."

Tango opened his eyes to see Aidan looking at his father questioningly.

"It's alright, isn't it?"

Ghost nodded. "Yeah. It will be."

"Shit," Tango whispered.

Ghost pulled something up on the computer and then angled the screen toward them so they could see it. A local news article. A fourteen-year-old boy who'd been…

The words blurred on the screen. Tango sat back in his chair, taste of metal on his tongue, breath lodging in his chest.

"Tango." Aidan put an arm around his shoulders. "Hey, it's okay, it doesn't say – we don't know–"

But Ghost's expression was knowing. "It's her," he said. "I just know it is."

"But…" Aidan said.

Tango gulped in a breath. "No, it's her. It has to be. Fuck." He scrubbed his face with both hands. "We should have killed her a long time ago." Though his stomach clenched at the idea; some latent sense of servitude, an aversion to murdering his captor and sole source of food for all those years. Damn, he was crazy.

"Tango," Ghost said. "Kev."

He lifted his head and faced his president, damp with fresh fear sweat beneath his clothes, heart trying to force its way through his ribs. "What?"

"I." Ghost took a breath. He looked nervous; Tango wasn't sure he'd ever seen the man look *nervous*. "I want to bring this up at church."

He was going to pass out.

"Hey, hey, listen. The last time, when they took you back, I kept your secret. Merc, and Aidan, and I handled it on our own. And we got you back. But I think it's time we totally dismantled that bitch, and to do that we need our whole club to help."

Tango drew his feet up into his chair and buried his face in his knees. Aidan rubbed his back.

"We don't have to tell everyone about you," Ghost continued.

"But you want to, don't you?" Tango whispered.

"They're you're brothers. They love you." But the nerves lingered, trapped in the sun lines around Ghost's eyes.

"Can I think about it?"

"Of course. It's your choice. Whatever you wanna do."

~*~

Whatever he wanted to do. Well wasn't that a foreign concept?

Tango spent the rest of the work day trying not to dissociate, fielding worried glances from Aidan, and wondering what might happen if he admitted to his club brothers that he used to be a sex slave.

Would they cut the dog tattoo from his shoulder? Or burn it off?

Would they look at him like some sort of creep? Like they thought he'd wanted them all this time?

What would he do without the club? Could he survive that? He had Whitney now, but...

What would he do without the brotherhood that had saved his life when he was fourteen?

He was grateful when quitting time arrived. He clocked out, assured Aidan he was okay, and headed home, to the little sanctuary he'd built with Whitney.

He found her in the middle of dinner prep, the kitchen redolent of garlic. He crossed the room to get to her right away, not pausing when she greeted him, wrapping his arms around her shoulders and crushing her to his chest as she tried to turn chicken breasts in the skillet with tongs.

"Oh," she said. "Oh, hi." She snuggled in closer, unable to hug him back with her arms trapped inside his. "You okay?"

"Well…"

A knock sounded at the door.

Tango stiffened. "Shit." He let go of Whitney. "Stay here."

He heard her turn the burner off and slide the skillet to a cold eye as he walked to the door.

"Whitney," he warned.

She followed anyway, a few paces back, and he sighed, because he wasn't willing to bodily restrain her. Not yet.

He probably should have expected it, but it was still an unhappy shock to see Ian standing on their front step, cold wind whipping his long coat around his legs.

Tango braced a hand on the half-open door, ready to close it. He felt that old familiar tug, deep in his gut, that Ian would always inspire in him. But stronger than that was the memory of how scared Whitney had been; the fresh wounds of Daniel.

"Why are you here?" He couldn't believe how sturdy his voice was.

"Did you see it on the news?"

"See what?"

Ian rolled his eyes. "For God's sakes, you know what. The boy. Did you see the boy?"

Tango jerked a nod. "Yeah, I saw."

"She's doing it again." Fear shivered across Ian's face, widened his eyes. "She's still in business, and she's bloody *doing it again.*"

"We don't know that."

Ian looked offended. "Are you mad? Or still just unbelievably stubborn because I spooked your little girlfriend?"

His eyes darted up and over Tango's shoulder, to where Whitney stood just behind him.

Tango started to close the door on him.

"Wait!" Ian slapped at the door, bracing it with a palm, tone going desperate. "I'm sorry, okay? I am. I need to talk to you about this."

"Why?"

"Because we need to do something about the bitch!"

For the first time in all their long years of knowing one another, Tango didn't feel compelled to admit anything to Ian. He could tell him about Ghost's plans, about the terrifying idea of coming out to his club, about the Lean Dogs finally ousting Miss Carla. But too much darkness lay between them now; a canyon full of finally-realized lies, obsession, and self-harm. He would always love Ian, but he saw how toxic it was now; it was a faded kind of love, an old watermark that wouldn't wash away.

And it paled next to what he felt for Whitney, the way her light and sweetness filled him up.

He ought to shut the door, turn the lock, and pretend this visit had never happened.

But Whitney said, "Why don't you come in so you aren't shouting out in public?"

"No," Tango said, the same moment Ian said, "Thank you," and shouldered his way inside.

Tango shot Whitney a betrayed look.

She shrugged. "I'm not sure that's something you want to talk about where the whole street can hear." She folded her arms and stood back, expression saying *handle it*.

Well, shit.

Ian strode deeper into the apartment, expensive shoes clicking on the boards, coat flaring behind him dramatically like a cape. When he reached the kitchen, he whirled to face them, and Tango bit back a sudden laugh – the operatic gall of the man. From dancing boy to rakish, Hollywood-worthy villain. What a climb.

"Quite the domestic little scene the two of you have here."

343

"Ian," Tango growled a warning.

"We were just about to have dinner, if you'd like some," Whitney offered.

Ian held up a declining hand. "Not that you aren't a lovely chef, dear, but no, thank you."

"I swear to God..." Tango started.

"Kev." Whitney touched his arm. Her expression said she appreciated him defending her honor, but that she was okay.

He didn't see how she could be, though, because he was *so* not okay, Ian smirking at them in their own kitchen.

Tango took a deep breath, lungs itching for a cigarette. "Let's just get this over with, okay?" He motioned to the couch and went and flopped onto it, grateful for Whitney's steadying presence as she folded herself against his side.

Ian made a theatrical show of falling into the chair and arranging his clothes and long limbs. He inclined his head toward Whitney. "Do you want her to hear this?"

"She already knows everything."

Ian's brows jumped, but he shrugged and said, "Very well." He looked at Tango like he was waiting for him to start the show.

The absurdity of the situation struck him: sitting here with his former and current lovers, contemplating murder. The sad part was: in his whole fucked up life, this wasn't all that strange.

"I saw the news," Tango said. "And yeah, I think it's Carla."

"What did she do now?" Whitney asked.

"Kidnapped a boy," Tango said, staring down at his hands, the dominos dark on his knuckles. "He's fourteen."

"God," she breathed.

"The police can't find any evidence. But...I just know. It was Carla."

"Which is why we've got to find her," Ian said.

"Find her how? I always assumed you'd...taken care of her a long time. You and all your pimp money."

"Excuse me," Ian said, affronted, "I am not a pimp."

344

"My mistake," Tango scoffed. "It's so much more respectable than that."

"Guys," Whitney said, voice a sharp little sliver through their brewing argument. When they both turned to her, she said, "So how can you find her?"

"Oh, I could find her," Ian said. "But the second I start tugging on threads is the second she packs up and skips town. She's in Knoxville; we've got to flush her out without tipping her off."

"So someone has to do some snooping," Whitney said, the gears whirring behind her eyes. "Someone neither she nor her people would recognize."

The small, dark grin Ian gave her sent chills running up Tango's spine.

"The club is gonna handle it," he said, and Ian snorted.

"Yes, of course, because it's not like Carla's people know who the Lean Dogs are."

"She…"

Wait.

Tango sucked in a breath. "She knows the Tennessee Dogs."

"Like I said…"

"No, I mean. She doesn't know *all* the Dogs."

"Someone from another chapter," Whitney guessed, gasping a little. "Like a mole."

Ian steepled his fingers together, gaze moving between the two of them. "Well, maybe she's not useless after all."

"Fuck you," Tango said, without much heat, because he knew Ian never did learn how to give a compliment. They were both ruined boys.

Whitney said, "Do you know anyone who'd be a good fit for the job?"

Tango smiled. "Yeah, I do."

~*~

"Ghost thinks it'll be good for me to tell all the guys about what happened to me. About Carla," Tango admitted later, after Ian had left and they were still sitting on the couch.

Whitney made a sympathetic noise and snuggled in closer beneath his arm. "What do you think?" She rested her head against his chest, fingers plucking at his shirt in a way that was soothing.

He took a deep breath. What *did* he think? It was a comfort to know that, by this point, he could say whatever he needed to say in front of Whitney, and she'd still love him. How could anything be worse than what he'd already told her? It couldn't.

"I think it's the scariest thing I've ever thought about doing. Scarier than slitting my wrists," he blurted, then winced.

Whitney managed to shift even closer, her voice soft and kind. "That's scary."

And then it all just poured out, like it had last night. His sick trauma word vomit. "MCs don't have gay members. They just don't. It's not 'bro' enough, or whatever. And I'm not gay – not that there's anything wrong with that, Ian is, I mean...But I'm bi. And I'm pretty damn sure bi is far enough away from straight that the guys will all see it as gay. And then when they know what happened, what I did...I just..."

"Hey. Hey, stop. Come here." Whitney sat up and slipped her little arm across his shoulders, managing to pull him into her chest like she was much bigger than she really was. "One thing at a time, okay?"

He nodded and dragged in a breath, breathing in the sweet smell of her skin off her sweater. And another note, a little punch of sour he couldn't place.

"Okay," he said. "Okay, um, the gay thing. Bi thing. Whatever. They don't know about it, and, um, it's not allowed," he said into her shoulder. "So that's grounds for stripping my patches."

"What does that entail?"

"They take my cut. I'm not in the club. And I have to lose any Dog-related tats."

"Do you have any of those?"

"Two. On my arm."

"What." And here her strength faltered a moment. "What do you have to do to get rid of them?"

"Sometimes guys get them cut off, or burned off."

She gasped quietly.

"But you can get them covered up with other tats. Or blacked out with ink."

"Okay." He felt the tiny thunder of her heart against his chest, through the softness of her breasts. "Okay, so that wouldn't be too bad. Having them covered up." She stroked the back of his head, his neck. "What would happen if you weren't in the club anymore?"

It chilled his insides to think it. "I'd have to get a new job, for one. Probably find a new place to live. I'd – I'd have to start over. Totally from scratch."

"Scary."

More than she even knew. He'd never been on his own, not really. From his mother's home, to Miss Carla's clutches, to the club that had raised him up as a son, given him a home, a livelihood, and a ready-made batch of friends.

"Is there any reason you have to tell them?" Whitney asked, pulling him back to the moment with gentle fingers sifting through his hair. "Can't it stay our secret?"

Our. Because they were together. Because she was *with him* in this.

"You know how we talked about someone else finding Carla? Yeah, if I'm gonna call in a favor, everybody's gonna want an explanation."

What he didn't say was that he was tired of living with shadows in his periphery, wondering if each day was the day one of his brothers found out all his dirty secrets.

"I don't know what to do," he admitted.

Her nails scratched lightly at his scalp. It was the most comfort he'd ever had from a woman, because his mother was mostly a smudged memory these days. Whitney was alive, and warm, and so good to him, right here in the present.

"I want to tell you something," she said.

"Okay."

"My boss sent me home early today because I couldn't stop throwing up."

"What?! Are you – are you sick? Do you need–"

"I'm not sick, I'm fine. Don't get up. I was…sort of freaking out about what you told me. I just kept thinking about you, being so young, and being forced to…" She gulped audibly. "It just got to me. And I puked in a trash can, and I felt really stupid afterward."

"Oh God." He wrapped both arms around her and crushed her hard. "Whit, Jesus, I'm so sorry. I never should have said anything. I can't believe–"

"No, no, stop that. I don't like it, but I'm an adult, okay? It's not that I'm not tough enough to hear it. It's just I care about you so much, and when I think about what you went through – you, sweet, wonderful, wonderful you – it just…it was awful. I just wanted to make it better for you. I wanted to take the hurt away, and I knew I couldn't, and I hated it. I felt so powerless. I felt like I'd do anything I could to help."

He sat back a little, arms still locked around her, and stared at her earnest face in wonder.

"You know why I felt that way?" she asked. "Because I love you. And you know what? I don't know how a club works, I admit it. But those guys love you too. And I can guarantee they'll want to puke and bash heads when you tell them."

His eyes burned, and he blinked hard.

"No one will be disgusted with you. No one will hate you." Her smile quivered. "That's just my two cents anyway."

Tango pulled her in close again, and this time he knew the sour scent was vomit, and he hated himself for making her sick.

But he loved her. And she loved him. And if what she said was true…If his brothers…

He had to try. To stop Carla, to spare other boys, he could do that. He could expose the dark marks deep beneath his skin and lay himself at his brothers' feet. They'd saved him, after all. So maybe…

348

Just maybe…

~*~

Ian fired off a text – *I want in when you find Carla* – and then laid his phone on the kitchen counter, resolved not to mess with it anymore tonight.

"Who are you texting?" Alec asked from his seat at the island, not jealous, just curious.

"My favorite frenemy." Ian smiled as he imagined Ghost Teague rolling his eyes. "Not to worry." He climbed onto the stool beside Alec and poured himself a glass of cabernet, ignoring the way his hand trembled. "What do you want to do tonight, darling?"

Alec had unbuttoned his collar and hung his tie on the coat rack just inside the door when he first arrived. Cuffs rolled up to his elbows, hair mussed from raking his fingers through it, he looked as casual and undone as Ian had ever seen him.

He shrugged. "I dunno. I don't really care about going out." He swirled his wine and sent Ian a sideways look, considering.

"What?"

Alec's eyes slid away, and he took a small sip of wine. "Nothing."

"Oh no. Nothing never means nothing." Inwardly, Ian groaned. He didn't have the emotional fortitude for the conversation that was obviously ramping up. "What is it?"

"It's nothing," Alec insisted. And then: "It's just that…I wonder, sometimes, what we're doing. You and me." And then came the bold, doe-eyed glance, full of longing and a dozen questions.

"Oh, Alec," Ian sighed. "Please don't tell me you're asking that."

"Too bad, 'cause I am. I'm just curious. I wanna know."

"Of course you do. Doesn't everyone?"

Alec stared at him.

"What do you want me to tell you?" Ian asked.

"The truth."

Ian groaned and put his head down on the cool marble of the counter. "Bloody hell."

"That bad, huh?" Alec deadpanned, but from Ian's vantage point, peeking out of the corner of his eye, Alec's gaze was full of hurt.

Ian straightened. "Love. Listen to me: you don't want to stay with me. This between us – it's good. It's *very* good. But you'll get tired of me."

Alec bristled. "Isn't that for me to decide? I may be younger than you, but I'm not some stupid kid you can just *decide* stuff for."

"And to think you were so docile and accommodating when I hired you."

Well if that wasn't the wrong thing to say…

Alec's eyes widened, and his jaw clenched, and for a moment, Ian was sure he was about to explode. But he swallowed his response. Said, "Are you just trying to push me away on purpose?"

"You tell me."

"You are," Alec said, with what Ian assumed was more certainty than he felt. "You're trying to keep me out." He tapped the side of his own head to demonstrate.

God, there wasn't enough wine in the world for this conversation. Ian drained what he'd poured in two long swallows and refilled his glass. "Don't presume to know what I'm thinking. Dangerous business, that, considering I write your paycheck."

Alec looked like he'd been slapped. "That's not fair."

"It's entirely fair, darling. Everything's fair in love and war, after all."

"When we're here, when we're not at work," Alec said, stumbling over his words, breathing hard now, "I'm not your damn employee."

"Oh no? Do you think because I let you fuck me that somehow the balance of power has shifted? That you're the big man now, and I'm just your little bitch?"

The stem of his glass snapped beneath the pressure of his fingers. Ian felt the bite of broken glass and didn't react, holding the fractured pieces together. That was something at which he excelled – keeping broken things contained.

Alec must have heard the muffled *crack*, his eyes flicking to the glass, and back to Ian's face. "I never said that, and I don't think it."

"Liar." Ian felt an awful sneer break across his face. "Every man wants his very own bitch." And maybe, in truth, he'd seen *Alec* as *his* little bitch, with his obscene politeness and deference. Turned out that was an office personality, though, and once he got comfy, the real Alec was an annoying asshole.

"Well let me tell you," he said, twisting on his stool so he faced Alec. "You picked the right one. I'm a professional bitch. I'm a genius at taking cock. I make it look easy. World Class Bitch, that's me. You won the fucking lottery when it comes to ass, love."

Alec stared at him, horrified. "Why are you saying this? I never wanted–"

"To acknowledge that you're gay? No, no one ever does, do they? They want to have their girlfriends, and wives, and mistresses, and *pretend*, deny what they are. And when they have a fistful of cash, they come down to the club so they can fuck boys. Just like all the rest, aren't you, Alec?"

The unobtrusive track lighting struck Alec's eyes at a strange angle, so he almost looked like he might cry. He said, "Ian, what are you talking about?" in the gentlest voice, as if he thought Ian might snap like his wineglass stem.

Oh, the glass. He glanced at it and saw dark red drips falling from his hand to the countertop; he didn't know if they were wine or blood. He leaned forward and carefully set the glass in the sink, staring afterward at the thin slices in the meat of his palm, the dark smears of crimson and purple.

"Ian," Alec said, voice cracking. "I'm not afraid to be gay. That's exactly the thing – I don't *want* us to hide. I want to be *with you*."

Ian curled his hand into a fist and watched the blood drip, drip, drip.

Over on the opposite counter, his phone beeped with a text alert.

"That'll be Kenneth," he said, and got to his feet.

Twenty-Seven

Whitney woke to the quiet black of the wee hours Friday morning, and found Kev awake, watching her, his eyes a shine of glass on the pillow beside hers. He was going to tell his brothers today, and her stomach grabbed, a brief shiver of fear. She was so proud of him, though. Grateful for the chance to be afraid, because he'd trusted her enough to lay his secrets in her hands.

This, she thought, was what it meant to be an old lady. To share his nerves in the dark, thrumming with quiet energy, the weight of love keeping her from flying off into madness. In that moment, she didn't wonder if he wanted to ink a proprietary tattoo into her skin, or if he thought of her that way. There was no room for doubt in the dark hours before dawn. Only certainty, and a quiet desperation.

"Kevin," she said, his name a flash of silver through the shadows.

He shifted closer toward her, and her hand slid up his chest, the warm skin of his throat, his pulse jumping under her palm.

Their kiss tasted like sour morning breath, and it didn't matter.

Whitney opened her mouth and let him lick inside, angling her head to give him access. His fine grain of stubble rasped at her chin, and she breathed in the faint salt smell of tears just beneath his eye.

He eased her over onto her back and settled between her thighs, braced with an arm beside her head, his other hand running slow patterns up and down her side. Easing her sleep shirt up inch by inch, until it was bundled up beneath her arms, and her bare skin, kissed silver by moonlight through the blinds, was revealed to him.

Whitney tugged at his shirt and he pulled back, ditching his clothes in a few practiced moves, not even leaving the bed. Then he was warm and naked against her, his cock hot and hard against her thigh.

He ducked his head to trail gentle, damp kisses across her breasts, teasing and sucking at her nipples, feathering his slick lips down her sternum in aimless patterns.

She whined quietly in the back of her throat and lifted her hips when his hand skimmed down her belly and found the damp place between her thighs. "Yes," she murmured. "Please."

But still he went slow, showing such care, fingering her until she was slick and ready. They hadn't used a condom the last few times, knowing he was clean and that she was on birth control. He eased into her entrance with measured, shallow little thrusts, finally sliding home, buried to the hilt. She was never going to tire of that possession, the fullness of having him so deeply rooted in her body.

She felt a heartbeat in every inch of her skin, and didn't know if it was hers or his. He didn't move at first, just held still, like he needed to feel that they were joined, soak it in.

He rested his forehead against hers, close enough she almost thought she could make out the blue of his eyes. "I love you," he said.

"I love you too."

~*~

"Are you sure?" Mercy asked, the picture of concern, all drawn up inside his huge frame like he intended to hit someone on Tango's behalf. Probably he did.

Tango raked his shower-damp hair back into a bun at the back of his head and secured it with an elastic. "I'm sure." And strangely enough, he was. That morning, snuggled deep into the afterglow with Whitney, listening to the birds start their four a.m. chorus, he'd felt his fear melt slowly out of his lax muscles. All he could do was be honest in an effort to help that poor kidnapped boy, and countless others like him. If his brothers couldn't handle that, then so be it. He still had Mercy, and Ghost, and Mags, and Ava, and Aidan. He still had his Whitney. He would survive, whatever the verdict, and for once – God – survival sounded like something he wanted.

It was a bitter morning, frost still heavy on the grass and the bikes that had spent the night parked outside the clubhouse. The sun limped gray and weak up a gunmetal sky, slowly by degrees, and their breath plumed in front of them, white smoke.

They both heard the approaching growl of what they recognized to be Aidan's bike, the ring of the pipes echoing off cold pavement. A moment later, Aidan drew into view, bundled up against the cold, and turned in at the gate, coasting to a halt in the empty parking space in front of them. He killed the engine and tugged the end of his tightly wound scarf out of his jacket collar. "He tell you what kinda idiot shit he's gonna do?" he asked Mercy.

"Yeah," Mercy sighed. He shoved his hands in his pockets, his huge shoulders drooped, and he looked sad. Sad enough that Tango's stomach hurt.

Aidan dropped his helmet on his handlebars and pushed his sunglasses up into his hair. His eyes were the color of rich hot chocolate in the early light. "I'm gonna ask you one more time: please don't do this."

Tango looked at his two friends, at the concern etched into their features, and he loved them so much.

But it was time to take his life in-hand now. So he said, "I'm sorry, guys, but I have to."

Aidan muttered something under his breath, but came to stand beside them, frame shaking with a little involuntary shiver from the cold.

The others were running late, or in RJ's case, not yet awake inside. Chanel brought them coffee; Tango figured that meant she'd spent the night. Then everyone started to trickle in: Rottie, Walsh, Michael, Carter, Dublin, Littlejohn. Everyone. A few cast curious glances toward the three of them standing together, but no one said anything besides "good morning" and "see you inside."

Ghost arrived last, which Tango had always thought he did on purpose, letting them all see that he was the boss, that he could make them wait if he chose.

He stepped up and put a hand on Tango's shoulder. "So what's it gonna be?"

"I wanna tell them."

Ghost nodded, expression serious, proud...fearful at the edges.

"And I have an idea about finding Carla."

"Oh yeah?" Ghost's brows jumped and he flashed a small smile. "Well let's hear it."

He told the three of them, and they all nodded.

"I like it," Ghost said. "Should have thought of it myself. Alright." Another shoulder squeeze. "You ready?"

"Yeah."

Aidan pulled him aside before they stepped into the chapel, hands on Tango's arms. "Whatever happens," he said, "you know I've got your back. Whatever you need, however we have to handle this, I'm there."

Tango flicked a smile. "I know."

Aidan hugged him hard, slapped his back, and they went into the sacred room.

~*~

Tango stared at his tattooed hands a long moment after Ghost opened up the floor to him. He held a cigarette between two fingers, its smoke curling lazily upward, the sharp smell grounding. He thought about where his hands had been that morning, the ways Whitney had allowed him to touch her, even though he was dirty and tainted. Because she loved him, no matter where *any* part of his body had been.

He took a deep breath, forced his head up, and started talking.

"There's something I need to tell all of you, because I need the club's help dealing with someone who's very, very evil.

"When I was seven, my dad stole me away from my mom and sold me to Carla Burgess..."

He told them an abridged, but informative version, focusing on the other boys, the way they were drugged, kept

356

under lock and key, starved and beaten, forced to service clients and dance for them. He told them about escaping at fourteen and meeting Aidan outside the school; about Maggie taking him home and bathing him, and giving him a soft bed where he shivered through his heroin withdrawal. He told them about being abducted in Walgreens, about the way he hated that he hadn't been strong enough to fight off the three thugs who'd knocked him out, bound his wrists, and then hauled him away to yet another basement.

He told them about trying to end his life. Twice.

He didn't tell them about Ian, because it was none of their business, and he couldn't just out the man like that. This was about *his* shame, *his* history, *his* club.

Tango tried to make eye contact, but found he couldn't, gaze skipping across blurred faces, too afraid of what he'd find in their gazes if he really looked. His cigarette burned down to the nub, burned his fingers, until he was forced to set it in the heavy crystal tray in the center of the table. At one point, Aidan's arm slid across his shoulders, solid and supportive, telling the whole table of men that Aidan stood beside him; a risky move for Aidan, but one that made Tango want to lean sideways into his best friend and absorb all the love and warmth offered.

His throat grew dry as paper, but he was too queasy to reach for his coffee. His heart lodged itself at the base of his throat and he forced himself to keep breathing as black spots crowded his vision.

Finally: "She's still around, and she's taking boys again. She...we have to stop her. That's why I told you all of that." He gulped. "It's just...it's really important that she doesn't keep doing this."

And then he was done, all the poison spilled out onto the table, billowing through the room like cigarette smoke.

Oh God, he actually *told them*. Oh shit. Oh *fuck*.

He braced himself inwardly for the flaying, and leaned a little into Aidan's solid shoulder.

Mercy wore an expression that suggested anyone who said something he didn't like was going to be put through the wall head-first.

Ghost managed to be impassive, but something feral and protective lurked in his eyes as they shifted across the table.

Surprisingly, Michael was the first to speak. "So let's kill the bitch."

"Yeah."

"I'm in."

"Absolutely."

"What do you need from us?" Walsh asked, face dark and harsh like Tango had only ever seen it when Emmie was in danger.

"We got your back, bro," RJ said, "always."

And…and they did. They were all looking at him, all with blends of horror and fierce determination on their faces. Not one of them looked like they hated him, or that he made them sick.

He darted a glance to Ghost, and the president looked proud.

"See?" Aidan whispered. "It's okay. They love you, brother."

Tango burst into tears and dropped his face into his hands.

~*~

The welcome burn of whiskey slid down his throat and filled his cold belly. He was shaky and chilled and emotionally empty after his purge and collapse, but in this moment, with his brothers' support, it was *such* a good feeling.

Aidan sat beside him at the clubhouse bar, their shoulders pressed together. Mercy was on his other side, warm, massive, and protective.

Ghost and Walsh were behind the bar, pouring drinks, much to everyone's amusement.

"Do you want me to make the phone call?" Ghost asked his VP as he sipped Scotch.

Walsh scowled. "No. I'll do it."

Mercy chuckled into his Johnnie Walker.

"Hey," Walsh said, "you've got an asshole half-brother. You should sympathize with me."

"Oh, I do," Mercy assured, "but I happen to like your half-brother."

Ghost laughed, and it sounded lighter and freer than Tango had heard from him in a while.

His own laughter tickled his ribs, stray little fingers of happiness he'd never expected.

"What can we do in the meantime?" Hound asked. "I mean, while we wait for Prince Charming to get here."

Walsh rolled his eyes.

Ghost said, "Nothing," with a wince. "We don't want to tip her or her people off, so we have to lay real low."

There were several groans.

"Wait," Aidan said. "Maybe that's not true." He grinned. "Don't we have eyes on the inside with the PD?"

"Yeah," Ghost said, going curious.

"We could go ahead and cover our asses."

Tango loved the way Ghost pointed at his son and said, "Now there's an idea."

~*~

"Kev, that's so wonderful," Whitney said into the phone, and blinked back hot, happy tears.

"You were right," he said, sounding a little emotional himself. "They didn't..." He sighed. "Thank you for encouraging me, you know?"

She dabbed at her eyes with her sleeve and said, "You're welcome." She hadn't really doubted the love of Kev's club brothers – in her heart of hearts she'd known they would accept him – but a small seed of worry dissipated in her belly to hear him say his confession had gone so well. The thing she was learning about bikers: they had a surprising capacity for love. The people in town who saw them as out and out villains could all pound sand as far as she was concerned; the Lean Dogs had saved her Kev not once, but three times. Whatever else they did, she loved them for doing *that*.

"Mercy said Ava's inviting us to dinner tonight," Kev said. "If you wanna go."

"I do, but I've got to make a quick stop first. Call you when I'm done?"

"Yeah, be careful."

"I will."

They said their goodbyes and hung up, and Whitney took a moment to stare up at the house, hands splayed across the steering wheel, gathering herself for the confrontation to come.

The strange but lovely Southwestern stucco house her brother had bought for his family was an eyesore. The architecture was punctuated by unmown grass, trees that needed trimming, and a dusty, leaf-strewn porch dotted with pots of dead flowers. The poor place told a story of neglect, one the home's owner was willingly allowing to play out.

Whitney took a deep breath and popped her door, stepped out into the sharp bite of the December afternoon. As she pulled her coat tighter around her, she tried not to think of previous Christmases in which Jason had strung white and multicolored lights in the trees, the tacky illuminated reindeer, the three-foot Santa he'd always perched on the roof. Back then, there had been wreaths on the doors and windows, a swag on the mailbox, and the house had smelled like fresh cookies and hot cider.

Today, when Whitney used her key and let herself into the kitchen, all she smelled was the ghost of something unappetizing that had been heated in the microwave, and moldy bread. The same wreck as before greeted her when she stepped into the living room, both girls in front of the TV when they should have been doing their homework.

They jumped up with shouts of "Aunt Whitney!" and rushed to hug her.

Whitney hugged them in close and asked where their mother was.

"In her room," Ashley said, eyes flicking to the carpet, like she thought she was being a tattle-tale. "She doesn't feel good."

Whiney patted her small back. "Okay, well I'm going to go see her. You girls keep watching TV, okay? Turn the volume up a little more – yeah, that's perfect. Good girls."

Her heart thumped a painful beat against her ribs as she slipped down the hall and turned the knob of Madelyn's door without knocking. The ripe smells of sweat and bourbon threatened to choke her when she opened the door, but she held her breath and slipped inside, closing the door behind her so the girls wouldn't hear so much.

Madelyn was a lifeless shape on the bed, snoring, arm flung over her eyes, bottle within reach on the nightstand.

Whitney thought of Kev, of how brave he'd been today, of what he'd been able to tell his club. She flipped on the overhead light and kicked Madelyn hard in the foot. "Wake up."

Madelyn came to with a loud snort, flailing, eyes shut against the light. "Wha...shit." She rolled over and pressed her face into the bedclothes.

"Nuh-uh." Whitney grabbed her clammy foot in both hands and heaved all her meager weight into a tug, managing to drag her sister-in-law down toward the foot of the bed. "Nap time is over."

Madelyn twisted around, flopping gracelessly onto her back again, squinting up at Whitney with a hand shading her eyes. "What the hell?" Her voice was a thick croak. "Thought I kicked you out."

"Yeah, well, that was a really stupid thing for you to do. You won't let me help, but you let some neighbor pick up the girls from work when you're too face-down drunk to get behind the wheel?" She spoke firmly, but not loudly, her voice a measured insistence, like what she imagined a doctor or teacher would have used on the girls.

Madelyn heaved upright, swaying, clutching at the covers for balance. She scowled at Whitney, the effect ruined by the way she flinched away from the light. "You little bitch, it's none of your—"

"Business? Oh, it absolutely is. Because, see, when Mrs. Patterson gets tired of playing chauffer, she's going to tell someone at the school about you, and then you're going to have a visit from Child Protective Services. And I'm guessing they'll have to force the door open and come in and find you just like I did. And then you know what happens? They take the girls away and put them in foster care. And my poor nieces, who lost their junkie dad, and who still have a mother, will be orphans, at the mercy of the system, and I won't ever see them again. *You* won't ever see them again. So it's *very much* my business that you stop drinking yourself to death and take care of your children."

Madelyn stared at her, and Whitney didn't know if the shaking was anger, DTs, or some combination of the two.

"Here's the thing, Madelyn. I watched my brother destroy his own life. I spent a week in a basement, being held as collateral, watching my boyfriend get beat to hell, because Jason couldn't stop using. I will not watch you throw your life down the toilet too. I won't let this whole family implode. I will literally drag your ass out of this house and take you to the hospital, see if I won't."

It was a confidence and a quiet rage she'd never shown to anyone before, tempered by all the shit that had happened in the last year. She was full of poison, and it was time to lance the wound.

"I'd like to see you try," Madelyn said, but it was a weak protest, her chin quivering.

"Okay, I can try. And if that doesn't work, I'll call my friend Mercy and he'll be happy to throw you over his shoulder and drag you out for me."

Madelyn's bloodshot eyes widened. "What?"

Whitney knew she shouldn't – she knew Madelyn's transformation should have come about because it was the right thing, because she wanted to get better for her kids, and Whitney certainly had no right to start throwing trump cards without anyone's permission. But throw she did.

"Madelyn." She stepped in close to the bed, aiming a finger at the woman's chest. "Don't push me. You're not just dealing with little old me anymore. I've got Lean Dogs connections now. You either get sober, or the MC is going to *help* you get sober. Understand?"

Fear and awe clashing on her face, Madelyn slowly nodded. "Shit," she muttered. "It really is always the quiet ones, isn't it?"

~*~

Maggie and Ghost and Aidan and Sam were also at the Lécuyers' for dinner that night. After Kev had retired to the living room with the rest of the guys, Whitney wrung her hands and said, "Um, I know I don't really have any business doing this, but I wanted to ask you all something."

The three old ladies looked at her, curious but friendly.

"Ask away," Ava said.

Whitney took a deep breath. "My sister-in-law is…well, she's an alcoholic."

"Your brother's widow?" Sam asked.

"Yeah. She just hasn't been able to cope, and she turned to the bottle. I went to confront her earlier today. For the second time. The first time she kicked me out of the house and it was a whole big mess." She shook her head, willing the bad memory away with a wave. "But I went back. And I told her how it was going to be, and that she was going to get sober so her girls don't get taken away. I got her to promise me that she'll go to AA meetings, and I've already made some phone calls and talked to some counselors, and I poured out all the booze in the house – even the airline bottles of vodka I found behind the toilet tank." She breathed a dry, humorless chuckle. "I guess I just…wanted some advice."

They studied her a moment, hands frozen in the act of preparing dinner, and Whitney really, really wished she hadn't threatened Madelyn with the club earlier. What had she been thinking? They might have been Kev's family, but they weren't hers, she had no right to...

"Oh honey," Maggie said, and dropped her knife, moved through the kitchen until she could draw Whitney into a one-armed, sideways hug. "We'll do you one better. We'll make sure she doesn't fall off the wagon, okay? No one's putting your nieces in the system, I promise."

Whitney bit her lip hard, eyes stinging. "You guys don't have to do that."

"Sure we do. Family takes care of family." She snorted. "Whether they want to be taken care of or not."

Over at the stove, Ava sent her a covert wink.

Family. She was family.

She just barely managed not to cry into the mashed potatoes.

~*~

The Lécuyers didn't have a dining room – something Mercy swore he was going to add on when he finally started expanding the place, which left Ava rolling her eyes – so the kitchen table and a folding table were wedged together in the living room and both heaped with food until the legs threatened to give out. The discussion was all about the approach of Christmas, and everyone's plans.

Maggie informed Whitney that the old ladies always decorated the clubhouse tree, and she was invited to come help. Sam was excited because it was going to be Lainie's first Christmas. The boys were planning a charity run to the children's wing at the hospital, delivering money and presents for the kids.

It was all just so *normal* and *good*.

On the way home, Kev's headlamp reflected in her rearview mirror, it started to snow, soft wet flakes that clung to her windshield wipers, and made her glad for the short trip.

Inside, Whitney made hot chocolate and they both perched on the window ledge in the living room, mugs warming their hands, watching snow spiral beneath streetlamps and collect like royal icing along the sidewalks.

"They kept saying it was gonna snow before Christmas, and it finally did," Tango observed. The ends of his hair were damp with snow, and curled slightly, framing his narrow, pretty face in a way that would have been feminine if not for the sharp cut of his narrow jaw and the masculine ridge of his nose. Whitney was convinced his eyes had come off a Disney character, beautiful and big and blue, silvered by the reflection of snow beyond the window.

"I'm glad they were right."

"Hmm."

Whitney nudged his knee with her own. "Hey, I'm really proud of you. It was really brave what you did today."

His smile was quick, rueful. "That's what Ghost said."

"Then I'm glad he and I agree on that."

Kev shook his head, hair sliding down to cover his eyes. "All I did was talk. I was so scared I thought I'd puke, and all it was was a story. I didn't fight anyone, or do anything." Another small headshake. "And for a fuckup like me, I guess that's brave."

"No. Hey." She nudged him again, harder this time, until he tucked his hair back and made eye contact, his gaze tinged with doubt and self-loathing. "Today, when I was at work, I may have...um, Googled some stuff about outlaw clubs. Trust me: what you told your club today – that was very brave. Very, Kev, I'm serious."

He snorted. "Clubs are changing, I guess."

"Everything changes, eventually. And they love you. Because, guess what: loving someone is maybe the bravest thing there is. Because they might not love you back, and they might hurt you, and it might all go to shit. But you were brave enough to tell them, and they're brave enough to love you. And every good thing that happens in the world is because of love. There's no bravery without it."

He cradled his mug in both hands, close to his chest. "It's pretty brave to love someone who's an addict."

She watched him, his slender fingers almost as white as the porcelain of the mug.

"Every day – every single day – I want to shoot up. But I talk myself out of it, and I don't. And isn't it stupid that there are people dying in wars, and bombings, and rescuing people out of burning buildings, and the bravest thing I do all day is keep myself from falling off the wagon?"

"Everybody's got their own war, Kev," she said, quietly. "Don't dismiss what you've accomplished, please."

"I'm not," he said. He glanced out the window, a small smile curving his mouth. "Trust me: I'm not."

Twenty-Eight

Walsh just knew. It was a prickling up the back of his neck, a stirring against his skin, like a ghost passing through the room. He was sunk down in the center of the couch in the den, fire crackling on the hearth, Emmie mostly asleep and snuggled up beside him, about to miss her favorite number from *White Christmas,* when the doorbell rang. He wasn't surprised, only disappointed.

Emmie jerked awake. "What?"

"I wonder who that could be," Bea said from her armchair.

Shane had managed to wrangle a date, and wasn't there to share a commiserating eye roll with Walsh.

"I'll give you one guess," he told his wife and mother, and got to his feet.

"Oh no," Emmie said with a laugh. "That's your Charlie face."

"Charlie's here?" Bea asked. "How delightful."

"Not delightful, Mum. Not a bit."

It was snowing, the night bright with it, the flakes sifting down in heavy clouds. A fresh stripe of black asphalt had been exposed on the driveway, visible in the moonlight, and Fox stood on the porch, boots crusted with rapidly-melting snow, pink at the tips of his ears from the cold.

"Evening, brother," Fox greeted, and looked like he was biting back a smile.

"I'm glad you left out the 'good.'"

Fox snorted.

"You know, out of town members usually just crash at the clubhouse."

"Not the ones with rich brothers."

"I'm not rich."

Fox took a dramatic look around the wide front porch. "Coulda fooled me." He hitched his rucksack up higher on his shoulder. "You're not actually going to make me stand out in the snow, are you?"

"No," Walsh said, stepping aside. "Wipe your feet."

"Oh, I always do."

"Did you come all the way from Amarillo?" Walsh asked, watching to make sure his brother took off his boots and wiped his damp jeans on the mat just inside the door.

"No. I was in Arkansas, helping out with something."

The sort of something Walsh probably didn't want to talk about.

Fox sniffed, testing the air with flared nostrils like an actual fox. "Do I smell Christmas biscuits?"

~*~

Albie decided the best time to have a word would be in the morning, right after the husband had left for work, when the wife was fresh and not expecting company.

It was an expensive area, even by Mayfair standards, with clean streets, iron fences, second-story balconies, and soothing winter gardens setting off the stone and brick facades of the lavish townhouses. Albie kept his gloved hands in the pockets of his best coat – a long wool number, only slightly frayed at the collar, a secret hole in the right front pocket where he'd once tucked a lit cigarette and it had burned the satin lining. He knew if anyone caught a look at his Docs and jeans and the bristly state of his face, they'd report him; he was out of place here, after all. So he walked with his head erect, unhurried, trying not to look squirrely.

The townhouse he was looking for was crisp white brick, marble front steps flanked by iron railings, its door blue. He caught flashes of curtains in upper windows, and a glimpse of a black grand piano through the naked first floor window to his right. He pushed the bell and raked a gloved hand through his hair, one last time, thinking for the tenth time he should have shaved. It wouldn't do him any good to get booted out into the street before he'd had a chance to even ask about the mistress of the house.

The blue door opened, revealing a black-and-white tiled entryway, and an employee in shirtsleeves and waistcoat.

"Yes?" he asked, expression cool.

"Hi, yes, my name is Albert, and I was hoping to speak with Mrs. Byron. I have some information concerning her son, Ian."

The butler looked at him a long moment. And then, against all probability, said, "Won't you come in?"

Twenty-Nine

The worst part about all of this was the waiting.

"So, hey." RJ leaned in until his elbow bumped into Tango's, dropping his voice to a stage whisper. "So that guy. That English dude. Shaman. Did he used to be, like, a customer or something?"

Scratch that: *this* was the worst part.

"Goddamn it," Mercy said, and by the way RJ jumped, Mercy kicked him beneath their favorite high-top table in Bell Bar. "What did I say about asking questions?"

"It's just a question," RJ protested, offended. "I'm just curious. I mean, it's obvious the guy's sweet on Ta—"

"He wasn't a customer," Tango rushed to say, now that Rottie, Dublin, and RJ were all eyeing him strangely. Shit, he hadn't wanted to spread Ian's business around, but he couldn't have them thinking he was one of those sick clients who'd used him. Ian was a lot of things, but he wasn't a rapist or a pedophile. "He – he worked there. With me."

"Shit," Dublin muttered, reaching for a smoke and then grimacing when he remembered he couldn't light one inside the bar. "Was he kidnapped too?"

Tango stared down into his beer. "Yeah. Back in London."

Dublin whistled and said, "Shit," again, a shocked little breath.

"Well how'd he get to be all rich and shit?" RJ asked.

"Dude," Mercy said. "I will fold you up and stuff you in this beer pitcher."

"But I'm curious!"

Tango sighed. "Ia – Shaman is a lot more resourceful than me. And a lot more focused. When he got out, he decided he wanted to be powerful for a change. So that's what he did."

"And we're not any of us gonna ask any more questions about it," Mercy said.

Tango waved at him. "It's okay, I get it. It's a lot to think about." When he risked a glance around the table, he saw that his brothers were just curious, and a little sad, and a little shocked. They were still processing. But they still didn't look like they hated him.

Sometimes, miracles did happen.

Rottie cleared his throat. "Anybody want hot wings?"

It was Tuesday night, and Whitney was spending the evening at her sister-in-law's house, getting in some quality time with the girls and helping Madelyn clean, trying to get back on some sort of solid footing. Tango was waiting for her call, so he could meet her over there and follow her home, and he didn't miss the irony of drinking beer so his girlfriend could take care of an alcoholic. He'd been sitting twitchily in front of the clubhouse TV, glancing at his phone every ten seconds when Mercy walked through and suggested they head over to the bar. No doubt Mercy would have rather been at home with Ava and the kids, but Tango appreciated the distraction.

On the table, his phone buzzed. "No wings for me." He chugged down the last half inch of his beer. "I gotta go; see you guys tomorrow."

He left to a chorus of goodbyes and some concerned looks. They were going to all mother hen him now, he realized. He'd worried that they would reject him, and instead they were going to smother him with worry and love. A bright ball of a laugh swelled in his chest, and he was smiling to himself as he stepped out onto the sidewalk.

It wasn't even six yet, though total darkness veiled the evening, and downtown was busy with shoppers and restaurant goers. Holiday lights kissed every metallic surface, glittering like earthbound stars. Even the sludgy remnants of snow in the gutters looked festive.

With a belly full of nothing stronger than beer, pleasantly warm but sober, Tango enjoyed the ride out to the Howard house. He pulled into the driveway, and was struck hard by the memory of the last time he was here.

It had been a year ago, and he'd lingered out at the curb, smoking, knowing he shouldn't be here, not when the family was grieving. The yard had been tidy, then. Whitney had seen him, and walked out, arms wrapped around herself against the cold. She'd touched him, and he'd wanted to lean into her until they fused into one being, and some of his terrible pain eased.

Now, he pulled out his phone and fired off a text, looking up at the warm glow in the window afterwards. *I'm here.*

His phone buzzed: *Come on in.*

He went to the side door, the one that led into the kitchen, because in his experience, no one used front doors. He had no idea what the room looked like normally, but it was sparkling now, smelling suspiciously of lemon cleaner and orange oil, cabinet faces gleaming, scrubbed tiles winking at him.

"Whit?" he called.

"In here!"

He followed her voice into the living room, and found her sitting cross-legged on the floor, mane of dark hair tied back in a ponytail, sorting through old magazines that she'd obviously dumped out of the rack a few feet away. She glanced up when he entered, flashed him a tired smile.

"Y'all should really have that door locked," Tango admonished, because it frightened him to see her sitting there so small and vulnerable, anyone able to walk right in and get to her.

She rolled her eyes, and even if he was worried about her safety, he was glad to see that kind of relaxed, normal response. He kept expecting everyone in his life to suddenly realize how awful he was, but that just wasn't happening.

"It was locked, but I unlocked it when you said you were on the way."

"Still," he insisted. "I could have knocked. It's not safe."

"This is a safe neighborhood," another voice protested, and he looked up over the back of the couch to see what must have been the sister-in-law. She was pretty, or would be, once she got her act together. Once the dark circles under her eyes and the hassled set to her face eased. She held an armload of laundry and glared at Tango, nothing about her expression suggesting friendliness or softness. No wonder Whitney had moved out.

"Uh…" Whitney scrambled to her feet. "Madelyn, this is Kev. Kev, this is my sister-in-law, Madelyn."

"Hi," Tango said, and got an unhappy snort in return. He waited for the "biker trash" insult her look suggested, but she just turned away and marched off with her dirty clothes.

"Sorry," Whitney said with a sigh as she walked to greet him. She slid her arms around his neck and pulled him down for a fast kiss. "She still hates my guts right now. It's not about you, personally."

"Oh, I think it has a little something to do with me personally." He plucked at the front of his cut, his other arm around her waist.

"Well…"

"Hey, we're all used to this. We're more infamous than famous."

"I don't like that, though." She frowned and it was adorable. "People shouldn't judge you just because you ride motorcycles and look all…leathery." She patted his leather-covered chest.

No, they judged them for the whole drug-dealing, illegal activity thing.

"Yeah, well, not everybody's as open-minded as you, baby."

"Guess you're right." She pulled back with one last pat and went back to her pile of sorted magazines. "I'm sorry, I'll be just another minute. I was all done when I texted you, but then I found this rack hiding under a pile of jackets." She shook her head. "It's one of those jobs that seems to get worse the longer you work at it."

"Take your time," he assured. "I got nowhere else to be."

And he didn't. They were all still waiting on Fox to track down the new Nest, which made him twitchy as all hell, but for once in his life, he didn't have a groupie, or a needle, or a razor blade, or even a guilty night of staring at the wall waiting for him at home. Home was where he lived with Whitney, now, and he was content to wait for her.

Tango wandered over to a floor-to-ceiling built-in bookshelf against the far wall, drawn by the promise of dozens of framed photos on the shelves. Most were of Madelyn and her husband, Whitney's brother. He'd been handsome: tall, and trim, and clean cut. No visible tattoos, no collection of earrings – or tattered scars along the edge of his ear where they'd been ripped out. He had Whitney's smile; or she had his. He didn't look like a heroin addict, not like Tango did. But poison didn't care what you looked like.

How terrible that the two of them had been brought together by something like that.

But what would he do without her?

"Alright," Whitney said, appearing at his elbow. "Let me just say bye and we can go." But she hooked her arm through his and made no move to go do so, her head resting against his shoulder. Tango wondered if she was staring at the pictures, too, and knew she was when she said, "It doesn't seem possible, does it?"

He didn't ask for clarification; just said, "No."

~*~

The change had been happening slowly – not really a change, but an awakening. A stirring of positive emotions and healthy ideas. Kev had made careful progress, a day at a time, and telling his club about his past seemed to have been some final hurdle. Whitney didn't kid herself, she knew there were more hurdles in the future, but she could see a peacefulness in him now that hadn't been there before, a softening of the tension around his eyes and mouth.

But he couldn't rest until the sex club that had warped him was out of business for good. The unproductive energy in him had transferred to her, and she knew they were both a little twitchy when they got home. Her fingers, as in all times of stress, itched for a brush.

"Hey," she said. "Since it's not that late…"

He glanced up at her from his place by the coat rack, in the process of hanging up his cut. Sent her an amused and curious half-smile. "Yeah?"

Why was she nervous, suddenly? "I was wondering if you'd sit for me."

"Sit…?"

"So I can paint you. Or, sketch, actually. I would need to sketch you first." She realized she was wringing her hands and forced them down at her sides. "It's kinda silly, I know, but–"

"I'll do it." His smile softened into something warm and wide. "But you can ask one of the other guys if you want. If you're looking for that whole bulging muscles, picture of masculinity thing."

"You know I'm not."

He ducked his head, pushing back a lock of hair that slipped across his face. "Okay. Um. Well, where do you want me?"

Now that the awkwardness of asking was out of the way, her right brain was taking over, throwing itself into the task. "One of the kitchen chairs would be nice, I think. And if you could take your shirt off, too. Jeans can stay, that's fine. I want to get all your ink, though." She rushed to get her pencil and sketchpad as he complied.

She took a moment to arrange him, one elbow resting on the edge of the table, his hair loose around his face, head turned toward the window so she had a view of his fine-edged profile. She dragged another chair a few feet back and settled into it, pencil poised above the paper, and took a long look at him.

The thing about it was: Kev knew he was beautiful. Not handsome, not rugged, not cute, but objectively goddamn beautiful. He could have modeled. He could have gone to Hollywood. He could have broken every female heart in a hundred-mile radius.

But he hated his beauty. Had tried to hide it beneath long hair, and tattoos, and piercings. Only that hadn't worked, the modifications becoming beautiful by default, because they were a part of him.

The lamplight dipped into the grooves between thin muscles, curved along the planes of bone, visible just beneath his skin, slid down the delicate lines of his hands, the dominoes on his fingers. Achingly *beautiful*.

Whitney's pencil scratched across the paper, sketching out the first faint lines of his profile. There was always something shocking about the first marks on the fresh paper, the foundation of an image captured in graphite.

"Sorry in advance when I don't do you justice," she said, the art haze stealing over her. When she worked, self-consciousness slipped away and the muscles in her hands loosened, the picture coming straight from her eyes, as if her fingers had nothing to do with it.

Kev snorted.

"I'm not kidding," she said with a quiet laugh. "You're too perfect. I only stand to mess you up with paint."

"Whitney," he said, so seriously she snatched her head up from the paper and really looked at his face, the expression he'd turned toward her. "Don't say stuff like that. Please."

"That you're perfect? Sorry, I can't promise I won't say that."

He sighed and rubbed a hand down his face. "I'm *not*. Please, just…praise is…it's complicated."

Because his horrible Miss Carla had praised him. Told him he was pretty. Had given him to men as a plaything.

Whitney set her sketchpad aside and stood, crossed the small distance between them. When Kev tipped his head back to look up at her, blue eyes full of pain and question, she took his face in her small hands, traced the hard lines of his cheekbones with her thumbs. "I won't say those things if you really don't want me to," she assured. "But don't let her keep taking things from you. Don't hate beautiful things because of her."

"Well, I don't hate you," he said with a weak smile.

Whitney tried to laugh, and realized her eyes were filling with tears.

"C'mere." Kev pulled her down so she was bent at the waist, their arms around one another, faces pressed into throats and tears fought with little sniffles.

"I do think you're beautiful," she said into the tender skin behind his ear, squeezing his shoulders. "And that's yours, you own it: it's *your* body. It's *your* beauty."

"She never woulda wanted me if I was ugly," he whispered.

"Oh, baby." She rubbed soothing circles between his shoulder blades. "Don't try to make sense of monsters. She did it because she's evil, plain and simple."

Kev took a deep, shuddering breath, and eased her back, hands on her waist. His eyes were wet, but he held the tears back. "Whit, will you do something for me, please?"

She smoothed his hair. "Of course."

"Will you…will you call me Tango?"

~*~

It came to him suddenly, a flash of inspiration. An epiphany, maybe. He was born Kev. Kev had been captured. Kev had been weak and hadn't been able to escape from Carla's clutches. And then Kev had become Loverboy, the dancer, the sex slave, the weak, weak heroin-addicted boy who'd allowed himself to be recaptured.

But Tango was a Lean Dog. Tango had a family, had friends, had people who loved him.

He swallowed, looking up at the surprise that rippled across Whitney's face. "I know that's what I told you to call me when we met. But I…I don't want to be Kev anymore. Kev was a lifetime ago."

"Tango." A slow smile broke across her face, her eyes shiny. "Okay. I can do that."

It wasn't much – it wasn't anything – but it felt like another of those steps. The careful trudging steps toward a livable life.

Thirty

It was five o'clock four days before Christmas when Fox sauntered into the clubhouse common room sporting several days' worth of beard and a smug look. "Well, I found the place."

Five minutes later, once all of them were gathered around the table in the chapel, he lit a smoke and expanded: "Bitch has gotten sneaky since you boys last had a run-in with her." The longer he talked, the more American his London accent began to sound. "The club runs for about week, and then they pack up shop and move it, which tells me she's spooked about a raid, 'cause what a bitch to move all those dancers and all that gear every time. Not to mention expensive; rumors I heard were that she's got a gentleman friend helping her foot the bill."

"And they say romance is dead," Mercy said with a snort.

Fox cut a tight, feral grin.

"Where is she right now and how long is she gonna be there?" Ghost asked.

"Warehouse downriver, bottom floor, no windows, guards at both doors. They'll be there for another night, and then they're gonna ghost."

"Tango," Ghost said, turning to him, and Tango realized he was dangerously close to spacing out, his heartbeat high and erratic in his ears, his palms sweating where they lay limp on his thighs. "You think she'll be keeping her boys somewhere offsite?"

Forcing his mouth to work, he said, "No. They'd quit doing that when I was…the second time. They'll be locked up somewhere onsite."

"Okay, that simplifies things." Ghost sent him a tight, grateful smile before turning back to the group. "Foxy, you got any suggestions while we're making plans?"

The Englishman stubbed out his cigarette and lit another, the only sign that all of this was agitating him. "If we go in while the action's hot, we've got the element of surprise, sure, and we've also got half the boys out on the floor, makes 'em easier to get hold of. But we've also got customers to deal with. If we wait until they start packing things away and getting ready to move, we've got them in disarray, but they're also mobile and ready to roll out. Chance someone will slip away."

"Yeah, but that's where Officer Bitchface can make himself useful," Ghost said.

Fox sighed dreamily. "I always forget you have your very own pet policeman."

Tango couldn't help it; his mind drifted. Participating in the planning sent him spiraling back through time, felt too much like disobeying. There were triggers buried deep within the folds of his brain, kneejerk desires to be good, to please, to keep his head down and not do anything to upset Miss Carla or her goons. She'd starved him and slapped him for giving her the wrong answers. What would she do if he tried to disassemble her precious club once and for all?

He pushed his chair back when he realized he was hyperventilating, muttered a hasty "excuse me," and fled. He ducked into the first dorm, not bothering to shut the door behind him, and sagged down onto the bed, head between his knees, fighting his own lungs. He felt like he had asthma, suddenly.

It was less than a minute before Aidan joined him, coming to sit beside him on the end of the bed without hesitation. "Hey," he said, and that one word managed to sound supportive. He nudged Tango's shoulder with his own and waited.

Tango blew out a long, shaky breath. "It's stupid."

"What is?"

"Shit." He breathed a sound that didn't quite become a laugh. "It's stupid that we're in there talking about the thing I've wanted most in my life, and all I can think about is the fact that I'm disappointing her. That she's gonna be so angry."

She didn't need clarification.

Aidan laid an arm across his shoulders and pulled him in tight, close enough for Tango to smell the cigarettes and cheap cologne on his collar. "You get that it's normal for you to feel like that, yeah? That it's just your head playing tricks?"

Tango managed to nod. "Doesn't mean it isn't stupid."

"Nope." Aidan jostled him back and forth, gently. "We're gonna do this for real this time, man. And if you can't do it, then don't worry about it. We're doing this because we love you, and we want you to get better. You don't have to come at all."

Except that he did. Even if his mind was in tatters afterward, he had to be there. He had to see it with his own eyes.

~*~

Tango's face, bloodless and blank with anxiety, convinced Aidan to follow him home.

"You don't have to," Tango said, and made a show of rolling his eyes – but he looked grateful.

"Nah, it's cool. Besides, I gotta see this Christmas tree I've heard so much about."

Tango groaned, but again, there was something brighter beneath.

Thick gray clouds tumbled across the sky on the way to the apartment, more snow threatening to join the dirty dregs that still lingered in shady patches and concrete gutters. It felt and smelled like Christmas in every way that counted, all the cliché aesthetics across town and in all of their homes. And they were planning battle and murder. How festive.

For Aidan's part, he couldn't wait to get this all over with. He felt helpless, watching his best friend battle demons that lived in his mind, that Aidan couldn't fight with his fists on Tango's behalf. Tango had come so far in such a short time: from the bathroom floor to admitting as much in church. But the fear and insecurity couldn't start to abate until Carla was dealt with once and for all. Aidan just wanted to skip ahead, spare Tango the trauma of seeing the woman again. But he would never deny his friend's need to see it through himself. He knew how that worked; you couldn't let something go until you'd turned it loose with your own bloody fingers.

Mercy's old apartment above the bakery, so cold and dim after Tango first moved in, was warm, full of buttery light, and rich with the scents of a home-cooked dinner.

He noticed the tree straight off, because it took up way too much space in the corner where a lamp used to be, and also because it was trimmed in colored lights and an eclectic mix of new and homemade ornaments. Aidan knew Whitney was a painter, and spotted some hand-painted stars, trees, and wreaths on thick craft paper. It was like a child's attempt at a tree, an explosion of color, light, and festive effort, and it plucked at Aidan's heartstrings in an unexpected way. They were just two kids trying to figure it all out, all the way down to the paper chains in the fir boughs.

Whitney was in the kitchen, dicing a large white onion, looking every inch the happy wife. "Hi," she greeted them brightly. "Aidan, are you staying for dinner?" she asked as Tango pressed a fast kiss to her cheek and then headed for the fridge. "I made plenty."

"Nah, I can't stay long." *Just here to make sure you guys aren't falling apart.* "Thanks, man," he said when Tango put a beer in his hand.

"How are Sam and Lainie?" Whitney asked.

"They're good." Lainie was growing like crazy, and Sam was worrying about Tango more than her job allowed, if her *That's fine* and string of concerned emojis she'd texted back to his earlier message about swinging by Tango's were anything to go by. "She wants to have you guys over for dinner sometime, maybe after Christmas."

"That would be fun. Just have her let me know what I need to bring."

"'Kay."

"Be right back," Tango said, and headed for the bathroom.

The second the bathroom door was shut, Whitney laid down her knife and met Aidan's gaze with one so direct he actually backed up a step, shocked by it. In a quiet voice, she said, "You guys are going after Miss Carla, aren't you?"

381

He had no idea what Tango had told her, and knew he shouldn't give her any intel, but he had a feeling she knew a fair bit by this point. He nodded.

She took a deep breath. "I don't know if he'll be able to go through with it, even though he wants to. Aidan, please, promise me: if Tango can't do it, the rest of you need to do it for him. Kill that woman."

When he stared at her, surprised as all hell and trying to figure out where this core of solid steel had come from, she said, "I'm serious."

He swallowed and got his tongue working. "Yeah, so are we. We'll do it. Don't worry on that front."

She exhaled and nodded, reaching for the knife again. "Good. Thank you."

It was the first time, Aidan realized, the girl had ever called Kev "Tango."

~*~

"There's a life drawing course at the college that starts in January," Whitney told him later that night when she was sketching him again. "Not really a college course, but an evening one that anyone can sign up for." She flicked a questioning glance up over the top of her sketchpad, and he wasn't fooled by her; he knew she wasn't just checking another line, but wondering what he thought about that.

"That's great. You should sign up," he said, immediately. Then: "Not that I mind modeling," with a self-deprecating smile. "But you're good enough to be in classes. In art shows," he pressed, because he wasn't going to let that go anytime soon.

"Yeah, well." Her eyes dropped to the paper again, pencil moving. "Maybe this could be a first step toward something like that."

"That's what you want, isn't it?" he asked, growing less certain. "To be a full-time artist?"

The pencil stilled; she glanced toward the window. "It's the dream. You know, like we talked about. Who knows if it's possible, but I don't want to work in customer service the rest of my life. I'm…" Her eyes darted over, bright and careful as he thought his own must be. "I'm starting to think about the future."

The future. Powerful words. It was something he couldn't see, and hadn't ever spent any time pondering. But now he had Whitney in his life, and she was thinking about the future. And…and he wanted to think about it with her.

Thirty-One

The day of the raid dawned gray and freezing, a few brave snowflakes drifting down to melt against the pavement. Ghost watched the snow flit against the kitchen window as he nursed a hot mug of half-coffee, half-whiskey. He would need to be sharp later, but right now, queasy and old-feeling, heaped with responsibility, he needed the bracing warmth and courage of the alcohol.

Maggie came into the room, almost silent, her favorite terrycloth robe cinched around her waist. He'd bought her a half-dozen slinky, black, clinging robes over the years, but she always swore this was the comfiest. She wore it in winter…and when there was trouble brewing and she needed its plush texture to give her a little emotional boost. It was her only concession toward any stress that befell the club.

She dropped a hand on his shoulder as she passed, let it linger there a moment, then went to pour herself a cup of coffee. Ghost heard the screw-cap come off the Jack as she doctored it. Then she joined him at the table, her usual place across from him.

Her hair was wild and snarled from sleep; it looked like she'd finger-combed it on her way down the hall. Without makeup, and in the pale wash of early morning light, Ghost saw the little lines streaking back from the corners of her eyes, the fatigue in the grooves around her mouth. He would never tell her he noticed the little physical signs of her aging – he valued the safety of his balls too much – but he always took the time to notice them in moments like these. She'd been with him all this time; she was the one who'd stayed. He loved those little lines for the reminder. And she was still the most gorgeous damn woman he'd ever laid eyes on.

Maggie took a bracing sip and said, "Well."

"Yeah."

"Tonight's the night."

"Mmhmm."

"You think he's ready?"

Ghost sighed and took a long swallow of whiskey-laced coffee. "Not in the slightest. But he says he needs to do it, and I think maybe he's right."

"Catharsis."

"Something like that."

The snow came down a little heavier, larger flakes swirling amongst the tiny specks beyond the window.

"You've always done right by him," Maggie said. "You've been a good dad."

He snorted. "I haven't even been a good dad for my own kids. Let alone Kev."

She hummed a disagreeing note. "You do have that overbearing cliché down pat." When he shot her a look, she flashed him a small, brief smile. "But what I mean is: you did something no one else could do, from the beginning, something he couldn't even do for himself. You accepted him."

"That doesn't feel like enough."

"Trust me, baby. That's the most important thing."

~*~

"It's snowing," Ava informed him when he stepped out of the shower. She stood in front of their bedroom window, the curtains pushed back, Camille propped up on her shoulder for a good post-feeding burp.

Wearing nothing but a towel around his waist, Mercy joined her at the window, looking through the panes over the top of her head. White flakes drifted down from the heavens like spilled powder sugar. "Huh."

Ava glanced back at him over her free shoulder. "Is that going to make things difficult tonight?"

"Possibly." He shrugged. He was in that state pre-mission where he felt invincible and pre-ordained. When a slow leak of adrenaline buzzed through his veins and left him breathless with anticipation. He knew it wasn't like that for the others, that they got nervous rather than excited. But he couldn't help what he was; he'd made his peace with these kinds of reactions a long time ago.

"Hey," she said, and he really looked down at her upturned face, searching for the fear in it. She only looked determined. "How's Tango doing with all this?"

Another time, another club, another old lady, it would have been sinful for Mercy to confide so much in his wife. The women of the club weren't supposed to know all the things she knew, for their own safety, and for the club's. But Mercy couldn't look at it that way: that she was his little woman and should be treated as such. She'd killed men. She knew the triggers for all the landmines in his head. She'd been born holding his leash. He would keep nothing secret from her; they were partners, fifty-fifty. And he had it on good authority his president had the same arrangement with his own old lady, so…

"He's rattled," he said, because that was the truth. "That bitch has still got some kinda hold over him, and it's turning him inside out."

"Bitches will do that," she said with a sigh.

"This one's bad, *fillette*. Worse than my mom."

Her brows lifted. "Jesus."

Camille finally burped, a fussy little grunt, and Ava lowered her back into her arms, bouncing her a little.

"I think he needs it, though," Mercy continued. "Not everybody gets a chance to kill their demons; when the opportunity comes along, you gotta take it."

"Your professional opinion?" she asked with a little smirk.

"You might say I've got some experience in that department."

~*~

Aidan slept like shit and finally gave in to the tremor in his hand around seven, pouring himself a liberal tumbler of whiskey and settling into the living room recliner with it. It was snowing, he

386

could see, the parking lot below slowly growing whiter and whiter as the minutes ticked by.

He didn't hear Sam come in, and jumped when he felt her hand in his hair. He settled, though, breathing out a deep sigh as she stepped around the chair and into view. "Hey."

"I don't usually get the chance to spook you," she observed, nails scratching lightly at his scalp. "Is there room for two?"

He smacked his thigh in invitation and she perched carefully in his lap, long legs hooked over the arm of the chair, snuggling in with her face tucked beneath his chin. The presence of her warmth and the familiar scent of her shampoo was instantly comforting.

He sighed.

"Oh, it's snowing."

"Of course it is. How else could the universe try to fuck up today?"

She stiffened a little against his chest. "Will you have to delay it?"

Aidan knew that Mercy was all about full-disclosure with Ava, but he didn't love that idea, not when it came to Sam. Ava didn't really count, what with being born into the club and having a body count of her own.

Sam though, while strong enough to take on the darkness, and had proved it last winter when she'd helped them free Tango from Ellison, shouldn't have to. That was Aidan's take on it, anyway. He wanted to spare her when he could. Let her live in a kinder, gentler world.

"Aidan." She prodded him back to their conversation with a delicious drag of her nails down the back of his neck. He wanted to purr and arch his back like a cat, lean into the touch. "What are you overthinking right now?" she asked, with no small amount of affection.

"Maybe I'm thinking just the right amount."

She chuckled. "Somehow I doubt that."

"You calling me stupid?" he teased, and realized what she was doing. She was helping him relax. She was always at least five steps ahead of him.

"Would I marry a stupid man?"

"Depends."

"On what?"

"How good he was in the sack."

She laughed quietly, not wanting to wake Lainie, and kissed his cheek.

A gust of wind drove snowflakes against the window, their icy centers rattling against the glass.

"We can talk about it, if you want," Sam offered. "If that would help."

"Nah, I...yeah. No."

"Informative."

He made an unhappy sound in the back of his throat.

"How about this," she said. "How about I tell you that whatever you're doing for Tango, I know it's the right thing, because you always do the right thing when it comes to him. You're a good friend. You always are."

Aidan wrapped both arms around her, buried his nose in her hair, and listened to the snow pelt the window.

~*~

By seven a.m. Tango was standing at the kitchen sink, watching the snow fall, working on his fourth cigarette of the morning. He hadn't slept at all, and around five had left the bed, not wanting to wake Whitney with all his tossing and fretting. The snow seemed fitting, poetic maybe, and he was looking forward to the way the damp cold would bite through his clothes and get to his skin later, when he left.

A quick burn against his fingers told him the cig had burned down, and he flicked it into the sink, dug a fresh one from the pack on the counter. He felt like one more would make him throw up, but he lit it anyway.

"Ke – Tango?" Whitney asked behind him, and he glanced over his shoulder to see her standing in the threshold, in her white sleep shirt and a pair of his thick boot socks, arms folded against the chill in the air. "Chainsmoking?" she asked as she shuffled up to stand beside him.

"It was that or…" He gestured to the air, full of smoke from his first exhale.

"Oh. Yeah." She shivered.

She stared out the window and he took the opportunity to study her, the delicate profile limned in silver snow light. She was so young. *Too* young. She should have been on the other side of the city, waking up beside her equally young, normal, well-employed, not-traumatized boyfriend. He hated himself for needing her, but he needed all the same. And she'd chosen him; he had to respect that this was her choice, he guessed, no matter how fruitless.

"I've always loved snow," she murmured. "It's like Mother Nature's giving you an excuse to rest a minute, and enjoy the quiet."

"Whit," he said, throat tight, and she glanced up at him. "Will you stay with Mags and Ava tonight? Please? So I know you're safe."

"Yeah, I can do that." And young, it turned out, wasn't without bravery, because she looked at him like he was steel-reinforced, like he could *do this* tonight.

Maybe he could.

~*~

At seven, Ian arranged his shirt collar over his jacket collar and examined his reflection with critical satisfaction. His shirt was ice blue, the jacket and slacks pale gray. His hair hung in a perfect, pressed sheet behind his shoulders. His shave was close and impeccable.

He couldn't breathe.

He stalked out of his bathroom and across to the closet, shrugging out of his jacket as he did so. He dropped it on the floor and tore at the shirt buttons. He was down to black boxer-briefs when Alec propped a shoulder in the closet doorway and said, "Um, what are you doing?"

"What does it look like I'm doing?" Ian found a black turtleneck sweater folded on the shelf and yanked it on over his head.

"Having a panic attack."

He spared Alec a glance as he searched for his black skinnies on the rack. His lover was appealingly rumpled from sleep, and looked very interested in going back to bed – with Ian.

"I'm not panicked."

"Coulda fooled me." Alec sighed. "Ian, come on, what is this? Those slacks are Armani and you just *stepped all over them.*"

Ian stepped into black socks and refused to be drawn into another bullshit relationship conversation. "Cancel all my appointments when you get to the office. Take messages. I'll be out today."

"What? Why? Ian." He grabbed Ian's sleeve as he tried to brush past him, just a light grip on the fabric between two fingers. A request, and not a demand.

Ian was pretty helpless when it came to beautiful boys requesting things. He sighed, and turned to face Alec. "I have something that I need to take care of. Something important. I don't know how long it will take, or when I'll be back. Don't plan on having dinner. Maybe you should stay at your place. If you want to," he added hastily when Alec's expression crumpled.

"Is that what *you* want me to do?"

Shit. He really couldn't do this.

"Stay if you'd like. Doesn't matter to me." Ian leaned in to press a fast, fierce kiss to his lips. "But I have to go. Don't forget to cancel the appointments!" he called over his shoulder as he left the bedroom.

"Fine," Alec muttered, sighing.

Sometime soon, possibly even in the wee hours of tomorrow morning, Ian was going to have to figure out what the hell he was doing with this kid. But it would have to wait, because tonight…tonight there was a witch to burn.

~*~

God knew how the long, snowy day passed. The clubhouse could have burned down around him for all that Tango was able to pay attention to anything. Aidan tried to play cards with him, but it turned into game after game of solitaire when Tango kept zoning out.

Finally, finally, Ghost stood up on a chair, clapped his leather-gloved hands together, and said, "Alright, boys." He surveyed them all as conversation died back and heads swiveled toward the president. "So here's the plan..."

Tango tried and failed to swallow the lump in his throat.

And that was before the door swung open, bringing a sharp gust of cold air and snow, and Ian entered, hair tied up and stuffed beneath a baseball cap, two bright spots of color burning on his high cheekbones, jaw set.

Ghost turned and spared the man a tight nod. Ian nodded back.

"I want to set up a loose perimeter," Ghost continued, "and then those of us on point can close in..."

Thirty-Two

The warehouse sat in the back corner of a cracked asphalt lot, its aesthetic not helped by a layer of snow, the surrounding patch of woods sinister and black. A starless, humid, frigid night.

The sole was starting to peel away on Tango's left boot, and he felt the cold, wet bite of snow nipping at his sock. It barely registered; it was taking too much effort to stay upright and breathing.

At his left elbow, Ian muttered, "Three cars left. Stragglers. The employees will be parked in the back, by the door."

"Thank you, Captain Obvious," Aidan muttered on Tango's other side. "Listen here, princess, don't go being a hero, okay? You stick to the plan. If you can't do that, then go back and wait in the van."

Ian said something under his breath; Tango caught "wanker."

The plan was simple enough: Fox would go in first. They were to give him ten minutes on the nose, then move in.

It had been two minutes.

The walkie talkie in Aidan's hand crackled. *"You in position?"* Ghost's voice floated through.

"Yeah," Aidan radioed back.

"Good. Stand by."

"What if she isn't here?" Tango asked, metallic tang of panic on his tongue.

"She's always there," Ian said, talking through clenched teeth. "She doesn't miss a night."

"Yeah, but what if…"

It had been three minutes.

"She's gonna be there, man," Aidan said. "And if for some reason she's not, then we'll find her. Wherever she is."

A strong gust of wind swirled snow around their ankles. The air smelled of frost, and garbage, rotting slowly beneath the cold.

Tango swallowed hard, contemplated puking, and reached beneath his jacket, curling his hand around the butt of his Glock for the hundredth time, just to reassure himself.

Reassure himself of what? That he was such a pussy he needed a gun to fight off a woman?

It had been four minutes.

"Just stop," Aidan said under his breath. "I can *hear* you going nuts. Whatever you're thinking, just put a lid on it and deal with it later. If you can't focus on this, then you need to wait out here." It was said with total gentleness, kindness, and concern, but it stung all the same, because it was true. He wasn't just dead weight, but an actual liability to his brothers. He could get one of them hurt; *killed*. And then what would he say to their wives? That he was sorry? Sorry he was such a stupid fuckup who not only caused all this, but couldn't even keep his head in the game when it came time to right the wrongs?

"Jesus," he whispered to himself, squeezing his eyes shut, willing his heartbeat to slow, his breath to steady.

It had been five minutes.

"Kev," Ian said. "Darling, maybe you should—"

"I'm not Kev, and I'm not your darling," he snapped.

"Dude," Aidan said.

"I'm not!" he insisted in an angry hiss. "I'm just Tango, and I'm not gonna fuck this up! Both of you, can it."

"Fine," Ian said in that flat, dry voice that said he knew Tango was lying. "Whatever you say, Rumba."

"Tango."

"Oh, right. Yes. Flamenco."

"Shut the fuck up, you asshole."

"Both of you need to shut up," Aidan said, "but I gotta say it's nice to finally hear you think he's an asshole."

"I'm deeply offended," Ian said with a sniff.

It had been five minutes.

"Darling," Tango mocked. "Don't you have a boyfriend?"

Ian sighed, long-suffering. "He seems to think that's what he is, in any event."

Aidan snorted.

"Not screwed up enough for you?" Tango asked.

"Too strong willed. He wants to have conversations. And go on dates. And do couple things. My God. He chastises me."

Aidan snorted again, and it turned into a dry cough that he muffled into his sleeve.

"You always needed a good chastising," Tango said. "On account of you being an asshole."

"Shit." Aidan leaned over and knocked his shoulder into Tango's.

"What about that bloody girl of yours? All sunshine and rainbows?"

"No, but it's really kinda cute when she's getting on my case."

It had been six minutes.

"Ian," Tango said, swallowing. "I…I do hope you're happy. You know that, right?" He glanced over at his ex, his beautiful profile stamped against the snowy forest floor, all his bright hair hidden under a hat. "I want you to be with someone who…who loves you."

Ian's blue-green eyes flicked over, his smile sad and tentative. "I want that for you, too."

It didn't bear repeating that they were toxic together. Too much poisonous history for there to ever be happiness between them. But there would always be love. They would always mean so much to each other.

"Is this turning into the sort of conversation I don't want to hear?" Aidan asked.

"No," Tango and Ian said at once, smiles widening.

It had been seven minutes.

"You know," Ian said, tipping his head back, blinking at the black sky laced with pine boughs. "The most fun I've had in my life has involved you Lean Dogs boys." It was an oddly tender and touching admission, said only because it was just the three of them, with no other witnesses.

"Wow," Aidan said. "That's…really sad. You not being a Lean Dog and all."

Ian turned a toothy smile on Aidan. "Wanker." And this time it was meant to be heard.

They all chuckled.

It had been eight minutes.

"Seriously, though," Aidan said. "Being in there, it isn't gonna…I dunno…*trigger* something for you guys, is it?"

Tango gave it serious consideration, and knew Ian did the same. It was a real concern. "We know what to expect," he said after a moment. "And I've seen worse than what's going to be in there." He'd been *subjected* to worse.

"No," Ian said firmly. "I'm fine."

They took a few paces forward, together as a unit, to the edge of the tree line. They couldn't see the others, and that was the point, all of them well hidden.

A fat customer, waddling and out of breath, folded himself down into one of the three cars, started it after a few tries and drove off the property.

"Get ready," Aidan said. "We gotta move fast when it's time."

It had been nine minutes…

~*~

For some reason, Whitney found the lack of charade comforting. When she'd shown up on the Walshes' considerable doorstep, she'd expected to be shown a guest bedroom or foldout couch and told that everyone was going to try and get some sleep. Instead, Maggie had answered the door in yoga gear and said, "Come on in. We're drinking wine and playing cards."

They sat around the massive dining room table, sipping white – save Emmie, who nursed ginger ale – and wagering little piles of Cheetos and Reese's cups against one another at Texas Hold 'Em. They kept their voices down for the sake of the kids tucked into bed upstairs, but there were no pretenses of sleep here, and for that, Whitney was grateful. These old ladies were old hat at this, but clearly, resting was off the table when they were worried about their menfolk.

Loverboy

"It feels very World War II, war wives or something," Emmie had confided when Whitney arrived. "But oh well. It is what it is. And I for one don't want to be raiding warehouses."

Whitney wondered how much of the story Emmie knew, but decided not to press.

"Another bottle, ladies?" Maggie asked, rising with an empty bottle of Chardonnay in her hand.

"None for me. Breastfeeding," Ava said.

"Yeah, I'll have another round," Mina said.

Considering her nerves were substantial as wet paper at the moment, Whitney said, "Me too. I'll come help." And stood up. She had a shit hand anyway, and folded before she left the table.

The farmhouse kitchen was cavernous, tricked out in industrial grade stainless everything. A cold room, if left to its own devices, but Emmie had added warm touches: framed photos along one wall, live green plants in colorful ceramic pots on the countertops, a bright red coffee maker, standing mixer, and toaster. A cork board where memos were pinned and mail was sorted.

Maggie opened the wine fridge – because this place actually had one of those – and pulled a fresh bottle, while Whitney took a chance to stand at the sink, dabbing cool water against the back of her neck with a paper towel and watching the play of moonlight and shadow across the snow of the back yard as the wind rustled through the trees.

"How's your sister-in-law doing?" Maggie asked as she pulled the corkscrew from its drawer.

"Better." Whitney sighed at the thought. "And by better I mean angry. Angry at me, angry at Jason – that one's understandable. Angry at sobriety. Angry at the world, really." Madelyn had had one relapse so far, getting piss drunk on vodka one afternoon. Whitney had locked herself in the freshly-scrubbed bathroom and wrestled with her tears for ten long minutes, reading articles on her phone about how common it was to have setbacks, about the way to handle them.

396

"There's not a straight line from addiction to recovery. But I guess you know that in more ways than one."

Whitney turned and put her back to the sink, found Maggie watching her, hand poised with the corkscrew over the bottle, gaze unreadable. "Yeah. Guess I do."

"How's he been?" Maggie asked. "Any relapses?"

"No, actually. He says...he says he wants it. That he thinks about it all the time. But he hasn't done anything about it yet." She forced a tight, frightened smile. "I should be worried, right?"

"Maybe. I dunno, actually. He's gotten clean twice and *stayed clean* both times, which isn't easy to do. Most people can't do that. Maybe it's because he never took it willingly – the control's worth more than the high to him. Or maybe he's just a lot stronger than everybody else."

"Both, I think."

"Hmm." Maggie spun the curved screw down into the cork, eyes leaving Whitney's. "I'll say this, though. Whatever happens tonight, it's gonna mess him up."

"I already kind of figured that," Whitney said.

"All you can do is be prepared, then."

And oh how insubstantial that felt.

~*~

Carla Burgess wasn't on the premises. They'd been through every damn room of the place, most of them Ghost never had a desire to see again, and the bitch *wasn't here*.

"Anything?" he asked Rottie as the tracker came into what had to be the office of the club, going by the hastily set up laptop and scattering of papers across the desk.

He shook his head. "She's not here."

"Fuck." Ghost pushed a hand through his hair. "Bring me one of her guys. And Mercy. I want answers."

"Right away," Rottie promised, and ducked out.

The raid had gone beautifully. And by that, Ghost meant that the remaining johns had been subdued and cuffed with zip ties, all the thugs had been detained in a similar manner, and the dancing boys had been released and piled into a van that Littlejohn was already driving to a halfway house that knew to expect them. But Miss Carla was nowhere to be seen, and Tango and Ian? Not handling it well.

"Hey," he said as he turned to them, both standing on either side of Aidan, gripping his strong arms like lifelines, breathing through their mouths, glassy-eyed. "We're going to find her. Mercy could get answers out of a stone, you know that. Just give us a minute."

Ian jerked a nod, but Tango didn't respond.

"Tango." Ghost walked toward him. "Kevin. Hey."

No response.

"Dad," Aidan said. "This—"

Rottie and RJ shoved a burly, black-clad guard through the door, smacking him in the shoulders with their telescoping clubs until the large man hit the floor on this knees with a grunt.

"Where's—"

Mercy entered, putting the thug to shame in every respect. Plenty of tall men ate lots of food and made themselves into physical blockades. And then there were men like Mercy, all stone and steel, more shoulders than anything, bright with bloodlust and vibrant with athletic intent.

"Go to work," Ghost told his extractor/son-in-law. "I wanna know where she is."

Mercy cracked his knuckles and a wicked little knife slid out of his sleeve and filled his palm. He twirled it between his fingers, the light glancing off the blade, and moved around to stand in front of his intended victim.

Shit, Ghost recognized that knife. He'd seen someone lose an ear to it once.

"Hey," Ghost said to the man kneeling on the floor. "Where's the boss bitch if she's not here?"

The man didn't say anything, jaw clamped tight in defiance.

"Alright. Merc." Ghost turned away, glanced toward the boys standing against the wall. "Don't watch this," he instructed, and meant it mainly for Tango. "Shut your eyes."

And of course neither he nor Ian did, both of them somehow paler and somehow delighted as they watched Mercy work.

The thug finally screamed. Then said, "Okay! Okay, okay, okay!"

Ghost redirected his gaze, studiously not looking at the blood. "Where?"

"She's with her guy," he panted.

"Who? What guy?"

"Her rich guy."

"And who the fuck is that?"

"Dad–" Aidan started, and cut off with a grunt.

"I dunno, she calls him Bernard," the guy said, eyeing Mercy's knife. "He pays for everything. Shit, man, I dunno. She's always with him now. He lives in this big fucking house. Used to buy boys from her and–"

"Dad."

Ghost looked over at his son, and saw that he was alone. Tango and Ian were gone.

~*~

Tango felt like he should have known all along somehow. The second the thug had started talking, he'd realized who Miss Carla's mystery benefactor was. Of course it was the rich client in the brick mansion. Of course it was the man Tango had run away from when he was fourteen, naked save a bathrobe, craving heroin and frightened out of his mind.

He'd never told Ghost and Maggie about the house and the man inside it who'd wanted to keep him for the night. At first, it had been because he was too afraid of tattling. Then it became a fear that said tattling would lead Miss Carla straight to him. And finally, he'd tried to push it all away, tell himself that nightmare chapter of his life was over and there was no sense seeking retribution.

But now…

Now he wanted blood.

They didn't have much of a head start, but Ian's Jag was quick and powerful, growling down the snow-lined streets like the jungle cat it was named after. In the bluish glow of the dash lights, his face was not his own, that feral mask Tango had glimpsed when they were kids in love.

Tango wondered if this was how Mercy felt when he was "working." This tight ball of nauseas anticipation. Somehow he doubted it, but he had no other references for the way he was *looking forward* to putting his hands around Carla's throat.

The house came into sight, a hulking dark sharp against the night sky, roof dusted with snow, grounds spreading white and flat around it.

Ian swung the Jag up into the driveway and jumped out, door open, engine running. In front of them, the heavy iron gates were locked in place, and Tango wondered, for a moment, if Ian actually thought he could push the things open. But Ian went to the key panel instead, the one affixed to a long arm so you could punch the code through your open car window. He produced a knife from somewhere amidst his all-black getup and pried the face off the box, going wrist-deep inside the wires within. A moment later, the gates slid open.

"You're kind of a genius," Tango said as Ian slid back into the car and put it in gear.

"Don't I know it."

From the exterior, the estate seemed deserted. Key word: *seemed*. There were no cars, no tire tracks in the snow. No footprints. Which meant Miss Carla and her sick beau were on vacation somewhere – and wasn't that a lovely thought; the bitch using her madam money to go to Tahiti – or they were buttoned up inside the house, cozy and hiding from the snow.

"I need to cut the power," Ian said.

"Yeah." Tango kept his hand curled around the grip of his gun as he slipped out of the car.

They both eased their doors shut silently, not wanting to alert anyone in the house to their presence. Though, probably they were already on security camera. Or an alarm had pinged when they came down the driveway. Something. But cutting the power was still good. Unless someone had already pushed the panic button.

"Don't freak out on me, darling," Ian said, and Tango didn't correct him this time.

"I'm not."

"Good. It's three in the morning, and we've got that on our side. Come on."

Ian produced a lock pick kit from his pocket and made quick work of the deadbolt in the garage pedestrian door. Inside, there were three bays: Range Rover, Benz, and a Cadillac that had to be Carla's; her taste never changed.

Ian found the fuse box against the back wall and flipped all the switches. "Torches," he said, and they both pulled out flashlights.

The house was cool, and totally dark. Without the power, there were no digital numbers on the microwave, no faint whirring of appliances, no hum of a furnace. Eerie. Tango's heartbeat sounded loud inside his head. He tried not to breathe. If there was anyone here, they were asleep.

They moved through the first floor as quickly and quietly as they could, walking up on the balls of their feet, flashlight beams tripping across expensive tile and hardwood, Italian-inspired furniture in warm browns, golds, and wine reds. It was exactly as Tango remembered it, and his lungs tightened with every step he took back into his nightmare. It was even worse than the crushing memories that had descended at the club; he'd never been in that warehouse before, and when he was at The Nest, he'd had the other dancing boys to share the violent attention. He'd at least felt like he wasn't alone.

But here...in this place...

He heard the soft *click* of someone thumbing the safety on a gun and reacted without thought. He shoved Ian down onto the floor and followed, shielding him with his body.

The shot was obscenely loud in the dark. Drywall cracked as the round embedded in the wall.

Tango rolled over onto his back, scrambling for his own gun, flashlight aimed at the dark figure who'd come down the staircase behind them. It was the client. Of course it was. Older, grayer, squinting against the brightness and shielding his eyes with one hand, the other holding a ridiculous pearl-handled semi-auto. And suddenly, Tango was fourteen, and tied to the bed, and a childish scream was building in his throat.

Then he felt Ian beside him.

Get your shit together! some inner voice screamed at him. Right. Because he wasn't fourteen, and he wasn't helpless, and it was time to get *off his fucking ass.*

He and Ian knocked shoulders in their haste to get on their feet. Tango kept the light trained on the client's face, who swatted at it and tried to aim his gun at them.

"Get out of my house!" he screamed, voice shrill and terrified. "I called the police!"

"Good. That gives us forty minutes," Ian spat, and Tango just caught his arm before he pulled his own gun.

"No," he said. "Not yet." And charged up the steps toward the man who'd once paid to rape him for a night.

"I'll shoot!" the man warned, and Tango batted the gun out of his hand. The client's fingers went limp the moment contact was made; he'd probably never fired the damn thing before in his life before tonight. He collapsed back against the stairs when Tango shoved him.

He stepped on the man's wrist, pinning him, earning a garbled shout of pain. "Do you remember me?" He shined the flashlight up onto his own face. "Huh? Do you?"

"N-n-no…"

"Oh love," Ian said, joining him, "he was never interested in our *faces*. Were you?" He kicked the guy, hard. "Maybe" – his teeth flashed white when he grinned – "he'd like to be on the *receiving end* of some of that attention."

The thought filled Tango with horror.

And that was when a woman came stomping down the stairs toward them, screaming bloody murder, what looked like a fireplace poker held above her head.

Miss Carla.

"Watch him," Tango said, and stepped over the client. Bernard. Whoever the fuck he was. Because right now, all his fear was burning away, and he felt nothing but *murderous*.

He met the woman mid-descent, caught her thin wrists in his hands, and the fireplace poker clattered down onto the wooden stairs, her hands curled into useless claws, the flashlight in his left hand digging into the bones of her forearm until he felt them shift.

She was fragile. This demon who'd ruined his entire life was breakable as glass.

He laughed wildly, crazily, at the realization, and backed her up the steps until they were in the upstairs hallway, Carla hissing, kicking, and screaming the whole time.

"Shut up." He shook her, hard, and backed her into a blue beam of moonlight let in from the window.

Time had not been kind to Miss Carla. She stared up at him with a face all too familiar, but deeply lined, her eyelids droopy and her lips seamed. Her hair stood up in messy yellow tufts, cut short now and dyed poorly. Her patterned silk nightgown was nothing new, though. And the sharp scent of her perfume was like a punch.

When she stopped screeching, and bothered to really look at him...it took her a moment, but she recognized him.

"God," she breathed. "Loverboy."

He slapped her. So hard she yelped. Hard enough that it hurt his hand. And unlike the times he'd done it in his nightmares, it brought no relief, only the crushing sense that he might be sick all over himself.

He heard footsteps behind him, and then Ian was there, gripping Tango's shoulder hard enough to leave finger-shaped bruises.

"Where's the other guy?" Tango asked the same moment Carla said, "Shit, it's Shaman."

"Out cold," Ian said. And then, to Carla, grinning: "That's right, Miss Carla. What's the matter? Didn't expect to see your little magic man again?"

She gulped and spluttered and…said nothing to them. Not a damn word.

Tango gripped her arms until she winced and flinched away. "What?" he asked. "Nothing you want to say to us? You *destroyed our goddamn lives*, and you're gonna, what, stare like a goddamn fish?"

It was stupid, so stupid of him, but he wanted – no, needed – her to say something. Anything. Call him names. Call him her pretty little Loverboy. Shout at them to leave. Tell them how worthless they'd always been…

The silence was terrible. It was soul-crushing.

"Speak, bitch!" Ian roared.

She closed her eyes and ducked her head, trying to shrink away from them.

Tango almost welcomed the sound of pounding footsteps moving through the floor below them, just because it signaled that something besides this ugly staring contest was about to happen.

One hand still clamped to Carla's arm, he turned, expecting the police to come barreling up the stairs. Instead, the hulking figure that reached the landing and stepped into the light was Mercy.

Tango opened his mouth to tell him to leave, that the cops were probably on their way, that this wasn't his fight, but couldn't form words. Could only whimper pathetically.

"Boys," Mercy said, approaching them slowly, like they were snakes he was trying not to rile. "Why don't you two clear outta here, huh? Just go on and I'll pick up the mess."

"She's seen our faces," Ian said, like Mercy was stupid.

"Yeah, I know, 'cause you geniuses came charging here like the damn Lone Ranger and Tonto – only without the masks. So get out before the cops show up."

Tango swallowed the lump in his throat and said, "This is what I came here to do." His fingers tightened on Carla's arm.

"No," Mercy said, gently, like he was talking to one of his kids, eyes soft. He eased a few steps forward, close enough to lay one of his big hands on Tango's shoulder. "Tonight was about rescuing that boy, the one from the news. And we did. And Fielding is gonna make sure all of this gets exposed to the public, and that everyone involved spends a long, long time getting gang-raped in jail. We took apart the club, Tango. We stopped it. That's what you came to do tonight: stop it, once and for all."

Tango blinked and realized there were tears pouring down his face.

"Brother," Mercy said, face gentling even further. "I have killed *a lot* of people in my time. Some deserved it more than others. But you're not me. You're a better person than me. So trust me when I tell you that killing her won't bring you any peace. It won't right the wrongs, or even the score. You'll only hate yourself. This isn't the way back home. Not for you." He glanced over at Ian. "Not for either of you. Go home. Everything's done. It's over now."

Tango wanted to argue. He wanted to scream and cry and hit things. But he...he felt the dark knot in his chest loosening.

"I won't go to prison for her," Ian said, but his voice had lost its heat.

"You won't," Mercy said. "Go on. I've got your back."

And...

And they left.

~*~

The woman, Carla Burgess, started to cry quietly as Mercy listened to Tango and Ian walk downstairs and leave the way they came in. When he was sure they were gone, he turned back to the woman, and opened the gate deep in his stomach, let out the devil that lived there.

He smiled.

"You know," he said, and her eyes snapped to his face, wide and terrified in the moonlight. "My mama always used to say this thing to me when I was real little. She'd say, 'You damn ugly brute, Felix. You ain't nothing but elbows.' I was a big kid. Nothin' like your pretty dancing boys." He heard his accent thicken, the Cajun coming out in full force now that he smelled fresh blood. "Guess I was always a monster, right from the start." He grinned at her, and she shuddered, stepping back.

"The thing about Tango," he continued, "which I guess you already know, is that he's a real sweet kid at heart. This woulda scarred him for life. He never woulda bounced back. And that woulda sucked, 'cause he's got a steady girl now, and a club, and brothers who love him. Tango wasn't built for killing.

"Me, on the other hand." He took her head between both his large hands and she gasped. "Do me a favor, would ya? When you get down there, when you go through Lucifer's gate, say hello to Mama for me. Tell her Felix sends his love."

And he snapped her neck in one neat, expert movement.

The body fell, juicy and limp, with a loud sound against the floorboards.

Down below, the unconscious man groaned on the staircase.

"Oh don't you worry," Mercy called and headed that way. "You're next."

Thirty-Three

"You can see all the stars after it snows," Ian observed. "Even inside the city."

Lying across the trunk and rear window of the Jag, they had a front row seat to said stars, the little winking diamonds set high in the black velvet of the sky. Along the horizon, the first dusky blue blush of dawn was beginning to appear. In just a couple more hours, this night would be over.

"Could you see the stars in London?" Tango took a long pull off the bottle of vodka they'd bought just inside at Leroy's, and passed it over.

"No, not that I ever noticed. Then again, I wasn't ever really looking for them. I was at that age where what was happening beneath my own feet was more important than the rest of the world." The bottle glugged as he took another sip, and then the cool glass was pressing back into Tango's palm.

"Aren't you still at that age?"

"Well, look who decided to show up: Kev's sense of humor, at long last."

Tango snorted. "I was serious earlier. About my name."

"Yes, yes, very well. *Tango*," Ian said with a sigh. "Bloody silly name."

"It's no worse than Shaman," Tango shot back. "And it's better than that. Aidan gave it to me."

It was quiet a beat, and Tango took another drink.

"He's sort of a bastard, your Aidan." Ian sighed again, and this one sounded like it was loosening something inside of him; a key turning in a lock. "But he's a good friend to you."

Afraid agreeing would only turn Ian into a shithead again, Tango said, "Maybe you should drop 'Shaman.' Maybe it's too much like having her in your life again."

"Hmm. Maybe. You think she's dead?"

"I know she is." The awful cold lump in his stomach was dissipating. In part from the vodka, but mostly because of Mercy. Because he *knew* that his friend hadn't let any of them down tonight; he'd done what Tango couldn't. "Mercy's very good at that sort of thing."

"Of that I have no doubts." He hummed quietly to himself. "Bikers," he mused. "Of all the places I thought you'd end up, it was never here, with this lot."

"They're not such a bad lot."

"I know that, darling."

A few cars slid past on the road; it wouldn't be long before morning rush hour.

Tango sat up, bottle resting on his thigh, and looked over at his…his friend, he guessed. He had no idea if labels would ever fit the two of them. For the first time in all of their history together, Ian looked tired. Peaceful, the sharp lines of his face blurred by the long night.

"Thank you," Tango said, quietly, and Ian's brows flicked up in silent question. "I wouldn't have survived The Nest without you. You…" He swallowed hard. "You could have picked a lot of boys, but you picked me. So thank you."

Ian's head rolled toward him, expression hard to read. "Of course I chose you; you were always special. Just not for the reasons Carla thought you were."

His eyes burned and he looked away, took another hit off the bottle.

In a small, vulnerable voice, Ian said, "Do you think it will be better now? Since she's gone?"

"I hope so."

Ian sat up, and leaned against Tango's shoulder, the warm pressure a comfort. It felt like apology and gratitude. Like friendship. Like letting one another go.

They watched the sun come up.

~*~

Whitney had planned on staying up all night until the guys got back. But sometime in the middle of a slice of Bea Walsh's orange marmalade cake, she slumped down into the corner of the couch and drifted off – a fact she didn't realize until someone took her hand in theirs and startled the shit out of her.

"What?" she shouted, jerking awake, and found Tango kneeling on the floor in front of her, trying not to laugh at whatever stupid face she was making. "You're here," she said. And then she realized that yes, he was here, and he wasn't covered in blood, and he obviously wasn't arrested, and he was smiling up at her like she was something really special, like he loved her. "You're here!" she repeated, and launched herself off the couch and into his arms.

"Morning." His voice was a little rough, but she could hear the smile in it. "How was your night?"

She pushed back, hands on his shoulders. "How was *yours?*"

His gaze slid away from hers. "Productive."

"Is she…"

"Yeah."

"Did you…"

"No. I…" His eyes came back, guilty. "I let someone else help me with that."

She exhaled in a shaky rush. "Oh good. I'm glad, baby." She hugged him again.

It should have been strange – congratulating someone on the death of someone else. But Whitney had done some thinking during the night. Some serious, what-am-I-doing-with-my-life soul searching. At her lowest point, when everyone else was dozing (or in Maggie and Ava's case, battling each other at double solitaire like the energized, supernatural creatures they were), and she'd been asking herself if she could do this over and over – waiting for news, wondering if her boyfriend was bleeding out somewhere – she'd never even considered leaving him. He was in her bloodstream now. Her love had reached a point past reason or question. She loved him, end of story.

But what about the rest? How could she rationalize the club, and the things it did in the dark of night?

She'd stepped out onto the front porch, breath pluming in the cold air, and watched the dancing, skeletal shadows of tree limbs tickle the snow. Whoever had built this house had spent a lot of time deciding on the perfect location, the spot with the best view. Because the farm lay beneath her, larger somehow, dressed all in white, the horses tucked away snug in their stalls, the world silent and restful.

She wondered if Emmie ever watched her farm like this, in the moonlight, and regretted the decisions she'd made that had led her here. If Ava looked around her little house, cluttered with kids' toys, and wished she was writing in an expensive office somewhere. If Maggie ever got tired of the vigils. Even if they felt that way…they were here. They were happy. They *wanted* to be here.

It had come to her then, on a frigid little gust of air. The decision to make wasn't about staying. Wasn't about enduring. It was much simpler than that. If you loved them, if you couldn't bear to love anyone else, then you stayed. And you handled each crazy, impossible, scary night as it came.

And then she'd laughed to herself, because she wondered if everyone inside had argued the same points to themselves.

"Let's go home," she said.

"Yeah. Let's do that."

~*~

Ian pulled off his hat in the elevator and shook out all his long hair, scratched his scalp with tired fingertips. He knew he looked rough, and that he smelled like vodka, and all he wanted to do was fall face-first into bed and sleep for a week.

But he had his suspicions that there was a not-boyfriend waiting for him upstairs.

Lo and behold, there was.

Alec was moving around the kitchen when Ian entered, wiping down the counters with a damp paper towel and going to the oven to crack the door and peek inside. He looked very domestic, and very young, and…so blessedly *normal*. He'd never been a dancer, or a stripper, or a hooker, never been forced over a table by a fat man with a little boy fetish. He'd been raised by loving parents, gone to school; maybe he'd been in a fraternity, a club, the swim team. So many ordinary little things American children took for granted, things he'd been denied.

Ian wanted to know all of it, suddenly. Wanted to bathe in the delicious stories of normalcy. Wanted to hear every boring detail of Alec's boring life.

"Something smells good," he greeted, his voice low and rough.

Alec glanced up like he wasn't surprised to see him; he'd heard the door open, after all. "That's the coffee cake," he explained. His smile was pleasant, but not all that warm. "It only needs another five minutes or so, and then it can come out."

"You bought coffee cake?"

"I made it. From scratch."

"You…what?"

"I also dropped off your dry cleaning, vacuumed, did some grocery shopping for you," Alec said, tossing the paper towel in the trash and coming to stand in front of Ian. "I also turned in my two-week notice."

"You *what?*"

"I'm quitting." He flashed a tight smile. "I've found another job. It pays better, actually. I'm not going to work for you anymore."

Ian could only stare, open-mouthed, like a bloody idiot.

Alec leaned forward and kissed the corner of his slack mouth. "Think about what you want, Ian. And call me when you do."

Ian listened to him leave, the smell of lemon cleaner and homemade coffee cake filling his lungs.

"Well," he said to his empty apartment. "Shit."

Thirty-Four

"How are you liking your NA meetings?" Dr. Jones asked, nudging up her glasses again with a knuckle.

Tango breathed a hollow chuckle. "I don't think 'like' is the right word, doc. They're going. And it's…I dunno. I think it's good to hear other people talk about it. The cravings."

She nodded sagely. "That's the hardest part about dealing with addiction: feeling like you're alone."

"Yeah." He hadn't even realized that – the lonely in his craving part – until his first meeting, sitting hunched in the back of the rec center gym, hat pulled low over his eyes. "I actually, um, did like you said, and let Whitney come to my last meeting."

"Good!" She beamed at him. "I think that will really help, letting her be a part of your recovery. If she can empathize, then she can be a good sounding board when you need to talk things out at home."

"Yeah, she always is."

Tango had started therapy with Dr. Tabitha Jones three days after Christmas with the expectation that he would hate every second of it. Instead, he'd showed up to the clinic to find a warm and inviting office that smelled like cinnamon, full of overstuffed furniture, a tropical fish tank in one corner. Dr. Jones was a small, fashionable woman who always wore bright colors that offset her dark skin. She liked blueberries and nibbled on them during their sessions. Had a passion for gardening and college football. Meeting with her was like catching up with an old family friend, and nothing at all like therapy. Before he knew it, it was February, and Tango had been seeing her for two months.

"You guys have plans this weekend?" Dr. Jones asked. "It's supposed to be unseasonably warm on Saturday."

"Just the usual," he said, smiling. "Maybe go for a ride. Have lunch out somewhere."

Her smile was warm and proud. "Sounds nice."

"It is."

~*~

"Okay, guys, there's just a few minutes left, so start cleaning up."

Whitney jerked, startled by her instructor's voice. She'd been so absorbed in her sketch that she'd lost track of time. Again. That happened pretty much every class.

Today's model was a member of the cross-country team, lean and hard with precisely-sculpted muscle, blonde, with a gentle face. He reminded her of Tango, a little, minus all the ink, and she'd found drawing him to be rather simple; she'd found she liked the challenge of committing all of her boyfriend's ink to paper.

She gave her sketch one last critical glance, then stowed it in her portfolio.

"See you next week," Megan said on her right.

"Yeah, see you!" Whitney said back.

She loved her life drawing class. In fact, she loved it so much she was starting to wish like hell she'd actually gone to college. She didn't think too much about her dashed art school dreams – her parents had passed and she hadn't been afforded the luxury of higher education; she didn't dwell on it – so long as art was just a private hobby. But in an academic setting, surrounded by other artists, she started to want things she couldn't have.

Which was just stupid, because Tango was doing so well, and they were both working, and paying their own bills, and she loved him so much. Madelyn was two months sober, and the girls were happy, and Whitney had this whole new biker family…

No. She couldn't complain. Not about something as silly as art.

It was a brisk night, but the promise of an early spring lingered in rare undercurrents of warmth on the breeze. Whitney shivered pleasantly as she climbed into her car in the dark parking lot, and didn't look over her shoulder in quiet distress as many times as she used to.

It filled her with indescribable warmth when she pulled into the alley and saw the glowing windows up above in the apartment. Her heart skipped like a schoolgirl's as she hurried up the iron stairs and let herself inside.

"Hi!" she called.

"Kitchen!" Tango called back, and she found him standing beside the table, contemplating a piece of big white poster board.

She slid an arm around his waist and cuddled up against his side, his arm landing across her shoulders. She took a moment to appreciate the clean laundry smell of him, reach up and tuck a stray lock of his new undercut back behind his ear; she'd liked his long hair, the feel of it through her fingers, but the shaved sides and back of his hair did things to her stomach, left her a little breathless. And don't even get her started on the long pieces on top.

"What's up?" she asked, looking down at the poster board.

His voice was pleased when he said, "I've got a project for you."

"A what?" Her eyes roved across the poster and she started to recognize what she was looking at: the blocked-off sections, the explanatory text, the quick doodles. "Is this a storyboard?"

"Yeah." His hand squeezed her shoulder. "Ava wrote a children's book. These are all the pages. She wants to know if you'll illustrate it for her."

"She does?" She glanced up at his face, incredulous, and found him smiling. "Are you serious?"

"Completely. She's got a contact at the school who's going to do a printing for her, and she thought maybe, if you weren't too busy–"

"Yes! One-hundred-percent yes!"

He chuckled. "I already told her you would."

"Oh my God." She tucked her face into his shoulder, shaking a little with delight. "This is...this is amazing. I never thought…" Her voice cracked and she closed her mouth, blinking back sudden hot tears.

Tango put his other arm around her and hugged her properly. "That's kinda our theme song, huh? 'I never thought.'"

It was. She had a feeling it always would be, too.

~*~

"No. We're not doing that. Absolutely not."

"Oh come oooonnnn." Alec hung his head off the edge of the bed, craning his neck back all the way, so the vein stood out in his forehead and he could look upside down at Ian where he lay stretched out on the rug. "It's romantic."

"Firstly," Ian said, holding up one finger. "Just because you've seen it in every terrible romance movie doesn't mean it's actually romantic. Two." Another finger. "For a man who didn't know he was gay six months ago, you sure do like being the sappy one in this relationship."

Alec laughed; it was a light sound, free of angst and heartache and all the dark things Ian brought to the table. "That's because I lo–"

"No," Ian said, not unkindly, and Alec's laughter faded into a soft smile. "Please don't say it."

"Not yet, huh?"

"Not yet, no. Getting there. Soon."

Alec's arm reached back off the bed and the very tip of his finger touched Ian's nose. A little affectionate boop.

"You're impossible," Ian muttered.

"Yep."

The doorbell rang.

"At this time of night?" Alec groaned, sitting up to check the clock. "Really?"

"Bruce!" Ian called, still tired and sweat-damp, and enjoying his expensive taste in rugs.

"You kicked Bruce up to his own apartment hours ago, babe."

415

"Shit, I did. Alright." With a sigh, Ian sat up and went to his dresser to find pajama pants. He caught his reflection in the mirror, grimaced a little at his sex-wrecked hair and tried to smooth it without success. He tugged on his robe and headed out of the room as the doorbell rang again.

"Coming! Jesus. Hey, no strawberries while I'm gone. I was serious about that."

"God, you're boring," Alec lamented behind him. "What if they're chocolate-dipped?"

"Still no!"

There was a sleek little modern sofa table right beside the door of the apartment. Ian pulled open the closest drawer and withdrew the Colt 1911 hidden within. With his other hand, he threw the locks, cracked the door and...

The bottom fell out of his stomach.

It wasn't an angry drug buyer, or an employee, or the building super. It was a woman, tall and slender, her dark hair shimmering in waves down her back, her face pale and lovely, high cheekbones and huge eyes. Their mother's eyes. His *sister's* eyes.

It was impossible. When he'd seen her last, she'd been just a little girl, in school uniform and pigtails. But...

The gun clattered as he set it on the table with shaking hands. "Janie?"

Jane gasped and pressed her knuckles to her lips – she'd done that as a child, unmistakable – and her eyes filled with tears. "Ian?"

"I..." He tried to swallow and couldn't. "Yes, it's me," he rasped.

"Oh my God." She flung herself at him, and he caught her around the waist, overwhelmed by the sight, and sound, feel, smell, and sheer presence of her. "It's you, it really is!"

Her hair brushed like silk against his face, and he wanted to crush her against his chest. Wanted the floor to swallow him, because how could he explain anything about his life to his little sister?

"How did you find me?" he asked.

She pulled back, crying freely, tears sliding down her cheeks. "There was this man," she said, voice strained. "He went to the house to see Mum. Albert Something. Some sort of horrid biker or something. And he said he knew where you were, if we'd like to—"

Ian couldn't decide if he wanted to kill Albert Cross, or send the man a gift basket. He hugged his sister again instead.

Behind him, someone softly cleared his throat. Alec, it was Alec, dressed again and watching the reunion with curious, but soft eyes.

Shit, here went nothing.

Ian towed Jane into the apartment and closed the door. "Alec, this is my long-lost sister, Jane. Jane, this is Alec…my boyfriend."

Jane's smile was blinding. "Oh, how lovely." She held out a hand to Alec. "It's wonderful to meet you."

Alec smiled back at her, warm and genuine in that way that had first landed him his job, back before Ian's stunted little world was turned upside down. "I've been told I'm not an expert about it yet, but I can make some tea if you'd like some."

"Brilliant."

Ian leaned back against the closed door and let it hold his weight, his muscles turned to jelly.

"Well," he said, smiling. "Shit."

~*~

Saturday was perfect. Cloudless, cold but not bitter, the roads dry and fast. Tango helped Whitney pack a lunch and they set off on the bike into the mountains.

Peace descended as the city melted away, leaving them alone on narrow roads that looped through serpentine curves, cutting through bare forest and undulating brown fields. It was far from the lush green that would descend in another few months, but Tango liked the quietness of the naked limbs and the sleepy color scheme. Even better, he liked the warm, slight shape of Whitney pressed to his back, her arms tight around his waist, her weight shifting with practiced grace on every turn.

He finally pulled off when they came to a place with a wide gravel shoulder, a path leading up through the trees, a little plaque marking it as a hiking trail. He stowed their helmets on the handlebars, took the backpack with their food from Whitney, and took her hand. "Come on."

She sent him a curious smile and fell into step beside him, though the trail was so narrow they had to walk with their sides bumping together.

"So I've been thinking about something," Tango said, squeezing her hand.

"Yeah? What?"

"Tell you when we get up there."

Though it was still winter, the forest was full of birds, cardinals, jays, and chickadees flitting between low branches. Tango heard the dull jackhammer thud of a woodpecker somewhere above them. Water trickled over rocks off to their right, light, musical notes. It was idyllic. And that was before they reached the top of the slow climb and stepped out into the dry, dormant grass of a clearing, and Tango turned Whitney by the shoulder and pointed back the way they'd come.

"Oh!" she gasped.

All around them the great humped backs of the Smokey Mountains stood blue, and gray, and cloud-dappled against the perfect cobalt of the sky. Leafless and cool, their smooth shapes overlapped and snuggled against one another. And just visible in the distance, like a jewel that had fallen into folds of dark velvet, lay Knoxville: the brick of buildings, the glittering ribbon of the Tennessee River. It was a scene straight off a postcard.

"It's gorgeous," Whitney said, voice low and reverent. "Oh my God, why haven't we come up here before?"

It was an innocent question, but the answer wasn't. They hadn't come up here before – Tango hadn't even been here himself since he was fifteen and Hound took he and Aidan camping – because four months ago, he couldn't have made the climb. Wouldn't have wanted to anyway. Would never even have thought of it. He'd been too thin, too exhausted, too rattled, too strung-out…too suicidal. He'd barely slept. Hiking up a mountain trail hadn't crossed his mind.

But now he had Whitney. And he had a tentative hold on his sobriety. He had his club, and a home, and he had the still-pink scars on his wrists to remind him of what he'd almost thrown away. And for the first time in his whole life he had hope. A thought that the future might be worth sticking around for.

A long answer, fraught with mental landmines.

So all he said was, "Because I was saving it for this." And he took Whitney's hand, and sank to one knee in front of her.

She said yes.

~*~

"My bloody sister, can you believe that?"

"Uh-huh," Aidan said, firing a confused look Tango's way.

"Oh forget it," Ian said with a sigh that was, as always, dramatic to the last.

"Ian's family thought he was dead," Tango explained. "He wasn't expecting anyone to turn up on his doorstep when he's not even living under his own name."

"Don't think I don't know you were involved with that." Ian aimed a chastising finger at Tango across their breakfast dishes. "Like I'm supposed to think a London Dog just happened to put all the pieces together? You insult my intelligence."

Tango rolled his eyes. "Yeah, well, sue me." Voice softening: "I wanted you to have your family back. If that's something you want."

Ian sighed and glanced down at his plate, the largely untouched bacon and hashbrowns. "It's…" He cleared his throat. "Out of all of them, I did miss Janie the most."

"See," Aidan said. "Happy endings all around."

Ian shot him a look that suggested he not push his luck.

Their waitress swayed pass. "More coffee, y'all?"

"Don't you dare ask about lattes again," Aidan hissed at Ian. "We're at Waffle House, your highness."

"No, thanks," Tango told the waitress with a smile, and she hurried off again shaking her head, probably still confused by the sight of two bikers in a booth across from the elegantly turned-out gentleman with the British accent.

"Alright." Aidan checked his watch and shoved the last bite of waffle into his mouth, talking around it. "We gotta clock in in ten minutes. So not that this hasn't been a fucking blast..." He made a *get to the point* gesture.

"Your father owns the place. You can clock in late."

"Aidan's trying not to be 'that guy' anymore," Tango said, and earned his friend's elbow in his ribs. He chuckled into his coffee.

"Fine." Ian rolled his eyes. But then his expression softened. "I wanted to say...well, I wanted to offer. Ugh. Bugger. Okay." He finally made eye contact. "I wanted to say that I wanted to be friends. With the club, I mean. Well, personally too or, yes, whatever..."

Tango had never seen him like this, nervous and awkward. It was *adorable*.

"I'm saying," he pressed on, growing more composed, "that I have considerable resources, and they will always be available to you Godforsaken Lean Dogs should you need them, no strings attached. No more favors. No more 'Dr. Evil' as you so eloquently put it," he said to Aidan, who smirked. "I want a real truce, gentlemen, with all of you. Friends." And then, still surprising them, he looked young and almost vulnerable.

"You want to be friends," Aidan said in a careful voice.

Ian twitched a tiny smile. "I haven't had many of those, I'm afraid, so I probably won't be very good at it."

Tango exchanged a look with Aidan, and didn't see suspicion in his eyes, only amusement.

Aidan shrugged. "It never hurts to have a millionaire on your side."

"No." Tango bit back a smile. "It doesn't."

"So?" Ian asked.

"Alright." Aidan stuck his hand across the table for Ian to shake. "Friends."

~*~

Even the waiting room at Dr. Jones's practice was soothing, though Tango guessed that was the point. Chocolate walls with white trim, deep, cozy armchairs instead of the typical plastic kind you found at doctors' offices. There was a fish tank out here, too, fresh water full of fat, slow-moving goldfish in orange, white, and black.

Tango was a little bit excited about his session today. He wanted to talk about proposing to Whitney – her saying yes! – and about being friends with Ian, and it feeling like that: just friendship. He wanted to talk about the way he'd awakened from a nightmare in the wee hours, but curling up with his arm around Whitney had lulled him back to sleep. About the way he didn't hate himself so much these days.

The door to Dr. Jones's partner's office opened, and Dr. Metcalf walked a slender teenage boy out toward the waiting room. "You did great today, Jamie. Just think about the things we talked about, okay?"

The boy, Jamie, had his gaze trained on the floor, chewing at his lip in a nervous tell, but nodded. "Okay," he said, quietly, the sound almost drowned out by the gentle bubbling of the fish tank's filter.

Dr. Metcalf clapped Jamie on the shoulder, Jamie flinched, and the doctor retreated back into the office to get ready for the next patient. Jamie shuffled over to the window, flicked up the blinds to peek through them, sighed, and fell into a chair across from Tango. He must have been searching for his ride and not found it.

And then the kid lifted his head, and Tango got a good look at his face.

A narrow, proportionate, almost dainty face. Almost feminine. Long lashes and high cheekbones and full pink lips. A face that belonged on a model. On a...*dancing boy*. A face that

Tango had seen on the news a couple months back, a photograph staring out at him from the TV, while his mother begged for her neighbors' help in finding him. The face that had been the catalyst for the night of the raid. For Tango's coming out to his club.

He sucked in a breath. "You're Jamie Long," he whispered, and the kid snapped his head around like he'd been slapped. There were only the two of them in the waiting room, so Tango pressed on. "Oh, no, I'm sorry. I didn't mean…I just recognized you is all. From…I'm sorry."

Jamie sank down into the collar of his shirt, the shame unmistakable on his face. An expression Tango had seen on his own reflection more times than he could count.

"Hey." He moved forward to the edge of his chair. "I'm sorry, I just…" He dropped his voice. "I wanted to tell you that I've been where you were."

Jamie's eyes darted to his face.

"Literally. For a long, long time." He tried to offer the kid a smile. "And it sucks, so bad, for a really long time afterward. But I promise it gets better."

Jamie looked unconvinced, but there was a spark of curiosity in his gaze now: *That happened to you?* His gaze flicked down across Tango's cut, all his patches, the tattoos on his hands.

"Yeah," he snorted. "Didn't exactly turn me into a model citizen. But. I've got a job. Friends. I've got a fiancée."

"You do?" Jamie's voice was rough, low, and much too old to belong to a pretty kid with a bright future. Carla had a way of aging people like that.

Tango nodded. "I do. It wasn't easy. But." He pushed up a sleeve and showed Jamie the scars on his wrists. "This wasn't the answer. It didn't help."

Jamie took a deep, shuddering breath.

"Do me a favor," Tango said, digging a gas station receipt out of his back pocket. He took a pen from the magazine display on the table next to him and wrote down his cell number. "If you ever start thinking like that, if it gets real bad, call me." He handed the receipt over, and watched Jamie take it carefully, reading the digits several times before he folded it up and put it in his wallet.

"The thing I've learned," Tango said, "is that you have to let it out. You can't live with it if you hold it in."

Jamie stared at him, a wealth of emotion laid bare on his face.

"Okay?" Tango asked.

"Okay."

~*~

"Thank you," Tango said one night, a beer in his hand, Mercy's solid presence taking up most of the couch beside him.

In the kitchen, he could hear the girls talking happily about something, the bright spill of Whitney's laughter like a gift. Aidan had taken a colicky Lainie for a walk out in the cool early spring air; the faint notes of his terrible singing voice could be heard when he passed close to the window.

"For everything," Tango continued, quietly. "I mean, for doing what I couldn't, yeah, but for...for listening." All those makeshift therapy sessions in the apartment, Ava's baked goods, the complete and total acceptance of all the terrible stories he'd told, the lack of judgement.

His eyes burned, suddenly. "I..."

"Hey." Mercy's huge arm went around his shoulders and pulled him in close. "I'm always here, okay?"

Tango nodded.

"Love you, brother."

He couldn't speak for the lump in his throat, but Tango nodded again, and hoped Mercy could read the love in it. He probably could; he was perceptive like that.

~*~

It didn't really hit him until March.

"Ugh," Whitney muttered against his shoulder. "Why is the alarm going off so early?" At least, that's what he thought she said. It got muffled in his arm and the bedclothes.

"Running," he explained. "Wanna come with?"

"Ugh."

He chuckled, pushed her hair back, and kissed her forehead before rolling out of bed. "Be back in a bit."

"Mmhm."

Running was a suggestion that had come up in therapy; Dr. Jones had suggested that positive physical routines could be important to his sobriety. The endorphin rush of a long run mimicked a drug high – that's what she'd said. Really, it wasn't the same. But the running had become addictive in and of itself, and the endorphin rush *was* pleasant. Each morning, he climbed out of bed at ten 'til six, tugged on sweats, plugged in his earbuds, and jogged through the city. He'd started with a mile, and now was up to six.

He'd discovered he loved this time of morning. By six, the bakery downstairs was open, as was every coffee shop and breakfast place along his route. He liked seeing the yellow lights through the windows, the tired but welcoming faces of the employees as they greeted early morning regulars. It was still dark, but not the desolate shade of black that accompanied three a.m. walks of shame; it was a friendly indigo, promising that daylight was only an hour off. It was a quietly busy time, a time just for the early risers, the go getters, the productive people who'd learned the secret gift of predawn.

And Tango…he felt like he was a part of that now. He waved to Janet through the window of Starbucks as he passed. And on the way back, he went in and she fixed him a tall cappuccino to go.

"How many miles this morning?" she asked. It was their thing.

"Seven," he said with a smile.

"Dude, go you. You should totally sign up for that five-K they're having."

"I think I might." And he did.

He walked the rest of the way back home to cool down, sipping his cappuccino, enjoying the blush of sunrise over the building tops, smiling to himself for no damn reason.

Back at the apartment, he downed two glasses of water, because hydration was important, and headed to the shower, stripping beside the tub as he waited for the water to heat inside the ancient pipes.

That was when he caught sight of his reflection in the medicine cabinet mirror.

He looked…*good*.

Sweat-damp hair slicked back along his head, eyes bright with exertion, spots of color high on his cheeks – cheeks that were fuller than they had been at the end of last year. His whole body was fuller; beneath his tattooed skin, he spotted muscle where there used to just be bone. Firm, smooth padding at his shoulders, his chest, down his arms. His hips still stood out as sharp points, but he had abs now, trim and distinct.

He looked healthy. Like he gave a damn about himself.

His eyes tracked across his reflection, going to the old scars at his wrists, the newer ones faded now. Someday, they would be silver like the old ones.

That was when it hit him. That was when he realized that the earth had shifted back in December. That it had started with Ava laying baby Camille in his arms, and that it was still happening now, slowly, day by day. That it would keep happening. The sea change. The healing. The rest of his life. He'd lived through actual hell…and that was over now. He was *past* it.

He turned around and looked at the white claw-foot tub, the water pounding behind the shower curtain. It was the place where he'd sliced open his veins and surrendered himself to death. He'd thought he'd always see it for what he'd intended it to be: his own personal crime scene.

But it was just a bathtub. The place where he washed away his clean sweat after every morning. Where Whitney read amidst a froth of bubbles, listening to George Michael and humming along off-key. The place where they showered together sometimes, soapy hands wandering.

He turned back around and faced his reflection again. Stared himself down. And smiled.

He was alive.

And he wanted to stay that way.

Epilogue

They didn't so much find Maya as she found them. Their own Isabelle was three, a tiny, golden, fresh spring day of a child. The living embodiment of Tango's second chance. She had Whitney's gorgeous eyes, and his own tendency toward anxiety, and for all that he hadn't wanted to procreate, he loved his girl more fiercely than anything. Whitney was an illustrator fulltime now, and could stay home with Izzie, making her lunch and singing her songs and being her mama in a way that made Tango ache with longing for his own mother. "We made it, Mama," he said to the stars one night. "We got to the other side."

That was when he heard a rustling in the grass, and the rattle of the trash can lid. And there had been Maya, six-years-old, dirty-faced, too thin and terrified, on the run from her most recent foster home. "Bad people," she called them, but wouldn't give a name, too terrified Tango and Whitney would send her back there.

Whitney coaxed her into taking a bath, gave her an oversized t-shirt to wear, and tucked her into the big girl bed in Izzie's room that Izzie wasn't quite ready for yet.

"Tango," Whitney said, soft sadness in her eyes, and he knew where this was going.

"You don't even have to say it," he said. "I'm already on board."

It had taken almost a year, countless home visits, and calling in every favor to every connection their friends and family had in the system. Erin Walton, Sam's little sister, had grown up to become a social worker, and she'd paved the way more than anyone. And in the end, Maya was theirs, and Tango slept a little easier at night thinking they'd saved one of the world's lost children.

Also, he loved the little monster.

He'd cried the first time she called him "Dad."

"Dad! Dad! Watch us!" she shouted now, delighted and breathless.

"Watch us, Daddy!" Izzie echoed.

"Daddy, are you watching?" Lainie Teague called, hands on her hips.

"We're watching!" Tango and Aidan shouted back across the white sand of the playground. Lainie's little brother, Jake, studiously ignored the girls and continued digging for whatever buried treasure he thought lay beneath the jungle gym. Probably discarded condoms, Tango thought with a snort.

With a tangle of happy shouts, the girls lined up one behind the next and shot down the slide together, shrieking with laughter when they all spilled out into the sand at the bottom.

"Okay, whoever said boys were rowdier than girls was a damn liar," Aidan said quietly, so the kids wouldn't hear. "Those three are gonna grow up and be Charlie's Angels or some shit."

"And just think: you offered to bring Camille along."

"Yeah, don't let me make that mistake again."

Tango chuckled. "Ava totally knew that was a bad idea."

Aidan frowned. "It sucks that she really is smarter than me."

Tango tried to turn his next laugh into a cough, but Aidan shot him a dirty look anyway. "Hey, you said it, man, don't look at me."

Tango heard the clip of heels against concrete and knew without looking, before he even heard their voices, that Sam and Whitney had joined them. He turned to see them coming down the sidewalk toward them, jackets zipped against the autumn chill, both talking animatedly about, probably, their latest project. Somehow, the three creative types in the family had teamed up and were currently working on a series of graphic novels for teens, Sam and Ava writing, Whitney illustrating.

Tango and Aidan secretly hoped their mechanic paychecks were about to become irrelevant.

As they neared, Whitney glanced up, caught his eye, and grinned so wide it looked like it made her face hurt.

His chest seized, a happy little heart attack, emotion moving like good whiskey through his veins.

The kids spotted their mothers with shouts of "Mom!" "Mommy!" "Mama!" and stampeded toward them, even Jake, flinging sand as he went.

Tango tipped his head back against the bench, staring up at the denim-colored evening sky. This was the most dangerous, the most wonderful, the most daring addiction of all: life.

THE END

Loverboy

Lauren Gilley is the author of eighteen novels and several shorts. She writes contemporary literary fiction which is sometimes mistaken for romance, and lives in the South.

Get connected:

Blog: hoofprintpress.blogspot.com
FB: facebook.com/Lauren Gilley – Author
Twitter: @lauren_gilley
Instagram: @hppress
Email: authorlaurengilley@gmail.com

Other Works by Lauren Gilley

Walker Series
Keep You
Dream of You
Better Than You
Fix You
Rosewood

Whatever Remains

Shelter

Russell Series
Made For Breaking
God Love Her
"Things That Go Bang In The Night"
Keeping Bad Company
"Green Like The Water"

Dartmoor Series
Fearless
Price of Angels
Half My Blood
The Skeleton King
Secondhand Smoke
Loverboy

Lean Dogs Legacy Series
Snow In Texas
Tastes Like Candy

Loverboy

Loverboy

Made in the USA
Coppell, TX
22 August 2020